Rock
Bottom

Advance acclaim for Michael Shilling's
Rock Bottom

"A rock-and-roll novel at once rocking and rollicking. *Rock Bottom* knowingly skewers the pretensions of the music business, while never taking them seriously, and the result is a simultaneously scabrous yet affectionate portrait of a band and its entourage in the final throes of a tour de farce. Michael Shilling writes with wit, fury, and an infectious gusto; it's the kind of high-energy prose that makes readers want to get up and strut their stuff."

—Peter Ho Davies, author of *The Welsh Girl*

"*Rock Bottom* is a raunchy, knowing, brilliant novel—a diamond-sharp, lightning-witted, sex-packed, hilarious account of the last days of a fallen-from-grace hard rock band, marooned in Amsterdam under the crashing ruins of a lost greatness. Shilling, himself a former musician, is our insider guide to the ravages and seductions of the rock-and-roll world, and he describes the sights with a tender, pitch-perfect savagery. But more than this, the novel is a remarkably accomplished piece of art—a complicated survivor's tale full of hilarious sadness, virtuous cruelty, beautiful destruction—the sort of book you pick up with high expectations and that, to your surprise and delight, surpasses them all. A book funnier, smarter, sadder, and more inventively composed than you could possibly have hoped. It's a hit—I mean, I was laughing all the way through, and singing along."

—Michael Byers, author of *Long for This World*

Rock Bottom

A NOVEL

Michael Shilling

BACK BAY BOOKS
Little, Brown and Company
New York   Boston   London

Back Bay Books / Little, Brown and Company
Hachette Book Group
237 Park Avenue, New York, NY 10017
Visit our Web site at www.HachetteBookGroup.com

First edition: January 2009

Back Bay Books is an imprint of Little, Brown and Company. The Back Bay
Books name and logo are trademarks of Hachette Book Group, Inc.

The characters and events in this book are fictitious. Any similarity to real
persons, living or dead, is coincidental and not intended by the author.

"To Be Someone" by Paul Weller © 1978 by Stylist Music Ltd. (PRS), all
rights in U.S. and Canada administered by Universal Music—Careers
(BMI), used by permission, all rights reserved.

Library of Congress Cataloging-in-Publication Data
Shilling, Michael.
    Rock bottom : a novel / Michael Shilling.
      p. cm.
    ISBN-13: 978-0-316-03192-9
    ISBN-10: 0-316-03192-5
    1. Musicians—Fiction.   I. Title.
    PS3619.H546R63 2009
    813'.6—dc22   2008014739

        10   9   8   7   6   5   4   3   2   1

                    RRD-IN

Printed in the United States of America

For Anna

There's no more swimming in a guitar-shaped pool.
No more reporters at my beck and call.
No more cocaine, it's only ground chalk.
No more taxis, now we'll have to walk.

But didn't we have a nice time?
Didn't we have a nice time?
Oh wasn't it such a fine time?

—The Jam, "To Be Someone"

It's about my gardener, actually.

—Keith Richards, on "Jumping Jack Flash"

PART

I

1

BOBBY HAD BEEN AWAKE for about ten seconds when his hands started to itch. His poor fucking hands, cracked and raw with eczema, stuck out of the blanket like rotting snails.

"Nice," he said. "Real nice."

He lay on a cot in Morten's living room. Morten, a friend of Helen, their European booking agent, was one of those starfuckers-in-spirit who put bands up so he could be part of the rock-and-roll underground railroad. No one in Blood Orphans had met Morten—he was a banker always away on business—and this time around he had apparently neglected to pay his heating bill.

"Fucking Euro icebox," Bobby hissed. "Unbelievable."

In the late-autumn half-light of the gloomy Amsterdam morning, Bobby stared at his hands with sadness and wonder. The eczema, a lifelong nuisance that in the past year had become a scourge, started off as little bubbles of lymph that, upon being opened by his stubby nails, caked into a yellow curd, burned like they had salt rubbed in them, and made playing the bass guitar a painful chore. Made him have to keep his semirancid left palm away from the pick guard and pluck gingerly. Forced him to play nothing but root notes, because every time his fingers moved, the fretboard bit them like a fucking cobra.

He gutted his left palm for a minute. It felt like he was getting to the bottom of something.

The blankets Morten had provided were for children, puny swatches of acrylic adorned with the actions of different cartoon characters. On Bobby's blanket, Underdog soared to the rescue in a long cape, his ears floppy, his grin light.

Bobby sat up and flexed his feet. Around him, in little Euro cots—always too short, always too narrow—slept Darlo and Adam, the drummer and guitar player. Shane, the singer, was missing, and that was fine with Bobby. He hated Shane, that faux-spiritual prick. And without Shane around, he didn't have to divide his attention. He could fully focus on his recurring fantasy of killing Darlo. Wiggling his freezing toes, Bobby imagined going into the kitchen, finding a big fucking knife, and slashing the drummer's smug, sex-addicted, square-jawed face until it looked like a Levolor blind. For fucking all the girls Bobby wanted to fuck. For constantly mocking his lack of musical ability. For exuding a smooth idiot confidence Bobby envied in a way that bordered on obsession.

Darlo slept with his hands behind his head, his mouth slackened into a smile, at perfect ease. Glyphs of Wonder Woman covered his blanket.

Blood Orphans had played in Amsterdam last night, and they were playing there tonight as well. The record company, determined to bury them alive, had conspired with the booking agency to get them a two-night stand at the new and improved Star Club. The original Star Club, in Hamburg, was where a band called the Beatles had spent four months in leather jackets and pompadours, honing their skills before they ate the world. Recently, some rich Dutchie had opened his own Star Club on the bank of the Amstel. Helen, who, like most booking agents, thought she was a strategic genius, had decided that Blood Orphans could really profit from bathing in the quasi-historical wave pool of an ill-conceived tourist trap.

"What a way to end a tour, huh?" she'd said. "Go out with a bang, right?"

More like a whimper, a peep, the distant screech of a rodent under the wheels of a truck. Bobby couldn't quite believe it, but here it was, the last day of their last tour. Tomorrow he'd be on a plane to Los Angeles, this grand failure over, and he'd be back in the world, where Blood Orphans was just some band that had blown its chance, and he was an unemployed loser.

He couldn't wait.

In ripped black T-shirt and banana-print boxers, Bobby shuffled into the kitchen and located the coffeemaker, an old, nasty Braun shellacked with the dirt of a thousand grubby rock musicians' paws. He poured ground coffee and grimaced. Dirt; there was a time when he wouldn't even have noticed. There was a time, on the first or second or even third tour, when everything had seemed part of some higher pattern of beauty. Back before they'd been branded racists. Back when all the teeth in his mouth were real. Back before the riot in Sweden, the jail time in Omaha, and a thousand utterly predictable days in that shitty van.

He paused in these ruminations to scratch furiously at his hands, rubbing and digging like a psychopath plotting with invisible allies. The dermal demolition proceeded so well, so much better than anything else ever did, that he kept at it until he felt a robust rip in his right palm.

"Oh fuck," he muttered, the rapture broken. "Oh well."

"Mommy!" Adam yelled from his bed. The guitar player often cried out for his mother in his sleep. His small blankets of shit acrylic were festooned with images of Mickey Mouse in top hat and tails.

"Shut up, please," Bobby grumbled. "Poncy little girl."

"Mommmaaa!" Adam howled in response, his voice echoing through the place, distant yet piercing, like something off a Pink Floyd record.

While the coffee brewed, Bobby went into the bathroom and looked for provisions to soothe his hands. In two years of touring he'd raided many a medicine cabinet for salves and ointments. He had tried Nivea and Aveeno. Doused his hands in shea butter and Cetaphil. Done a dance of olive oil and calendula and minerals from the Dead Sea, prayed to the gods of aloe vera, camphor, and almond blossom, worshipped at the dark altar of cortisone. For all this he had been forsaken.

He stepped into the shower, the soap-spattered curtain of which showed the Justice League doing its thing, wrinkled up and warped from countless hours of rank musician scrubbing. Dried rivulets of mold ran down the plastic.

If there was one thing Bobby missed about America, it was bathroom life—how hot water was hot, cold water was cold, and both were right on time. Here in Europe the ham was meatier, the beer was hoppier, the sex was another thing completely, but the plumbing was ancient, the pressure in the pipes was anemic, and the toilets had the hole at the back of the bowl, allowing one to examine one's waste for approval before signing off. This variance in toilet architecture had spooked Bobby into a long month of constipation. Now he only played when his body went into the red. He only played to a sold-out crowd.

When the soap touched his raw right hand, the lather turned into a mass of bees.

"I am so cosmically fucked," he said, and stared into the sputtering showerhead.

He dried off with one of those tiny Euro towels—thin and nonabsorbent—applied Eucerin to his hands, shook them like they were on fire, and retrieved ten Band-Aids from his stash. Soon his hands were covered. The Mummy, back in black.

Navigating the uselessness of hands covered in latex, he put on the same clothes he'd worn for a week, including jeans so ripe they could walk away. Then he poured some coffee, procured sugar and milk, and lit a cigarette.

Euro cigarettes were not fucking around. Instantly the day improved. But then his phone rang. His bell tolled.

It was Joey. The manager. The fucking day tripper. That bitch.

"Yeah?" Bobby said. "What?"

"Hey, babe," she said, in a cocaine hum. "Good morning."

"What the fuck do you want?"

"Don't be like that, Bobby. Play nice."

"Play nice?" He growled. "Come on tour and see how much you want to play nice."

"How are your hands?"

"I said, what the fuck do you want? Why are you calling me?"

"I'm calling you," the manager said, "because I just got to Amsterdam, and I'm sitting here at a café outside my hotel."

"And?"

"And I knew you'd be the only one up."

"And?"

"And I thought you'd want to come over here and imbibe, partake, and otherwise dilate."

He put the coffee cup down. "Is that so?"

"Yeah," she replied. "It is so."

"You and that bindle of coke getting a wittle wone-wey?"

She waited for a second. "I'm trying to reach out to you, Bobby. Don't be a dick."

He hung up on her.

Fucking Joey. Her talents, which had seemed so formidable at first, had a wicked fucking half-life now. The conniving witch hadn't delivered shit for them since the day the ink went dry on their Warners contract.

Had she stopped the absolutely career-crippling racism charge? No.

Had she kept Aerosmith from dropping Blood Orphans from their tour of America's finest sports arenas? No.

Had she stopped their slow slide into booking agent hell, from favorites at William Morris to the laughingstock of the interns' desk at Who Gives a Shit Booking? She had not.

At least she hadn't slept with Darlo. At least, if only for reasons involving power and control, she had denied the drummer a place between her slamming little legs, kept him hurting, kept him frustrated. That made Joey a little bit of a saint to Bobby, carved out a special place for her in his weary, bitter heart.

Big deal, he thought. She was still an incompetent cokehead shill, and they were still the worst fucking band in existence.

A wasp flew by his head and started banging itself against the cold windowpane. This wasp had missed the last flight out of summer and would soon die a cold, exoskeletal death in a bland Amsterdam apartment.

Bobby always appreciated others with whom he could find kinship, and this wasp fit the bill nicely. Like the wasp, he too had been led astray by his instincts and was now at the whim of vast forces, forces beyond comprehension in the complexity with which they had ruined his life. Every day was a cold window to bang one's head against.

"Oh, little wasp," he said, "ye I shall free."

And with that he smashed the insect against the pane, exploding its rust-orange exo-body but also creating a solid fracture in the glass, a flat skein that resembled the interstate in North Dakota, upon which they had often trod.

The wasp, splattered in the center, was reborn as Bismarck.

"Bad omen," Bobby said. "I'm outta here."

He donned his bomber jacket and went down the Dutch stairs,

into this last miserable morning of tour. On the banister, he left behind a goo of rot.

Morten's apartment lay on a fashionable street. Lanterns decorated the sidewalk. Scanning the storefronts, Bobby saw three posh clothing stores, a pharmacy with a hand-carved dove for a sign, and several restaurants with thousand-euro signage. Next door to Morten's, an Internet café was opening.

"Oh, sweet," he said, and flicked his cigarette to the pavement.

The café had that chic modern primitive vibe that plagued European hipster establishments, and smelled of sandalwood, cloves, and espresso. Behind the counter, a skinny aging hippie in overalls read a copy of *De Telegraaf.* Brown dreadlocks accentuated his receding hairline. He was smoking a fat spliff, and smiled as Bobby approached.

"Do you mind speaking English?" Bobby asked. "I no sprecken ze Dutch."

Natty Dread nodded. "Sure, man. Sure."

"A double espresso, please." He looked in the glass case. "And that pastry."

"The mazette?"

"Yeah, I guess. What's a mazette?"

The hippie's sallow stoned eyes gazed at him. "French for fool."

"Perfect, then."

A short, foxy girl with shoulder-length henna-red hair came in. She looked like that chick from *Run Lola Run,* wearing black eye shadow and something in the vein of a Catholic schoolgirl's uniform. Bobby's hands tingled. She smiled at him and sat down at a computer.

If Darlo were here, he thought reflexively, that girl wouldn't stand a chance.

Chewing on his mazette, which was just a safe house for powdered sugar, Bobby stared at the front page of yesterday's

International Herald Tribune, which someone had left on a stool. He read the headlines, America this and America that, but nothing registered. After five futile weeks combing Europe for an audience, America was just a dream now. Until he emerged from the gate at Long Beach, America would feel no closer to him than Atlantis.

"What is that you are humming, man?" asked Natty Dread.

"Jethro Tull," he said. "'Aqualung.'"

The man smiled, then pointed to the ceiling.

"You are staying with Morten, no doubt?"

"Roger that."

"Over and out." He made a thumbs-up. "Sweet, dude."

Europeans all spoke American differently. Each had cobbled together a personal mishmash of idiom, cliché, and insult. Marta, the band's continental publicist, punctuated everything with "to the max!" She consistently described people she didn't like as "total blowjobs." President Bush was "a cowboy fascist" and Ronald McDonald was an "American materialist ass-clown." The one time she and Bobby had slept together, she had whispered "Hit that magic kitty" over and over into his ear, her breath a mixture of pork and whiskey, until he went soft.

Naturally, Darlo had refused her first. But whatever.

"She's a cooze," he'd said, and left the club with twins.

Natty Dread introduced himself. Ullee. Another wimpy Euro name.

"I am a musician too," he said. "We play a lot here in Amsterdam. Jazz and rock, kind of together, kind of at the same time. Simultaneously, dude."

"Jazz is nice," Bobby said. He hated jazz. "Cool."

"We are called Past Tense," Ullee said. "We played Rotterdam once, and Maastricht too. Groningen, we never played there."

"I was mugged in Groningen," Bobby said.

"Ah, mugged," Ullee said wistfully, as if remembering the most beautiful sunset. "Mugged is not fun."

"No. It's not."

"And what is the name of your band?"

"Blood Orphans."

Ullee scrunched his face up. Bobby waited for the sad smile of recognition, for all those ad buys that Warners had taken out in a hundred magazines to pay off. But those ads had been pulled long ago. And that smile never came.

"Blood Orphans," Ullee said. "What does that mean?"

"Fuck if I know," Bobby said. "I used to think it had to do with brotherhood. But now I'm pretty sure it's about death."

The *Run Lola Run* girl giggled. He stole a look at her, but she appeared to be giggling at the screen, not his weak attempt at wisdom.

Ullee giggled too. His onion skin stretched into a smile. Some real light showed up in his eyes.

"OK," he said. "That's a good name."

Bobby decided that Ullee was his guardian angel, come to grant him three wishes. That was how it worked in *Twilight Zone* episodes, and Blood Orphans had long since fallen into that fifth dimension little known to man, of sight, of sound, of mind.

The first wish would be two years of his life back, before Blood Orphans existed, so he could be scrubbed of the different emotions that accompanied this downward spiral: excitement, joy, confusion, worry, disappointment, and finally despair. He didn't need these emotions anymore. He would find others. Just put me back in my apartment, up there in the loft with the Sabbath posters, the autographed Jet Li lithograph, and the vague smell of cat piss, tuck me in, raise the moon high over Costa Mesa, and let me sleep it all away.

The second wish would be for Jessica to fall in love with him again, truly, madly, deeply. Give her a tattoo of his name over her carotid artery. Make every dream she ever had be about what a self-assured, centered, and well-endowed guy he was. Have every one of her paintings be epic scenes of him in Viking gear, standing at the mast of a mighty warship, ready to fight the hordes, singing and crying. Her strong prince. Her Nordic master. Her Overlord.

The third wish would be for someone to slice up Darlo's face until it looked like a Levolor blind. Then Jessica would never have fucked him.

"We broke up a year ago!" she'd said. "You have no right to get mad!"

Bobby took another bite of the mazette, moaning in approval. His dreadlocked guardian angel smiled, and Bobby smiled back, held his breath, anticipated the good news.

"I am trying not to be rude," Ullee said. "But dude, your hands look like cottage cheese."

A warm wave of shame, like pissing on oneself, passed through him.

"What happened to them?" Ullee said, but the bass player was already drifting, humiliated, over to a computer, his head down, pastry and coffee held in his itching putridities.

Run Lola Run looked up at him and smiled. In pity, no doubt.

"Hi," she said.

"Hi," he said, and looked down.

While you were lost in the swirling toilet of tour, e-mail was one of those valuable life preservers that kept you from going right down the hole. It gave you some sense that there might be a more humane life somewhere over the broken-glass rock-and-roll rainbow, an engagement with those unenslaved by the wet dream of stardom.

Three messages awaited him. First up was Dave, his roommate in LA, saying, No, I can't pick you up at the airport, and anyway, what do you want a ride for, you're the guy on MTV, why don't you get a limousine? Next up was Giles, a small, androgynous slip of a boy they'd met on their second tour of England, wondering when they'd be back on the sceptred isle. While high on ecstasy, Bobby and Giles had made out in the bathroom of the London Hard Rock Café.

"I can't forget you man," wrote the androgyne. "Think we'll ever cross paths again?"

Bobby winced. One more dumb fucking thing he'd done on the long march to show-biz irrelevance.

"Kill me," he said, deleting the e-mail. "Please kill me."

The third and final e-mail was subject-lined *Proust Personality Test for Blood Orphans.*

"Hi Blood Orphans," wrote Rachel from Los Angeles. "I saw you guys on *Carson Daly* the other night and thought you were great. So funny and rocking and hot. Really hot!"

They were showing the band in reruns? More likely her brother TiVoed them a year ago and she was confused.

"I went out and bought *Rocket Heart* like, the next day, though it was kind of hard to find. But the Tower in Anaheim had it. Totally awesome! Your publicist at Warners gave me your e-mail addys. He said you guys had been on the road for, like, a *long* time, and needed encouragement."

Back in the days of wine and roses, interviews were everywhere, swirling around them like palm fronds over Egyptian monarchs. But they hadn't had an interview request in forever. And if one showed up at Warners, there was probably a standing order to flush it down the toilet.

Some intern hadn't got the memo. Awesome.

"Anyway," Rachel continued, "I'm a psych major at UCLA, and in my seminar on cognitive dissonance my prof handed out this crazy thing written by Marcel Proust, a questionnaire used to gauge one's personality. They use it in *Vanity Fair* to interview celebrities—I'm also a freelance journalist for music webzines—it's really fun!—and I've been using it for all my interviews. It's attached. Would you mind filling it out? It's normally like thirty questions but I've narrowed it down to eight because I know you're busy."

Proust. He had always wanted to read Proust, but the books were so big.

"Thanks a lot! You guys rawk!"

Bobby looked at his hands. Could they take a little typing? Why not. He hadn't imagined the band still had fans. Maybe Rachel was a portent of happy days ahead.

"What," read question one, "do you regard as the lowest depth of misery?"

"Right now," he replied. "Stuck two-plus years into the worst experience of my life. All my dreams dead and my hands destroyed."

A little tension left his neck.

"Where," the next question read, "would you like to live?"

He tapped on the dirty keyboard, stained with the muck of backpackers and itinerants. "Somewhere I never have to fucking see the faces of my bandmates ever fucking again."

He tapped too hard and opened a crack in the well between thumb and forefinger. A little powdered sugar fell into said crack. It looked like lime in a fresh grave. Run Lola Run smiled at him, then walked outside and lit a cigarette.

"What," read question number three, "do you most value in friends?"

He typed away, as hard as he could, in the hope of waking the sleeping bandmates above him, in the hope of robbing them of their peace. His hands burned, and the cracks running across his life line and heart line opened wide.

"Friends?" he replied. "I value that they don't completely laugh in your face when you return from a long journey, with little money to your name, your pride a memory, and your soul ripped to fucking shreds."

The computer wobbled under the rickety Old World table.

"How about you, Rachel?" he typed. "How about you, Proust?"

He took a breath. Maybe he should stop. Maybe he should go for a walk.

One more question, he thought. I can handle one more.

"What," the screen asked, "is your idea of earthly happiness?"

And that question kind of killed him. The answer, even a year ago, would have been that this life is my idea of total happiness: on tour, free of the shackles of middle-class expectation, just me and my boys, screaming down the highway to hell, on through the night, just another moonlight mile down the road. The answer would have been set in a clarion call, for once they were righteous soldiers of the cause, purveyors of the swindle, ready to engage in battles cultural, social, and economic, whatever it took to sing the rock-and-roll body electric. The answer would have been two words. The answer would have been Blood Orphans.

But now the answer was a giant sucking sound. Happiness? Happee-ness?

He forehanded the keyboard like a tennis pro, and it crashed to the floor.

Patrons looked up from their coffee and papers. Ullee came out of the kitchen. His dreads seemed thinner. He looked at Bobby like he'd taken a shit in his café.

"Whoops," Bobby said. "Sorry?"

"I think you should leave now," Ullee said. "I think you ought to go."

"You do, huh?"

"Now, man," he said, and cursed in Dutch. "Now."

The keyboard lay there, bent and twisted, torn and frayed.

"Now!" Ullee yelled. "Go!"

Bobby put on his jacket and stomped out into the Dutch mist. The old buildings looked down on him with their cockeyed dormer windows. Fog blotted out their roofs.

"Good job, dude," he said. "Could you be a bigger asshole?"

Run Lola Run stood there with her cigarette. Her legs, Bobby thought, looked like a fishnet ladder to a hot Dutch heaven, one that, with these ragged hands, he could never climb. Another beauty out of reach. Another sexy sprite who would fall into the arms of undeserving men. Men who never knew regret, never thought twice, and never looked back.

She flicked her cigarette into the street and bounced on her heels.

"Hey, rock star," she said. "How's it going?"

2

JUST ONCE, Joey thought, they could appreciate me. Just once, they could call her up and say, Hey, Joey, we know it must be tough wiping the spit of humiliation off your face each and every day, but we just want you to know we never forget how hard you work for us, how tirelessly you advocate our interests, how completely you sacrifice everything else to make sure we're happy. Just once, she could call them and not get insulted with nicknames: Nazgûl, the Crippled Crone, Amphetamine Annie. She had a proper name and it wouldn't kill them to use it once in a while.

They had no idea what it was like to be the ambassador and evangelist of the biggest joke in the music business, the defender of terminally damaged goods, the sunny shepherd of the walking dead.

Of course, calling Bobby had been a mistake. She had no love for Bobby. Bobby was hard to love, always fretting like the rabbit in Wonderland. It wouldn't have done her any good to have him sitting here, scratching his hands. Generally, your enemy's enemy was your friend. But with Bobby she'd rather take on failure all by her fucking self.

Failure was going to show up any minute now at this sidewalk café, in the form of John Hackney, their European A&R guy, who, back in ancient history, had the task of assuring the success of Blood Orphans on the continent. Hackney, whom Joey had made the mistake of contacting before her trip, just to see if he could get some press to these final shows, only to find out that he would be in Amsterdam too, on unrelated matters.

"We need to get together," Hackney said. "We have to talk."

Very fucking funny.

Her trip had been an act of desperation. She'd gone stir crazy at the world headquarters of DreamDare, her management company with an employee roster of exactly one, that ridiculous office on Wilshire and Westwood she rented to show what a budding Brian Epsteinette she was, a low-ceilinged, dusty room full of unopened boxes and a phone that rang only with complaints from creditors, a quiet place where she sat at a desk doing crossword puzzles and checking her e-mail while in the offices around her, boutique offshoots of the movie business—editing and animation and postproduction—hummed and thrummed. Out of boredom, she'd forced herself on all these adjacent people, hanging out until they had to ask her, Uh, Joey, don't you have work to do? 'Cause we do. And she would say, Oh, of course, what time is it oh shit I have a meeting over at Capitol, I have lunch with an agent over at ICM, I have to meet with the accountant and figure out what to do with all this revenue. I just can't count it fast enough!

Upon which she would go back to her office and cry.

So she decided to cross the pond and see what the four stooges had been up to, witness the end of an era, make a clean break with that which had brought her almost-fame and several hundred thousand dollars that she'd frittered away on expensive dinners, rebuilt hot rods, and sky-high office rent. She wanted to see her blessed band's last show, even though seeing them now, at the tight end of the career noose, would do little more than fill her with any number of different angers: at the band, at herself, at the record company. But anger on a first-class transatlantic flight was a fuck of a lot better than watching sunlight move across the Hollywood sign from your window, waiting for someone who wasn't a collection agency to return your phone calls.

Not that she knew anything about running a company, or even going to work. When Joey was seventeen, an old man had driven up onto a Santa Monica sidewalk and plowed right into her. The accident provided her with two things: a settlement that meant a decade's worth of financial security and a bum left leg with a nasty limp. At first she'd alleviated the pain with prescription painkillers, but then she put her purple Camaro into a guardrail while loaded on Vicodin and malt liquor. Now she just hauled around an infirmary-sized bottle of Tylenol, and a well-hidden bindle of coke.

You could get anything on a plane if you stuck it far enough up your ass.

In her wildest nightmares, Joey had never imagined that Blood Orphans would fail so completely. There had been Darlo and Bobby's night in the Omaha jail, and the riot in Stockholm. There had been Bobby's tooth loss and hand decay, and Shane's descent into comically condescending religiosity, and Adam's annoying art-school philosophies, his crushed velvet, his Fu Manchu.

But that was just rock and roll. The real problem, the quandary that turned folly into failure, was one very small number: 3,451. The number of copies of *Rocket Heart* sold. Figuring out who was responsible for that number would take the rest of her life.

The breeze picked up, spun leaves on Dam Square. She lit a cigarette and felt some postnasal drip. Eau de Cocaine slid down her throat.

"Nice day," she said, smiling, as if she were on a date.

Conventional wisdom said that Blood Orphans had set themselves up by taking that advance. No one wanted to like a band that hadn't earned it. Everyone from radio promoters to fellow bands to hipster blog bullshit artists looked upon them as some rogue element, as if their big record deal had forever polluted the workings of a pure and untainted pop music ecosystem.

But none of that would've mattered if *Spin* hadn't gone after them. *Spin*'s hatchet job rendered them stillborn. The editor, some butch British fuck named Arthur St. George, took it upon himself to turn his review of *Rocket Heart* into an editorial on the evils of irresponsible rock-star life and made this screed the Editor's Note, right under a picture of him looking smarmy at his desk in skyscraperland.

"You've no doubt heard about Blood Orphans," St. George wrote, "the foursome from Silver Lake that went from unknown in their hometown to a multimillion-dollar act for Warners. Bully for them. We root for the lucky. It's what makes rock and roll great. Still, it's no surprise that their record, *Rocket Heart,* is terrible. Just flat-out criminally terrible, a hodgepodge of old Kiss riffs, vocals that make David Coverdale look like Placido Domingo, and guitar pyrotechnics so lame Steve Vai could do better with a ukulele. That's not surprising. What is surprising is that Warner Bros., proud home to generations of musical legends, has signed a bunch of racists. Yes, that's right. Blood Orphans are racist. Stop me if you've heard this one before—I know, it's only rock and roll—but 'Double Mocha Lattay' makes 'Brown Sugar' look like an appeal for tolerance. The track features lines like 'Once you go black, you'll never go slack' and 'Sweet little white boy, you're the best don't you know/buy me a mink fur coat and I'm your personal ho.' Another example of this idiocy can be found in track three, 'I Also Have a Dream,' with the lines 'I just want a cock as big as MLK/So I can walk down the street and yell, Ladies, this way!' And finally there's 'Ultra-Apache': 'She was a squaw so fine, I loved to grind her gears/full lips, brown skin, and a trail of fucking tears.' Blood Orphans deserve a fast burial in an unmarked grave, the entire print run of *Rocket Heart* burned in a fire of purification. Shame on you, Warner Bros. Shame on you."

Within a week Warners had recalled the record and released another, in a vastly smaller print run, without the three offending songs. One hundred thousand discs and one hundred thousand inner sleeves into the shredder. Darlo, author of said lyrics, refused to apologize, make a statement, stage a benefit for the NAACP.

"These lyrics are a joke," he said through their new, smaller, cheaper publicist. "It's rock and roll, everyone. Besides, I'm one eighth full-blooded Cherokee. I know how racism feels. Lighten up!"

The label withdrew the offer for them to spend two months opening for Aerosmith, and suddenly Steadman, their domestic A&R man, could not be reached for comment. Steadman, who had listened to every one of the offending songs over and over and never made a peep of protest, who liked to party with them like it was 1999, was always out, gone for the day, or had just stepped into a meeting.

"Don't worry," Steadman's assistant told Joey. "We'll get them on tour in more suitable markets. Youthcentric markets. Cutting-edge markets."

"Cutting-edge market" is code for "very small club."

Not that the band themselves, lost in the funhouse, noticed.

And I am the one who takes it in the face today, Joey thought. I am the one who gets fucking dunked in it. Double Mocha Lattay, coming right up.

Joey adjusted her mohawk, which had grown out into a thick blond lump that defied all attempts at order, and watched John Hackney, their soon-to-be-former A&R man in Europe, arrive at the café.

"There she is," Hackney said, and they rose to cheek-kiss. "Joey."

Hackney, Joey thought, sure was one hot piece of ass, complete with thick lower lip, sleepy-but-knowing gaze, and sultry half-smile. They had met only once before, in London, back at the start of this long, strange trip, before the road to riches went from shiny yellow bricks to sticky black tar. The two meetings were bookends to the miserable epic of Joey's ineptitude.

At that first meeting—drinks in Notting Hill, dinner in Soho, just the two of them talking strategy—Joey had made a pass at Hackney, but he'd declined, leaving her on a misty street corner like a poor man's Twiggy. Maybe this time he'd want to show her his record collection.

Hackney was dressed in top Brit gangster gear, and smelled of oranges.

"Foggy day here in Amsterdam," he said. "But it has its drama."

"Does it?" Joey wrapped her coat tight. "I didn't notice."

Even though Hackney was supposed to be their Euro champion, the A&R executive had never been able to pretend excitement. Joey knew that Hackney thought Blood Orphans were that once-in-a-career clusterfuck he just had to grin and bear — that the fact that they'd been signed at all, let alone for a sizable percentage of the A&R budget for business year 2003, was a travesty.

Sometimes shit didn't break a band's way. That was one thing. If you were John Hackney, you felt bad about that. You did your best. But with Blood Orphans, Joey knew that he was thinking, Thank fucking God, and let's just forget this ever happened.

"Talked to the band lately?" Hackney asked, sitting down.

"No." She tried to look indignant. "They're not talking to me."

"Why is that?"

"Darlo says I'm a shit Midas. All I do is bring bad news."

"You're their manager," he said. "Wouldn't it be —"

"— a little self-defeating not to talk to your manager? The lunatics run the fucking asylum. It's been a month since I spoke with them." She thought about it for a second. "Actually, that's not entirely true. Sometimes Darlo sends me text messages, one-word sentiments like 'Lazy' and 'Lesbian.'"

Hackney lit a Players, and Joey mooched a light.

"I saw them play in Rotterdam," Hackney said. "About two weeks ago."

"How was it?"

"Memorable."

"You'll have to elaborate. With those morons, that could mean so many things."

Hackney laughed at that, and so did Joey. But insults, even now, made her feel like a suck-up betrayer.

"Let me guess," Joey said. "Shane's still a Tantric Buddhist."

"He sure is." Hackney took a long drag. "And how."

"Did he mention it onstage?"

"Between every song."

Shane had started off as the closest thing to a normal person in the band, despite the fact that when they all met, he was a most devout Holy Roller, part of some scary Orange County clan. But he wasn't vicious like Darlo, or pretentious like Adam, or neurotic like Bobby. He'd been a pleasant kid whose blond good looks and affable personality could have fit in anywhere. But delusions of grandeur had fucked them all in different ways, and in Shane's case had made him a preachy, annoying mouthpiece for a number of successive spiritual dead ends.

"Let me see if I can remember it right," Hackney said. "The cock is the lingam. The pussy is the yoni. The cock is also the jade stalk and the pussy is the emerald lagoon."

"What else?"

He blew perfect smoke rings. Some calf hair peeked out where his cuff broke. Joey wanted to lick his legs bare.

"A most comprehensive retelling of the Kama Sutra," he said. "Which some drunk in the crowd kept calling the Come On Sarah."

"Did you get the guy's address?" Joey asked. "I want to send the fucker some flowers."

Hackney laughed. Joey fixated on his pearly British chompers.

"The heckling didn't dissuade him," Hackney said. "He kept on, into a discussion of Ashtanga yoga, and the virtues of ten glasses of water a day, and the magic aphrodisiac qualities of yohimbine." He looked to Joey. "I know I'm missing some things."

"Genghis Khan died having sex," she offered. "He was a brave warrior."

"He had many wives," Hackney said, "and practiced the downward dog, the chanting hyena, the oracular ostrich, the galloping goat."

"You're killing me over here," Joey said. "Killing me softly."

Hackney puffed. "The lectures really thinned the room. By the end of the set the band was playing to their shadows. I introduced myself after the show, and they couldn't have cared less. They practically pushed me out of the way to get to their beers."

Had there ever been a cuter man? Joey fixed a fuck-me-anytime smile on Hackney and looked deep into his eyes. This gaze, a little sleepy and full of dirty vibes, had worked extremely well in her days as a bartender, when closing time approached and she didn't want to go home alone.

"Are you all right?" he asked.

"Of course." She sat up straight, tapped a cigarette against the table. "Just a little tired."

He looked polite, confused, suddenly boyish. Boyish in a big strong man drove her crazy.

"Thought you were going to pass out there."

She smiled professionally, took a healthy, outdoorsy breath, and imagined that this meeting was, in fact, an interview for a job at Warners, that they hated Blood Orphans but thought Joey's talents wasted. Sure, why not? That would work. Maybe she and Hackney could negotiate the position while she fucked that polite-British-boy confusion right off his face.

"The drummer," Hackney said. "What's his name?"

"Darlo Cox."

"Good-looking kid. Strapping. His dad's the porn king?"

Joey nodded and uncrossed her legs.

"David Cox. Dirty Darling Pictures of Van Nuys. He bank-rolled the band. Before you guys."

The phrase *not for long* passed over them like a flock of starving doves.

Hackney took a long drag and continued his impressive gangster slouch. He really had that charming throat-slitter thing down pat.

"Shame that he's the best-looking," he said. "That face is wasted behind those drums. Looks like Jim Morrison. Lovely hair."

"He writes the lyrics," Joey said. "Some of them are almost clever."

"Personally," Hackney said, "I think the lyrics are very funny."

"So did a lot of people, before we were racists."

Hackney tried to look sympathetic. "Really unfortunate press, that," he said. "Unfair."

When Joey first heard about the racism problem, she was cruising up Laurel Drive, on her way to Darlo's in her just-bought, completely restored gold-with-blue-trim 1977 TR7. Steadman, their stateside A&R fair-weather man, called her up with an advance copy of *Spin*.

"It's bad," he'd said. "It's really bad."

She'd felt the blood leave her head, there in her new British steel, and pulled over to the side of the road.

"Racists?" she'd yelled, as the good times rolled into a ditch. "You can't be serious!"

"Anyway," he continued, "when Shane shut up and they played, they weren't half bad."

"You're lying."

"No, really. Kind of reminded me of Blink-182 meets Sabbath."

"OK, come on," she said. "Blink-182? That's cruel."

"They've sold millions of records."

"Hmm." She nodded. "Can't argue with that."

"Honestly," he said, "they had their moments. And that poor bass player. His hands!"

Disgust and contempt for Bobby rolled in Joey's gut. That weasel. Bobby was only in the band because his ex-girlfriend knew Adam and every other bass player in LA had been busy. Bobby was the fucking passenger.

"Eczema," she said. "Don't get me started."

"He wasn't faring so well up there."

"He hides behind Adam's guitar."

"Yes," Hackney said. "Brilliant boy, our Adam. Funny mustache, though."

"I hate that Fu Manchu. He's had it for as long as I've known him." She lit a cigarette. "Anyway, Bobby." She blew some smoke. "We're going to fire Bobby, I think."

She had to try something, and maybe Bobby was the problem. Maybe without Bobby they wouldn't get dropped. Maybe it was that simple.

Sometimes she could really amuse herself.

They ordered drinks. The label was paying, Hackney said. Knock yourself out. So Joey drank her vodka tonic and, grasping at some shred of pride, quit the whole this-is-secretly-a-job-interview fantasy. She couldn't go over to the dark side, live on the Death Star, suck off Vader for a hundred grand plus bonus. Expense account, paid vacations, 401(k): she didn't need the creature comforts that came with being a vampire. All her life she had been about the music, the sheer love of it, the might and the majesty, and working for the label would be a repudiation of everything she'd ever stood for.

Pretending to have principles really made her heart race.

"Look," Hackney said. "You know why I'm here."

Joey's throat tensed up. The slow trot to the guillotine was over.

"This isn't easy for anyone," Hackney said. "We wanted to make this work." He cupped the cigarette in his hands, leaned forward, and put his elbows on the table. A lock of black, professionally greased hair fell forward like a salute to his cheekbones. The knot in his tie was way past Windsor. Joey's eyes gravitated to his gold wedding band. She wondered what his wife looked like.

"What I want to know," Joey said, "is why this didn't happen sooner."

"An attempt at return on investment, I think."

"Right." She nodded. "I guess our lawyer will be in touch...to tie up loose ends."

Hackney cocked an eyebrow. "Loose ends?" He smiled. "There are none, Joey."

She puffed and laughed, a nervous wreck. "Right. Just reading from the 'got dropped' script."

She had always wanted to be the woman in the know, the mover, the shaker, the closer. That was her dream. Some people wanted to be doctors, astronauts, firemen. Joey wanted to be the manager of the biggest rock-and-roll band in the world, and she couldn't even bluff her way into a lawyer's due diligence.

Hackney lit another Players and drained his Limonata. Joey's compromised left leg started to ache deep down in the workings of her thigh.

"I'm going to see this band tonight," Hackney said. "The Soporifics."

"Bad name."

"If we sign them, the name'll change." He pocketed the matches. "They have this gorgeous singer. He's a real tall glass of chocolate stout. A good swinging boogie of a group. You want to join me?"

She stared at his wedding band. "Maybe after the Blood Orphans show," she said.

Hackney shook his head. Wind blew the leaves down.

"May I suggest," he said, "that you spare yourself the pain?"

"I can't," she said. "Closure."

Hackney sat back, looked a little deflated in his ultracool way. It pained her to resist his overture, but saying no was a nice way to create the illusion of self-respect. He stood up.

"All right, then," he said, laying down a hundred euros. "Good luck, Joey."

"Cheers, John."

He lingered for a moment, looming over her, a big hunk of English granite. Then he reached into his jacket pocket, took out a leather-covered pad and a tiny pen, and wrote something down.

"Here," he said, handing her a piece of paper. "Where I'm staying."

"Uh-huh," she said, acting nonchalant. "Oh, sure."

She watched Hackney walk away. He grew thinner, as in comic books when someone disappears into a crowd, losing shape, abstracting into anonymity, until the body becomes a jagged vertical streak, a simple black line, the closing of a gatefold on a double album.

Joey, she thought. You fucking loser.

She stretched her feet—her left leg was tensing up for real now—and ran her hands through her outgrown faux hawk. A hundred euros and keep the change on a two-drink tab. It seemed a huge insult, the financial equivalent of a pity fuck, about which Joey knew a great deal. A car drove by, playing the Rolling Stones, songs about the truth between men and women, defining the narrow space between evasion and protection, mapping the porous DMZ between anger and vanity. Unlike all the other men in Joey's life, Mick and Keith had never lied to her. She leaned in and listened for clues.

3

HOW HE'D EVER GOTTEN STUCK with such a bunch of boring, cowardly, pretentious, panty-waisted faggots he would never understand.

Hadn't his dad told him that the world was full of people like this? Had he not explicitly stated that everywhere you looked, morons were in your path, trying to gum up the system, trying to disrupt your flow?

Anger drove him now. Glory was still within his grasp. Glory was still possible, even if he had to carry them all on his back. Glory was a hot little bitch, waiting, hiding, coy.

Damn, it was cold in here.

So thought Darlo, lying in Morten's apartment, hands on his balls.

Darlington Archibald Cox was born on August 12, 1981, in Encino. His father, David Cox, was an adult-film producer who had the supreme luck to be panning for porn gold just when a whitewater torrent called videotape came rushing down the river. Consequently, his company, Dirty Darling Pictures, spearheaded porn's great migration from theater to living room, making Cox, whose real name was Samuel Forest, a fantastically rich man. Twenty years later he was the dark analogue to Hugh Hefner, the kind of guy who was invited to B-movie premieres, who gave vast sums of money to the Cato Institute under a fake name, who had five Rhodesian Ridgebacks and one small man named Frederico, whose job it was to clean up all the shit the dogs left on the white shag rugs that covered the living room floor of Cox's Laurel Canyon mansion.

Darlo's dad was not without a sense of humor. He'd produced numerous film series based on the happy marriage of fetish and farce; for those who liked to fuck outside, there was *Garden Ho;* for those who liked to watch men have sex with girls half their age, there was *Poppycock;* for those who had a yen for girls with glasses, there were seven volumes of *Four Eyes.* With flawless, sleazy precision, David Cox understood the turn-ons of lonely men in prefab, cookie-cutter apartments, and riches followed.

Where other kids grew up with a white noise of television commercials, sibling rivalry, and mundane parental chatter, Darlo roamed in a bandwidth of ecstasy both real and put-on—the giggles, the moans, the screams. You could turn any which way in the Cox house and find reminders of sex, in the form of toys, wrappers, the heavy sweet musk of it floating like a demon firefly. Rampant, boundary-free sexuality was an everyday fact of life, like garbage collection or grocery shopping.

His friends were always begging to come over, but what, Darlo thought, was the big deal about seeing a young woman walk down a hallway naked? What was so special about passing by an open door, on your way to pee in the middle of the night, and seeing a mass of bodies pounding against each other? What was so odd and unusual about your dad saying, "Show him your pussy, baby. Give Darlo here a little sneak preview of what's in store for him. Give him a little smell of the heavenly body. Do it, baby. I said do it."

Didn't it all come and go, like the weather?

Darlo sat up and put on his clothes—a stained white T-shirt, old black leather pants, and muddy motorcycle boots. He walked over to the window, lit a cigarette, and looked at the posh, empty street.

"Amsterdam," he said. "It ain't Hollywood."

The first thing to do once he was back in LA, freshly shaved and laid, was set the label straight. They were going to get the Darlo treatment, all right. Less money spent on turning the band into a post-punk Spinal Tap, a little more cultivating them as a serious outfit. Irony in the service of truth had been Joey's line. Wasn't it brilliant? Didn't it have a certain brilliance? How could they not see the brilliance?

"Shortsighted motherfucking record company," he grumbled, and went to brush his teeth. In the living room, his acrylic Wonder Woman crumpled in on herself, upside down, headfirst onto the floor.

Blood Orphans was his band and he had to take it back.

After dealing with the label, he would do the next logical thing: fire Joey. Joey used to know what she was doing, but Darlo had grown tired of her capitulation, her weak bargaining stances, her utter inability to stand firm in the face of bluff. No record label would drop seven figures on a band and then wash its hands as soon as the ink was dry. The band had two million dollars' worth of leverage, yet Joey treated every interaction with Warners as a plea. She had been so sharp back when they were starting out, but once she got the direct deposit of her percentage, once she was in the big show and got an expensive office and started managing other bands, she couldn't keep her sloe eyes on the prize.

He stumbled into the bathroom, felt a dryness in the back of his throat, and sighed. Just like that, the libido had its tenterhooks in him. In robotic fashion he pulled one off, feeling helpless but also feeling fine. Oh please God give me the serenity to accept the things I cannot change, the courage to change the things I can, and the wisdom to know the difference.

"Fucking Joey," he said to his reflection, reaching for some toilet paper.

In the beginning, Joey and Darlo had been an unstoppable force. They'd met at Spaceland, where Joey tended bar and Darlo played with his shitty band, Big Broom. They hit it off immediately. Joey was every boy's rock-and-roll wet dream, a foul-mouthed fox who could snort coke like an aardvark and had mastered the aesthetics of street-punk chic, stomping her little self around in motorcycle boots, short skirts, and ripped wife beater, yet coming across like the black sheep in a royal family. Darlo was a smarmy, broad-chested Adonis-in-training who made Rod Stewart look insecure. They recognized in each other kindred spirits who had only one true desire: world dominance.

Joey had just started managing bands, but her acts, Dame Wicked and SaberTooth, were no good—"ironic" bands that wanted to make it as camp, which meant they calculated every one of their moves. To curse or not to curse, that is most definitely *not* the question. Joey had done everything she could with these bands: lobbied all the music journalists until they came to shows, bought them food and drink so they would write nice things, even purveyed drugs on the cheap so they could better glean the brilliance of Dame Wicked, an electroclash girl group without anyone hot enough to remember, and SaberTooth, who were after a Blue Cheer vibe but had too much of a preoccupation with hiding their faces while singing about cavemen abducted by aliens.

Big Broom and SaberTooth had shared many bills. Joey and Darlo had got to talking.

"Your bands suck," Darlo told her, sipping whiskey on some forgettable night at Spaceland. "But you make the most of them. You pretend they're the Beatles. And how the hell did you get that Peter Murphy opening slot at El Rey?"

"The way you get any good opening slot," Joey said, chewing on peanuts. "Mediocrity. Openers can't be embarrassing and they also can't present the possibility of blowing you off the stage." She slugged her Jameson. "Basically, we've peaked. What about you guys? How long are you going to keep banging your head against the door of No One Cares Incorporated?"

"Not long. And besides, I'm fucking the singer's girlfriend."

Joey laughed, poured them both a shot of Cuervo. "Let's start a joke band," she said. "Something campy, something ridiculous and cocksure and anything goes, Poison meets AC/DC meets Kiss in a darkened alleyway."

"I'll drink to that."

They threw back their tequila, sucked on their limes, and stared each other down in a predatory way.

"So," she said, wiping her mouth. "You have anyone in mind for this joke band of ours?"

Memories. Stardust. Innocence.

"Do you?"

Brushing his teeth in Morten's bathroom with some nasty Dutch toothpaste—Fennel? Mint? Topsoil?—Darlo shook his head. Oh yeah, I know some people. I know a bass player with leprosy, and a singer who's up a fucking tree about God, and a guitar player who shreds and writes slamming hooks but must be the most precious tear-jerked little bitch this side of Joan of Fucking Arc. Oh yeah, I've got a fucking crew.

"Idiot," he told the reflection. "Shortsighted pussy-hound idiot."

Darlo had approached Adam, who was playing in an obnoxious weep-rock band named Angel's Sweat. They had a cello player, and sometimes Adam even whipped out the flute. Sometimes he also whipped out the mellotron, the Hammond B-3, and the oboe. That was the point. He could play anything.

At the time Adam was vegan, so Darlo suggested they meet at the Burger Master off Wilshire. Lunch and dinner had been free lately for Adam, as every New Age imprint was on to Angel's Sweat. There's always one doofus at every label, major or indie, who thinks 1973 was the high point of rock, who subsists on a musical diet of Hawkwind, Gentle Giant, and King Crimson, who thinks Yes are the Beatles and will go to the mat arguing that John McLaughlin is a better guitar player than Jimi Hendrix. For these losers, Angel's Sweat was the only game in town and Adam was the new Robert Fripp.

Prog rockers, Darlo thought. *Fuck.*

Adam brought a pamphlet on veganism to the Burger Master. He wore purple crushed-velvet pants and a scarf and that Fu Manchu mustache. Darlo, standing in the parking lot, rolled his pretty brown eyes, shook his shaggy, shiny black mane, rubbed his full lips.

"Jesus," he said. "Why don't you color that 'tache into a fucking rainbow while you're at it. Do you have any idea how bad you look?"

Adam went blank. "I—"

Darlo grabbed the vegan literature out of Adam's hand and chucked it to the ground. "Trash," he said. "This is Burger Master. Show some respect."

Adam retrieved the pamphlet, astonished. "You don't have to be so rude."

Darlo took the pamphlet from Adam, looked at it, tried to be thoughtful. "I'm sorry. I'm not into all that shit is all."

"Oh, no problem," Adam said, and emitted a weak smile.

A capitulator, Darlo thought. Weak of conviction. Noted.

Over the course of a few nights of drinking in Darlo's poolroom, the two of them wrote ten songs. That they were complete musical opposites was essential; they came up with radio-friendly riff rock with moments of prog flourish, the occasional unnecessary accents, the when-you-least-expect-it time change, five chord progressions instead of three—subtleties that would keep Adam amused, give the music journalists something to write about, and provide Joey with one more angle.

Darlo suggested they call themselves Blood Devils.

"Over the top," Adam said. "How about Blood Orphans?"

"Nice," Darlo said, rolling the cue ball in his hands. "Done."

Now the drummer spit out toothpaste into Morten's little Euro sink.

"Fuck memories," he said, and popped a pimple on his chin.

His cell phone rang in the cold Dutch hallway. Fucking phone was a tri-band; he couldn't get America from it. He went into the hallway and looked at the ID, saw it was Joey. He wondered if the manager had prevailed on Warners to get them a good opening slot for the winter tour. He wanted to open for the Shins. They were cool. A little bit of cool was all they needed to get back on track. Just one break. He smiled and watched the gray Dutch sky and turned his frown upside down. All he needed now was some pussy.

Get back on track. Fresh turn. Recharge their energies. He didn't want to start over. He was loyal. He didn't need to fire Joey. He and Joey could still make it work. Loyalty was an important trait in a man. Loyalty to your beliefs, and your conviction, and the dudes who were your fellow climbers up the craggy mountain of fame, connected by the carabiner of desire.

Where was that conniving opportunistic gimp ho staying?

The phone beeped with a new message.

Needed to get some action. Back on track. First things first.

"Amsterdam," he said. "Pussytown."

In curdling cotton and leather, motorcycle jacket, and aviator sunglasses, he left for the ATM.

4

SHANE FELT SOMETHING in his dreadlocks. He grabbed a piece dangling in his eyes and looked it over. He hoped it was peanut butter. Not too many things were this color, and the alternatives were hummus, new concrete, and baby shit.

He lay in what was definitely a teenager's room. There was a certain undeniable smell to a teenager's room, a fruitiness, innocence not yet completely leached. A man's voice called up the stairs in Dutch.

Shane smelled his hair, bunched into shortish dreads. Definitely peanut butter.

He heard a child running back and forth in the hallway. Then the child opened the door and peeked in. She was about five, blond and cherubic, a real slice of master race. She asked him something in Dutch.

"Ja," he said, unsure what language he was speaking. There had been so many beds in so many countries. "Ja," he said again, as if to pop some balloon between them.

She let out a peep and ran down the hall.

Danika, the teenager in question, lay beside him. He pulled back the covers. She had a slamming body—martini-glass tits, a stomach you could bounce a quarter off, an ass that saluted the sky—topped off with a witchy set of black dreads. She too was strafed in peanut butter. He felt a rush of blood to his crotch.

The walls of Danika's room were kind of black. Like maybe she had only put one coat on before her parents caught her.

"Fuck," he said.

Without makeup, Danika was still in the proto-pubescent stage. He prayed to every god he had ever worshipped—Jesus, Buddha, and Yahweh—that she was seventeen, or whatever street-legal was in Dutchland. But either way the blood continued its express trip to his pieces and parts.

She'd been standing at the front of the stage of the Star Club with her friends, wearing a black push-up corset, upside-down crosses for earrings, and a blouse that resembled a spider's web. Her eyeliner ran down her face in what appeared to be a strategic, symmetric drip. She smiled at him and did funny hand movements in the air like a clumsy Shiva. Her bottom lip had rings pierced through both corners, and she wore a black bindi. Bindis on pale white girls killed Shane. He sang to her, trying, as in every other show he had ever played as a member of Blood Orphans, to transcend the lyrics. Through Darlo's disgusting, loveless words, he tried to affect a tone of kindness and grace and the most organic types of desire, so that his speeches in between songs about Tantra and Buddha would seem natural. He did all of this, crooning and emoting, while keeping his gaze on her fashionably tearstained face.

Danika, he said later, as they stood at the bar. That sounds like the most delicious seeded fruit. That sounds like the wind through the palm trees. That sounds like a glorious, sacred mantra.

"Fuck me," she said, and pulled him into a closet.

Now a tall man stood in the doorway, sporting a billowing head of salt-and-pepper hair and a bushy mustache. All the blood left Shane's crotch, and his balls retreated into his pelvis.

"Hello," Shane said. "I was just—"

The man yelled at Danika, spewed Dutch words.

She jumped up as if a prod had been put to her. Gasping, she gathered up her sheet, covering those martini-glass titties.

"Marcus, get out!" she said in English. "Gett owd!"

They stared at each other for a minute. She started to lower her sheet. Marcus retreated.

"Danika," he warned, eyes unable to settle on a latitude.

She looked at Shane, smiling, then giggled. "He's not really my dad," she said. "Are you, Marcus?"

Shane felt a little bit sick.

Marcus cursed crazily and stomped off.

She looked at Shane, touched his face. He jumped back, almost fell off the bed. His balls were caught in the undertow of his retreating body, and he let out a cry.

"You're silly," was her response. "Silly rock star."

Marcus was back in the doorway. He marched over, grabbed her by the arm, and shook her little frame. "Slut!" he yelled. "Dirty slut!"

"Fuck you!" she said, sheet barely hanging on her. "Pervert! Like to look at Danika's titties! Like to spy on me in the bathroom! Pervert!"

For Shane, the scene was a new and improved version of the morality movies he had watched in church when he was growing up.

Marcus pulled at Danika the wrong way and her sheet fell off. The peanut butter, combined with the smell of sex and sweat, created a Dutch BO tsunami that made Shane quiver. Marcus looked away like a vampire staring at the sun.

"Pervert!" she yelled.

He shrieked some quality Dutch horror-words and ran from the room.

She smiled at Shane, tousled her mane, and moved to him, crawling on the bed, a ragamuffin prowler. The lamp on the black night table shone on her sparse ebony pubic hair.

"Come here," she said. "I have ten minutes before school. Come here."

He was going to do the right thing and leave this twisted scene, but then the stench hit him. The stench, sweet and yeasty, sucker-punched his best intentions. How helpless he really was, after all this time.

"Come here," she repeated, her bindi still in place. "Come here."

Being a Christian rocker didn't mean you didn't have a sense of humor. Shane hated that. Of course he had a sense of humor. Jesus had a sense of humor, for Christ's sake.

Back when he was starting out, singing in The Dragon Slayed and trying to get shows in Silver Lake and Hollywood, *Christian* was a dirtier word than *pedophile*. When he stated his faith, other musicians stared at him as if he'd stopped halfway through a joke. When he said he was guided by God's love, bartenders smiled at him as if he'd lost his mind. When he mentioned the importance of meditating on Christ, booking agents hung up on him.

Even then he had wanted to branch out. The three other members of The Dragon Slayed expected all his lyrics to speak of the King of Kings, but he didn't care if every song was about Him. He mentioned the Beatles to his girlfriend and she said, How could you like the Beatles? They wrote all that music on drugs!

Then Darlo, the vulgar guy in Big Broom, had asked him to be in his new band, which he described as "over the top, incredibly stupid, morally bankrupt, and full of killer hooks." Well, why not? He had a sense of humor. He could hang. Darlo was an atheist and his dad exploited women, but all right. Shane wasn't a fool. He could roll with the dirty dawgs. He could have some fun and still believe. His faith wasn't everything. Of course he took issue with the way that Darlo and Joey chose to live their lives, but he could, you know, *bro down.*

"Whatever, Bono," Joey said at the first band meeting. "Spare us the theology."

He didn't like being in a box. He was more than the sum of his beliefs.

"What are you, deaf?" Darlo said. "We don't care. And don't be late for practice again."

Shane's girlfriend, Donna, hadn't approved of his new band. She came from a strict Anaheim fundamentalist flock and had recently agonized deeply over her belly-button piercing. Was it an adornment? Did it make of her a false idol?

Shane thought, I'm sorry, Jesus, but her belly-button ring gives me a violent, worldly erection. He stared at it when they sat on her porch swing, across the street from a lemon grove.

"You're going to start doing drugs, Shane," she said. "You won't be pure in body."

He touched her hand. "Christ taught us to understand ourselves," he said. "And I'm sure that in the desert, there were strange roots and berries."

"Strange roots and berries? What strange roots and berries?"

"All cultures," he continued, "have used substances native to them to explore their relationship with their god. It's completely—"

"*Their* god?" She shook her head. "There's only one true God, Shane."

Her promise ring shone in the sun.

"I don't want to talk about this," she said. "Drugs are for losers, for people who don't wish to be pure of mind and spirit, for fools who represent the moral antiforce of the mob."

The fish on the back of her Subaru Impreza glimmered. She'd been reading C. S. Lewis.

"Don't make me feel bad about personal discovery," he said. "Be a fellow seeker with me."

She let go of his hand. "Come on, now, Shane. Stop it. You're starting to freak me out. My parents already would prefer I date someone who wasn't in a rock band, no matter how righteous the cause. Don't make me have to justify your living a life that isn't right."

Why did she have to wear such tight tops, showing her shallow cleavage, the sweat running over her silver cross, into her valley of the shadow of good times? Why did she have to be such a hypocrite?

He wanted to roll his tongue through that valley. He wanted to gather her up in his mouth. How could that be wrong?

"Are you listening to me?" she asked.

No, he wasn't.

"Shane? Hello?"

No, he could exist in his own place. He could love Jesus and still play in a band with those of weak spirituality. He could ride the line.

Wet dreams of fame came nightly.

Blood Orphans was a test of Shane's beliefs. Here was an opportunity to walk among the sick and lame and do good, even if he was singing about sex with girls who had no legs, going back in time and assassinating President Nixon, and dropping a neutron bomb on the state of Mississippi. Shane had a sense of humor. He could keep it balanced.

What unbalanced Shane James Warner was popularity, for Blood Orphans, with their raucous, who-gives-a-fuck shows, were an instant hit among the jaded masses of Silver Lake. Onstage, the four wielded a strange magic, and the hipper-than-thou dropped their blank game faces and submitted to the spell. Joey emceed the shows, evangelizing the new gospel like a late-night Sunbelt preacher.

"Behold the very example of rock-and-roll miz-ajesty!" she'd scream into the microphone, favoring her right leg. "Behold the merrymaking, God-dust-tasting, pleasure and pain shaking and baking Blood Orphans!"

Within a month, Blood Orphans became the band to see. Stupidity abhorred a vacuum and they were there to fill it, having successfully—or successfully enough—blurred the intersecting lines between tragedy and farce. All they had to do was lay down a steady diet of decent boogie, rampant chest-puffing, and crotch-thrusting hullabaloo, and the crowds came. The crowds, teeming with unfettered female lust and abandon, shredded the perfect pages of Shane's Christian playbook; all these girls saw him as an idol at the altar of the rock-and-roll stage, at which they wished to receive the most blessed postadolescent communion.

Good Book this, Good Book that. None of it made sense anymore.

"Christ teaches us to be seekers!" he told his girlfriend, Saint Donna of the Subaru Impreza, when they broke up. "Does not Paul say that without wisdom, all is lost? His teachings cannot be real without—"

"What the heck are you talking about?" she said as they sat on her porch together one last time. "How could you possibly twist his words to justify playing music that dishonors everything good? All these songs are about—"

"The temptations of the modern world! How can we heal the lost if we do not understand what brought them to a sorry state?"

He took her hand and looked into her eyes, but he was thinking about a girl he had recently met at a show who could knot a cherry stem with her tongue.

"Seriously," he said, "how can you not see the irony of the situation?"

She twisted at her promise ring. "*Irony?* Is that a Darlo word?"

"What does that mean?" he said, his mind's eye drifting into a sea of wet female lips and slick, smooth tongues. All those tongues! "Donna, you're lost in doctrine!"

She twisted at her promise ring until it came off. "It is *so* over, Shane," she cried. "I don't know you anymore. Who are you? Where is my Saint George? Where is my slayer of the dragon?" She threw the promise ring into the bushes. "Shane Warner, you break my tender heart!"

Shane stared at her belly-button ring and thought of her as just as much of a seeker as he was, yet unknowing, unaware of the different paths one could take to God. So he chose a winding path that, to his friends and family, looked sacrilegious and misguided, ill-conceived and paved in sin. He chose the path marked Blood Orphans.

"Danika!" said a woman's voice in Dutch. "Danika!"

He had obeyed her. He had come to her, and was about to slide into home when she hit reverse.

"Oh, that's my mom," she said, and moved away from his embrace. "I'm up, Mama!" She put on her black terry-cloth robe, shook her dreads a little, and went down the hall. Shane rubbed some peanut butter between thumb and forefinger. The shower began to run.

He smelled bacon cooking. That smell hit him before he could remember that he was vegan. Nose hairs stood at attention, begging for the heavy scent.

Closing his eyes, he tried to imagine the Buddha, walking through the forest in ancient lands, among grains of peace, trees of tranquillity. But his erection stayed put, and the fantasy went haywire. The Buddha disappeared in the shadow of an enormous canopied tuber.

Shane looked out the window, seeing low clouds, feeling cold suddenly, remembering how miserable his life had become. Buddhism was the oasis of hope that he could turn band life around. He'd thought that it would be a bulwark against bad vibes, sad times, problem realities, but he was starting to see that it was as flimsy as any other faith he had tried, a cruddy last theological stand against utter, complete, and stunning foolishness.

Danika peeked in from the hallway. Where her robe opened, soft teenage hip beckoned.

"Are you coming?" she said. "The water's nice. Très sympathique."

These Europeans could speak, like, twelve languages.

"Mon petit chou," she said. "Allons-y!"

He smiled and made a face. "Une...minute...s'il vous plaît."

She galloped back into the bathroom.

"Merde," he said. He got out of bed and put on his clothes, which reeked of cigarettes and beer and sweat. He wondered if perhaps he should take her up on that offer, but no. Prime Dutch pussy would be nice, but he had to get out of the house before Marcus the pervert stepdad showed up again.

A yearning for the warmth and palm trees and surf of Los Angeles stabbed at him. It didn't seem possible that he would be there in forty-eight hours. Like a prisoner who's always known his release date, he felt like the closer it got, the more distant it was.

Buddha said to reconcile your dualistic nature. Put away your desire. Let it flow from you. Let it become a focus point in your mind and watch it drift away. Smaller, smaller. Out with desire, in with peace.

Every once in a while this worked.

Something felt wrong—a strange weight distribution in his body. He opened his wallet to find that somewhere between the Star Club and Danika's sticky teen bed, someone had stolen all his money, two hundred essential euros. He scanned the room, hoping that the money lay here, thrown aside in the black-magic moments of the previous night's passionate disrobing.

No time for that, though. He heard Danika's mother's voice climbing the stairs. He put on his jean jacket and, falling out of harmony for a moment, stuffed a pair of Danika's dirty panties into his pocket.

Duality could be a real bitch.

He peeked out into the hall and spotted a back set of stairs, which he rushed down, bursting through a mud room and out a side door. He made his way through a yard littered with children's toys, but then he ran right into Marcus, standing between him and freedom, taking out the trash. In each of his hands, Captain Dutch Mustache held a galvanized steel garbage can top.

They locked eyes.

"Scum," Marcus said.

Shane felt in his body a negative nostalgia. Buddha didn't discuss premonition, but here it was. On the other side of the next thirty seconds, a memory waited for him.

"Hi, Marcus," he said, the way you speak to a rabid Doberman, and walked toward him.

"Little American scum," Marcus said, and lunged.

Shane tried to dodge him, but the fucker was fast. Marcus smashed Shane's head with the tops, one clang, a Venus flytrap.

"Asshole," Marcus said. He cursed in Dutch, triumphantly threw the lids to the ground, and marched back into the house.

Though Shane reeled from the pain, he was also trying to be at peace with the dualistic nature of the universe, the mixture of pleasure and anguish. He stumbled off, feeling Danika's dirty underwear bulging in his pocket. He was whimpering, his inner peace blown completely.

"Ungh," he unghed, and tumbled into the bushes.

He tasted dirt, felt twigs against his scalp, and imagined himself as an ape, a dirty blond ape who got beaten up by weird, pedophilic Dutch family men. He had devolved into a primate, and no amount of half-baked synthesized theology was going to get him back up the evolutionary ladder. What if his mother, sitting on the porch of their house in mostly sunny Anaheim, saw him now? What would she think as she sipped her decaf English Breakfast? Reeking of over two years of mistakes, of every bit of windborne errata he'd acquired in his long fall from grace to defamy, he buried his broken head in the brambles.

5

IT WAS NOT EASY being the kind, sweet, vulnerable one. Just ask Ringo. Everything you thought, felt, imagined, you couldn't keep it in because you were a flower, an artist, a sensitive soul. That was what made your music so sublime. That was what made you such a standout. That was what got you taken for granted and laughed at and prodded by the animals you shared a van with. You couldn't hide your nature, yet you were stranded in the regiment of rock, where kindness meant being left alone for a few hours to sketch and daydream without interruption while the animals said their words — pussy, cunt, ass, tits — over and over outside the walls of your earphones, banged those words against your consciousness like barbarians at the falling gate of calm.

It was not easy being Adam Nickerson, guitar player of Blood Orphans.

Adam was the soft rose in a garden of black orchids. His pollen had been sent by an evil wind into the wrong field, a field of machismo gone mad, cruelty, greed, lust serving the insatiable master of testosterone. His role in Blood Orphans was a replay of his role in his family, a bunch of REO Speedealers in Bakersfield. Darlo and Bobby were like his brothers, Dave and Ike, always working on another car, always bleeding from putting their hands in the wrong spinning places, always throwing a punch on their way to the next mess, while his dad said boys will be boys and his mom hid in her room, smoking Kools and watching *Oprah*.

She had given him a paint set for his tenth birthday. Saved his ass. He never forgot.

When Blood Orphans was through and Adam was back at CalArts, he planned to do a series of paintings on the history of the band, a fresco of their march from holiness to damnation. To the viewer, it would be a combination of Narnia, Middle-earth, Dante's Inferno, and West Hollywood. He would tell the story his way.

In the morning murk of Morten's apartment, having been awoken by Darlo's slam of the front door, Adam stroked his Fu Manchu, Mickey Mouse blanket at his chest. He thought about the night before. How pathetic they'd become.

There'd been maybe twenty people at the Star Club, two hundred fewer than Darlo had promised.

"We've moved units in this town," the drummer said, dismayed. "Another example of bad fucking Warners publicity."

Adam wondered how Darlo could have deluded himself so completely. The SoundScans for *Rocket Heart* told a stark tale; the record had sold, in the entirety of the greater Amsterdam metropolitan area, forty-three copies. Marketing-budget-wise, that broke down to about seven hundred dollars a disc.

"We've been on the radio and everything," Darlo continued, backstage in the green room, glugging Stella. "I fucking hate Holland."

"Holland hates you too," Bobby said, wrapping his hands in new bandages for the third time that day. "Holland rightly thinks Blood Orphans are—"

"Shut up, Mummy!" Darlo said, and threw an empty bottle at him.

Bobby picked up the bottle and tried to throw it. But with his hands all fucked up and slippery, he just bobbled it, and it crashed to the floor.

"Loser," Darlo said, and Bobby kicked an empty at him.

Shane came in from the bathroom, sporting tight black underwear and nothing else. "Could you guys keep it down?"

"Oh, sorry," Darlo said. "Are you trying to meditate? We'll *totally* keep it down."

"I would appreciate that."

"Swami wants total silence," Darlo said. "Inner-peace bullshit train coming through."

"Leave him alone," Adam said.

Shane threw him a dirty look. "Fight your own battles, please," he said in a bitchy voice. "I don't need your help."

"Spoken like a true Buddhist grand master," Bobby said, and kicked a bottle at the singer.

Matters deteriorated when they hit the stage. Darlo, a mass of hair behind his six-piece kit, immediately introduced Shane as "our sensei Buddhist faggot, just our top Buddhist faggot bro." Shane returned the favor by calling upon the audience for a moment of silence for "the animal behind the drums who, many tours ago, lost his way."

They stumbled into the first song, the infamous "Double Mocha Lattay." Being the band musician was Adam's greatest asset and his largest liability. He had a recurring dream in which he was the favorite son in a family of two-fingered children, the kind on the front page of *Weekly World News*. The other children, all of whom were jealous of his perfectly formed, five-fingered hands, looked suspiciously like the other members of Blood Orphans, and chased him with their webbed scissorhands until he thought he would drop, promising that they would kill him by cruel, slow, and unusual means. In the dreams, he screamed for his mother but no mother came.

When shows were going badly, it never had anything to do with Adam. But in the pretzel logic of a rock band, when shows went badly, it had everything to do with Adam. It was Adam's fault completely. How could he let them down and let the show go bad? It was his job to hold it together.

So it went after "Double Mocha Lattay" ended thirty seconds early, on account of Bobby burning himself with his cigarette while trying to play and smoke at the same time. He'd reached for the Marlboro resting on his Marshall, but with his mummy hands he dropped it down his black silk shirt. At that, he broke into full-on ants-in-my-pants, throwing off his bass, which bounced on the stage like a monster truck running over a bunch of subcompacts, and pulling at his shirt until the offending cigarette dropped to the ground.

"That's a new shirt!" he yelled. "Fucking silk!"

Sometimes when these mishaps occurred, the crowd was with you. They were in on the joke. They had your sympathy. But not this time. Just a dead silence and a few wincing giggles. Everyone stared at Bobby. A little chunky and a lot of greasy, with a hairline that one could only describe as proceeding, Bobby just wasn't a sympathetic figure.

"All right over there?" Shane asked.

"Like you fucking care," Bobby replied, wiping ashes from his shirt.

Standing in the crowd, one could be forgiven for thinking that this hatred would dissipate; one could easily imagine, if one really didn't know anything about how a band worked, that a little collective sympathy would rise up, providing time for the hurt band member to compose himself. But the knowledgeable ones in the crowd knew the laws of rock-band interaction. They knew commandment A-number one: find kindness and destroy it. Pick on the small. Kill the weak.

"Seriously," Adam said into the mike, worried about poor, afflicted Bobby. "Are you OK?"

Genuine concern was chum in the water. And here came the sharks.

"Oh, the artist has spoken," Bobby said, peeling his hands like they were bananas. "Oh, quiver quiver, shiver me timbers!"

Darlo laughed and chucked a stick at Adam. "Ladies and gentlemen, Mother fucking Teresa!"

Shane became the emcee of a roast. He picked up his beer and toasted the universe. "Well, the little precious artist musician has spoken. We should all be careful not to hurt his feelings." He turned to Adam. "Wouldn't want your pussy all sore, now would we?"

Adam shrank in his velvet and thought, Why are you still standing here? Where is your self-respect? There would never have been any Blood Orphans without you. You are the one in control. *You write all the music.*

It was the nature of their taunting that put him over the top. Their disdain for him was a bond, and this bond made Adam feel doubly alone. In their mockery, they recognized each other but kept him out.

"All right," Shane said, trying unsuccessfully to sweep back his dread-nots. "While Adam over here can never get enough of the punishment, I think you fine Dutch people have suffered plenty watching us attack our pathetic guitar player. So let's play a little music?"

"Oh yes, please, faggot!" yelled Darlo, and they launched into Bobby's favorite, "Dave's Really a Girl."

"All right!" the bass player said, and turned up his Marshall.

Jealousy kicked in Adam, and he felt, for the hundredth time, a profound sense of being used. They sure hadn't shat on him in the beginning. Quite the opposite—they'd treated him like a fucking Jedi master, a musical Rosetta stone, a walking hit factory. They bowed down to his every quietly uttered suggestion. They acted like he was the lost son of Jimmy Page, here to bestow melodic genius upon their crass musical plan.

Unappreciative pricks.

From his Euro cot, Adam looked down Morten's hallway. He had woken up briefly an hour before to the sound of a window-pane cracking, and had watched the elongated shadow of Bobby in the kitchen as he lifted his hands to the heavens for forgive-ness. For a moment Bobby was a saint, the poor suffering fool, the lost one, tearing himself apart. Then Adam snapped out of it. At least Bobby was part of the club, the merrymaking fellowship of rock-and-roll stupidity. Granted, the club had no front door, the windows were smashed out, and shit riddled the walls, but it was a club nonetheless, and Adam wasn't allowed inside.

He'd watched Bobby's sainted shadow-hands lift to the gods. Then the bass player had taken to the stairs and let the door slam.

At which point Darlo had let out an orgasmic groan. "Yeah, baby," he said, far away. "That's right."

Even when Darlo's asleep, Adam mused, he has a good time.

He thought of his family, deep in the macho misery of Bakersfield, in the dirty depressed basin of the Central Valley. He thought about his father, the cop, his leather gloves filled with buckshot. He visualized the Cadillac Ranch in the backyard, which Dave and Ike spent endless hours restoring and recalibrat-ing. They were good at two things: fixing cars and selling drugs. Rage ran in his family, and Adam, the mellow aberration, wanted to extract some of that rough ancestral mitochondria, graft it to his cause, use it for a good end against his bandmates.

Being the one everyone picked on had at least one advantage: it provided some objectivity, allowed Adam to see the mess that they were without any mitigating delusions of grandeur. There was no way the record company would continue flushing money down the toilet on their per diems, their gasoline, their van, their accommodations, and, on occasion, their bail bond. Maybe Warners had long ago decided to use them as a test case, to see how long a bad thing can keep on trucking before it completely self-destructs.

But the last show was tonight. Joey was coming. How could she not be the bearer of the final nail?

The Final Nail. If Adam were in charge, that would be the title of their live record.

The other three were in their own worlds of pain, consumed by different addictions: gnarliest eczema, flabby spirituality, sex as oxygen. They had constructed realities of their own, and for these realities to keep on keeping on, they couldn't fathom the band ending.

He was on the outside, denied entrance to the clubhouse, but that meant when the house burned down, he would survive. When the whole thing incinerated, any minute now, he would watch from across the street with other passersby. When Darlo and Shane and Bobby came running through the rotted doorway, choking on soot and ash, he would crack his knuckles, shed a tear, and walk on by. His jealousy of exclusion turned to relief, and his relief turned to contempt. He had finally found a way to contempt, that shiny, brand-new, antiseptic room in his mind. For a while he walked in this new room, untouched, unstained. Then two cars honked at each other, breaking the spell, and Adam rose to his last day as a Blood Orphan.

PART

II

1

BOBBY STOOD OUTSIDE Ullee's Internet café, talking with the girl who looked all *Run Lola Run*. Her name was Sarah, and she was an art student at some school Bobby couldn't even begin to pronounce.

"Blood Orphans?" she said. "Are you lying?"

"No. We're on Warner Brothers. We were the next big thing once."

"Oh, really?" She lit another cigarette. "You sure?"

"Yeah. We used to be the shit."

She French-inhaled. "Sure. I totally believe you."

But it was true. Back in the beginning, Blood Orphans had roamed in fields of goodwill, picked apples from the tree of rock-and-roll goodness, and rolled in the green grass of collective bump-and-grind dreams. Bobby had a weakness for the medieval metaphor, and so he had a fixed image of Blood Orphans as pied pipers at the gates of dawn, wearing bells and vibrant-colored patchwork clothes, rousing up the people of all the good villages to follow them to a place of cultural harmonic convergence. It had been amazing. Elysian, even.

Elysian was one of his favorite words. One time Shane had tried to lecture him on the Elysian nature of Tantric Buddhism, and he had flicked a lit cigarette at the singer's face.

"My word, you prick," he said. "Find your own fucking word."

And truthfully, getting their wings had been effortless. Having played the ironic/not ironic card masterfully—Adam's heavy riffs, Darlo's parody lyrics, Bobby's stupid-basic bass parts, and

Shane's blond-sylph caterwaul, fused into a package by Joey's fast-talking impressariette jive — the A&R hordes arrived in a tizzy. Within five shows, representatives from all the major labels stormed the barricades of Silver Lake in a blazing idiot wind. One of these walking expense accounts claimed that Blood Orphans was the missing link between Aerosmith, Korn, and the Strokes. Another described them as a nucleus around which a completely new musical style could be constructed. Yet another said that in his twenty years of A&R, he'd seen three acts that blew his mind: Nirvana, Jane's Addiction, and Blood Orphans.

You could always tell a normal human being from A&R. They had an extra chromosome of utter insincerity, a covalent ion of free-floating bullshit, making them unlinkable to other, more stable molecular structures. This insincerity most often manifested itself in their appearance — always too dressed up, or not dressed up enough, or wearing a chain of precious metal around their neck, or sporting an extreme version of a hairstyle that went out of fashion six years ago. No one but A&R wore a white suit to a show. No one but A&R would go on and on about how great it was to drink top-shelf vodka. And no one but A&R, except for Darlo, would speak of Caribbean vacations, the crystal blue water, so perfect for snorkeling, the deep-sea fishing trips. Caught a swordfish! It was sweet!

And so the A&R hurricane arrived, in a flurry of free dinners, free whiskey, free lap dances. No independent labels needed to apply; Joey made that clear to all.

"Blood Orphans doesn't have the bandwidth for small fry," she'd declared. "We want planetary dominion and total wealth accumulation. We want France and Greece and Brazil. We want it all. Street cred, you ask? Does it pay my bills? Does it help my stock portfolio? Fuck the little panty-waisted Buddy-Holly-glasses-and-V-neck-sweater-wearing emo shitheads! Zeppelin wasn't indie. Sabbath wasn't indie. Fuck the fifty-fifty split after cost. I want distribution in motherfucking Nowhere, Idaho. I want to see our faces in fucking Bulgaria, Romania, all the eastern bloc countries that never made it to the twenty-first century. Blood Orphans isn't looking to be the house band of white ghetto cool. We want to rock Wembley! Rock the Coliseum in Rome! Rock the LA Forum! Twee, integrity-bound motherfuckers, look upon me and despair!"

The band resembled a new Maserati coming off the line, souped up and tricked out, mad, bad, and nationwide. But beneath the slick exterior, Blood Orphans was Pinto through and through. Rear-end them the wrong way and they'd explode all over the big rock interstate.

Luckily, Warner Bros. saw no need to take them for a test drive.

Bobby longed for those early days, now that the downward spiral was something he looked up to see.

"Yes," Sarah said as they walked down Kalverstraat, a boulevard of tourists and consumer goods. "A very sad story. But are you sure you're not totally full of shit?"

"Very sure," Bobby said. "If you think I'm so full of shit, maybe you ought to leave me to my misery."

She made a contemplative expression. "I was going to spend the day studying, but that can wait. This is more fun. You are more fun."

"That's funny," Bobby said. "I was just stepping out to get a coffee before I killed myself. But this is more fun."

His hands itched so badly he wanted to bite them off. He had actually bitten at his hands before, like a rodent pinned in a trap; Shane had caught him doing so in the bathroom of the Bowery Ballroom, before they played the thousand-capacity venue to about fifty hecklers. It was like getting caught masturbating.

Please bite me, his hands said. Bite me now. But if he did, he would lose his hot new Dutch friend.

"It looks like you stuck your hands in a furnace," she said.

"They've been like this for months," he said. "I don't know how to turn the corner."

She gingerly took them, examining. "We should get you to my doctor," she said. "I wonder if we can get you some painkillers."

"Painkillers sound lovely."

Even at the darkest moment of this two-year experience, he found that being in a touring rock-and-roll band afforded special treatment from the large chunk of the Western world known as Females Under Thirty. He had small but authentic powers; he was a traveling spirit, a little bit holy, a metaphor for adventure. Being a rock musician was one of the last good ways to catch a break.

"Hey, rock star," she'd said, and here she was, Florence fucking Nightingale with a perky rack, vintage clothes, and fire-red hair. She stroked his hands like a fortune-teller.

"It's your mind acting up on your body," she said. "My friend picked out his hair from stress for a long time."

"I feel like a cripple," he said, and looked into her eyes. "It completely changes your life. There are all kinds of everyday things I cannot do."

She looked over his hands with a clinical expression. "Your band must be so worried about you."

He twiddled his fingers in the air. "Are you kidding?" he said. "They call me the Mummy."

She laughed, then covered her mouth to try to be polite, which was the best response he could hope for. So he laughed along with her, milked the wounded monster card. Mee a funny monsterr. Mee have feelings too. People they passed tried and failed to keep their eyes off the deformed American fool.

"What was the name of your band again?"

"Blood Orphans."

"I'm not sure if I've heard of you. What was the name of the record?"

"*Rocket Heart.*"

She lit a cigarette and winked. "If we went to a record store, then I would know if you are lying. You could just be trying to get with me, huh?"

"I wouldn't do that," he said. "I have a rotten imagination. I'm no good with girls. Not smooth at all."

"But you're cute." She took a drag. "Still, I want to see your record. See if you're legit, you know?"

"We won't find it," he said. "The record's as rare as a three-dollar bill."

She giggled, undaunted. And he wasn't cute, he knew that. He looked like a Baldwin brother, but not Alec. Billy, maybe, but minus the raffish charm.

"Amsterdam's big record store is this way," she said, her tight little plaid-covered Dutch ass leading the way. "Let's settle this, huh?"

In every city, it was as if Warners had erased the memory of Blood Orphans from history. The last time he'd seen *Rocket Heart* in a record shop was in Gainesville, back in August, and even then it was an accident. Adam found three copies hidden in the torch song section, behind *The Best of Billie Holiday.* Darlo had demanded an explanation, loudly enough to get himself forcibly removed by a girl wearing a Bettie Page haircut and a Misfits T-shirt. "I heard about you and your stupid band!" she screamed. "Racists! Disgusting!" Darlo, who normally had a retort for every occasion, scurried backward, a crab swallowed by the rising tide of public opinion.

On Kalverstraat, armies of young Dutchies bearing colorful

scarves zoomed by on rickety bicycles, the kind Bobby's old hippie grandmother rode down the streets of Venice Beach. These bikes shouldn't have worked at all, but they had a mysterious Dutch efficiency. Everything worked better here. Despite the congestion, the cyclists moved like water rolling through perfectly oiled urban cogs.

"My stepdad is a musician," Sarah said. She wore chunky heels and still barely cleared five feet. "He plays the ukulele and the guitar. Folk music mainly. I think that he wanted to be a professional musician too, go live in a van, screw girls he barely knew."

"We never do that," he said. "That's a myth. It moves product."

"Yeah, right. Now he's a house builder with an anger management problem. He has a wine cellar and loves to ski. I wouldn't describe him as an unhappy guy. But when I play the Sex Pistols or the Clash in the car, it's like he goes into another world. I wonder if meeting you would break his heart a little."

"He has no idea what he didn't miss," Bobby said. "I promise you."

His cell phone rang; the number had no ID. Maybe Darlo had died a violent death, his face slashed, yes, why not, like a Levolor blind, and the morgue needed Bobby to ID the body. That would be an honor well earned.

Dream on.

"Hello?"

"It's Shane. Hello?"

"Yeah, I'm here. What do you want, Siddhartha?"

"Oh, Bobby, thank God."

"What *is* it?"

Static overcame the line, then faded off.

"I need money," Shane said. "My money was stolen from my wallet."

"What makes you think I have any?"

"Because you *always* do," Shane said. "Come on, man, just help me."

It was true that Bobby had plenty of money. Bobby actually lived on his per diems. But hearing Shane's voice, a little tinny and gravelly, leached all the generosity right out of him.

While listening to Shane recount his shitty morning, Bobby exchanged a glance with Sarah that transmitted all kinds of undeserved affection. He had never felt more fortunate than Shane, so it was so very satisfying to hear the little Christian Buddhist whatever-the-fuck-he-was whine away from the bottom of life's well while Bobby hung out with his new Dutch fox.

"On top of that," Shane said, "my hair's covered in peanut butter."

"Peanut butter, huh?" Bobby said. "Kinky."

"Are you going to help me or what?"

"Hmm," he said. "Actually, no."

Shane huffed. "Why are you doing this?"

"Because I hate you."

"It's an emergency."

"Talk to God about it."

"Fuck you, Bobby," he said. "Fuck you and your fucking—"

Bobby hung up, satisfied. Contributing to Shane's despair cast a dazzling ray over his already bright mood.

"Your bandmate?" Sarah asked.

"That's right. The singer. Piece of shit."

"That's not a nice thing to say," she said. "Really."

"I have my reasons," he said, and cracked a rotting knuckle.

They'd come upon the superstore, which was called Fame.

"This is silly," he said, stepping back. "We're not going to find the record."

She raised her eyebrows. "You're not making all of this up, are you?"

"Of course not."

She took his hand. "Let's go in. My curiosity is killing me."

The bass player felt the familiar hum of humiliation coming on. Aerosmith's new record, *Rockin' the Joint*, was prominently displayed, and Franz Ferdinand blasted through the speakers, their ferocious, angular, and undeniably pro stomp coming down on Bobby to call bullshit on his very soul.

"Oh, I love this song!" Sarah said, and shook her plaid ass.

Bobby had been in this situation before, experienced the awfulness of not being able to find the record in a megastore while trying to impress a girl, saw the way he shrank in said girl's eyes when the store clerk tried not to laugh when she said that he was in Blood Orphans, and come on, there must be one copy of the record here! No? Not one? *Not one?*

And then Bobby's heart skipped a beat. In a corner, in the farthest shadowy reaches of the pop/rock section, he saw his face.

"Oh my God!" Sarah said. "Look at that!"

Bobby's mouth dropped wide open, gaped at the wall display. An oversized poster of their album cover. The four faces of Blood Orphans gazing up from some primeval darkness, looking tough, righteous, and blissfully unaware of the misery ahead.

They were arranged like a compass. Darlo was north, Adam was west, Shane was east, and Bobby was dead south.

Below them, in Old English font, *Blood Orphans,* and below that, *Rocket Heart,* and below that, *June 23.* Down at the edge, someone had tagged a small Post-it note and scrawled *Star Club November 24–25.*

Four faces in the shadows, come from mighty Los Angeles to completely fucking fool themselves.

Sarah grabbed his arm and jumped up and down. "Holy shit!" she said. "That's totally you!"

"How?" he said through the fog of war. "What?"

A clerk stopped, looked at the picture, looked at him, pushed his lower lip out, tapped his clipboard. "You?" he said while blasts of Scottish melody and syncopation thundered out of the speakers. "You?"

"Him!" Sarah said, and pulled Bobby close to the poster. "Wow!"

Bobby stared at himself and barely recognized the kid he saw. He looked healthy and free, happy and cocksure.

"I totally thought you were lying," she said. "I don't believe it!"

As he stood there with this adorable girl suddenly holding on to his arm with both hands, a certainty about the finalities of time settled and took hold. The boy in the picture, his head pushed defiantly upward, could never have imagined anything that Bobby felt here, without the use of his opposable thumbs and two weeks before his twenty-seventh birthday. The picture was a relic from a lost place to which he would never return, from that Elysian time that had been rubbed out of his memory, from the endless summer, from the perpetual kiss of the warmth of the sun, from the frolic in the lush fields of future fame. He knew that he was now, at this moment, officially in the twilight of his youth.

2

DARLO'S MOTHER, ANN ATCHISON, had helped found Dirty Darling and had performed in many of the company's early films. She shouldn't have been one of the big stars because she would only fuck girls on camera, but that didn't matter, because she looked like she should have been emblazoned across the Mexican flag: pneumatic tits and ass, mocha skin, a smile that could start a revolution, and black hair that rose over her head like storm clouds. She stood just over six feet tall. Her license plate was *Inca Fire.*

That didn't last long. By the time Darlo was three, she had left her husband and young child, pulled a Linda Lovelace, gone Moral Majority. She remarried, to an oilman, got a J.D. from Texas Christian, and worked for a right-wing legal organization determined to stamp out everyone's constitutionally guaranteed right to watch complete strangers rut on each other. She wrote to Darlo once a year, on his birthday, but aside from that, Ann Atchison was a stranger.

"Your mother's the poster child for all the suppression and rage of American sexual life," his dad would often say. "When I met her she was a lovely flower, the softest of sweet red petals, the most delicious glass of *agua fresca* I'd ever tasted. Now she makes Ed Meese look like a friend to the industry. But don't let me stop you. You're old enough to make your own decisions."

Darlo saw his mother as the crazy woman who'd abandoned him, and considering that sex had always been waiting for him, a best friend and a comfort, any enemy of its free-flowing goodness was highly suspect. His dad seemed to live a happy polygamous life, rich and rejoicing 24/7, while she sat in the middle of *west fucking Texas* with the idiots who had tried to impeach President Clinton for doing only the most natural thing in the world: getting a little on the side. How could anyone turn down a hot piece of twenty-year-old intern ass?

But when Darlo was seventeen, his mother gave up being all God Squad, got divorced, and moved to Iowa to become a farmer. She met a man there, an Allstate agent. She mellowed and tried to make things right with her son.

"Your father has surrounded you with the trappings of Sodom," she wrote in a letter. "You think that pleasure is holy. Pleasure as an end *and* a means. Pleasure at all costs. Satisfaction without accountability. That is the thrust of your father's philosophy. It is a dead end: morally, spiritually, ethically. You must think about your actions in life. Do they serve a higher end? Do they enrich the lives of others beside yourself? Do they connect you with a higher purpose? Ask yourself. We would love to see you anytime here in Iowa. Fares are cheap. American has very good fares. Have you ever ridden a horse? We have many beautiful fillies in our stable. But ask yourself, seriously, Darlington, if—"

Darlo crushed the letter. His mother was a crank. But when he went to tear it up, his hands went still. Deep in that thick young-pirate head of his, he knew she was on to something. That awareness reached up through the tar of his testosterone.

She was on to something. He kept the letter.

She wrote again. "We were out in the meadow today, Darlo, and I was thinking of you. I was with John and Robert, your stepbrothers, and the wind was in our faces, cold and crisp and fresh, and I thought, wouldn't it be great for you to be with us? I remember when you were a little boy, how we would go to the park in Encino and you'd love the bees and the birds, the flowers and the grass. You were a clear nature baby. You were Adam in his garden, and had His blessing. How I wished, I said to your stepbrothers, that you could be out here on the plain and see the real unfolding of nature, as opposed to the false idols that are daily painted upon your young eyes. Eyes so inured to kindness. Idols drawn across them, a jaded shroud."

Darlo was fun-loving. He had a party-hearty nature like his dad. But he was not his dad. Who was this strange woman, from whom half of him had sprung?

"Your mother," his father said, smoking at the pool. A blonde massaged his shoulders. "She was peaches and cream. Peaches... and cream."

After a bunch of letters, Darlo wrote her back. Hi, I'm Darlo, uh, I read what you wrote, uh, it was good, I have a pretty good average in school. Uhh.

They went back and forth for a while. Darlo kept meaning to rip up her letters, but he didn't.

When he told his dad about this continued correspondence, David Cox adjusted his jock strap, fingered his graying chest hair, and shrugged. "Good for you," he said. "Now the son goes looking for the mother. He goes off to the wilderness. The biblical, the biblical. It had to happen. Find out who you are. Hey, can you call the caterer and make sure he doesn't bring turkey to the shoot? Turkey gives the actors gas. Maybe I ought to have a series about fuckers with a fart fetish! Call it *Blowing Smoke!*"

Her letters, intense as they were, did not illuminate any corners in his past, did not inform, effect, or mitigate his burgeoning sex addiction. For how could you grow up in a world where bodies had no autonomy, when the images of them contorting, twisting, and malleable were more common to you than a family, at a table, eating a meal, and not just roll right into it?

Yes. Sex. The problem with sex.

He lost his virginity at twelve. Her name was Sandy Rose. She was a short, long-lashed, small-bosomed Latina who got paid extra to be his dad's fluffer. She opened his door one sunny afternoon as light from the swimming pool danced on the windowpane. He was watching *Stripes*. Her bikini was the color of unripe bananas.

"Your poppy says it's time," she said, and mounted him.

Seventh grade, eighth grade, ninth grade; the years were a blur of afternoon interludes, morning glories, night visions. Comic flesh configurations, maximum sweat, the rippling of muscles, girls on him, in public and private, among crowds and in churches, dare you to do this, bet you won't do that. Oh, do that again. Do that again. Over here and over there. Over under sideways down. Clench your teeth and arch your back. Hold still. Over and over till his fucking knees buckled.

Compulsion.

His friends treated Darlo like the luckiest guy alive. But they didn't see what had happened on the inside. They didn't see his brain rewired. They didn't see how his life resembled that of a lab rat, overloaded with sensation, glutted with pleasure, fattened up with ecstasy until the taste went bland and only one feeling was left.

His body ached if he went without it for a day. He couldn't sleep until he had the smell of it on his fingers, the faint taste of it on his tongue, the assurance of it upon waking.

What people didn't know was the pain of it. What people didn't understand was how saying no felt like reversing gravity, how pulling away from pussy was like rending muscle from bone. He could never get in far enough. He could never really touch it.

Compulsion. Cold sweat.

In eleventh grade he started playing the drums as a way to calm this ache. He leveraged his horny groove into four-four rhythm.

His girlfriend, Jenni Feingold, had encouraged this hobby when she broke up with him.

"You should see a fucking shrink, too."

"Fuck that."

He went and bought a kit at Guitar Center. The bottomless aching hole started to fill up. He could bash away and feel less empty. Still, she wouldn't get back together with him.

"So you can fuck me and another girl at the same time?" she asked. "So you can pay me to slap her? Darlo, I want a commitment. Not a life in porn."

Jenni Feingold. Putting the Fine back in Feingold. The only girl who ever understood him. The one who started off as a drug buddy from the estate next door and ended up trying it all with him. Never a kink for her. Never slumming it. They just wanted the same thing. Until she wanted the weakest thing a person could want. Monogamy.

He practiced his drums. The more he practiced, the less he wanted to spend all night looking for tail. Even his dad, the Captain of the Mighty Cumshot Exxon, thought it was good for him.

"You have talent," he said. They were walking around the fulfillment warehouse in Pasadena. Stacks of tapes and DVDs surrounded them. College boys in USC caps stood at counters, processed orders, stuffed packing popcorn and product into boxes. "I hate it when kids with money just sit around and count it. You've got good rhythm. I hear the noises the girls make upstairs, by the pool, in the den. I hear all that. Put that to good use."

The letters from his mother kept coming. He was starting to maybe, uh, *like* her. She was honest and relaxed on the page. She seemed to be at peace.

"I think I want to go visit her, Dad." They were sitting in the kitchen: copper pots hanging from the ceiling, a pack of Trojans sitting in the napkin drawer. "So what do you think?"

His mother's latest letter included a promise of airfare to lovely greater Des Moines, where the buffalo roam and the skies are not cloudy all day.

"Why would you want to?" the old man asked, sipping a Virgin Mary.

"Obviously she wants to get to know me."

Père Cox swirled his tomato juice and looked as if he was actually thinking before he talked. He only looked that way when he was choosing box shots.

"Your mother never forgave us for the lifestyle we chose. She says I chose it, but she knows that it was a joint decision. She liked to swing. She liked other guys and me at the same—"

"That's my mother you're talking about," Darlo said, because that's what they said on TV. Indignation seemed like a thing worth trying. "I know that you guys used to—"

"—fuck other people. Your mother led the charge. Off-camera, she wrote the book on double penetration. She's just Linda Lovelacing it." Darlo heard fracture in his father's voice, actual hurt, a knife piercing hard ground. "Really, Darlo, you don't know the half of her world-class denial. And now she's gonna save you from de old debbil David."

"I just want to meet her."

"You spent nine months inside her. Wasn't that enough?"

Darlo tabled the issue. He stuck with the drums.

"When you're ready," she wrote, "come see us."

Darlo's first band was called Salvage Yard. Four guys from Hollywood High. One of them was Darlo's drug dealer, a poor man's Beastie Boy named Jesse. He lived in a French Normandie mansion near Darlo. Jesse's stepfather, a British film executive at Universal, had built in the basement a nice little sixty-four-track, all-digital recording studio for himself, complete with isolation booths, a six-figure bank of compressors, and a two-hundred-gallon exotic fish tank. This was where Salvage Yard practiced, and it was also where Darlo brought his conquests, until the day that the British film executive stepdad caught him taking a girl over the mixing board.

"Can I have a piece of that?" he said, and unzipped his fly.

"I'm into it," the girl said, and moved to oblige.

Darlo had been reading his mother's letters over and over, letters that described the calmness of nature and the kindness of strangers, letters like blades, the words slashing through his fattened-up lab rat mind, confusing everything, rearranging nothing.

"You bitch!" he yelled, and went for her eyes.

Now he was under some heat. Now he had to go see a shrink.

"You are one sick puppy," his dad said after the incident. "Good thing Poppa Dog and Jesse's stepdad have deep pockets. But that doesn't change how disgusted I am."

"You hit girls in your films. You hit girls in every room of this house."

"Please." His father scoffed. "Acts of consent."

Once, Blood Orphans had done ecstasy. They'd gone out to the desert, to Darlo's house in Palm Springs, and loaded up. All the others were bonding about how much they loved each other, man, and can I touch your arm, it feels so good, and oh man, we're just going to fucking take over the world, dude. But Darlo had wandered off into the Coachella Valley scrub and cried about that girl all night.

Outside of Morten's, he adjusted his jock and slipped on his aviators.

"Pussy," he said, sniffing. "Which fucking way to the tail?"

Lately he'd lapsed back into the kind of sex that was, to put it mildly, problematic. Girls were different here in Europe. They didn't bother so much with the pretty scents. They didn't mind smelling of themselves, and they fucked like animals.

American girls fucked like the idea of animals. These Euro carnal trysts hooked him into a part of himself he didn't understand, some murky spiritual swamp where right and wrong were indistinguishable.

Another problem was the flab he was starting to get around his midsection. He hated it when he couldn't see his abs. His abs were drowning in a sea of chocolate beer. He hadn't done his hundred situps a day since this second trip to Europe started. Where was his willpower? When he got back to America he needed to hit the gym.

His phone rang again and he ignored it.

He was so looking forward to giving interviews about the next Blood Orphans record. He would talk about all they had learned about hard work, and say that just because you get a big advance, it doesn't mean that anyone owes you a living. Also, people say we don't get along. That's crazy talk. I mean, sure, we're competitive, that's what makes the music shine, but enemies? Are you kidding? We're totally bros! All that onstage banter is just that. To call it what one reviewer called it, what was it, oh yeah, "a shit shower of bad will," that's just crazy, man! And Europe was totally a gas, a balls-out great time. There's no anti-American sentiment there, no way! That business in Sweden was so completely a misunderstanding. We *love* Sweden.

When he saw Joey later, they really had to map out talking points for the whole band. Especially Shane. Shane needed to ix-nay the uddism-Bay.

But first Darlo had to get some pussy. The sweats were not far away. And he was in the right town for pay-to-cum.

He found an ATM a few blocks from Morten's, housed in a superclean kiosk shaped like a thatched Dutch country house, but there was some kind of problem with his debit card. The screen blinked *Your account cannot be accessed.*

"Fucking Dutch technology," he said, and failed to catch the eye of some hot piece passing by. "Nice coat," he purred, but she didn't even glance his way.

He put in his credit card, and another error message came up. He punched the screen and a small crack appeared in the side.

"Fucking bullshit," he said, and went to find another ATM.

He really didn't want to have to call his bank and complain. He had loaned Citibank many thousands of dollars for them to do what they pleased with, and for a very small amount of interest. And this is how they said thank you?

Another ATM appeared. In the distance lay the main thoroughfare of the red-light district. He stared at the glittering Sinstraat like a child nearing a candy store.

"Come on, you bitch," he said, and entered his PIN.

Another error message. *Funds not available at this time.*

He was beginning to shake.

"Fucking ATM bullshit," he said, and looked behind him. A young woman held the hand of a little boy. He tried to smile.

"It'll be just a minute," he said. "My card isn't—"

She looked down.

He tried another credit card. No dice. His phone rang again. He ignored it, grabbed his card from the ATM, and punched the screen. Another fracture. That was two for two. The woman looked up, horrified. Horrified and superior. Fucking Dutch, he thought, and strolled to the avenue, taking in the wares, laughing at the Museum of Cannabis, looking for a woman who resembled Winona Ryder or Kirsten Dunst. He saw a girl in a window who looked, well, sort of like Winona Ryder. At least she had biggish tits and black hair. She sat on a chaise longue in red-and-black frilled lingerie, trying to look alluring, leaning to one side, showing her little rump. Her office space was candy pink.

Aside from his two trips to Amsterdam—one on tour and one

accompanying his father when he filmed the first three volumes of *Awesome Amsterdam*—his experience with legalized prostitution was limited to the Mustang Ranch, outside Las Vegas. There you had to go to some parlor and actually have a conversation with a few different women before you got to go upstairs, play the whole howdy-sailor routine. Here you smiled, swiped your credit card, and got down to it. You did have to do this funny little thing where you knocked on the door, whereupon the girl acted demure and unsure of what you were doing there, like maybe you were lost and wanted to know the way to the Rijksmuseum.

The Winona-frau watched him cross the cobblestone street. He knocked on the door and she opened it a crack, showing shoulder.

"Good afternoon," he said. "I'm a stranger in town, looking for a good time. Are you a good time?"

Her smile seemed to flag, like a car struggling not to stall.

"I am a good time," she said in a smoky voice. "Come on in." She shut the door, pulled the curtain closed.

"What's your name?" he asked. "Mine's Steven."

She smiled. "I will run your credit card, Steven. And then my name is whatever you want it to be."

Winona disappeared behind another curtain. He had taken off his jacket and shoes and started thinking about positions when he saw, through the little section of window that remained exposed to the street, the faces of several college-aged boys. They smiled and looked mildly retarded. Darlo walked right up to the window and spat at their faces. They reeled back.

"What are you *doing?*" she asked, emerging.

"We had spectators," he said. "I had to teach them a lesson."

"Don't spit on my window," she said. "Draw the curtain. Jesus in heaven."

"I'll show you heaven. Are you ready?"

She rolled her eyes and disappeared back behind the curtain.

"Can't wait to get inside you, baby!" he said, and took off the rest of his clothes. "You are one sweet-looking bitch."

He heard the swipe of his card, and another swipe, and the tap of her nails, and one more swipe. He thought some more about interview talking points. Had to keep Bobby from whining, and make sure they plugged the Shins, and Spoon too. Had to lay the groundwork for some new strategic relationships. You could reinvent yourself in the music business. It had been done before. U2 did it. Madonna did it. All they had to do was—

She reappeared, tapping the card against her palm.

"Denied."

"What?"

"Don't act stupid." Black pubic hair teased out from her panties. "Give me cash or another card or you can go."

"I'm not going anywhere." He pulled at himself. "Fucking try it again."

The giggling face of one of the kids had reappeared in the corner of the window. He grabbed his crotch. "You want some of this?" He shoved his crotch at the kid, who had birthmarks dotting his face. Spittle grew on the corners of his mouth. He laughed and shoved off.

"Listen, man," she said, "if you don't have the funds, we can't play. Got it, *Steven?*"

He tugged the curtain shut and turned to her, hard, stiff.

"Fucking try it again, please."

"I don't think so."

"Please," he said seriously. "The card works. It's just your fucking stupid Dutch computers that have everything all fucked up, for fuck's sake."

She smiled and went in the back. He turned to the window to see if there were any more eyes peeking through. He heard footsteps behind him.

"Did you finally get it to work?"

Darlo turned to find a big blond white guy in a three-quarter leather jacket staring him down. He wore all the right pimp accouterments: rings, greasy hair falling into his eyes, motorcycle boots, and a bulge that indicated what, exactly? A gun? A knife? A copy of the Dutch constitution?

Darlo began hastily putting on his clothes. The guy threw his credit card at him and said some Dutch in the key of get the fuck out of here.

"I thought the idea with regulated pussy," Darlo said, "was that it cut out guys like you."

The large fellow said nothing.

"I thought," Darlo continued, flexing his arm, "that the police handled problems."

"Shut up," the man said, and cracked his knuckles.

"Oh my God, are you kidding?" Darlo cracked his knuckles too. "Woo, scary sound. You need a better trick than that if—"

Leather Jacket Man picked him up, opened the door, and threw him out. Darlo landed on the right side of his face. A few pebbles found a home in his cheek. He jumped up, and the passers-by parted fast, as if he were a ruptured sewer pipe, and then, as the door slammed, he realized that he didn't have his aviators.

"Give me back my sunglasses, asshole!" he yelled, and banged on the door. The door opened, and the man stepped out and shoved Darlo back to the ground. A few seconds passed, and then he heard his precious shades die under the heavy's heel. His phone rang and he didn't answer it.

Darlo looked up. A long, spindly loogie emerged from the air and landed on his cheek.

"Prick," the man said, and closed the door.

Enough was fucking enough. He went into a smoke shop and bought a phone card. One euro a minute.

"You guys really are a bunch of rip-off artists," Darlo told the cashier, who stared at him. "You know that?"

He marched over to a green KPN phone booth, shining in verdant hues, and dialed his voicemail. His cock, pressing against his leather pants, was still hard from the nonevent with the prostitute, and he wondered why he felt queasy. There were seven messages awaiting him, and the first six, cooing from LA fuck buddies, shed no light on the subject. The last one, however, did.

"Darlo, my sweet boy. Greetings. It's Dad. I'm calling from the North Hollywood police station. I've been arrested is all. Some bullshit entrapment. Tax evasion, they say. Money laundering, they claim. My arraignment is tomorrow and then we can celebrate. Of course I'm innocent. I'm the subject of a witch hunt by the FBI. They're trying to suppress freedom of speech. Anyway, the bad news is that they've temporarily frozen all assets, which includes your bank cards. No money will be available for a few days. Yeah, it's a bummer, man, so stretch those panties—I mean pennies. Gotta keep a sense of humor! Rock-and-roll hootchie-koo!"

3

JOEY HAD HEARD IT a million times, like an invocation: Amsterdam, golden Amsterdam, totally awesome city of good times. Smoke pot all day! Have sex with hot prostitutes! She'd listened to these claims while tending bar, nodding at the hipsters who swore Amsterdam was a flat-out heaven on earth.

"My brother went there, Joey, and it's all true."

"My cousin lived there, man, it was heaven."

She'd nodded and polished glasses, imitating Ted Danson on *Cheers*, a mild smile, sagacious. But Ted Danson didn't drink. And she was no sage.

"My uncle married a Dutch woman, and she took him to sex clubs all the time. Fucking sex clubs, Joey! All! The! Time!"

Lies, she thought, dodging cyclists and trams. Everyone here was perfect and buttoned up. The pot shacks, such as the Grasshopper, which Joey entered to drink away the morning, were places no Dutch citizen would be caught dead. She went downstairs into the fetid tourist grotto, sat at the bar, ordered a Stella, felt her morning cocaine course through her blood. She dangled her high heels, massaged her lame left leg, and surveyed the scene: British football drunks watching BBC1 and playing pool, backpackers checking their e-mail, and young Americans gazing about like they were at Disney World. Oh my God, is it true that we can buy pot in here? Dude, they have a fucking *marijuana menu* at the bar, just like ordering a drink. You do it. No, you do it. OK, I'll totally do it, but you've got to come with me! Get the sensimilla! Get the

Panama Red! No, get both, dude! They have Hawaiian Gold too? Dude, get all three! Taste test! Taste test!

She was satisfied with this purgatory; the pot shack was a fine location to lick her wounds, wipe herself off the heel of John Hackney's boots of Spanish leather, and accept the idea that, truly, today was the culmination of two years of downward momentum.

Joey remembered a picture from *National Geographic* that hung in the break room of Spaceland, a snap of the southernmost road on earth, in Tierra del Fuego: a dirt lane fading to grass, and a sign in Spanish saying, *You are officially at the bottom of the world.* Next stop, the South Pole.

Darlo would be calling soon, and what would she tell the deluded porn prince? All is lost, friend. We are drifting into regions of ice. We are through.

Of course he wouldn't believe it. Darlo had no conception that the end was near. The sun will rise in the west before we get dropped, he'd often promised Joey, in moments of managerial doubt and dismay. Darlo would put his arm around her and squeeze her shoulder pads and say, It's all good, babe, we shall overcome. Put your chin up, Ms. Manager.

It had to be nice having an über-dad, she thought, arming you with a heavy dose of the sociopathology necessary to succeed in the world. Joey had always thought she possessed some quality Ayn Randitude, but this entire experience had proven her to be so fucking bush league. At least when it was all over, she would be able to carry on. Darlo, when the news actually punctured his resilient dream world, would deflate, shrivel up, and float away.

She listened to a pool table of English dogs argue about the merits of the Aston Villa, Nottingham, and Wigan squads. A crew of college girls, de facto American in their Juicy sweats and Ugg boot sorority tourist bling, baited each other to buy pot, while the guy behind the counter, an old, mutton-chopped tough who could have been the Who's European tour manager in the seventies, looked right through them and sipped coffee. Soon the English dogs were hitting on the girls, buying them drinks and doing everything short of humping their legs in a scene of total thoughtless pleasure. Joey could not have envied them more. At the same time, she wanted to smash their faces against the oak bar.

She recognized these feelings as a sign to go somewhere else. And then she heard it, coming from the TV.

"Oh no," she moaned. "No, no, no."

It was the Sharpie Shakes commercial. Sharpie Shakes, the formerly unknown ice cream company that two years back had approached Blood Orphans with an opportunity. Please write our jingle. Please be on our commercial. Please be the Sharpie Shakes house band.

Everyone but Joey thought it was a great idea. The Sharpie Shakes people had been so hooked by the advance copy of *Rocket Heart* Steadman had slipped them that they'd offered a sweet licensing situation and a fat fee up front, one that would have netted each band member a hundred grand and the manager even more.

But Joey, back then, had leverage with her boys. After all, she'd just gotten them the record deal of the century, hadn't she?

"Terrible idea," she'd said, swinging a pool cue in Darlo's basement. "It'll turn the Blood Orphans brand into a kiddie joke-metal band. We'll be like Smash Mouth, with a fan base whose average age is ten."

"Not with those lyrics we won't," Darlo said.

The cue flew out of her hands and clanged against the wall, dropping the dartboard.

"It's a slippery slope," she said. "We need smooth longitudinal thinking, not flash-in-the-pan antics. Aerosmith would never have done something like this back when they were starting out. I'm begging you guys to listen to me."

"If you think it's right," Darlo said, and sank the eight ball. "I trust you."

"Fine, fine," Shane said, thumbing through a copy of *Penthouse.*

"That's crazy!" Bobby said, and no one had cared.

In the intervening two years, Sharpie Shakes had become the biggest success in ice cream since Häagen-Dazs. And that damn jingle, performed by some band from Los Angeles that sounded like every other bastard son of Nirvana and Green Day, followed them everywhere. That jingle made it cool for teenage white kidz to love ice cream. It made ice cream Wylde and Krazy.

She covered her ears but resistance was futile.

It's the razor-sharp taste of good times to come.
It's a cool summer day, smooth, fresh, and homespun.
It's the most awesome times with your friends…
It's the half-pipe, the pipeline, the raddest weekend!
Sharpie Shakes, the fun in the sun, you betcha!
Sharpie Shakes, creamy and smooth, it'll getcha!

The sorority girls, in the middle of the first legal joint of their life, jumped up and giggled.

"I *love* Sharpie Shakes!" one of them said. Lovely tits bounced in tight red fleece. "Awesome!"

Joey had really told those ice cream executives what was what.

"We're not a shill for the ice cream business," she'd said in a corporate conference room in Burbank. "Our target market isn't little kids. They'll buy a Sharpie Shake and then they'll buy the record and then the parents will hear the lyrics and lose their mind. They won't understand the irony. Warner Brothers will never forgive us."

Forget that Steadman's only words concerning the matter were *Go for it.*

Now Sharpie Shakes Inc. was the lead sponsor for this year's CMJ Music Marathon. They were cross-marketing with *Rolling Stone*, Adidas, and British Knights. They were putting up mass kiosk action on the Warped Tour, at Bonnarroo, at Coachella. A Sharpie Shake hadn't been near a teenybopper since the rebranding. Smooth longitudinal thinking, my ass.

The pop-punk jingle, performed by some band that made Blood Orphans sound like Zeppelin, reverberated out of the Grasshopper's projection-screen speakers.

. . . fun in the sun, you betcha!

Every time she heard it, Joey died a little. Every time Darlo heard it, he called Joey.

"I'm just listening to the sound of more money going down the drain, you shortsighted poser. How's your day going?"

Well, she thought, if she heard it, so did the band. All over Amsterdam. Her incompetence in every grocery store. A reminder to the four of them of what a fuckup she was, all over the pretty, foggy city.

"So unfair," she mumbled. Draining her Stella and feeling her leg tense up completely, she dropped twice the amount she owed on the bar — damned if she was gonna get cheap now — and limped up the stairs.

The Grasshopper lay on Oudebrugsteeg, which on this any-other-Friday resembled a perfect location for a Fodor's photo shoot, teeming with tourists framed by thousand-year-old, skinny buildings. Diesel engines went *toot toot,* pigeons fluttered around, sharply dressed businesspeople went about their perfect Dutch business, and everywhere, moving around them like plasma holding tissue together, ran the army of three-speed bicycles. Amsterdam was gray all right, here in autumn's final trimester, but it had a level of adorable quaintness that, if you were, say, a rapidly intoxicating, coked-up, small-time failure of a rock band impresariette, had a moderately soothing effect. She took out a pack of cigarettes, sat on the nearest bench, and let the sound of church bells ring in her ears.

Bleary with beer, she had been ignoring, from the depths of her red Kate Spade bag, the ringing of her Iridium satellite phone, a thousand-dollar-a-month, three-pound piece of hardware that ensured that if she were ascending the peak of Everest or kidnapped on a freighter in the Black Sea, she'd still be able to check her voicemail. But now she thought, Shit, why spend all that money if I'm just gonna let it ring? What if it's Hackney taking it all back and ordering me to his hotel room? She pulled out the hunk of beeping black scrap metal.

"Joey, it's Adam."

"Oh, hi, Adam."

In one way or another she felt bad for all the members of Blood Orphans, but Adam was special. She had an extra shot of sympathy for him, even though he'd retained all his money, stayed above the fray, and suffered with the silence of the eventually validated.

"Today sucks a fat rod," she said. "Know what I mean?"

"Yeah. Morten's apartment is freezing and smells like mold. I was wondering if you wanted to go to the Van Gogh Museum."

"No."

"But it's our tradition."

"Tradition. What's that?"

"Come *on*, Joey."

She grunted in grudging assent. On the first tour of Europe, she had gone along for a week, and the two of them had been the only ones who didn't say, Tate Gallery what? And Louvre shmovre! And Prado shmado! What is that, like, a clothing museum?

"Fine," she said, hangdog, "if you're prepared to deal with me drunk and coked up."

"Like any other day?"

"Mean," she said. "So mean to me."

"You started it."

"Half an hour," she said, and dropped the phone back in her bag.

Joey headed south, crossed canal after canal, muttering to herself over the astounding foxiness of Amsterdam boys, pressed and coiffed, riding their dingy grandma bikes, scarves flitting around their heads, with their smooth side parts and slim-cut suits, with their ankle boots and alabaster skin and pointy noses, modern Von Trapps. Said cute boys kept almost running her over, though, but the pointy noses and milky skin made up for it.

A tram whizzed by. She felt the grit of the coach graze her skin. She retreated to the sidewalk and dry-popped a few Tylenol.

These Dutch had a completely different orientation toward public space. They had to be, like, ten times as aware of their surroundings as Americans. The trams went through the *middle of the city*. In America the streets would run with blood, but here everyone weaved and bobbed and hopped around each other, danced between the civic raindrops with their navigational sixth sense. She was just a small, slow-moving American lump to be avoided.

Fucking Dutch with their extra Public Space Gland.

But at least the Dutch weren't looking for a fight. Blood Orphans was the very personification of every cliché about America, arrogant and materialistic, and the band's behavior had grown steadily worse, from practiced bratty to full-on revolting. What other band could go to Sweden, the least belligerent place on earth, and start a riot? If they had sold a million copies, they would just be considered roguish or difficult. But they hadn't. They'd sold exactly 3,451 copies. Joey wasn't sure what that made them, besides losers.

Ah yes, Sweden. Halfway through the first European tour, they were showing signs of acute decay. Shane had grown pale and gaunt while practicing something called "Sensual Asceticism," which the rest of the planet called white powder, pussy, and beer; the singer had long since ditched the basics of hygiene in order to become more connected to his "natural aura," and his band nickname had become Operation Shock and Awful. Adam was in the middle of a month of enforced silence, because, as he'd scribbled to the other Blood Orphans, "my energies need to be recirculated back into me, and then thrust forward through my guitar. Also no one listens to a thing I say." Darlo had contracted crabs, and Bobby had ballooned from all the backstage deli plates and chests of beer. He'd also grown a red beard, and his nickname had been changed from Ovary to Gimli.

Changes in nicknames kept everything fresh and new.

Joey had been in Los Angeles during the first few tours. With Blood Orphans as her not-so-slowly depreciating leverage, she'd formed her management company, DreamDare, and spent her days trying to get record deals for the other three acts under her wing. Success eluded her, however, and after several months of smashing her head against the hard rock, she'd flown to Stockholm, thrilled to be part of the gang once again. But when she walked into the dressing room, her heart sank.

"Jesus Christ," she said. "You guys look like shit."

Darlo had been running toward Joey with the most loving embrace-to-be. But the dressing room was so big that somewhere en route her words sank in, and by the time he reached the manager, his love was gone, and he body-checked her into a table full of food, covering her Stuart-plaid Vivienne Westwood suit in herring salad.

It was like the general coming down to the front lines and complaining about the mud. And the general was a fucking *girl*.

"I have crotch rot!" Darlo cried. "How's the Jacuzzi?"

The entire world had not yet gotten the memo that Blood Orphans was radioactive. In a place like Sweden, there was a five-month lag for such memos to fly the length of the zeitgeist. So the band was running on the final fumes of the Warners European marketing machine, reflected in a) the size of the club they were playing, which was almost a theater, b) the guarantee, which was still informed by some actual booking agent muscle, and c) the packed room of young blond kids, including a not insignificant number of completely shit-hot, very tall, twenty-one-year-old girls.

Joey had introduced the band, just like old times, but the carny-circus-show-barker routine resonated not one bit with the Swedes. To them, she was just some American in a herring-salad-stained suit who spoke loudly and made stupid promises, like her president. They stared and booed. Someone screamed "Nazi oil thugs, go home!" Joey ranted like the Big Bopper, Robin Williams, and Huey Long cramped into one Drew Barrymore-esque tart from the San Fernando Valley, and knew, for the first time since Blood Orphans had been born, that she had wildly overestimated her charm.

The band sauntered onstage. Shane had really become the anti-Shane by this point, without any semblance of the earnest and sweet New Fundamentalist Baptist Church parishioner. Now he was just an emaciated waif wearing torn cotton, grade-Z leather, and eye shadow.

He looked out from sad, underfed, forsaken eyes.

"Good evening, tall Swedish people," he said. "We're Blood Orphans and we do not support the war in Iraq. In fact, we agree with you that it is the most craven act yet from an already craven, power-drunk administration. We want to make that clear. *I* want to make that clear. For it is most certainly written, in the religion that I grew up in, Christianity, that one must respect all races and faiths, and..."

The band had started to play over him, a midtempo number called "Landing Strip Blues ('Taint What You Think)," a common tactic the other three used to get Shane to stop his monologues. Sometimes they had to cycle the same opening of a song for ten minutes, until Shane grew bored and caught the boat as it came round, segueing into the vocals. But that night Gandhi just kept talking.

"I mean, I grew up in a microeconomy of armaments, in Orange County, and my dad was an engineer at Lockheed. You guys don't understand what it's like to, uh, grow up in that kind of military-industrial shadow complex, because your government doesn't actually sell weapons. I mean, I don't know what the main industry is here, besides snow and hot blondes, but..."

Joey stood behind the stage, horrified. Adam and Bobby stood in their corners, statues in this torture garden, and cycled the chord progression. Darlo bared his teeth. Every time they came around for the verse to start, he would count out, as if a little orientation were all Shane needed. But Preacher Shane's train kept a-rollin'.

"Certainly in books I've been reading, like the Kama Sutra and *The Seventeen Storey Mountain*, wait, I mean *Seven Storey Mountain*, issues of peace are first off the most important. That's what good books teach, peace. Any of you girls down here want to show me your idea of peace? But I'm serious, I'm just as upset as you with the war. It's so lame. You know. Uh. Maybe it is *Seventeen Storey Mountain*."

Joey watched the Swedish kids start to fume. Darlo chucked a drumstick at Shane, but it missed and ricocheted into the face of some girl in the front row. She yelped and dropped, and that got Shane on board. He jumped in like a bargain-basement Jerry Lee Lewis:

> It's the big uh-huh ah-ha! the part between the yin and
>   the yang.
> It's kind of sweet, it's got a precious tang.
> I go down there to read between the lines,
> When I'm on my way to that sweet meaty bee-hind.
>
> I heard about it from a cool cool gal,
> She had a brother named Six-Dinner Sal.
> Forsooth! she said, Go now and taste that plunder.
> Don't be a Johnny-one-note when you're down under!

All four of them jumped in for the refrain.

> It ain't here, and it ain't there!
> It has the smell of just 'bout everywhere.
> It's a full-on combo-nation of sin and pride,
> It's the motherfuckin' altar of her Lower East Side.
> It's the Taint! It's the Taint! It's the Taint!

Swedish faces, dumb with disgust.

> It's the Taint! Makes me Faint! It's the Taint!

Every time the band yelled "Taint!" Joey felt the temperature in the room drop. Blood Orphans was supposed to be a joke; no matter how offensive the lyrics, they were to be delivered with a smile and a wink. But touring had dredged the joy of the music right out of the band, and now the lyrics rode in on the scaly wings of scorn and hostility. When Shane began the last verse, Joey watched the Swedish faces lose all semblance of color. So did hers. Darlo had rewritten the lyrics for the occasion. Shane grabbed the mike and bent in:

> Sometimes I think that NATO is all shit.
> You Europeans, you Swedes, are the pits.
> Why do we keep on giving you schmucks a pass?
> Grow some stones and save your own sorry ass.

> But wait, I think I lost the plot or two.
> This ain't no song about no *Pierre le Fou.*
> It's about the places that I like to go,
> With all you natural-blond babes right after the show.

> It's the Taint! No restraint! It's the Taint!

The Swedish faces hardened, their days of neutrality over.

> It's the Taint! Makes me faint! It's the Taint! The Taint!
>   The Taint!

The song ended, ushering in howls and boos and a hail of plastic cups.

"Stock-mother-fucking-holm!" Bobby said. "Good evening!"

A female voice lobbed a Swedish-toned grenade from the back of the hall. "Fuck you, American scum!"

Shane laughed, locking eyes with a male member of the audience, and thrust his hips a few times. Shane had been a sweet kid—all full of religion, perhaps, and kind of naive, but without a bad bone in his body—and now he was an underfed, leering monster who had embraced the persona of obnoxious rock star, one who resembled Sebastian Bach in his "AIDS Kills Fags Dead" stage.

"You want a piece of this?" he asked the audience member. "I'll have your little girlfriend instead."

Another verbal mortar sailed over no-man's-land. "Go home, Blood Orphans!"

This soon became a chant, like at a football match.

"Go home, Blood Orphans!"

"I think they want us to go home," Darlo said into the microphone.

"I think so," Shane replied, surveying the crowd. "What do you think, Adam?"

Adam looked up from his guitar. Come on, Adam, Joey thought, you're the voice of sanity and professionalism. Bring it down a notch.

"Fuck 'em," Adam said. "Let's play 'Hella-Prosthetica.'"

"He hath spoken!" Bobby yelled, and mangled the opening bass line.

Shane continued to taunt the front row as the band started up a song about having sex with a girl without legs, a song much more offensive than the ones that had earned them the racist tag. The singer posed in a torch song affectation, holding the mike gingerly in his hands while giving the front row the finger. Joey hoped that these were, at heart, mild-mannered Swedes who would never deign to take Shane's bait.

Two tall, thin, equine boys jumped onstage and tackled him.

Before the mike thumped to the ground, Shane's surprised laughter moved through the hall like the last amazed gasp of a man going under.

Darlo trampled up and over his drums, a West Hollywood warlord out in the wilderness, happy finally to have cause to attack the natives. One of the Swedes squared up to meet him and received a bull's-eye kick to the groin, a kick underwritten by the full-body frustration of a profoundly tweaked son of a pornography empire. One perfect kick to the crotch and the whole crowd jumped onstage.

Guitars and microphones hit the ground and fed back, slathering the riot in steel noise.

Of course now Joey had to get into it. She had to have their back. So she ran to the dressing room and hid behind a couch.

The Swedish police were exceedingly polite. They escorted the band to the Stockholm Grand Hyatt and asked for autographs.

"Finally!" Darlo said, blotting a bloody lower lip back in the hotel room. "Something to get us on *MTV News!*"

"Yeah, great," Joey said, gunning a Carlsberg. "You wish."

Darlo threw an empty bottle at her. "Shut up, you fucking coward. Jesus, how much of a pussy could one girl be? Take your heels off and get in the fucking ring, Joey. Even Adam got my back. Adam!"

Bobby took his hands out of an ice bucket. "Did you see me bite that guy!" He whooped and threw his hairy hobbit feet on the coffee table. "It was awesome!"

Now, traffic swirled around Joey. She dodged and weaved and favored her right leg. Darlo's voice in that Stockholm hotel room rang in her head, accusing, indignant, and unappreciative.

Yeah, Bobby, she thought. *Awesome.*

A school of Dutch male fish rode by, so close that Joey smelled their cologne. There were certain scents, apparently, that never made it to the States. Certain scents that had never been on the same acres as a pesticide. These guys smelled like new grass. They smelled great.

This isn't easy for anyone, Hackney had said. *We wanted to make this work.*

"I'm worthless," she said, and hobbled toward the Van Gogh Museum.

4

ADAM STOOD IN MORTEN'S bathroom, meditating on his newfound contempt. Fun as it was, he wouldn't let his contempt consume him. The way to happiness was through peace with that which you cannot contain, said Professor Harold Sweet, the head of Adam's open studio his first year at CalArts. Sweet was a wizened old man who had studied with De Kooning and partied with Pollock, so everyone hung on his every word.

"Art informed by ego is trash," he said, and tapped his cane. "You can never escape cliché if you are using art to assert yourself. You can never justify your existence on earth with your art. It's not real then. It's not universal. How can the universal and the ego coexist?"

Adam counted to ten, stared at himself in the mirror. He stroked his Fu Manchu and brushed his teeth and hummed one of his favorite guitar parts, the soaring solo in Tom Petty's "The Waiting," where Mike Campbell turns sorrow into sunrise.

"Art and anger are not bedmates," said Professor Sweet, leaning over Adam's canvas, pointing at his painting of a face not unlike his father's. "That is the anger of your ego informing your work, resulting in undue force." He grabbed Adam's hand. "This isn't a portrait. You're not using the brush to draw out the figure. You're using it just to hack at the face. Are you trying to leave scars?"

But you couldn't apply these truths to rock and roll. Rock and roll was ego and anger and the universal mashed together in struggle, shoving their way around the head of a pin, fighting for the smallest prime emotional bandwidth.

How many times had he said he would leave? How many

times had he threatened, in that reedy little voice of his, only to be laughed at?

"Leave?" Darlo said. "And do what? Go back to painting your little paintings and working in a coffee shop? Now that you've got your quarter mil? Please."

He dressed and went outside, called Joey and persuaded her to meet him at the Van Gogh. Those times with Joey, roaming through the museums while he talked about Truth and Meaning and she hit on young museum attendants, always cheered both of them up. One time in the Guggenheim Bilbao he'd pondered the genius curves of Frank Gehry's architecture while Joey did some dude in the bathroom.

He went into the café. Behind the counter, a middle-aged dreadlocked guy smoked a clove and read the paper. His dreads ran almost down to the small of his back. They looked like the broken arms of a giant spider.

"You are another one of the band, yeah? The Blood Orphans?" He stuck out his hand. "I am Ullee."

"Adam." They shook hands. "Hi."

"Your bandmate was in here...an hour ago, maybe? Bobby?"

"The guy with the ripped-up hands?"

"That's right." He drew Adam two shots and squinted from the smoke of his clove. "We talked. Nice young man. But those hands..." He shivered in disgust.

"It's actually really sad," Adam said. "Bobby's completely screwed up. His hands are an expression of that."

"Yes, man, completely," Ullee said. Apparently that was the Dutch way of saying *whatever*. "How's the coffee?"

"A delight."

Adam was pleased to meet Ullee. Like so many Europeans, he seemed to be missing that underlying principle of aggression that marked Americans.

"So many American bands," Ullee said, "they come in here to get their breakfast and check their faraway e-mails. They complain about Morten and how cold his apartment is. They do seem so very sad."

"They are," Adam said. "Touring is miserable unless you're famous."

"Ah yes, if you were U2, that would be fantastic!" Ullee looked at Adam as if they'd just come upon a truth together. "Fantastic, man. But still, there must be something good that happens on the road, no?" He motioned to a stool. "Why not tell me about it, hmm? One good story, ah?"

A story? He had no story for Ullee. He didn't want to revel in the misery of a terminal group psychology that had long since scarred him enough. He wanted to spend the day in Amsterdam, this last day of what had to be their last tour, going out on a good note. He was going to stay above the fray.

"Sorry, Ullee," he said. "No new tales to tell."

"Ah, yes, OK," Ullee said. "Sick of talking about it, no doubt."

"Yeah. That's right." He laid down a fat tip. "Could you tell me where I could rent a bike?"

He had weathered the storm of the months of bullshit, and now he was but one show away from freedom. All the times that he'd thought of quitting, promised, sworn up and down that he would, only to find himself tongue-tied and backtracking when he saw Darlo's thug face: he'd cursed himself for being such a doormat, but now he felt as if he'd suffered through to a more evolved state. He could leave this band with his integrity intact, without telling strangers stories of woe, without submitting to the weakness of complaint. He could walk by that bombed-out clubhouse, *Blood Orphans* spray-painted above the doorway, with his head held high, proud of what he had done and how he had acted as a participant in, if not a member of, this band. Couldn't he?

5

SHANE STARED AT his phone. He hated it when Bobby hung up on him. If he couldn't exert some kind of power over his most despised compatriot, then this was going to be a shitty day indeed.

And who was that girl who had been giggling behind Bobby, giggling at everything the Mummy said? Fucking Bobby, always picking up the scraps at Darlo's endless sex feast.

He sat down on a bench, cracked his back, wiped a piece of peanut butter out of his eye, and tried to meditate. Buddha taught that money and issues of the material world were just—

"Oh, fuck that," he said.

The scene before him felt insidious: the well-dressed Dutch looking at him as if he were a gob of acidic spit burning a hole in their newly painted Euro bench; the pitter-patter of rain that fell from the Goth sky; the barking of Dutch pugs, running in circles with their crushed, buglike faces as their owners chattered, their posture excellent.

His mother had a pug named Rosie. Once a week you had to dig the slime out of the ridges in the dog's face.

It is not good to blame others for the fault of one's self, he thought. You can make of this day an opportunity, not for self-pity and misery but for taking stock. You could make this day a meditation on modesty, and be humble, like Buddha, and integrate your failings. You could practice Shamatha, and devote an hour to Vipashyana, and perfect the task of Vipassana.

You could also make of this day a time to reflect on how badly your quasi-religious bullshit has served you, and how perhaps just once it would be better to think like the people who surround you, think like Darlo or Joey or Bobby, with nothing but your own interest at stake.

He checked the time on the pink Swatch that Donna, his ex-girlfriend, had given him as a peace offering the day he left for tour.

"I wanted to let you know I cared," she said. "This way we'll always be together."

He held a soft spot for her. She was the representation of all he had forsaken to take on this life, and though he thought she was hypocritical, judgmental, and wouldn't take him in her mouth, he still associated her with cleanliness and clarity.

He breathed deep, trying to clean out his bad karma, just like that Seattle yoga instructor he'd fucked had told him to.

"I wish you lived here," she'd said, pointing out the window at the snowy peaks of the Cascades. "You have such a clear aura. Totally clear. Even on coke!"

Though it was unpleasant to sit destitute in a foreign country while your ears ached from the percussive talents of some crazy foreign stepdad, it was less unpleasant than waking up next to girls like that yoga instructor, who looked at you after one night of amphetamine passion like they were going to turn you inside out, find everything they thought was wrong with you, and change it all while you were sleeping. And it was also less unpleasant than waking up in hotel rooms next to Bobby as the bass player scratched his hands and cried.

"Bobby," he said, and made fists.

He tried to recall what day it was but could not. Being on tour took you out of civilization's circadian rhythm. A weekend was meaningless, a respite from nothing at all. At first all of them thought this was the best possible proof that they'd escaped the clutches of society's grinding ways, but as time went on they mused aloud that it would be nice to have a part of the week to have something to look forward to. Their lives were suspended, floating, and they were never sure which direction they should be headed in, borne by currents that had long ago turned into a churning rock-and-roll riptide.

"Friday," he said. "It must be Friday."

He exited onto the street. Before him lay a Starbucks inside an old mansion. Through the windows, he watched hot Barista-Frau serve more superswank Dutchies, who then repaired to tables to read their crisp, perfectly creased newspapers, not a bit of ink on their hands. Shane was in the habit of pretending he knew something about art—why should Adam have all the fun?—and he tried to compare the scene to that of a famous painter, as if someone were there waiting for him to prove he was smart. He scratched at some peanut butter itching his ear.

"Edward Hooper?" he said. "Is that his name?"

Some church bells rang, off in the clouds, bringing to mind his decision to give most of his advance—which, after everyone got his cut and his taxes approximated, was a hundred and twenty-three thousand dollars—to the New Fundamentalist Baptist Church of Anaheim.

"Sounds like a bank," Bobby had said. "Why would you do that?"

The two had been sitting on the Venice pier, eating hot dogs. They were leaving the next day for their first tour, and Shane felt compelled to tell someone about his decision, to, yes, fine, show what a selfless seeker he was. He would rather have told Adam, but here he was with Bobby, and he couldn't hold it in.

"I want to give back," the singer said. "The church has provided me with the moral backbone I'll need to make it through this journey with my integrity intact. I can't even imagine the temptations we'll find."

"I can," Bobby said, and smiled. "Can I ever." The bass player chewed thoughtfully on his hot dog. "I think that's admirable, really," he said. "But it sounds like guilt money to me—like you're just trying to make yourself feel better about what you're doing."

"Well, it's not," Shane said, indignant. "I am honoring His works by tithing. Tithing is a practice by which the—"

"You know I'm an atheist, right? Like, I have no idea what you're talking about and I don't care." Bobby lit a cigarette and shook his hands, which at the time showed only traces of eczema. "I don't know, man. Giving all your money to some fascist church sounds pretty stupid to me. One day you'll really regret it."

That day, at the dawn of the Blood Orphans anti-empire, Shane's bank balance showed twenty thousand dollars. This was spending money; the band received a per diem check once a month, a direct deposit in the amount of four hundred and fifty dollars, which broke down to fifteen dollars a day. The balance, fifteen grand, was the part of his advance he hadn't tithed.

Now, seventeen months later, all of his remaining money, all two hundred tax-free euros, lay, most probably, in a gutter. The rest of it sat in a vault beneath his childhood house of worship in Anaheim.

Squatting against a Dutch wall, his stomach growling and his wallet empty, he thought his decision to give back was the dumbest thing he could have done.

"Pride comes before a fall," he said, and went into the Starbucks.

How strange it was to be looked upon as slime. So much of his life had been spent pronouncing upon the failings of others. One does not see one's own vanity until groveling in personal decay. He thought of the Buddha before he became transfigured, a prince dressed in the finest silk, awaiting his enlightenment, and tried to meditate while standing in line, now a pauper, now one of the outcasts asking for alms.

I am a beggar, Shane thought, free of material want. I am sweetness and light, joy and radiance. He imagined chirping birds perched on his shoulders. The beggar approached the barista.

"Hel*lo*," he said in the most joyous voice he could. "Hel*lo*. I come to ask for coffee. I come...to ask...for coffee."

The girl—short, blond, and looking as if she'd just jumped out of an ad for Dutch waffles—did not regard him as a fallen prince receiving enlightenment. A beat-up scarab, maybe. A frayed Teutonic leaf, perhaps. A peanut-butter-stinking American poser with matted albino stubs for hair, most likely.

"Bathrooms are for the customers only," she said in a rattled English. A black-suited businessman pushed ahead of him.

He wondered which noble Buddhist truth this beggarly moment qualified as. Was this dukkha or nibbhana? Then again, perhaps it was tanha. It was hard to keep track of these things. He had to eat something.

"Please," he said. "I'm a...starving...muzish-an."

He wanted to sound like one of his prophet-heroes, but mainly he sounded like Captain Kirk talking to an alien life-form. His ears ached.

"I...must eat...some...food."

He understood that he had devolved. He had indulged. He had lost his way. But wasn't losing your way part of the way? To go against nature is part of nature too?

"Please," he asked the little Dutch barista, nudging his way up. "Please give...me some cake...and coffee?"

She smiled politely, as did the whole counterful of green-aproned and black-polo-shirted Dutchies, and said nothing.

He looked around at the line of pensive, productive people.

"Please?" he said, smiling. "I'm in...a rock band. My bank account is empty. I'm...so...hungry."

The Starbucks employees spoke to each other, staring at him.

Then their noses wrinkled. Peanut butter could really get rank. All in line kept a healthy distance from His Royal Aromaness.

What would his mother say if she saw this? Oh, why did he have to think of his mother now, driving through Orange County in her yellow Miata, listening to James Dobson's latest book on tape, nodding along with every fifteenth-century idea he threw out there.

"Here," the girl at the counter said, handing him some coffee-cake, reeling at his stink. "Take it and go. Please go."

Outside, he wolfed down the burnt offering. It couldn't be just the peanut butter that had them so revolted. There had to be something else. And then he looked down and gagged.

Dog shit. On his leg. On his shoes. At some point he had fallen in a mighty fresh steaming pile.

He thrust his head into the bushes just a few feet from suited Dutch people enjoying their civilized morning and vomited. Right in the middle of the pretty Dutch scene. Welcome to the jungle, baby.

A businessman almost tripped over him. He stared at Shane, let out a volley of curses, and kept walking.

He needed to get cleaned up, go to Morten's place and get a fresh set of clothes and a shower, but he had exactly no idea where Morten's was. Danika had pulled him into that closet backstage, and then they had run off, drunk and cavorting, before he got the information. And he had no idea where Joey was staying, either. He dialed, but Joey wasn't answering. He left a message that made everything sound a lot better than it was.

"You know, so, no biggie," he said. "But if I could use your shower before the show, that'd be great."

Joey would not get the satisfaction of hearing him beg.

He belched up some cake that he hadn't puked. A car drove by, and he heard the Sharpie Shakes jingle.

…creamy and smooth, it'll getcha!

That really hurt.

Shane ran across the street to a little park, grabbed some leaves off the ground, and wiped off as much of the dog shit as he could. Nothing brought failure more into focus than wiping manure off yourself. Bile bubbled up in his throat.

A few bicyclists zoomed by and knocked him over.

"Assholes!" he yelled, and rubbed his shit-stained hands in the grass.

There had been triumphs, hadn't there? There had been moments of glory, sweet glory, where it all seemed worth it, right? He scoured his memory: the time they played in Times Square on the *Carson Daly Show;* that three-night opening slot for Motley Crüe at the Henry Fonda, right after they finished the record; the photo shoot for *Rolling Stone,* and their cover story which never saw daylight because of that stupid charge of racism, that prick editor of *Spin;* the first American tour, rolling thunder in summer, everyone getting along, before Darlo got beat up by that crippled girl's brother; doing LSD in the desert outside Tucson with those twins, taking off their clothes, mixing his lingam with their yonis, piercing them, a live wire into their energy fields, and the greatest good time of all, whether or not he cared to admit it, the money, that insane advance, and why did he have to remember that now, goddamnit? Why had he given all that money away to satisfy his shame?

Bobby being right galled him.

But all of that still didn't even begin to explain how he had gotten to this wretched place. It didn't explain shit. And speaking of shit, some of it had gotten on his hand. He wiped it on the ground, scratched his arm, and felt a little lump in the chest pocket of his jean jacket. That lump was a counterweight to his light wallet, a key to another door, behind which lay calm and happiness. He pulled out a twenty-euro note. He had no recollection of putting any money there. The flimsy scrip was a gift from the universe, a reminder of fortune.

"Thank you," he said to his arm. "Blessed be, thank you."

He shed a few tears of relief, making promises in his head and apologies to the sky. "I am so sorry," he said, "that I let my anger divert me."

The Buddha didn't let anger get him. The Buddha didn't get consumed with rage, step in dog shit, and lose track of the money he had in his pocket.

"O thanks to the peaceful ways of thee," he said, and stumbled on.

The first food establishment he saw was where he would eat, he decided, even if it meant he would have to eat meat. So hard to find anything vegan in this town. So hard to find anything vegan anywhere in Europe. And there, like a mirage, stood a McDonald's. He hadn't eaten McDonald's in years. It was the vegan Antichrist, the herbivore's Beelzebub. But philosophy seemed like a luxury that cost a lot more than the twenty euros in his pocket, and suddenly he missed meat even more than he missed his long-lost sense of who he actually was. The golden arches beckoned like the arms of Shiva.

6

YOU PEOPLE ARE CRAZY!"

Joey bobbed and weaved in the tangles of another throng of cyclists.

Ring ring ring! Dutch Dutch Dutch!

"Jesus fucking Christ!" she yelled, but they didn't give her the satisfaction of a glance. "Gonna kill me!"

Her brain floating in a pool of Stella, she stopped at a soup bar and sucked down minty split pea while a trio of teenagers made a bunch of noise about how great Ryan Adams was. "So cute!" one of them said. "So talented!"

She hobbled out, dry-popped a few more Tylenol, and approached the line at the Van Gogh, which ran halfway down the block. Adam stood near the front, reading a copy of *Siddhartha*, looking like an extra in Cirque du Soleil. Joey frowned. "Oh God, please don't fucking tell me that you're getting into that Tantric Buddhist bullshit too."

"No," Adam said. "I just wanted to see if anything in the book matches up with anything that Shane says."

"Does it?"

"Not yet."

Adam smiled at her in that annoying heartfelt way. The guy had a sincere streak five miles wide. But Joey knew she shouldn't be sitting in judgment of anyone, and after all, that syrupy look felt kind of nice. No one else in the band was going to give her that look, especially with the bad news from Hackney. She wondered where in Amsterdam she could buy body armor.

"I went into the Grasshopper," Joey said. "Have you been there?"

"For about ten minutes. Such a bummer. Like an opium den. Tour is already depressing enough."

"Well, it's almost over."

Adam nodded solemnly as they shuffled forward. "I've been waiting months for touring to end, but now I really don't know what to feel. It's weird that we're going to be in limbo, you know?"

"Roger that," Joey said, but of course they weren't going to be in limbo. One show was all that stood between Blood Orphans and the dustbin of rock-and-roll history.

"Darlo completely humiliated me onstage last night," Adam said as they filed in. "It's the last time."

"You've said that before."

"This time I mean it."

"You mean what?"

Adam said nothing, took out his wallet.

"That's what I thought," Joey said. "Don't worry, I'll get it."

The Van Gogh was packed with happy faces: the American upper-middle-class tourists with their new REI-approved hooded winter parkas; the hostelers with their water-resistant Thinsulate anoraks; the young Dutch couples arm-in-arm; the shutter-happy Japanese traveling in packs. But there wasn't an ounce of happiness, Joey thought, in the work before them. MC Van Gogh sure had rocked the most miserable of painterly mikes.

Joey had minored in art history at UCLA, and she thought about painters in rock music comparisons. Monet was straight-up Lovin' Spoonful. Mondrian was Kraftwerk with strings. Canaletto was two parts Beatles and one part ELO. But Van Gogh was his own thing.

"You're really hobbling," Adam said. "You OK?"

"I'm fine," she said, and tasted lipstick. "Don't bring it up."

They stopped in front of *The Cottage*. A little rural house, the sun going down, a fire within through the stone window. Rough filters.

"I love this one," Adam said. "I wrote a paper on it in art school. It was like a creative writing/art crit course, where we took paintings and extrapolated on what we thought the story was. I said that it was the house of a local murderer, a nineteenth-century serial killer."

Joey scanned the crowd for hotties. Slim pickins.

"Where did you get *that* theory from?" she asked.

"It's so sinister. Look at the wet olive tones and the burnt orange."

Joey picked a cocaine crumb from her nose. "What, now olive and orange are symbols of death?"

Adam looked exasperated; she wasn't playing her part. "No," he said. "Jesus, Joey."

"You're not explaining it very well."

"Well, quit being so literal. Just *look* at it, for fuck's sake." He stuck his hands out and made a scrunchy motion. "Just feel it."

Joey stuck her hands out the same way. They looked like two people poking through an invisible pound of raw hamburger.

"Feel it?" Adam said. "Murder on the menu."

"Hmm," Joey said, and crossed her arms. "Do you think Van Gogh had a big cock?"

Adam looked down, exhausted.

"I should have been an art critic," she said. "I should have followed my bliss. I could have been the art critic who writes about imagined artist cocks. Could have written a whole fucking book about it. I'd call it *The Angle of the Dangle*. An awesome muh-fugging title. Don't you think?"

"Quit mocking me," Adam said.

She still had that cocaine crust on her finger. It almost constituted a bump. She wiped the residue on her skirt. "Do you think I was a good manager, Adam?"

"A good manager?"

"Just check your reticence at the door and answer the question."

Adam stuck out his lower lip. They had moved on to a series of paintings of flowers. "I think you did the best you could. I mean, I'm so wiped out it's hard to say. Maybe in a week I could tell you."

She squinted. "A week."

"That's right."

"Why?"

"Because it's a complicated question."

She looked deep into his eyes. He wasn't kidding.

"Just say yes or no. Just go with your gut."

Adam looked as if he suddenly had to take a raging piss. "I just don't know, Joey." He tried to move, but Joey grabbed him.

"Say yes or no," she said. "Don't write a letter. Don't consult your genie in a bottle. Don't call your mommy for advice. Just tell me what you fucking think."

"Adam?"

A slight, beautiful hipster boy in the eighties-revival style emerged from the crowd.

"Oh, hey," Adam said. "How are you? This is Joey, our manager."

The boy introduced himself as Charlie Darling. He had photographed the band for British *Vogue*. For the shoot they had frolicked in the topiary of some thousand-year-old English manor dressed up like dukes, all Adam Ant–like. Charlie caught them in midair poses à la *Hard Day's Night*. After, they had all done ecstasy. Bobby and Charlie Darling had made out behind the stables.

"Wow," Joey said. "Bobby, huh?"

"Indeed," Charlie said, playing with his headband. "And how is Bobby? Boy with the thorn in his side, eh?"

"In his hands, maybe," Adam said. "What brings you to Amsterdam?"

"Long weekend of sexcapades," he said. "You can't beat this town for hobbying, and the price is where it's at. But how have things *been?*"

"Terrible," Joey said. "We've been abandoned by our label."

Adam looked at Joey like, What the fuck is wrong with you? He actually looked disgusted. This improved Joey's mood a hundred percent.

"Oh yeah," she continued, "we've been fucked three ways until Wednesday by Warners. Left out to dry. Screwed, blewed, and tattooed."

"Uh-huh," Charlie said, because no one ever said stuff like that. You always kept up a bullshit front. You always acted like you'd just been asked to headline the Super Bowl. "Sorry to hear that. Such a good band."

"You're not sorry," Joey said, disgusted with Charlie, a real Captain Disingenuous. "You probably think it's funny. You're probably just as fake and backstabbing as the—"

"*Shut up,*" Adam said.

Ah, fuck it, Joey thought. This was sweet, being able to speak her mind. But wait, she had always spoken her mind. That was the problem.

"I'm so sorry about the way things have gone," Charlie said. "Hopefully things will improve."

"Doubt it, Charlie," she said. "Nothing personal. I'm sorry. But fuck you and fuck British *Vogue* and fucking fuck all of you."

She winked at Adam, whose mustache had withered completely.

"See you outside?" she asked, and tried to skip away. But her bad leg wasn't doing so hot, so she hobbled off, clutching herself, moaning in pain.

7

THEY'D BEEN HAVING such a nice time, Adam thought, and then Joey had exploded all over the fey photographer. Which made him think that maybe they hadn't been having such a nice time, that in fact Joey had been acting strange since the moment she appeared in line, dim-eyed, beer-breathed, and limping, carrying a vibe that said, It's over. Curtains. *Sayonara. Auf Wiedersehen,* Blood Orphans.

Joey, he knew, was a good soul; she may not really have known what she was doing, but if nothing else, she was a buffer zone between Darlo and the universe. Their only trouble-free tour had been the one she'd been along for; Darlo hadn't gotten in a single fight, and Darlo could no more avoid fights than he could avoid semianonymous sex. The drummer's feelings for Joey were hard to determine, but he sure as shit straightened up when she walked in the room.

Yes, they were having a gay old time, there in the Van Gogh, until Joey started going on about whether or not Adam thought she was a good manager. Got right up in his face, so that Adam saw the network of lines around her eyes, lines that ran down her cheek so she looked old, as if she'd smoked too many cigarettes and had lost the elastin in her face. He could see the process of decomposition starting to happen underneath the smooth Sephora sheen, like in a horror movie where the young, beautiful girl is revealed to be three hundred years old, and a bloodsucker.

"See you outside?" she had said, and scampered off like Quasimodo.

Adam found her out front, talking on the phone with Darlo. Joey hung up, smiling. "Darlo's got his panties up in a bunch. Something with his dad."

"Hope it's not too bad."

"I hope it's bad." She smiled tightly, cigarette smoke enveloping her. "The guy's a fucking scumbag. I told Darlo from the day I met him that he needed to distance himself from the old slime-stain. And did he listen? No. God forbid he should listen to me."

"You're the *only* one he listens to."

Joey looked at him, disbelieving, smoke shrouding her face. "That's ridiculous."

"Is it?" Adam's eyes went sharp. "You know what's up."

Adam watched confusion settle in Joey's eyes. She looked around as if she stood in a cage, trying to find the lock.

"These bike riders are crazy," she said. "I almost got hit too many times to count. Vast armies of them. Battalions of them. Or would that be batallia?"

She kept looking around, frantic to change the subject.

"You're not a bad manager, Joey," he said. "You're a great manager. There's the answer to your question."

Her eyes came to rest. She brushed off her suit jacket. She even managed to look a little bashful.

"Thanks, Adam. Your lie is most appreciated." She squeezed his shoulder. "The whole fucking time this band has been together, you've been playing Gandhi. Maybe it's the best approach to all the bullshit."

"It isn't." He unlocked his bike. "I can promise you that."

She leaned on the bike rack, pulled her aviators from her hair, and put them on. "Anyway, this will all be over soon, which you probably know better than the others because you're not all fucked up, you're still the same person, no better or worse than you were when you were playing in Angel's Sweat, and I hope in your post–Blood Orphans existence that you stop being the one everyone laughs at. The long-suffering martyr act didn't serve you well in this band, and it won't serve you well in life."

Adam nodded, and thought, *Joey, poor Joey.* But behind those words, he smarted.

"I say this," she said, wincing on her bad leg, "because I care about you, and Darlo, and even Shane, though I shouldn't."

"What about Bobby?"

Joey dropped her empty Players box. "Bobby sucks. I fucking hate Bobby. Little Darlo suck-up."

"He's all right."

"Is he?" She stamped on the box again and again. "No one with hands like that is *all right*. I wish I could fire Bobby and fix the whole problem. But that would be too easy."

Now the box was impaled on her heel. She shook her foot, but it wouldn't come off, hanging there like a little baby trash panda. Adam remembered when he'd met Joey, in the booker's office at Spaceland. She'd been such a laser beam then, a hot little Colossus striding across the LA scene, her tight mohawk most fashionable, with glitter makeup shading her eyes and her red-stained diamond ring shining despite the dim backstage light. Back then, Adam had truly felt like he'd wandered into some culturally Promethean moment; she'd had some kind of aura to her. She just fully believed every fucking word she said, and that was enough to spin a spell. Now she stood in a stained suit on a windy corner, one hand gripping his arm, as she snagged the cardboard off her stiletto heel.

"*Got it*," she said, as hair fell into her eyes.

8

DARLO RARELY EXPERIENCED DOUBT. Doubt appeared only when he drove his M3 just a little too fast on the downward curves of Laurel Drive, or when Shane stumbled around onstage, babbling about Buddha, unable to catch the beginning of a verse, or when he was riding some almost nameless trick too hard and thought he'd blow his wad too soon. But now doubt crawled up his dirty pant leg and seized his balls. His balls, normally so big and burnished, experienced a sense of entrapment. Doubt shrank them down, filling him with a lightheaded sense of foreboding.

Tax evasion. The all-purpose proxy charge. The prosecutorial straw man. And no access to his money. All tied up.

What the fuck.

His dad, in dulcet tones of nonchalance, made it sound like getting arrested was a common nuisance that you had to deal with year in and year out. But the old man had never been arrested; investigated, yes, for almost the entirety of his career, but never served and cuffed. Back in the eighties, the Meese Commission had a hard-on for David Cox. They'd bugged his house, and all they'd heard was a bunch of rutting. But arrested? Arrested had to mean that the problem had scaled above the heads of the legal teams his dad retained for First Amendment rights, racketeering, and employment discrimination. Had to mean surveillance and dots connected. Had to mean the lawyers hadn't seen it coming.

How could this fucking happen?

A commotion to his left. Music, amplified in watery echoes and tinny accents. A kind of tiny riverboat, à la Mark Twain, moved up the canal, full of reveling blond people and a Dutch Dixieland band marching in place on a little stage. Darlo grimaced; Dixieland music always gave him the creeps, ever since he saw *Live and Let Die* as a kid, that opening scene where the marching band stops its parade to become a hit squad. Gave him nightmares for months.

That grimace turned to anger, because the scene also reminded him of yet another one of Joey's great ideas gone amok, a publicity stunt that even Warners thought was of dubious worth but what the fuck, we just gave them seven figures, might as well try everything. Let's get a flatbed truck, load it up with a wall of amps and some of America's next top models, put the band in feather boas and leather, and drive it up Fifth Avenue in the middle of the day. It was a trick that the Rolling Stones did back in nineteen seventy-whatever, so that means it has to be a good idea, right? We'll make a little backdrop, a plywood wall with *Rocket Heart* posters, and the models will rub up on the band, and they'll take rush hour hostage. What a photo op, huh?

No. Ninety minutes in bumper-to-bumper traffic was what it was. Open season for hecklers was what it was. Harassment from the cops, as in, You got a permit for that? was what it was.

The Rolling Stones did it, officer. Don't you like the Stones?

Just tell me who the hell you are and why there's no license plate.

Come on, it's good times all around, Officer...Blake.

Yeah, right, kid.

Don't be a cooze, man.

Excuse me?

Don't mind him, he's just the drummer.

You just watch it, kid. This ticket's got to go to someone.

Honk honk! Get out of the road!

And then it started to rain.

Teen taunters threw tomatoes. Someone spit on Shane. Warners got a fine for not having the right permits.

The Dixieland band and the good-time revelers waved to him, rolling on the canal. Darlo gave them the finger. The band played on. Doubt scratched at the surface of his indomitable soul.

He wondered if Blood Orphans had done anything right. Maybe they should tell Warners to fuck off and then get on an indie. That would help. It would complement the strategy of touring with someone cool, anyone on one of those hip labels. Take a hundred-dollar guarantee to show the proper humility. Perfect first step for the band's reinvention. Totally.

Either way, the next record needed a power ballad.

His phone rang. The Mummy on line one.

"What's up, faggot?" he said.

"Nothing, faggot. You ought to —"

"Fuck your mother?"

"Yeah, you ought to fuck your mother. That would help you figure shit out for sure. Once you roll off her, you ought to go down to a record store called Fame over here on Kalverstraat. There's some pretty amazing shit there."

"What, like Aerosmith?"

"Yeah, like Aerosmith," he said. "You can finally get that remastered version of *Toys in the Attic*. Other stuff too."

"Like what?"

"A poster of us. Two copies of *Rocket Heart*."

"So what?"

"When's the last time you found any trace of us in a record store?"

Darlo said nothing. Point-of-sale issues were a soft spot.

"That's what I thought," Bobby said. "It'll fuck you up, seeing what you used to be."

Fucking Mummy. Whiner. Passenger.

"Hello?" Bobby said. "Paging the band sex addict."

Darlo couldn't speak. An unseen hand covered his mouth. Tax evasion?

"Signing off," Bobby said. "Kiss my hairy ass!"

Dead line. Euro static. Fucking Bobby. Sore loser in the pussy wars. Disgusting hands. No self-respect.

The Dixieland band drifted on, the people in the boat waving their arms in the cold Dutch air like they just didn't care. He needed money, now that his dad was in deep. Now that doubt flickered around his tarnished spirit. He dialed the manager. She would understand.

"He had it coming," Joey said. "Nasty old fuck."

"He's innocent."

"And I'm the pope, bitch."

"Fuck you, babe," he said. "My dad's totally on the level."

"On the *level?*"

"That's right."

She tittered, amazed. "So on the level that you had no idea your money was tied to his?"

"It's not illegal."

"No, but it is forty kinds of fucked up."

"I don't want to hear it." The riverboat drifted out of sight. "Just loan me some money. Please, babe."

She sighed, and Darlo wished she wouldn't. When she sighed, something inside him unhinged.

"That fucker's been taking you for a ride for a long time, *man.*"

"You're just jealous," he said. "Jealous of people who understand power."

She laughed. "Nice to put up a brave face while you're getting your ass fucked."

Doubt, falling faintly.

"Don't tell anyone yet," he said. "No one."

"Just hurry up," Joey said. "I'm at the Van Gogh and I ain't got all day. Wait—yes, I do!"

Darlo lit a smoke and started on his way, hurt at Joey's utter faithlessness. He knew that his dad had long since stopped operating at full strength. His killer instinct had gone all Fat Elvis. He wasn't staying on top of things, walking around in his silk robe all day, but not like Hugh Hefner. More like Brian Wilson. And those mob guys had been sucking him dry.

Back when David Cox was getting started, after he quit assistant-directing for VCA, the seventies porn powerhouse, and went looking for capital, the seed money came from the mob. There weren't any weekend libertarian day-trippers who wanted to drop bills and invest. There was no such thing as porn chic until *Boogie Nights*. Ask anyone who'd ever purveyed pussy in the Valley. Nowadays the porn industry chilled with freewheeling congressmen and chorused about government oppression. Back then you went to Tony and Fabrizio and Ricky and secured a little control. All these men, Darlo remembered, wore strong cologne, but their heavy goaty smell pushed right through the Aramis, the Paco Rabanne, the Old Spice. These guys would hug little Darlo—and whadda fuck kyna name is dat?—so tight he thought his eyes would pop. Then they'd crouch down and put out their palms. "Come on," they'd say. "Show us your jab, Darlo. Show us your right hook. Give it whatcha got!"

These men used the Cox house as a brothel. They banged girls left and right. They slapped girls silly. Sometimes Darlo, eight or ten or twelve, wandered upon such moments. No doors closed in the Cox mansion. Sometimes the girls, under punches, locked eyes with the boy in the hallway. Faraway eyes. Doll's eyes.

"Hey, cherry!" the man—or men—would yell to him. "Wanna get up in this bitch? She's good to go!"

Dead doll's eyes. Nodding out.

But the men looked so strong. The men could not be hurt. They were like thunderous skies over small lakes. They became Darlo's heroes.

His dad said, Respect women, but it was like an oilman saying, Respect the environment.

After the Meese Commission report, after what his dad called "the year of the fucking knives-out cockless Republican fuckwad witch-hunt," organized crime gave up the porn hobby. But David Cox kept the dregs around. He admired them. They were his friends. He kept them around and he became one of them, loansharking. He told Darlo he loved shaking people down.

"I'm not going to get any fucking AVN awards acting like Nice Guy Eddie," he said. "But you find some prick bigger than his britches and you put his ass out on a line. You stretch him and then you let him snap back. You take him cleaning and then you take him for a swim."

He talked to Darlo in this seminonsense; the house had been bugged for years, and the old man thought this gibberish was clever *and* effective. How he had escaped the Meese Commission was anyone's guess. So much talk of blackmail and blood spilled and legs broken. And for all those taps, no one tipped off enforcement. No criminal charges.

"They keep me out," Cox told his son, "because I'm bait."

"Are you an informant?"

"That's a terrible thing to say!"

So now the bait had run rancid, and they were hauling him in. The bait was used up and rotting. That's what it was.

Is that what it was?

Such bad timing for Darlo. Everything connected to his dad. All his credit cards. His American Express. His *Hustler* house account.

And then he thought about the sack of cocaine hidden in his closet. Had the authorities seized the house? Had they torn the place apart?

Freaking out wouldn't help. He had to get Joey's big stupid phone and make calls pronto.

As he headed over the canal toward the Van Gogh, a bunch of earnest-looking Dutch college kids came toward him, holding banners and cloth signs that said that the U.S. sucked, blood for oil, all that shit that Darlo hated so much. Out of Iraq, Boycott the Oppressor, yadda yadda yadda, a big stuffed Bush doll they were no doubt going to burn. Fucking clichés, Darlo thought. They acted like America was some Nazi state that didn't save their ass every thirty years. Where was the respect for history? Why couldn't they separate shit out? Why did his dad have to go and get arrested for tax evasion? Why was his band so irrevocably fucked?

He grabbed a *US out of Iraq* banner from the hands of some hot hippie girl with long, shiny hair.

She said something in Dutch that indicated her displeasure.

"Fuck you!" he said, spit flying, teeth bared. "Get your own army!"

She held up her hands and walked away backward. Leaves swirled on the ground.

"Bitch!" he said. "Surrender!"

Dead doll's eyes. In the hallway. Good to go.

She was away now, in the river of faces, some of her fellow protesters looking back at him as he stamped the banner into the ground, grinding it with his boots.

"Bitch!" he yelled, as if she were still there.

Dead eyes. Looking through cracks in doorways. Skies over lakes.

He walked in the direction of the Museumplein, chain-smoking, and wondered what the fuck else they were finding in that house when they tore it apart. His fucking dad's house. His house. Their dirty fed hands. Just because some prosecutor wanted to make a name for himself.

He felt the knife in his jacket pocket. The oversized switchblade he'd bought on that Sioux reservation in South Dakota. The Magic Wand.

"That is so fucking illegal," Bobby had said as they stood in the most weapon-filled gas station minimart they'd ever seen. "You get caught with that, you'll get so fucking busted."

"I'm shaking," Darlo said, and left a hundred-dollar bill on the counter.

On tour, he'd pulled out the Magic Wand a few times and watched people scatter. It was asshole kryptonite.

If cops searched the house, they would find the other knives he'd bought through unregulated channels — the foot-long fillet shiv and the serrated buck knife and the mini-scimitar. Damn, he would miss those. And his guns — the Bren and the Beretta and the Glock. All unlicensed, bought from Cox mansion hangers-on. Well, shit.

What kind of lawyers did his dad have, anyway? What was he paying them for if, in two thousand fucking five, when porn was practically being sold in Wal-Mart, the man could get singled out. Tax evasion!

He called Joey. "I can't find the fucking place, babe."

"You're across the street from it, you fucking idiot."

He looked up. Joey gave him the finger, which curled into a come-hither.

"Get over here," she said.

"No, you get over here."

"Who's got the money, asshole?" she said. "Now's no time for stubborn."

Darlo ran through traffic, middle fingers up at drivers like guns blazing. Seeing Joey's messy early-drunk face helped ease his troubles.

He kicked a piece of dog shit at the museum line and no one noticed.

"Where's Adam?"

"Rode away on a bike," she said. "So cute, our little Adam."

He shrugged. "I gotta have a talk with him."

"About what?"

"The next record." Darlo spat a loogie to the curb. "I have ideas."

Joey winced.

"What?"

"Nothing."

Darlo hadn't seen Joey in over six weeks, since New York at CMJ. The previous year they'd played with Queens of the Stone Age at the Hammerstein Ballroom, but this year Warners wouldn't even get them a showcase at a fucking piano bar in Queens. Still, they went trolling; Darlo had nabbed a publicist from Interscope, a fat Irish girl named Moira, right under Bobby's nose, and they tried to get Joey to go back to her hotel room with them. Moira had that condition where your eyes look too big for your sockets.

"I want both of you," she leered, eyes bulging in her skull. "I love the girls and I love the boys and I want your bodies in my mouth."

Darlo had smiled and put his arm around Joey. "Come on, babe," he'd said. "It's time."

She had demurred. "You take her," she said. "You like the fat girls way more than me."

Now Joey stood there, small and coke-eyed. Seeing her made Darlo think about TV movies where lovers are reunited; his confidence softened a little, and his desire to just run everyone over subsided. He felt framed by some phenomenon that he hoped was not love; he had the urge to take her feet out of those shoes and stroke them. He had the urge to carry her in his arms wherever she wanted to go—a zoo, a department store, another museum, all the places he hated. But he couldn't trust these feelings, couldn't imagine from where, in his porny past, these feelings could have derived. He saw no path to them, no back alleyway, no hidden passage to any of these emotions, so he knew they had to be fake. Or at least wrong.

"So," she said, breaking the fog. "Your dad."

"My dad." He nodded. "Tax evasion. That's what he said on the message. Can't figure it out."

"Never heard you say that."

"He never got arrested before."

They walked in the direction of the brouhaha. Leaves spun in little tornadoes on the ground. Parts of Darlo separated and drifted off into autonomy, like the continents a million years ago. Between them, seas of unknown emotion appeared and made him dizzy.

"My feet are fucking killing me," Joey said.

"Cry me a river," he replied, and sped up.

9

HE WAS REALLY an Untouchable now. He had gotten what he wanted, standing in line at the McDonald's, eyes of disgust upon him, noses wrinkling. Was Jesus not also an outcast? Was Buddha not an outcast? He was part of a most fantastic line of questers, seekers. He was, like them, a cross-pollinator, a mixer of cultural influences, a journeyman, a missing link!

"Four cheeseburgers," Shane said. "Two fries. Large Coke."

He went to the back, where a trio of old Dutch men sipped coffee in three-piece suits. The ethics of eating meat for the first time in a year wasn't something he could navigate just now. Just now, this cheeseburger was a lifeboat upon which he would float until he hit the blood-sugar shore. Then he would walk upon the sand and assess the damage.

His mind focused on a series of questions. How had he managed to let everything get so out of hand? He had become so preoccupied with his search, with his seeking, that he had let Darlo run the band into the ground. Endless touring, and for what?

"They want to work us to death," Darlo said each time he announced more touring plans. "But they don't know how strong we are. Bring it on!"

Why did it have to be adversarial? Why didn't they just stop the madness and make a record that wasn't full of disgusting lyrics? And why, he thought, did I not speak up?

All those girls and their pagan ways. Pleasures of the flesh shining in his eyes like God dust. That was why.

Forgive me, Gautama, Shane thought, but what a delicious

fucking cheeseburger! He sucked ketchup up from deep within the bun.

A chunk of peanut butter, colored like earwax, dislodged from his hair and fell to the McTray. An old man missing most of his teeth walked by, and Shane, bearing down on reminiscence, felt that mixture of remorse and pride that accompanied the memory of knocking out Bobby's front tooth in that Charlottesville Super 8.

"He deserved it," Shane told his fries. "Not my fault. Stole my Bible." He unwrapped another cheeseburger. "My fucking *Bible*."

On the first tour, Shane had taken his Extreme Teen Bible — a gift from his pastor, Richard Olmer of the New Fundamentalist Baptist Church of Anaheim — on tour. This was the least Olmer could do, considering that he'd just started his second full-time job counting the hundred grand Shane had just tithed. The singer took the Bible, with its monogrammed leather case and silk bookmark, and placed it prominently in the glove compartment of the band's brand-new, jet-black V8 Ford Econoline. Well, not entirely new; Darlo's dad had a film series called *Back That Shit Up*, which involved men paying women they saw on the street to have sex with them in said van. They'd shot only three scenes when Darlo requisitioned it, and he wasn't about to let Bibles hang out in the glove compartment.

"That's where cigarettes and maps go," the drummer said. "And besides, no one wants to see it. The rest of us are Satanists. So put it in your fucking backpack."

"Have you ever thought," Shane said, "that the Bible is *my* map?"

"Priceless," Bobby said, and cracked open a can of Black Label. "Here's to you, loser."

Shane had expected Darlo to be his scourge on tour, but instead he and Bobby developed an inexplicable negative chemistry. When Bobby did his neurotic worry-wart routine, scratching at his hands and complaining about every little thing down to the amount of fizz in his soda, Shane felt like something was picking at the inside of his head. He prayed for understanding, but that didn't work; the fact was, he'd been too busy fucking girls whose last names went unsaid to have much time to pray.

With rare exception, Bobby drove, and every time he came upon the Extreme Teen Bible in the search for maps or Marlboros, he'd chuck it to the back. Shane would say nothing and put the Good Book back the first chance he got. This was the standard routine for the entire six weeks of their first tour.

Then one day the Extreme Teen Bible was gone.

"I left it right *here*," Shane said, tapping the glove box. "Give it back, Bobby."

"I didn't touch your fucking precious Bible," Bobby said as they passed through the industrial Jersey swamps, through the American fens. "Christ."

"That Bible was a present from my pastor," he said. "*Please* give it back."

"The pastor you gave away your entire advance to?"

"That was supposed to be a secret."

Darlo laughed. "Bono says a secret is something you tell one other person," he said, and snapped his copy of *Hustler* back in place. "What an interesting article I'm reading."

Bobby adjusted the AC. "That book's a mockery of Christianity," he said, and broke into an imitation of the book's cadence, in the vein of a used-car salesman. "Hey, boys and girls, do you know what Jesus said about forgiveness? He said it was way rad! Isn't that extreme? Isn't that just totally awesome? Jesus plays guitar better than Hendrix. Jesus makes the very sweetest chocolate cake. Jesus has a better jumpshot than Michael Jordan, and he makes Aristotle look like a copycat. Jesus is so cool!"

In truth, Shane was starting to be not so into the Christian thing. Really, this was about him and Bobby. But he wasn't going to let on. Matters of principle were at stake.

"Mock all you want," he said. "That book's important to me, and I want it back, you faithless jerk."

Shane knew Bobby had that Bible; however ephemerally it currently fit into his daily life of thoughtless sex, that Bible was the wall separating him from the amoral compass of Darlo and Bobby and Joey, and he wanted it around.

Adam wasn't involved; he was too busy sketching in his notebook, speaking in a whisper, and playing the guitar like Kirk Hammett. To Shane he wasn't there most of the time.

"Give me the Bible back" became the normal breakfast conversation.

"Repent, sinner" became the normal breakfast reply.

Then, a week later, in a Charlottesville Super 8, he found two pages of the Gospel of St. John on the door of his room, with the words *Eat Me* written in marker across its hallowed pages. When Bobby opened his door, Shane, suffering from irritable bowels and so already short-leashed, attacked.

"You piece of shit!" he yelled, and shoved the bass player back into his room. "Give it back!"

Then he saw the book on the bed in pieces. Bobby had ripped out more than a few extreme pages; paper was strewn all over the room. The leather coverlet peeked out from under a sheet, hiding until the coast was clear.

Bobby smirked and cracked open a can of Black Label. "Adam was talking last night about some artist who did this," he said. "Some idea about the inner meaning of the text, the poetry of cut and paste. Thought I'd try it myself." He glugged some beer. "What do you think?"

Shane threw a sharp jab and knocked out one of Bobby's front teeth.

Though punching someone in the face wasn't exactly his area of expertise, Shane immediately knew he'd connected. When he felt the tooth go, right on his middle finger, he had the same sensation as sliding his cock into a warm, wet, welcoming pussy. He went rock-solid, standing there breathless as Bobby fell to the floor, clutching his face.

"Son of a bitch," the bass player yelled, writhing as blood streamed from between his fingers. "Oh my God!"

Picking at the crusts of his final cheeseburger, Shane reflected on the incident, a marker of epochs come and gone. He had always gloated that Bobby had never been the same, but now he knew that he too had been changed in full by that action, and not for the better. When he saw Bobby's front tooth lying on the dirty Super 8 carpet, he should have thought, I've become lost. But what he thought was, Serves you right, prick. If Bobby hadn't been bleeding so badly, he would have hit him again. Looking at it now, the Extreme Teen Bible seemed more like a coloring book than anything else, but that didn't change the utter sacrilege of the act, the downright insult.

Losing his tooth had really broken Bobby's demon dam. The smirk on the bass player's face just before Shane clocked him was a smirk Shane hadn't seen in at least three tours. Until his tooth went flying across the Super 8 carpet, Bobby had been an edgy but happy-go-lucky guy. Not long after, his hands turned to shit, Darlo started fucking every girl he wanted, and his questionable utility onstage disappeared altogether.

The Buddha taught love. Jesus taught love. But something about Bobby was beyond Shane's grasp of love. Something about the way he smelled. Like pears turning.

Shane's method of self-forgiveness was to imagine them meeting years later in a neutral space — say, at Adam's wedding, to celebrate the guitar player's discovery of his perfect sensitive fairy-girl. Like other great rock bands who have broken up — the Police, the Faces, three members of the Beatles — they would do a ceremonial onstage reunion jam, and he would find all of Bobby's habits and tics endearing: how he stuck out his lower lip when excited, how he bounced in his seat *every* time Soundgarden came on the radio, and even the way he played the bass, stooped down like he was trying to squeeze one out and eat at the same time.

Shane wanted to think that the past two years had been part of some deliberate quest. He wanted to believe that everything that had happened, including knocking out Bobby's tooth, had been a product of his spiritual deliberation. But sitting under the warming lamps of McDonald's with a gut full of cow meat, he felt like a leaf blown to and fro on the winds of fate and circumstance, caught in a farce of his making.

As if he could sit here, peanut butter in his hair, smelling like the back end of a dog and some unnamed Dutch pussy perfume, and claim that he was any better off than the day he had met the other members of the band.

He needed a shower. He needed help. Joey owed him a thousand hot showers. You bet she did. He ate his burger crusts, sipped the last of his Coke, and dialed the manager.

10

SINCE CHILDHOOD, Bobby's life had been defined by eczema. And considering how many people suffered from the problem, he always thought it surprising how little could be done, how deep this problem ran, hardwired into one's genetics. Dr. Adler, his pediatrician, had said, "Not my specialty!" and sent him to a dermatologist, Dr. Lawler, who should have given Bobby a punchcard for the amount of business he provided. Time after time he reappeared in Lawler's office, his mother fretting and disgusted, her shame hanging over the room. His mother, a successful corporate lawyer at Melveney & Meyers, a proud member of the Sherman Oaks PTA, and one hundred percent free of the slightest rough spot on her ring-covered hands. All Lawler could say was, "That's truly an amazing condition you've got, Robert. Truly amazing! Want a lollipop? Want Dodgers tickets?"

People who lived normal lives would never understand. If you could play basketball, spend ten minutes using a shovel, or help a friend move without having everything you touched feel like sandpaper, you had no clue.

As Bobby grew older, his eczema improved enough for him to take up the bass. His real desire was to play the drums, but his hands were too wrecked to build up the proper calluses. Those years, in retrospect, seemed a golden age, without his cracked jelly-skin as the organizing principle of his life.

That golden age ended the day he signed that contract with Warners and imagined his cut in the mail, a hundred and twenty-three thousand dollars. And his hands began to itch, ever so faintly, like the first cricket singing of the coming evening outside your twilit window. By the time Blood Orphans hit the road, his hands were inflamed, and soon went from private annoyance to public problem. People started noticing—Carson Daly, for instance, when they played his show. Daly was walking around meeting all of them as they soundchecked. Then he shook Bobby's hand and his eyes went wide.

"That's looking pretty rough," Daly said. "What's that all about?"

"Gangrene," Bobby replied, and squeezed harder.

Shane punching his tooth out had proved some kind of dermal event horizon, and the rot had set in hard; for relief, Bobby would run the shower to scalding and stick his hands under. The burn was so lovely, so rounded and complete, that his body shook, a direct line to a twisted joy; the burn uncovered some hidden happy nerve as his lips quivered with a paralytic grin. During this ritual, he thought of the descriptions of heroin's rush through your body. The scalding water was alchemy, transmuting the base metals of his pedestrian pain into pure pleasure gold.

This habit also peeled his hands raw, and thus the Mummy was born, its shadow rising high over the terrain of their third U.S. tour, their trek across America in winter. Snow, sleet, and decomposing fingers.

"I'm recovering from an accident," he would tell girls at shows. "It's a long, horrible story."

Responses varied.

"You poor thing!"

"That's awful!"

"I know something that would help!"

"Does Darlo have a girlfriend?"

His scarce musical abilities went south. No more attempts at being fancy or melodic. Now he had to imitate Michael Anthony,

Van Halen's bass player, the king of the root note. Michael Anthony had made a career out of playing the simplest parts this side of incompetence, and so could Bobby. That was fine with the rest of the band. Adam's playing was chock-full of the swells and screams of his pedalboard, Darlo's drumming was busy and loud, like a poor man's John Bonham, and Shane's Steven-Tyler-meets-Justin-Timberlake routine filled the rest of the spaces, his voice a blurred Technicolor to the musical two-tone. No one noticed that Bobby wasn't doing anything.

Anyway, he wasn't a very good bass player, so he didn't really mind. Oh, no one ever said, not even once, You're the band passenger, but he knew. Using the P-word out loud was the utter humiliation, though. He dreaded it every time he fucked up a take, or stifled Adam's solos by switching to the wrong key, or ran over Shane's voice with a mangled part. Actually, ruining Shane's whiny flow was the only silver lining of his condition that he could find.

Well, there was one other thing: when people saw the crud, they feared you. They wouldn't want to run the risk of getting too close to what looked like a flesh-eating virus. At the mess in Sweden, Bobby'd had the pleasure of rubbing his hands all over the faces of a great many shrieking blond kids.

But here was this sweet girl, sweet Sarah Van der Hoff, with her full lips and pale blue eyes and hot elfin curves. Here was his guardian angel in her henna-red tresses, wearing those fishnets, sporting that ridiculous Nine Inch Nails tattoo on her arm, escorting him around the foggy city.

"Have you ever been to Burning Man?" she asked. "I so want to go!"

European girls always had the cutest naïveté.

"Burning Man is pretty silly now," he said. "It's so commercial."

"It sounds beautiful to me," she said, and skipped along. "I'd love to, you know, screw in the desert. So natural. Kissed by the sun."

"Now you're talking."

Bobby always had trouble with silence when it came to girls. Silence felt like a loss of momentum.

"We might record our next record out in the desert," he said. He had never spoken of the next record, never really pondered it. "One of the guys from Queens of the Stone Age has a studio out there, and he said we could record any time we wanted."

"I like Queen," she said. "Freddie Mercury is so great."

"No, Queens of the Stone Age," he said, starting to jog along to keep up with her skipping. She was a little sprite, all right. Her body, a sinuous little piece, was built for speed, not comfort. Bobby thought about all that red hair going up and down on his crotch, then chastised himself, then quit thinking about anything because she was skipping even faster.

"Could you slow down?" he asked.

She laughed. "Come on, Bobby. We're almost there!"

She skipped as if she were on one of those airport conveyor belts, and he barely kept up, thinking about the time in St. Louis when he had chased a Goth brunette with big tits and a clit ring all over the room of a Motel 6, while Darlo threw up next door after losing a drinking contest with some old biker. That had been an event of supreme satisfaction.

They stopped at a corner. A tram lumbered by. She stole a glance at his hands.

"I saw that."

"Sorry." She sashayed a little and took one of the mitts in her gentle palms. "Don't be mad, but I don't know why it doesn't make me sick."

Bobby stared into her eyes and thought, *She must not meet Darlo.*

"Come on," she said, "Dr. Guttfriend is waiting for us."

They passed a man lying on the sidewalk, a young man, strung out, who looked just enough like Shane to fill him with glee. He imagined the singer, dead on the concrete, mouth open and filling with flies, Captain Condescending Christian Buddhist Fuckwit being eaten alive by minions of Satan.

Sarah stopped in front of a modern-looking building, the kind that in America would have been a constant target of mockery.

"We're here," she said.

Dr. Guttfriend's office ghost-smelled of baby vomit, despite the fact that it was germ-freak clean. Toys were neatly stacked, and the white walls were covered with images of the smiling toddlers of socialized medicine.

"Is he a children's doctor or something?" Bobby asked.

She nodded.

"How are old are you, Sarah?"

"I'll be nineteen on December fifth." She made a face. "How old are you?"

"Twenty-six. I was just making sure that you were street-legal."

Her brow tightened. She didn't know what *street-legal* meant, but she sure knew the letchy tone. That tone was global. Every woman recognized it.

"I'll let him know we're here," she said, and went through a door.

Stupid ass, Bobby chastised himself. She's a great girl. She'd never be a Blood Orphans fan. You don't talk to normal girls like that. Darlo must *never fucking meet her.*

He scratched his right hand, loosening the bandages. He scratched and scratched. Stupid guy, you're so fucking stupid. Always say the stupid thing. Always have to ruin everything. Some bandages detached, flapping like untethered sails in choppy water. Fucking stupid jerk. Ruin everything stupid fucking band never going home ever it'll never end oh fuck that feels so fuck-ing g-good —

"Hey, *stop*," Sarah said, and grabbed his hands. "Stop, Bobby. He's ready. Let's go in."

Dr. Guttfriend looked like Mr. Rogers with a big bushy Euro tache. He stuck out his hand, and then he saw what he was dealing with and put the hand on Bobby's shoulder. His face contracted just a touch. Even doctors, Bobby thought. Even fucking doctors.

In the examination room, Guttfriend tried to make small talk but stared at Bobby's hands like they were the missing dermatologic link.

"Eczema, eczema," the good doctor said like an incantation, putting his hand to his chin in a thoughtful pose. "Such a mysterious ailment. How long have you had..."

He gingerly took one of Bobby's hands in his, then said something in Dutch a few times.

"Sorry, I don't speak Dutch," Bobby said. "What are you saying?"

Guttfriend looked at Sarah, like, Where have you been trolling, little girl?

She said something in Dutch, and Guttfriend smiled at Bobby.

"I'm sorry," he said. "Please, go on."

Bobby gave him the backstory, and Guttfriend examined his hands, nodding and tapping his pen on his cheek. Bobby watched the lymph grow in the wells of his cuticles and saw the yellow stains it made on the bandages. His right hand was more inflamed than the left, but the left had more open sores. His wrists looked much too small to be connected to his inflamed hands, and Dr. Guttfriend seemed to express displeasure at the mention of cortisone.

"Cortisone appears to work, but it only undermines the condition in the long run. It makes the outer *dehr*mis fragile, like onion skin."

"Well, it has saved my ass."

"But not enough, as you can see."

Bobby looked up at the posters of the little kids, going Dutch tra-la-la down a sunny northern European street. "I mean, I don't know what I would do when the itch comes. It's like a wave taking me out. It's so powerful."

"You've tried cod liver oil?"

"Bottles of it."

"Cutting out coffee?"

"Check."

"Avoiding nuts and wheat?"

"Like a carnivore."

"Not scratching?"

"Oh, never," Bobby said, and he and Guttfriend laughed like old friends.

Finally, Bobby thought, someone who understood. This was the most fun he'd had on this tour. He felt like the two of them were priests talking theology.

"When did you say your hands became unmanageable?"

"Sometime on the third tour."

"When was that?"

"About a year ago."

Dr. Guttfriend nodded, and Sarah grabbed Bobby's shoulder. "Your hands have been like this for a year?" she said. "Bobby, no."

"You get used to it."

"That's crazy, babe."

Bobby's world always froze for a second when a girl called him *babe* for the first time.

"You can't live like that," she continued, and looked at Gutt-friend. "Please do something."

He had the strangest feeling, a heat on the left side of his face, the warmth of a fireplace in a ski lodge, rosy and comforting. Sarah was there, lying in front of the flames, wrapped naked in a bearskin rug. She gave him a look.

"I could refer Sarah to a dermatologist," Guttfriend said. "How long are you in Amsterdam?"

"I don't know," he said. "Tonight's our last night, and then I don't know what's going to happen." He turned to her. "I have a plane reservation for tomorrow, but I could change it."

Sarah nodded ever so slightly and smiled, showing her teeth, her ivory jewels. Bobby thought of tulip fields and his face on an EU passport. His hands pulsed like a go-ahead.

"I could change it," he said. "Why don't you give us his name?"

11

DARLO CRAMPED HIMSELF into the small Dutch phone booth, green and covered with KPN logos, holding Joey's fat phone in his hand while she sat next door in a bar. He felt private in there, free of Joey's all-seeing gaze. Fucking thing weighs a ton, he thought, and popped the phone against the green handset, making a crack down the middle.

Bob McFadden, the Cox family lawyer, picked up on the fifth ring.

"Why are you calling me in the middle of the night, Darlo?"

McFadden, the old family counsel who'd seen them through Ed Meese and John Ashcroft and two investigations for syndicalism. The guy who'd collected thirty grand in fees for negotiating the Blood Orphans contract and then applied exactly zero pressure to Warners when they dropped the ball.

"Don't sound too excited."

"You woke me up," McFadden said. "How do you want me to sound?"

Fucking McFadden, Darlo thought. On this day, where my dad lands in the clink, you should be up around the clock, hauling legal ass.

"Look, Bob," he said, "what's the deal? I'm in fucking Amsterdam and none of my cards work. I can't access any money."

"Your dad—"

"I know, *I know*, Bob."

"Don't you want to know how he's doing?"

"Fuck him. I can't get my money because of him. Why can't I, Bob?"

McFadden did that lawyer sigh. "I can't believe he didn't tell you."

"Tell me what?"

"That when the DA froze all his accounts, yours would freeze too."

"When the DA...Did you know that this was coming?"

He groaned. A bed creaked. "Yeah, Darlo. I did. So did he."

Static overrode them. Weather shifts over the North Sea. Seagulls over the Arctic. Wasn't the idea with this thousand-dollar phone that you avoided interference?

"Well, he didn't tell me." He kicked the wall. "I can't believe he'd do this to me. He said the money would be safer tied to his."

Another lawyer sigh. "In all honesty, Darlo, I don't know why you would ever have taken that to mean anything."

That hurt like a paper cut. Implying that his dad took advantage of him. It hurt, Darlo knew, because it was true.

"Yeah, well, then why didn't you tell me how stupid that was?" he said. "I mean, aren't you my lawyer too? I mean, like how much have you leached off us and now you can't help?"

"Darlo," he said, "I'm not a magician."

"No, but you are a crooked little fuck."

Another lawyer sigh.

"Stop with the fucking lawyer sighs. I fucking hate those."

"Look," McFadden said. "I know you're upset. I wish I could help. There's nothing I can do. But this business with the missing girl—"

"What business?"

"The girl that showed up yesterday at the Encino precinct who said she'd escaped from the house of a man named Jeffrey

Brown, who'd been keeping her in a dungeon. She named a number of men as part of a sex-slave ring. Your dad was one of them."

Darlo felt a gust of sulfurous wind shoot through him. He turned in the booth, fast, as if some noxious ghost had just blown into his ear. A hot ball of memory threw him over, lathered him up, flattened him out.

"Darlo?" McFadden said. "Hello?"

"I'm here." He ran his hands through his hair. He looked down at his pants. A new spot of urine. He smelled weird all of a sudden. "I can't even figure out what that means." Another gust moved through him, a windy metallic shiver. "What does that mean?"

"It means that come tomorrow they comb your dad's house for real, and if they find anything..."

Darlo felt like he was being lifted up right there in his shoes. Those cops would find signs of a regular Inquisition chamber down there in the catacombs.

"But what about the money, Bob? *My* money."

One more lawyer sigh. Echoes of waves cresting in the Bering Sea.

"Nothing I can do right now, Darlo. I'm sorry. Borrow some from your bandmates."

Darlo hung up. "Yeah, thanks, Bob!" he said. "Real swift."

Creating a false image of one's father wasn't easy. To be the lone crusader for his good name, the defender of the faith, you had to drink the Kool-Aid and even lick the rim. All reason was against you. And look where it's gotten me, Darlo thought. He imagined the house in Laurel Canyon, knew his dad was somewhere in there, maybe with one of those GPS bracelets around an ankle, celebrating the day he'd made the illustrious list of Those Who Have Been Indicted. This was, to David Cox, an honor.

"What bullshit," Darlo said, and cracked his knuckles.

And how would his dad commemorate this exciting day, now that he could present himself as a bona fide outlaw? Probably by the pool, his no-longer-indestructible body taking in a fat line of prescription speed, eighteen-year-old nubiles at each corner of his vision like holes in a pool table, though the man wasn't really much into sex anymore. He just wanted the pussy close, the ass in reach, the wet mouths at the ready to take orders. Viagra was all that kept him up anymore; he often went overboard with the drug, complaining to his son, whose erections were natural and never-ending, about the unique discomfort of the hard-on that wouldn't die.

"Guess you can get too much of a good thing, eh, Kemo Sabe?" he'd said on a number of occasions. "Guess you can shoot the moon and hit the sun."

Violence was his thing now. Daddy Cox would pay girls to get hit and tape their screams. Darlo had long wondered when one of these girls was going to turn her scream into a lawsuit. You could hear those screams through the bushes, down the street. How was it that no one had ever complained? How was it that no policemen had ever stopped by to chat?

He went and sat down at the bar next to Joey. The manager smoked a cigarette and looked through her bag for something she couldn't find.

"That phone is a piece of fucking work," he said, handing it over.

"Try carrying it around all day," she said.

Darlo watched Joey wolf her bourbon and make smoke rings. The mohawk had grown too long in front, and blond hay fell into her eyes. Man, he wanted to kiss her. Nausea washed over him like a bore tide. Quicksand trapped him in place.

Darlo had gone through life thinking he was like any other

guy. He was like Bobby, but cruder. He was like Bobby, but his dad was in porn. He was like Bobby, but no. He was of this, from this, destined to be this. He was not Bobby. Bobby's parents were not people who taped the screams of desperate girls who fucked strangers for a living.

And then he snapped out of it. He rolled up on the shore of logistics and plans. Logistics and plans kept him safe.

Keep the band alive. Make the band your focus. Dad is lost.

He came up through the kelp. Logistics. And. Plans.

"Double bourbon," he said, and lit a cigarette.

Joey quit looking for her lost item. "How'd it go?"

"For shit. I have to fucking call him back later. No funds."

"I got your back." Joey smiled, and then her nose wrinkled. "You really smell, babe."

"I think I pissed on myself a little." Darlo looked at his pants, shrugged. "You still haven't told me what Hackney said." He lit a cigarette. "Spill it."

"Nothing to spill."

Darlo didn't believe her, but he could harbor only one worry at a time, and his father had taken that mooring.

"Can't even imagine what kind of shit is waiting for me back in the States," he said. "You think maybe I should move out and find my own place?"

"*Yes*," Joey said. "That would be a start."

"Maybe being too close to the old man is holding me back."

"I could have told you that."

"Yeah, well, why didn't you?"

"Maybe because you worship the ground he walks on?" She made a face. "You've been clear that Thou Shalt Speak No Ill of Thy Father."

Darlo shook his head and gulped his drink. "You know when you get, like, a feeling in your gut that everything is not what it seems? I mean, I don't mean any mystical shit, I'm not about to get all Shane right now, just an unsettling sense that shit is off? In your life? A lot more than you thought? That's how I feel. You know?"

Joey kept a straight face. "I have no idea what that's like."

"You don't?"

She rolled her eyes. "Darlo, is this the first time you've wondered if Blood Orphans is fucked?"

"Fucked? We're not fucked. I was talking about my dad."

Joey looked at him in utter amazement.

"What?" Darlo said. "Babe, we're not. We need a vacation is all."

"Oh. Is that all we need?"

She spoke in a tone that said, You are fucking deluded, but Darlo was inflating again. Logistics and plans.

"We need more discipline," he said. "I have all kinds of ideas for the next record."

"Like what?"

"A power ballad, for one."

She blew smoke and smiled. "Like covering 'Home Sweet Home' is going to fucking fix anything."

Darlo looked at their reflection in the circular chrome that lined the bar. Their faces were elongated, like the eerie masks in that stupid Kabuki porn series his dad had done called *Yellow Fever*. Guys marched around in those masks and cock rings in some pagoda-type house and fucked Japanese girls dressed like geishas. Not one of Dirty Darling's bestsellers. Still, he lingered on the image, staring hard.

"Enough," Joey said. "Let's quit ambling and go back to my hotel. You need a fucking shower."

As they walked, Darlo tried to keep his head clear, but the dungeon in the basement of his father's house reared up. The dungeon and the closet full of guns, knives, cocaine. They were coming upon Museumplein again, and the sound of the protest rose up.

"I need to use your phone again," he said.

She lugged it over and crossed her arms. "Don't take too long. That shit is a squillion cents a minute."

He went into a booth and punched numbers. Satellite noise thrummed in his ear. Arctic blasts over Hudson Bay. Electrons bouncing through the ionosphere. The sound of Jesse's voice had its own tweaky comfort.

"Oh, damn!" Jesse yelled. "My nigga!"

"Yo, Adamson."

He clued Jesse. He told his drug dealer what needed to be done. "You know where I keep all of it, right?"

"In the pool house?"

"No, man. In the closet. In the shoe box. Next to the guns."

Some coiffed art-student type in a black turtleneck and coat knocked on the booth. He spat at the little Dutchie. Loogie congealed between them.

"Can I have one of those guns?" Jesse asked. "As payment for services rendered."

"Not a chance," Darlo said, "and enough with the fucking thug life. This is serious shit."

"I could hang up," Jesse said. "I could do that."

Darlo growled. "Take the Bren, if you want to be a bitch about it. But not the Glock."

"You have a Glock?"

"Dude, this isn't a joke! They're going to search the place."

"And that means your house is under fucking surveillance, *dude.*"

More Canadian static.

"What do you expect me to do?" Jesse continued. "Flash a badge?"

Drug dealers. You'd think they'd be more resourceful.

"Wait until five in the morning," Darlo said. "That's in a few hours. There won't be anyone there."

"You bet there will."

"And what if there is? You get caught, it'll be like that fucking time we broke into the Sharkey house down the street. Once they see your address on your license, they'll scatter. Your fucking dad pays their salary. Now stop being a pussy, *bro*, and go get my shit."

Darlo breathed out frost and lit a cigarette. Joey sat on a bench, looking pensive—looking, Darlo thought, like she was hiding something. Fucking knew it. That bitch is full-on withholding.

"Fine," Jesse said.

"Yeah, look, just do it and—"

Static over Iceland. Birds over Newfoundland.

"—if it, if you can't—Jesus, what is that?"

"Bad connection. Technology, man."

"Just try, all right? And call me when you're in there. OK?"

Jesse moaned. Darlo couldn't believe how difficult he was being. "In the closet. With the guns. Leave the Glock."

"Roger that," Jesse said. "At your service."

"Leave the Glock. I mean it. Go."

12

SO HOW WAS THE MEETING?" Darlo asked, handing over the phone. "With Hackney?"

Joey never thought the day would come when Darlo looked spooked, but here they were, walking toward Vondelpark, pretty sure they were going in the wrong direction from her hotel, and the drummer seemed so preoccupied and nervous she thought he'd walk right into Dutchie tram traffic. Of course, she understood that his dad's arrest would rattle Darlo, but still, she expected him to put on a brave face. Darlo was the heart of Blood Orphans, righteously pumping, keeping the rotting body intact. Darlo showing vulnerability, however stunted, deflated what was left of her optimism.

And he really smelled. The smell of him made Joey's eyes water in ways good and bad.

Joey shrugged and lit one of her matches. "Fucking Hackney thinks he's so slick." She wasn't going to let on, not here. "Talking loud and saying nothing."

"What *nothing* did he say, though? Are they upset? Are they happy?"

"We didn't really talk about it."

Darlo looked skeptical. She'd blown it a little there, underplayed it.

"What do you mean, didn't talk about it?"

"He just wanted to party."

"With you? At breakfast?"

"I'm attractive and easy."

"Real virtues."

"You don't seem to mind."

Darlo looked at the manager, who recognized, in his blood-shot valleys, profound problems that had nothing to do with her or the band. They were the red tangled map of a deep and fermented sorrow.

"Your eyes," she said. "Jesus, Darlo."

"I'm having a bad fucking day, babe," he said. "My dad's in fucking jail and I can't get any money. So pardon fucking me if I look a little shitty."

She resisted taking his hand. "We can talk if you want."

He drew back, smirking. "About fucking what, exactly?"

Joey thought of pictures of rock musicians not long before they died: Brian Jones by the pool in which he drowned, pasty-faced, wearing a shirt of American flags; Jim Morrison, pig-faced and stringy-haired in a Paris café; Janis Joplin, slouched on a velvet couch, cradling a Jack Daniel's bottle in her arms like a baby. Darlo had the same end-of-the-line vibe, and he hadn't been famous in the bargain. She waited for feelings of guilt, as if, in her capacity as manager, she could have alleviated this condition. But no guilt came. Only worry that Darlo would start breaking down in ways she could not predict.

If I fuck him, she thought, finally and completely, will that do the trick?

Darlo picked something out of his hair. This took a minute. Her phone rang.

"Who is it?" he asked.

"Shane," she said, and pulled away as he tried to grab it from her. They rubbed against each other. Kiss me now, she thought. But he wavered.

"I wanna fucking talk to him," Darlo said.

"Tough shit," she said, and took the call. "What's up, white bread?"

"Hi, Joey. You're in Amsterdam, right?"

"Fine," she said, "and how are you?"

"Fine. You're in Amsterdam, right?"

"Oh good, I'm glad you're well. How was the show last night?"

"You're in *Amsterdam, right?*"

Darlo stared off into space, his square-jawed profile measuring up well as black hair flopped beautifully over his eyes. She lit a Players and passed him a match.

"I need to use your hotel room," Shane said. "I need a shower."

"What about Morten's?"

"I didn't stay there last night, and I could really use a nice bathroom right now, and besides, I don't even know where Morten's—"

"Find a hostel." Silence. "Did you get that?"

"Joey, do me a fucking favor for once."

"Apologize for telling Helen that I'm a shitty manager."

"I didn't tell Helen—"

"See you later."

"Fine! I'm sorry. Where's your fucking hotel?"

Joey stared at Darlo's hair. Such good hair. "I'm at the Grand Hotel Krasnapolsky. On Dam Square. Get a key from reception."

Shane clicked it right in her ear.

"Dickwad," she said, strangling her phone, and turned to Darlo. "Why does the singer always have to be the baby?"

"Gets him attention," Darlo said, and blew smoke rings.

They continued to stroll in the wrong direction. Joey chainsmoked and gamed out dinner. How would everyone take it? Adam would act like a normal human being; Joey was sure the guitar player wanted out but was too spineless to quit without such a major development—this would be his chance. Bobby would laugh and scratch at his disgusting hands and pretend that he was thrilled, they had it coming—the Mummy was such a future-fucker—but inside he would be dying. Shane was a wild card; he could be sanguine or damning, biding his time, that careerist shit. Darlo wouldn't accept it. He'd demand satisfaction, the phone numbers of all involved, just so he could embarrass himself even more deeply than he already had, as if two years were not enough to forever disgust everyone who pledged to help him. Or he'd skip the Rolodex, jump across the table, and throttle her.

Darlo had that thousand-yard stare on. Despite thinking that Père Cox was largely subhuman, she hadn't thought he'd fuck over his son. But he had, right in the keester.

The drummer shook his head, as if breaking free from a spell. "I just can't believe my dad would mismanage things like this," he said. "He's got an aging outlaw problem, man—he just wants to be young forever. It's making him do weird, crazy shit."

"You mean the snuff films?"

Darlo looked at her. Was that *hurt* on his face?

"They're not snuff films," he said.

"Close enough. You told me about that one girl."

"It was just a black eye. He paid her for it."

She laughed. "Please tell me you're not defending him."

"I'm not," he said. "But it was acting."

She too blew smoke rings, feeling competitive. "The sooner you start understanding that violence is wrong, *always* wrong, the sooner you and I can do business."

"You mean fuck?"

"No, Darlo." She stretched her aching leg. "Something deeper than that."

Darlo changed the subject, started in on one of his diagnostic sessions, where he catalogued all that had gone wrong with the band and made recommendations for how to fix it. This was the vestigial, ossified version of the bull sessions the two of them had once so enjoyed, back when they were going to take over the world, back when the world was the length of the Sunset Strip and thick enough to spread all over the globe. Glory on a small scale was suitable for all kinds of dreamers. You could really plot that graph. But the bigger stuff required real mathematicians, required an actual and quantified understanding of the algorithms of celebrity, the positioning of image, the discipline to stay with the plan. Sting and McCartney and Steven Tyler had discipline, Joey thought. Jim Morrison and Sid Vicious did not. Neither did Darlo, or anyone in Blood Orphans except Adam, Mr. Anticharisma.

Adam had discipline. No wonder they hated him.

The intimacy of those bull sessions. The authenticity. Their collective ability to imagine it fully and enact it. Beautiful. Sunshined. Beers at the Silverlake Lounge and hamburgers at Tommy's and cocaine at Peppermint Castle. And now here was Darlo, a little bug in the rainforest of fame, trying to drag the mighty leaf of perseverance across the jungle floor. Here he was, all alone with broken antennae. What could Joey do? She got down there in the dirt, stretched her mandibles, and gave a pull.

"Mistakes were made," she said. "I won't dispute that."

Darlo lit up, managing to burn his hand on the match a little.

"One mistake we made," he said, "was 'Hella-Prosthetica.' That's a bad idea for a song. Fucking cringe-tastic, dude. Some kid e-mailed me a drawing of what it would look like to actually fuck some chick without legs."

"Not to mention the fight you got in because of that stupid song." Joey took a drag. "That didn't wise you up?"

"No. That guy was a prick, man."

"I'm sorry," Joey said. "But it seemed totally reasonable to me."

"Why? Because his sister had no legs?"

"That sounds about right."

"Fucker had a strong punch," Darlo said, in a tone of contrition. "If I had it coming, I sure as shit got it." The bloodshot in his eyes had increased, as if he were crying on the inside of his sockets. "A real strong punch."

They continued on, into Museumplein. Joey wondered how they had just gone in a circle. On the green, a couple hundred kids protested America's involvement in every little thing. Hippies, straights, and a few modern primitives, a smattering of dreadlocks and old furs, and polar fleece like icing.

"The old devil America," Darlo said. "Get a new hobby."

The crowd grew fast, coagulating like hair in a drain. Banners waved under the gray Dutch sky, watched over by the old buildings, scoured and prettified. Joey wondered about all the different demonstrations that had occurred through history upon this Dutch square: greater chocolate tariffs, better representation for tobacco traders, anger over burgher-mandated funny hats. In this context, anti-McDonald's-ism couldn't match up.

"Look at these assholes," Darlo said, motioning to the protesters.

"They're not assholes," Joey said. "They're angry."

Darlo ran tongue over teeth. "Spare me the fucking sociology, babe," he said, "because you were sitting in your fucking office filing your nails while we were stuck in a van wasting time, wasting our fucking time because Warners didn't do their fucking job, because *you* didn't do your job. Fucking stuck in there going insane at eighty miles per hour, the black hole of rock-and-roll fucking Calcutta."

They stood at the fringe of the mass. A young man with a blond beard, a real Dutch Guevara, stood on a platform, raised his fist, and railed. Joey didn't understand a word, but the strident tone said it all.

Darlo pointed at a few choice female backsides. "We're all the same, man. The way they put their ass in the air in those European beds, it's no different from American girls. Except European girls like it more. Euros love getting fucked in the ass. Let history be my guide."

Joey thought it best to not continue this line of conversation. It would end in an entanglement of her mind and spirit, and right now she needed to feel elevated over Darlo.

"All of them," the drummer said. "Ungrateful worms."

No one turned to look.

"All of them. Just like my band."

Worrying about her dudes ran deep in the manager's blood; Joey enjoyed the privilege, the exceptional vantage from which she could watch, diagnose, and take care of her boys. Even Darlo. Especially Darlo. Her old partner in crime, who now, in the midst of this bracing autumnal moment, at this late, late hour, was cracking hard and cracking ugly. Oh, to the untrained eye the young man appeared to be like any other snot-nosed hottie in a leather jacket, just another chauvinist-cum-tourist-cum-two-week-drunk, some frat boy with a little clothes sense. But Joey knew better. Darlo, waving his arms and mumbling about the undeserving, was a magician throwing blank spells. His abrasion and bravado, usually a vibe that came off him in feral waves, had lost transmission.

He continued to piss and moan. His ill-fitting amalgam of pettiness, bitterness, and flat-out incoherence looked to passersby like nothing more than the whinings of a sulky and privileged American son. But actually, this stink bomb of emotional dry charges constituted Darlo's cry for help.

"Babe," she said, grabbing his shoulders. "It's OK."

Darlo's eyes popped at her. "Don't look at me like that," he said.

"Like what?"

"You know."

"I don't."

"You do. Like you're gonna let me in. Like you're finally going to let it happen."

"Jesus Christ."

"You know how hard it is for me," he said. "You totally know."

Joey knew that she couldn't go the tenderness route. Her sentiments hardened. "I'm worried about you. Look at you. You're a mess."

Cheering came up from the crowd. Dutch Guevara left the stage.

"Maybe I am," he said. "But you can't fucking help."

"Because I won't *let it happen?*"

He shook his head, as if he'd grown tired of explaining something important.

Everything was lost. Her band, her career, her twenties. The weight of it sank in while people around her grew louder, became strident, thought about things outside the purview of the radius of their collective navel. Joey wished she had any fucking idea how to navigate the maze of Darlo's heart without getting lost in its bloated curves.

And then they were burning a replica of President Bush. Joey thought of the footage she'd seen as a child, of Iranian protesters parading the hostages, chanting, dancing, doing the anti-American hokeypokey. Hopefully they would circle her and Darlo and try to rip them to pieces. Bring it on, you bitches, she thought. Bring it on.

13

ADAM IMMERSED HIMSELF in the rush of cyclists moving along the Amstel. Joey's behavior at the museum had freaked him out. Something about her mania felt dead serious, felt steady-on bad, portended doom. He was starting to feel as if today was a special day, profoundly special.

He wondered what had happened with Darlo's dad. When the two had met in the Cox kitchen, the old freak's eyes had climbed over him like spiders.

"You're an artist, huh?" Cox asked. Wearing a karate outfit, he'd been practicing his forms on the back lawn while the band was swimming. Now he stood by the butcher block, sweaty, sipping water, thinning hair slicked back, looking at Adam as if he wore a stolen heirloom. "An artist, I said?"

"Yes. I'm at CalArts, studying—"

"My sister was an artist." Sip. "Acid casualty." Sip. "What do you think of that?"

"Think of what?"

"Art's relationship to being fucked up."

"Sometimes an intense vision comes with an inability to cope."

"Ooh, smart guy." Sip. "I think that art is for people who want to cover the walls of people with real jobs." Sip.

"You're entitled to your opinion."

"Damn right—" Sip—"I am."

Cox adjusted his black belt. No way, Adam thought, that black belt was real. Cox spit water into the sink. The man's skin looked like distressed leather. Adam felt retchy.

"At least you play the guitar," Cox said. "You can make some money out of that. And play quite well, Darlo says."

"That's very kind of him."

"Kind?" he said. "No, not my son."

Following the flow of traffic, Adam imagined Cox being escorted away from his porn palace in cuffs and thought maybe, a few years down the road, when all had been forgotten, he'd paint that scene, but switch Dad out for Darlo.

Now and then Adam had lobbied for changes in the music. Blood Orphans could evolve if they wanted, away from songs about girls who imitate vacuum cleaners, florid nuclear scenarios, and motorcycles that talked.

They had tried to learn one cover, early on: "Eighties," by Killing Joke, because Darlo heard it in *Weird Science* and thought it sounded tough. They recorded it for the record, but Shane did Jaz Coleman about as well as George W. Bush did Abraham Lincoln.

"No good," Sheridan, their stoner producer, had said from the control room. "Too soft."

On the third tour, Adam broached the subject of adding acoustic elements to the next record, suggesting covers — Neutral Milk Hotel, Cat Stevens, Nick Drake — as a way into the soft parade.

"Neutral Milk Hotel?" Darlo had said. "The fuck's a Neutral Milk Hotel?"

They were driving on I-15 through Idaho, one of the ugliest stretches of interstate, second only to I-20 across west Texas. Shane was at the wheel, which meant they were stuck in the right lane, cruise control set at sixty.

"They're really amazing," Adam said.

"They sound gay," Darlo replied, and turned up the AC/DC.

Adam looked to Bobby for support. The bass player lit a Marlboro.

"Fu Manchu is right," Bobby said. "You should listen to him for once. All the cool girls like it."

"Is that so?"

"Yup. And you know who cool girls don't like?"

"Who?"

Sometimes the drummer could be so thick.

"Us, Darlo. They don't like us. Cool critics don't like us either."

"No critics like us," Shane said. "We're racists."

They all laughed. It was still early enough in the game for them to laugh together, once or twice a week.

"We need some cool points, that's for sure," Darlo said. "Neutral what-did-you-call-it?"

The next day Adam stuck *In the Aeroplane over the Sea* into the car stereo while Darlo was driving.

"This is the band I was telling you about."

"Uh-huh," Darlo said, picking his nose. "Fine."

They listened to about half the record, and Darlo seemed to be enjoying it. But then he reached for his soda, pulling through the piles, and came up with one of Shane's Gideon Bibles, which, since the demise of his Extreme Teen Bible, the singer had begun stealing en masse from motels. He lobbed the volume back and popped Shane, asleep and drooling, in the head.

"I thought I told you to stop stuffing the van with these."

Shane threw it back. "I'm collecting colors."

"You can't do that shit, dude. It's not funny and it serves no purpose and we *get* it that you're mad."

Shane put the Bible under his pillow to prop his head. "I'll do what I want, sex addict."

And then it was on. The Shane and Darlo Show.

Darlo grabbed the CD out of the player. "This fucking whiny gay music is driving me fucking crazy!"

The next time Adam brought up the idea, a week later in a Nashville green room, Darlo rolled his eyes. "Oh my God. Will you just give it a rest, Adam?"

"This is only the second time I've mentioned it."

Darlo adjusted his balls and threw an acidic smile. "Then I guess it's two times too many."

Adam looked at Bobby, but Bobby appeared to be operating on his hands. He squared up his weak jaw.

"We're going to have to—"

"—shake it up for the next record. Yeah, yeah, I know, Adam."

"That's not what I was going to say."

"Shut up about it!" Darlo chucked a drumstick at him. "Stop trying to undermine what we're doing with your faggy folk-music ideas! Can you imagine me writing lyrics like 'Double Mocha Lattay' to some stupid acoustic music?"

"That's his point," Shane said. "You retard."

Everyone, even Darlo, knew that the second record had to be different. They weren't even the laughingstock of the music business anymore; other bands had taken their place. They were simply a synonym for utter lame-itude. As in, man, that song's a real Blood Orphan, or, Jesus, that tour routing is just utter Blood Orphans, or, Fuckin' A, the turnout tonight was full-on Blood Orphans. I mean, was *anybody* there?

Getting along was the least of their problems. At some point, Adam would have to go to Darlo and say, We're fucked and you know it. Give me a turn at the wheel or I quit.

"That's right," he said, moving through traffic. "I'll quit."

He cursed his mousy voice. He rode his Dutch bike along some canal and contemplated years of big talk and no walk.

How many times had he promised to make things right? At least thirty.

How many times had he actually threatened to leave? Maybe two.

Degree to which he felt like he was a chickenshit loser? Priceless.

The little part of Adam with some cojones, tied up in the cellar of his sensitive-guy mind, marveled at his ability to get all the lessons of his childhood wrong, to come from a family of bullies, get attacked and ridiculed for being a sweet sensitive boy with feelings, and simply take it. To go out in the world and, at his first real opportunity, get into exactly the same dynamic of abuse that he'd promised he would forever be free of.

Adam had always found excuses. In childhood: the brotherly trouble ends sooner when I do nothing. In adolescence: soon I will be done and gone, no use dragging it out by antagonizing the Bakersfield apes. In Blood Orphans: but look at all the money, and the chance for glory, and the publishing money on top of it. Look at my bank balance!

Excuses.

But now the end of the line was here. He really had nothing to lose. Go ahead. Call my bluff. This time he meant it.

"Sure you do," he said, riding down another beautiful Dutch straat. "Please."

He took a turn into Vondelpark. He'd find a nice tree and clear his head, make his mind's eye a blank screen, imagine that he was on some lonely Caribbean beach. The white sand, the deep blue water. Under an almost barren oak, he parked his bike on the grass and conceived the scene, spread a blanket out on the sand, rolled a cigarette, imagined sandcastles and the lush roar of crashing surf.

But no. Here came Darlo and Bobby, over the dune. They had beers in their hands. Bobby didn't even have eczema. Here they came, infringing even on his meditative dream, and behind them

Shane, walking slowly, stiff, trying to approximate a penitent, a pilgrim, a seeker. A poser.

Soon Darlo and Bobby were kicking sand in his face and pouring beer on his head while Shane read a section of the Extreme Teen Bible. *Jesus is the deepest philosopher. Jesus could make better water than Perrier. Jesus makes a better burger than In-N-Out.*

They stomped on his sandcastle. He opened his eyes and sat up.

Adam watched, straight ahead in the distance, as kids walked with banners in their hands. *Down with America* sounded fine to him. All America had ever done was saddle him with a shitty family, a crazy-sadistic band, and a hundred thousand guilt-soaked dollars.

To his left, about a hundred yards off, two skinheads passed by. Adam tried to take his eyes off them but could not. He found images of power to be irresistible, and this pair in flight jackets and black jeans strutted across the green like conquerors. They looked over, making eye contact; Adam looked down, fumbled in his pockets for nothing at all. He heard them laugh. When he looked up, they were disappearing into some trees.

He took out his sketchbook and started doodling, trying to relax his mind to a place of creation, from which narrative would flow. You needed a narrative to draw. That was the first rule Michael Samuels, his composition instructor at CalArts, had said as they sat in front of dry, untouched easels. You needed to let your unconscious run free all over the image, let it map out a story, tap your own fears and joys and make commentary on the world around you. Narcissism, he'd said, is not a limitation. Narcissism is the key to a unique worldview.

"Narcissism melting into humanism," Instructor Samuels had said, "creates a win-win strategy."

Samuels, even more than the other instructors, sounded like a cheap guru.

"Get moving on your opus now," he had said, circling the studio, tall, ponytailed, and rapidly balding. "Do not wait for the right subject. The right subject is the known universe."

That much was true. Production was the key to insight.

"Plumb your narcissism," Samuels had said, while staring at some hot art-school ass in black wool.

So Adam plumbed his narcissism and returned to a sketch he had started the day before, when he had walked the Amsterdam streets, imagining life here four hundred years back, imagining he was Rembrandt walking in slippers and hose, staring into the windows at the burghers who ran the city, imagining how he would line them up in the portrait for which he had just been commissioned. Standing there channeling the old Dutchmen had filled Adam with a sense of continuity, of being in the right place in the right time, carrying on a tradition, keeping up the magic of collective memory. Perhaps he would make a painting, after Rembrandt, of Blood Orphans. A portrait, hundreds of years later, of four fake nobles. Group pride and individual sorrow, jockeying for space on the crusted canvas.

"Take your smallest motivation and inflate it," Samuels had said, eyes glued on that coed ass. "Make it epic. Find the epic kernel."

Adam drew wrinkles on the four of them. He tipped a hat on Darlo's head, drew mustaches, laid a heavy aspect on the eyes.

"Find the epic that lies in your most mundane obsession."

He put more facial hair on Shane. He drew Bobby in such a way that his right hand touched his chin, revealing flickers of dry skin. All of them appeared sallow-skinned, drunk with mead, scurvy-bound. His phone rang.

"Hi, Shane."

"Hey, what's up, man?"

He counted to three, to purge all niceness from his voice. "What is it?"

"Do you know where Joey's staying? Fucker told me, but I didn't have a pen and I forgot what she said."

He shadowed some capes on the four of them, then realized he had to make room for Joey. Would he paint her in milkmaid dress, or as the head mayor? He added more hair to Shane's beard.

"Adam?"

"Oh, sorry, you faded out there. Hold on and I'll get the info."

He put his cell phone down and started counting to one hundred. A shiver of excitement went through him.

"Hello?" came the voice on the phone, faceup on the ground. "Adam?"

He picked the phone back up. "Here it is. The Grand Hotel Krasnapolsky. Near Dam Square. You know how to get there?"

"I'll find it," Shane said, the line crackling. "Everything's going wrong today. But some days I guess the pilgrimage is rough."

Smoke rose from the park. Cheering rose higher. He dropped the phone and sketched out Joey in burgher dress, looming over them, the head of the landowners. Her blond hair peeked out the sides of her tall black hat.

Adam tried to map his narcissism onto the scene, the way his instructor had said to do. What element in himself was he ashamed of? How could he apply that to this portrait of the dead, the drunk, the disaffected?

Some issue of perspective clicked in his head. Some relationship became apparent. He drew downward lines in the faces. He sharpened corners on hats. He picked the phone up again because Shane was yelling for him.

"I'm here. What is it?"

"Just want to say thanks," the singer said. "Thanks, man. Thanks a lot."

What was that weird semitone hidden in Shane's voice?

Regret.

"You're welcome."

He made the hairs on Shane's face sharp, pointy, a touch of the porcupine.

"Hey," Shane said. "I'm sorry about last night. We're just so mean to you. We're always picking on—"

Adam hung up on him. Shane apologizing was just another off-key moment in their song of failed connection. Not today. He stretched his velvet-trousered legs.

He tried to keep sketching, but the magic was gone. The moment of pure synthesis, as Instructor Samuels called it, had abandoned him. But soon he would have all the time in the world to channel the synthetic moment. Soon he would be able to sit on the sand at Venice and let the natural world bring the synthesis of this disparate world to him. He closed his eyes and imagined the beach again, cool and calm. This time he was on the Oregon coastline. Seastacks blocked out the sun. He was alone and reaching for the pure synthetic moment. He was free.

And that was when he heard the yelling. He closed his eyes, trying to keep the dream alive, but rough voices cut through like solvent into grease. The two skinheads were walking across the field toward him.

Maybe they weren't. What would they want out of him? But then he remembered that he was a poncy little rock musician, in his leather jacket and spiky black hair and motorcycle boots. Then he remembered the Fu Manchu.

They pointed at him like they'd finally found their man.

"Dutch, dutch, da-du-dutch dutch!" they said. "Dutch da-dutch, *ausländer!*"

In their open green flight jackets and suspenders and T-shirts with swastikas, they were just too ridiculous. They couldn't be real.

"Dutch, da-dutch, *ausländer!*" said the other one. "*Ausländer,* Dutch!"

Bad acne scarred one of them, deep like a carved-out delta. Anyone with acne scars that bad would be pretty pissed off.

"Dutch, dutch, *Juden!*" the other one said. He did not have acne but was the kind of short that passes the true threshold of utter shortitude, like five-three maybe. He had a body like a bulldog's, and his blue eyes were on fire.

Studying them carefully staved off fear for a few seconds — the stubborn dispassion of the artist — but soon Adam's body felt as if it were sinking into rapidly hardening goo. "What's the problem?" he said, which might have been the least tough thing he could have said.

"*Ausländer* dutch-dutch *Juden!*" said Pizza Face, and raised his hands like Godzilla.

He waited for them to vaporize. He had fallen asleep and this was a nightmare, brought on by a shallow nodding-out.

Pizza Face grabbed Adam's backpack and shook it, pointing, as if to say, Look what you've brought into this country. Look at the filthy backpack with which you are defiling the pure, undecadent backpacks of Holland.

Images of past harassments began to overlap each other like misaligned transparencies; the hands of his two brothers, Ike and Dave, who would come to him while he was drawing out in the yard, pick up his stuff, and say, You make us look bad acting like such a faggot. Ike and Dave, who worked on their motorcycles out in the shed and resembled the Hanson brothers. Ike and Dave, who filmed their own porn in the Motel 6 off I-5 and sold it at their demolition derbies, at their pit-bull fights, at their Aryan Nation meetings.

These two casts of characters toppled over each other, slippery and out of sync.

Pizza Face threw the backpack down. Adam went sweaty. His body felt covered in Astroglide.

"Leave me alone," he peeped.

They looked at each other like maybe they'd heard him wrong. He wanted them to start laughing, to temper the anger with some levity. But these mindless freaks seemed to have no sense of humor whatsoever. They seemed to have hot pokers up their asses and to be sure that Adam had put them there.

"Ausländer!" the short bulldog said, and kicked him.

Adam could see everything, slowing speed down, an endocrine aberration that gave him just a little more time to react, so that instead of getting a steel-toed foot in his face he dodged left and swatted at the leg—swatted, he knew, like a little girl.

Waiting for him on his right was another foot, which got him in the shoulder.

"Stop!" he screamed. "Help!"

He rolled and tried to cover his head, muffling his cries. Some dirt got into his mouth, tasting acidic.

The skinheads were just barking now, punctuating their kicks with grunts.

"Help!" Adam screamed, but his voice disappeared into the ether.

14

STARING INTO THE MASS of protesters, Joey grew increasingly aggro. She just wanted one person to resemble someone who had wronged her, and she'd rush in. The crowd grew, over two hundred strong, exercising their right to hate America.

"Can you call McFadden?" Darlo said. His voice was akin to her father's waking her up to take out the garbage. "Fucker won't listen to me."

"And why would he listen to me?"

"You helped him negotiate our contract."

Joey gritted her teeth. "That's some totally different shit from the thing with your dad. I'm not getting involved in that. Besides, the last time I saw him, I called him a fat faggot."

"You did?" He French-inhaled. "Well, just call him and apologize and then help me—"

Joey held up her hand. "Some things are not cleared up with an apology," she said. "Some things sting for a while. Like, when you talk to your dad, are you just going to accept an apology from him? No, maybe you're not. Maybe you're going to hope that wild dogs eat him slowly. Maybe one of those Rhodesian Ridgebacks of his will freak out on him like Abby freaked out on you."

"Don't you ever fucking mention that."

"He set you up," Joey said. "He set that dog on you."

"Shut *up*."

"He's a piece of shit, Darlo. He's a fucking turd."

Now, as the crowd roared in the pastoral urban square, Joey

pulled her meager suit jacket to her body. A monochromatic blur of sun peeked through the clouds.

"I still think you should have pressed charges," she said, popping some Tylenol. "Seriously."

"Nah. Stupid whiny thing to do."

"He sicced a killer dog on you because you sold a few of his baseball cards." She stepped closer to him. "It's in the way you walk. You limp a little."

"You're one to talk."

"I was hit by a car."

Darlo lit another cigarette. His fingers shook. But she knew he couldn't let it out. That would break him.

"Victims whine, babe," he said. "I'm not a victim."

Darlo's voice went a little flat; the flatness encompassed so much to Joey that was lost in his life, her life. She wanted to take his face in her hands and kiss him gently, coax him from where he hid, but she couldn't get around her wall of worry about balances of power. Anger at her own inabilities tightened her spine, and now the faces of the crowd became those of the Warners publicity department, the army of young hipster women who had ignored the record to death, the same women who would come into Spaceland and expect Joey to give them free drinks because they shilled for the label. What had happened to the Blood Orphans street team they'd been promised, an army of college reps in Blood Orphans T-shirts, distributing CDs on every college quad in America. Where were those T-shirts now?

Ah yes, the publicity department, which greeted every inquiry as if it were a hot pebble up their collective ass, despite all assurances from Steadman that everyone was lined up, geared to go, ready to roll. Every call greeted with stony indifference or snobby disgust.

Did they think she enjoyed eating shit?

"What can I do?" Steadman said the day after Aerosmith dropped them from the bill. Joey had stormed—well, tried to storm; she wasn't really tall enough—into his office in her café au lait Gucci knee boots and matching suede suit from Nudies, demanding justice.

"The racist tag kind of ties a hand or two," he said. "It's a millstone around the label's neck." He lit a cigar. "Don't you think?"

"Like you don't know the editor of fucking *Spin!*"

"He's a very independent man. He serves bigger masters than me." He smiled. Like that smile was going to make anything better.

"We can't get the booking agent on the phone!" Joey said.

"You're the manager!" He puffed on a Cuban cigar. "Not my job, amigo."

Buck-passing slime. And now she saw them all in the crowd; Steadman and his publicity minions, hidden in the fight against the American Century.

"Fuck you!" she screamed, pushing forward. She charged at the mass of them, began to climb onto the backs of the progeny of the burghers and traders, low-country smarmy shits, namby-pamby pacifists, but some high-octane patchouli choked her up. She hated patchouli as much as the next person with any self-respect. These passé Euros didn't even have the integrity to steer clear of that most revolting of scents, which they probably discovered via an American exchange student.

"Hey!" shouted a black-haired English girl in a blue Polartec hoodie. "Hey, get off me!"

Jack Fredericks, Joey's father, the corporate executive, had laughed and said, That's what you get for tying your fortunes to a bunch of idiots. That's what you get for taking your entrepreneurial steam and running a faulty train down broken rails. Joey took a few million dollars and shredded it! Burned it in the pyre of her stupid fucking bad judgment! Got in too deep and drowned! She refused Sharpie Shakes and trusted the wisdom of her unproven hubris.

"My hair! Get off me!"

She remembered the day of the signing. They took pictures and ate a cake in the Warners offices. Drank Lucky Lagers because Lucky was going to sponsor them—another endorsement ruined by racism—to be the official beer of the Blood Orphans (Blood Orphans want you to get Lucky!), and she shoved Steadman's face in the cake, ha ha, Steadman, you genius!

"Joey!"

She shoved cake into Darlo's mouth and Shane's ear and smeared it on Adam's face and in Bobby's hair and everyone laughed. Groupies and hangers-on were there like frames on a frilly pastoral picture, like a crocheted Bless This House that goes above a kitchen doorway, girls who had later taken turns with each of them; even Adam couldn't resist because the rock-and-roll fantasy was real for them and here they were, chosen for it, and Joey had made it happen! The wet lips on their cocks and Joey had made it happen! She had cake in her hands and smiled at the camera in her pink vintage Chanel suit and matching pillbox hat and thought, Next time we're here I'll have platinum records in my little hands, plaques of platinum, and we'll be holding them aloft like the heads of our enemies, medieval warriors come from the land of the ice and snow, all my late-night childhood fantasies fulfilled, Valhalla we are coming—

"Joey!"

Valhalla we are coming.

"Joey!"

Valhalla we are coming.

"Joey!"

15

THE MORE DARLO THOUGHT about it, the more he felt like a sucker. His loyalty, rewarded with a fresh load of trouble. It wasn't fair that his money was in hock because the old man had gotten sloppy. He thought of the old porn stars who came over for dinner, mournful, pathetic, their bodies wasted by speed, disease, and sorrow. They showed up in their tracksuits and their business-in-front-party-in-the-back haircuts, ate the steak and drank the wine as a windup for the sympathy pitch.

"I need help, Dave," they'd say, and break down over their sirloin. "I'm in a fucking bad place, man. I fucked it up. You're all I've got."

His dad would give them a hundred dollars and a hug. "It's all *I've* got," he'd say. "My poor brother. It's all I can do."

Their faces would contort, gratitude sodomized by disappointment.

And now his dad looked like them. He had a gazillion dollars, but he looked like a husk, a permatanned phantom.

Tax evasion. That was the cute part, and Darlo knew it.

They were in the square now. Some blond trustafarian was on a soapbox, complaining about American guns, germs, and steel.

Joey shot down his bright idea that she should call McFadden and then had to go and mention the time his dad sicced the dogs on him, a memory that was salt rubbed in the wound of his dad's betrayal.

When Darlo was sixteen, he'd stolen his father's baseball card collection. He'd stolen the collection because the old bag had hit on Jenni Feingold, his girlfriend from next door, whom he thought he might love. Jenni kept it quiet, but then David Cox ran into Aavram Feingold over at Canter's and told him all about it.

"You oughta look out," he said, chugging a Cel-Ray soda. "I might have to tap that ass."

Consequently, Jenni's parents forbade her to see Darlo. He and Jenni had to sneak around. She was never really the same with him.

"I only told him an obvious truth," Cox said. "They ought to be proud their daughter's such a little fox. What's the big deal?"

In retaliation, Darlo stole the cards, burned them on the lawn, and left the ashes. Several hundred bits of cardboard, valued at over five thousand dollars, reduced to charred mold. But price was nothing. The cards were Daddy Cox's visa back into childhood. Now that visa had been revoked. Now he was cut off from any and all palimpsests of innocence.

"You son of a bitch!" he said, and cuffed Darlo's ear.

"You're a fucking scumbag!" Darlo replied, and punched his father in his fat nose. "A pedophile!"

Darlo figured that was it. The man never stayed angry at his son. His son was all. But when Darlo came home from school the next day, Abby, the most ferocious of the Rhodesian Ridgebacks, was waiting for him.

Abby was stone-cold insane. Darlo's dad used her in the dog-fight ring he and his fellow pornographers and hoodlums held out at the Malibu estate of Bon Charles, the burgeoning king of American bukkake.

Abby had been brought up to kill. David Cox kept her separate from the other dogs, fed her red meat and cow brains, and deprived her of any affection whatsoever. So he let Abby out to teach Darlo a lesson.

She charged Darlo, threw him down, and planted her teeth in

his side. Darlo ripped at her eyes, punched at her face. The dog ran around the property screaming. She banged into trees and tripped over herself. Darlo went into the house, got his grandfather's service revolver—a gift that Darlo's dad had protested—and shot Abby through the temple. He held the blinded dog down, crying an apology, drooling an apology as his hands went red, and put three bullets in her head.

He threw up on the patio, then wandered over to Jenni Feingold's house, weeping, blood running down his side. Her father answered the door to find him sprawled out, stained crimson, unconscious.

But underneath the trauma, in some hidden fold of his soul, Darlo had expected his dad to retaliate. This was just the way life was. Some part of him never even flinched. Some part of him respected his dad's actions.

Every time he looked in a mirror, he saw the toothmarks above his waist. Sixteen stitches. Another bite or two and the dog would have taken a kidney, plucked it right out with that vise grip.

When he told Joey about the incident years back, she had not been impressed.

"Siccing a dog on your fucking son is a Saddam Hussein kind of nuts," she'd said, throwing down a shot of Cuervo at a Westwood strip club. "It's a Pol Pot kind of nuts."

"You don't understand. My dad's been good to me."

"No. Wrong. Now take that shot, pussy."

Down there, in his soul, that tight part of him had cried out. Up here, Pretend Land. No Big Deal Land. On the green of Museumplein, the trustafarian blathered on and on.

Joey stamped out her cigarette. "Fuck you," she said, and rushed into the crowd.

More cheers came up. Some hot piece of milky-white Dutch ass walked by, and Darlo remembered that he hadn't fucked anything today except his hand. A deep throb rose in his chest, and under normal circumstances he would have followed after, hit on her, capitalized on his distinct feral charms. But those charms were MIA, and besides, he was too busy thinking about the coke in the cupboard, the Adderall in the attic, the Vicodin in the vestibule.

The police would find it for sure. They would bust his dad some more. They couldn't link it back to him. There was no receipt on the shit. So let them tag the old man with his son's cache. Served him right.

His loyalty to the paterfamilias loosened up a little, an airtight seal losing pressure, an engine without enough compression.

His dad was at home, probably, celebrating his arraignment by sport-fucking a bunch of eighteen-year-olds. He would get in all his fresh talent, call a bunch of his scumbag underworld friends, pepper the girls with cocaine and crystal—Darlo's, probably, found nestled in the DVD collection in the screening room—and just line 'em up. After the first round in the living room, he'd follow the routine and take them down to the basement, press the code on the keypad behind the bookshelf—664, the neighbor of the beast—and open the secret door to the fun-guy dungeon, the S&M cellar, with the hoses and the clamps and the rubber bats, and make service animals out of them.

They'd think it was all fun and games at first, but at some juncture, watching the arc of men's spanking hands change as they moved through the air on the way to their asses, their wet lips would go crooked with fear. Their doll's eyes would tighten in their heads. They would panic and scream. Stupid girls. Naive girls. Didn't everyone know that David Cox was a sick old fuck who had done everything but make snuff? Didn't they know that he liked to draw blood and twist back arms over the warm leatherette and the olde-tyme rack?

Darlo pretended that his father hurt no one, that the man was only kink and fetish, feathers and hot wax. But screams came up from the cellar like bad smells.

He ignored the screams. Night after night month after month year after year. He smoked, drank, snorted, fucked himself into a cloudy stupor so the screams would go soft, sound like birds singing in April.

But one time he had not been able to make the sound go soft. The sound had cut through the stoned haze, cut through the floor, the ceiling, the door.

So he went down there, because the screaming was making him bite his lips, making him draw blood.

He went down there and found his father and a few other men with thick necks and silver watches taking turns with a tied-up girl. Sitting on couches, sweaty, they were naked but for their jewels and rings. The girl was bent over some kind of leather pommel horse. She was bleeding and crying. They were laughing.

"Stop, Dad," Darlo said. "Stop now, you sick fuck, or I'll call the cops."

His dad was in a leather mask, a whip in one hand, his hard cock in the other. He stared through his son.

"Oh, come on!" one of the men said, lighting up a cigar. "Come on, Darlo, don't spoil the fun!"

Mascara ran down the girl's face. She was so scared she shook; drool hung from her mouth. Darlo untied her. She blubbered and moaned and held on to him. She moaned in thanks. She gripped his arm. Blood ran from her.

Darlo surprised himself with nausea.

"She wanted to do it," his dad said, scratching his wet balls. "Don't be such a killjoy."

She held on to Darlo. Moist walls, old man stink, jazz on the stereo accentuating the lies. Didn't jazz always accentuate the lies in a room?

"Help me," she said. "Please help me."

She bled all over her body. Darlo saw the story. Blood ran down her leg, drying on the way. He barely kept his dinner down.

"Please," she said.

Darlo grabbed his father by the neck. He grabbed his father and squeezed as hard as he could. The girl ran, screaming.

"I'll fucking kill you," he said, and punched his father in the eye. Punched him hard enough to burst a bunch of capillaries. Punched him hard enough to break two bones in the man's face.

There were things people could never know.

He broke the old man's left zygomatic and maxilla. But all Darlo knew was the fat crunch under the girl's screams and the jazz.

And out in the world, aboveground, people thought he was a piece of shit. They thought Darlo Cox was bluster and meanness and selfishness, the sex addict, inhaler of alcohol, a regular ripper. All they saw was one side.

But there are two sides. There is night and day, and everyone is at a different latitude. Darlo's latitude was way up north. In Darlo's genetic code, there was one hour of light in the day. He barely made it over the horizon, but in that hour he shot up, burned as bright as anyone else. He burned with jealousy of those whose sun rises high in their sky, whose emotions are not tethered by that fixed point, whose light also gives heat.

Darlo had punched his father's face. He had risen over the horizon so his light shone, and he broke bones. He had attacked the man who tried to restrain the girl. He had grabbed the man's balls and squeezed until the man made the sound of air escaping through ice.

"Help me!" the girl screamed, and ran out the door, up the stairs.

Darlo ran after her. She hid from him in the kitchen.

"It's OK," he said. "Hey!"

But then he heard yelling from the dungeon, stomping up the stairs.

He ran to the stairs and met two dudes. "Darlo!" they yelled. "You fuckin'—"

Darlo barreled into them and they fell down against each other, still yelling. Behind him, he heard running and the slam of the door. By the time he was out on the street, she was gone.

A naked girl, gone? A naked barefoot girl, gone?

"It's OK!" he shouted into the trees, into the canyon. Wind and dirt. "It's OK—I'll help you!"

He knew he heard breathing.

"I'm not one of them. He's disgusting!"

Nausea up in him. The house shaking. The house crumbling.

"Not one of them I'll help you not one of them!"

Sick on the ground. All of him rushing to escape. His light struggling to stay over the horizon.

"Not one of them!"

On the ground. He heard her crying, but too late. He was on the ground, shoveling it all out of him. But the sun was sinking. His ancestral gravity dragged the sun down.

"Not one of not one of them notoneofthemnot!"

A protester shoved him. Darlo's feet were numb. He almost fell over. Joey was up near the podium. Her head bobbed as if she were moshing.

What would his mother say to all of this?

"Come back to the open spaces," she'd written. "The vastness of the land cleans the soul."

A lasso in midair, spinning.

"The land lets a person breathe. The land connects you with the benevolent forces of grace."

What separates the old man and me? Give me something to separate us. I don't torture. I don't hurt.

The differences felt like small ones. The differences felt like abstractions.

How could he push his sun higher into the sky? How could he escape that ancestral gravity?

He hung his head, daunted by the sense of impossibility. He needed that Iridium phone again. He had to stop it from happening.

Joey was in the crowd, head bobbing, arms flailing. Space opened around her.

He needed to get Jesse over to Chez Cox. Logistics and plans. See what Jesse can do. Jesse, you owe me.

The manager had the black hair of some girl in her hands, and it looked like the two were dancing on mud.

Darlo pushed through to her. He experienced a clarity of seriousness, the need to protect, and lunged forward into the fracas.

The man on the podium pointed at Joey like a hunter.

"Get off of me!" the girl screamed.

Darlo threw people aside and grabbed Joey's wrist and bit it.

"Fuck!" Joey said, and lost her grip so the girl pulled free.

"Babe!" Darlo said. "Babe, what are you doing?"

Joey looked at him, panicked, like How did I get here?

"Babe!" Darlo said, and pulled her. "Come on!"

That was the thing about Euros, Darlo thought. They didn't put up a fight. Here he and Joey were, two wasted Americans, and all he had to do was shove. All he had to do was stiffen his back, bare his teeth, and they backed off. Darlo stiff-armed and dispersed them like snow under a plow.

And then he was running. Catching up with the light over the horizon, his light, trying to break that latitude.

"Darlo!" Joey yelled. "I can't run!"

Joey would catch up. Darlo heard the scurrying of the girl through the steep dirt woods of Laurel Canyon.

"Wait!"

Darlo was going to catch her. He was going to protect her. Lab rat testing out new feelings.

"Stop running from me!" he said. "Fucking stop!"

His dad would be in the dungeon, rosining up the bow. A girl would be there. Some hot little number looking to spread for the living legend of extreme pornography. His stomach lurched.

How do you feel about pain, baby?

A nervous shrug, indigenous to girls from small towns. Sweat forming on the lip. A giggle that said, Where am I going, and where have I been?

Down there, hiding in the canyon, naked.

Or here, ahead of him, his manager falling behind.

"Stop!" he said, and ran the memory down.

16

JOEY BROKE FREE OF THE CROWD and ran across the green after Darlo, but with her shitty leg she couldn't keep up.

"Wait!" she yelled. "Darlo!"

Darlo ran through traffic, whooping, yelling his way through all those polite faces. He turned back.

"Come on!" he yelled, and ran on, promising all kinds of whoop-ass to the crowd of formally placid, constructive, client-state Dutchies. "You wanna hit me, Mr. Car? You want a piece of this? I'll fucking rip your throats, you dumb fucks!"

Joey ran after him, her leg working better than it had a right to, and she thought it was funny that no one chased after them. Try to rip out some girl's hair and suffer no consequences? She looked back; the crowd swarmed in on itself, as if the two Americans were hiding in the throng. The effigy of George Bush flopped in the wind like something you see on the top of a used-car lot.

Darlo disappeared from view and she tried to pick up the pace, yelling for him to stop. She hadn't been this out of breath since she'd had that threesome with the two interns from *Rolling Stone*.

Clouds turned over and over in the sky, shapes wrestling, tumbling.

Darlo stood at an intersection like a mad, tweaked-up mouse in a maze, smelling for the right direction. He saw her hobbling toward him. His hair lay in a greasy mop, and he laughed, exhilarated. She couldn't help but hear strings as she slouched toward him.

"Fredericks!" he yelled, panting. "Holy shit! What the fuck was that?"

"Gonna fucking kill someone or something!"

"Fucking Dutch!"

"Praise it!" she yelled. "Sing it!"

They laughed like they were back in the Spaceland bar, the world spread before them, happenstance and skill throwing elbows for bragging rights at the helm of their ship. Laughing, two friends at the dawn of their reign, having just lit a fresh wick on their explosive, dynamic future. Laughing, and Joey heard the joyous howl of introductions in a hundred sold-out arenas.

Can you hear me, San Francisco?

Blood Orphans!

Can you hear me, New York?

Blood Orphans!

Can you hear me, Los Angeles? At the back of the arena, way back there in the nosebleed seats, we love you, Los Angeles, can you hear me?

Blood Orphans!

Their name in pulsing lights above them, huge lights pulsing their name.

Blood...Orphans...Blood...Orphans.

Laughing like it was all to be just...like...that.

"What the fuck, babe!" Darlo yelled, smile wide as the Nile. "Trying to get us killed!"

"Fuck them!" she said. "Bitching and moaning like record company publicists! An army of them right there. Every face like a fucking Steadman." She growled. "Fucking Steadmans, the whole bunch of them."

Darlo shook his head. "You've lost it. Lost it!"

"I have lost it. Absolutely goddamned right."

Darlo looked up. Joey saw watery eyes.

"I love you, Joey," he said.

Oh, no. That was dewy. Dewy eyes.

"I really love you," he said, and inhaled.

What she wondered was, How did this never happen before? How could we go years without Darlo going dewy?

"Don't be a fag!" she yelled, and massaged her ankle.

His face went dark. "Bitch," he said, "I mean it!" And then he went running off again.

"Darlo!" she yelled, and hobbled after him. "No, come on!"

Darlo ran like he had a thousand volts up his ass, bolting by all the old buildings, all the fashionable Dutch youth, all the protesting Euro complainistas.

"Darlo!" she yelled, limping, pathetic. "I'm sorry!"

Back in the halcyon days, they'd raced down the beach at Venice like two boxers in training, right along the shore, laughing at the freaks and turds, the waste cases, the whole throng of those born without the gene of opportunity in them. Joey would run along that beach and think, That's right, I *am* running right the fuck by you, I *am* leaving you in the rotting dust, I *will* make something of myself. I won't be an executive like my dad or a banker like my mother, I won't be a dentist like Uncle Phil or a philosophy professor at UCLA like Aunt Grace, I won't be a premed like sister Annie or an engineer like brother Rob, but I will have use, have a point, be a legend.

Running, leaving them all in the dust. Pacific mist and spray.

I will be remembered.

Darlo ran, barreling through the entrance to Vondelpark, plowing right through those few mellow park revelers, over blankets spread out and students reading. Seconds later, Joey came hobbling by, sweating hard, passing a family of four—a man, a woman, and two toddlers—who'd been swamped in the undertow of Darlo's pure rude-itude, and they looked at her for some explanation as she yelled for her friend like a dog owner who'd let go of the leash.

"Sorry!" she said. "So sorry!"

The drummer had straightened out his path, and he ran as if he actually had a destination. And it turned out, he did have a destination, for at the end of the field, as Joey's leg and ankle started working together to screw her, at the end of the field in the shade of some trees, two skinheads were kicking some helpless dude who appeared, in Joey's shaky running vision, to be putting up no resistance.

"Hey!" she screamed, and picked up the pace.

The matter of virtue had appeared. The chance to do something selfless was upon her. The opportunity to transcend her navel-gazing had reared its rosy-cheeked face. So she found a second wind, fought against the weight of the various aches and pains, and charged in to help save the day.

"Nazi punks!" she screamed. "Nazi punks, fuck off!"

The guy the two skinheads were attacking was up now. His backpack whirled about, exploding with pens and paper, and a sketchbook went airborne. He was up and trying to fight back, but with little success. The entire contents of his backpack fell out like from a shattered piñata and he screamed, "Leave me alone!"

She knew that voice.

She knew that lament.

"Adam!" she yelled from across the green. "Adam!"

The guitar player flailed and rolled like a kid being dragged underwater by a great white. He didn't seem to have any idea that half of the people he knew in all of Holland were barreling crazily toward him.

"Leave me alone!" he howled, spinning.

Ahead of her, Darlo was just about to hit the beach. He gurgled a cry of attack, lifted his arms, and hurled himself into the scene.

17

COVERING HIS HEAD with his arms, Adam figured that his assailants would soon grow bored and move on to whatever pint of neo-Nazi beer awaited them on the other side of town. They were angry, but they weren't psychopaths—except that they were. The kicks kept coming, and Adam realized that this was for real. He windmilled his arms, hands in fists, flailing.

"Help!"

The short one tried to tackle Adam, but he pushed him off. The Nazis smelled like beer and cigarettes and vomit.

"Help me!"

Pizza Face came at him the other way and threw him down, tried to get on top of him, pin him down. Each moment escalated Adam's panic, and he felt a hum in the back of his neck.

Is that my soul leaving?

"Help!" he yelled, struggling under Pizza Face, whose dog collar was too tight around the neck. Adam heard the crowd again, alive and free, and a charge went through him. He threw Pizza Face off, but then the short one was wrestling him down and he was screaming again. He heard the crowd coming toward him, stomping in unison. Voices rose up out of the crowd, and he screamed back in a blues. The skinhead reached for Adam's throat, put pressure on his windpipe as the hum in his neck grew, rubbing against the sounds of the crowd, but the crowd was going to cover them all.

From nowhere, some guy came charging in, followed by a hobbling girl, a cut-and-paste out of some dreamscape. He thought, with his soul leaving and all, that his mind was playing tricks. But then the skinheads held up their hands in pointless protest, and this black-haired guy tackled Pizza Face, tackled him and started punching, a whirling dervish of anger.

"I'll kill you!" he guttered. "I'll ghill-yuuuuu!!"

The hobbling girl ran at the other skinhead, bopping and howling like a Caucasian Pocahontas, and sprayed pepper gas in his face. "Die, you fuck!" she screamed, and sprayed him, sprayed him, sprayed him until he fell back against a tree, clutching and clawing at his face.

Adam scampered back while these transports from a dream railed against his attackers.

"Ghill youuuuu!" the black-haired guy said.

Darlo?

Adam felt the hum in his neck move to his spine as the Astroglide sweat poured down. This was a fantasy his mind was enacting, brought on by lack of oxygen. It was all wrong and soon he would be back underneath Pizza Face, being strangled. Soon he would wake up from his suffocation-induced delusion and find himself dying.

But no. That was Darlo. And that was Joey. And he was here, in a foreign place, at the end of many things. And he was going to live.

Joey's skinhead writhed against the tree in a spasm, grabbing at his cheeks, whimpering like a dog. She had her arms out, shaking, and every few seconds she hobbled in and sprayed him again, as if he were a big wasp that wouldn't die.

"Sick fuck!" she said in a phlegmy growl. "Nazi fuck!"

Darlo had Pizza Face pinned and punched away, little spats of blood rising up under his blows. Adam's ears were pressuring up, like on airplanes, and sound went murky. He watched Darlo take out that knife of his, that scimitar switchblade, the so-called

Magic Wand. And truly it glittered with the spirit dust of the lonely Sioux spirit plain from which it had been forged. It glittered even in dour Dutch fog.

Darlo raised the knife up high, like he raised up a drumstick at the start of a song, counting off before they blasted into power-chord infinity.

"Ghill yuuuu!" the caveman gurgled, and reared up to strike.

18

JOEY HAD ALMOST DECIDED against taking the pepper spray with her to Amsterdam; the damn thing was so old she wondered if it even worked. Now she pulled it from her bag and fired away.

"Die!" she screamed. "Die!"

That little atomizer packed a real punch.

"Die! Die! Die!"

She heard the crunch of sticks in Darlo's direction. Darlo, on top of his skinhead, was in the process of losing his mind, bearing down like Godzilla over Bambi. He'd pinned the kid, put his arms under his legs so he was defenseless, and was throwing his fists.

"That's my friend!" he screamed. "My friend! My friend!"

She realized that Darlo was crying.

"My friend! My fra-heh-heh-hend!"

Joey went numb. For a second this had been fun, high adventure, but now she bore witness to a meltdown.

Adam crawled away like a man emerging from quicksand.

"Oh, God," she said. "Darlo, stop!"

Darlo raised his red hands above his head like a rabid ape.

"My friend! Rrrruuuggghhhh!"

Darlo landed punch after punch, and blood peppered the drummer's face. Then he leaned back and, from his back pocket, took out the Magic Wand.

Joey realized that Darlo was going to kill the skinhead. Rage had taken him. The knife, built by those who struggled every day merely to exist, snapped open in a rich boy's hand.

The dream was over.

"Darlo!" she yelled. "Stop!"

She kicked the knife out of the drummer's red paw, then tackled him.

"We have to go now!" She put her hands on Darlo's face. He looked like a panicking dog, eyes rolling in his sockets. "Now! Look in my eyes! Look in my eyes! Now!"

Darlo's cries were sorrowful. He rolled and sputtered, rage and anguish going at each other behind mad eyes.

"Think of his mother!" Joey said, because that's what an ex-con she'd dated had said to say to a person contemplating the taking of life. "Think of his mother!"

"No I can't no!"

"A mother, come on!"

She looked around. Adam had disappeared, and the skinhead she'd pepper-sprayed crawled to his friend, who was just a bloody mess. The knife was barely visible in the grass, had blended back into the ground, was melting back into the earth.

"Oh I'm sorry!" Darlo said. "Oh God I'm sorry Oh God I'm so sorry—"

"Run!" she yelled.

"Sorry oh my god oh no—"

"Now!" she said, and heard the roar of protesters calling themselves to arms against the evil empire. Adam appeared on his bike downfield, escaping from them, getting all the distance he could between him and them and every little thing they were. Wind blew through the bare trees.

"My hands!" Darlo yelled, already running. "My hands!"

19

BLOOD WAS ALWAYS STICKIER than he expected. Fighting was always more fun. They balanced themselves out.

Darlo kept swinging. He'd swing until his father went straight, his cock quit straining against his pants, and Aerosmith took them out on tour. He'd swing until that girl from the dungeon was safe at home, in her bed, at peace. He'd swing until Adam was safe from harm.

Below him, a face lay covered in red, the bones shifting to the left side, sliding like a seashell into the ebb tide. Now he was an artist like Adam, painting it black.

The skinhead made a noise, whimpering, the sound of fear before the time of the wheel, stripped down, raw tracks unmixed, just like the girl Darlo had found in the basement among the thugs, blubbering in her nakedness, scores on her back, sweat burning down her face.

Darlo thought, You may not share that noise with her, and took out the Magic Wand. You may not dare make that noise. I am a good person. I am not my father. I do not hurt the weak.

He took a second to look at the curve of his precious possession, and the barbs along the blade, and then Joey kicked the knife out of his hand.

"No, Darlo, no no no!"

Joey threw him off the skinhead, and Darlo heard the sound of his own crying and babbling and felt the wetness on his cheeks.

"No, Darlo, no, come on, no!"

Joey pulled him up and he was running. The world rushed

at him, mistakes on mistakes, ill-fitting. Darlo fell to the ground again, his legs jelly, but Joey pulled him as if he were weightless.

"Can't stay, come on, cops, come on!"

He looked back. The skinhead rolled on the ground, no longer imitating the innocent. Darlo had done what needed to be done. Though his father would be putting on gloves right now, wetting his lips, laughing at another nervous girl in black negligee right off the damn bus and there was nothing he could do, he had started to make things right. His proof lay there, in crimson, wiped out.

"Now Darlo, *get* the fuck *up!*"

He ran past Joey. He couldn't wait for her. He bolted into the mass of well-dressed unbloodied Dutchies, over another lovely canal, and spun on the sidewalk.

God if you exist deliver that girl from him. God if you exist deliver that girl from him. God if you—

Joey slammed into him. He wasn't running. When had he stopped running? Her breath climbed all over him. She pulled him, but he wasn't running; she pulled him down into the canyon. She would help him find that girl. Into the canyon. She was always there for him. He wanted to tell her. He wasn't running.

Doors opened, and Joey pulled him into a room. Faucets and tile. Coat of arms and Guinness signs. Leather seats like in the dungeon. Green leather here, black leather there. Going down into the canyon. Not running anymore.

20

ADAM HID BEHIND A TREE while Darlo whaled on the skinhead. He knew that, hidden deep inside a number of less savory motivations, Darlo's act of extreme violence was payback for the time Adam had saved his life at Crow Head.

Crow Head was a big chunk of rock that jutted out of the water about two hundred yards from the shore at Paradise, the five-hundred-dollar-a-day studio in St. Croix where they made *Rocket Heart*. During low tide a sandbar emerged, and Adam would walk out to the end of it to draw and listen to music. People avoided the sandbar, an incongruity to the perfect, smooth aspect of everything else in sight, but Adam loved being out there. A former member of the Bakersfield High swim team, he would often leap off the sandbar and breast-stroke the fifty yards over to Crow Head. He hit riptides now and then, but he knew how to handle them, and would sometimes end up on one of the adjacent beaches, appearing to people in the shallows like some castaway from Faggy Boy University.

Darlo hated it when someone could do something he couldn't do. Adam could play every known instrument, and that grated on the drummer.

"I'm gonna come out there one day and we're gonna race to that fuckin' rock," he said one night at dinner as they broke open lobster. "Yeah. I'm gonna come out there and school your ass."

Shane smashed a claw. "Drown *your* ass is more like it."

Bobby sucked at a leg and nodded. "It's rough out there, man. People go down every year."

"That is such bullshit," Darlo said, and pointed at Adam, who was trying to be delicate with his sea bug. "I *will* school you."

Bobby ripped open his lobster's middle, spraying green liver goo on his Iron Maiden T-shirt. "Goddamn," he said. "This is a collector's item."

Darlo made his lobster dance. "School you," he repeated.

Adam nodded, and Shane laughed.

"So fucking arrogant," the singer said. "God did not—"

"No God at the table," Darlo said. "None. Nada."

Shane stuck his nose up. "You'll drown, Darlo. That's all I'm saying."

A few days later, Adam was out there, trying to make good on Instructor Samuels's dictum on sketching out one's narcissism, when Darlo came stumbling up the sandbar. The day was out of a Club Med ad, with little white wisps against a deep blue sky and the sound of steel drums echoing from the shore. Darlo coming toward him was the lone storm cloud fucking it all up.

"What's up, faggot?"

He just stared at the drummer.

"What are you doing out here all day, anyway?"

"Drawing. Thinking."

"Well, la-dee-da," Darlo said, and plunked down.

Adam had been there an hour, his only visitors a few Jet-Skidiots, silly Frenchies who made Adam look masculine. The Jet-Skidiots would splash him and call him dirty French names while he detailed the curves of a bodacious, war-lusted maiden in a plate-mail bustier.

Darlo looked at Adam's sketch. "Hot," he said. "You wanna race?"

"It's not as easy as it looks."

Darlo looked at Crow Head and grunted in contempt. "It'll be a piece of cake."

Adam pondered the ethics of dissuading Darlo. "There's riptides."

"Is that your way of saying no?"

"It's my way of saying you'd better really know how to swim."

"Watch me." The drummer pulled off his shirt and cannonballed in. Adam rolled his eyes, annoyed.

"Come on, dude," Darlo said, sweeping back his luxurious black mane. He looked strong enough to swim to Africa. "I'm gonna get one hell of a jump on you."

You're gonna need it, Adam thought. He put down his sketchbook and dove in. On down the watery line, Crow Head resembled the Loch Ness Monster, a big inverted *J* of black stone.

Darlo's strokes were sloppy and uneconomical. Adam knew that the drummer would tire halfway and, like a fucking tortoise, Adam would catch up and easily overtake him.

The sound of steel drums rose from the beach but seemed to be coming from above, like a rogue god tuning the atmosphere. Adam did a sidestroke and watched a cloud change shape from a mouse to a dragon.

"Hey, what the fuck, Adam?" Darlo treaded water, huffing and puffing, maybe twenty feet ahead. "Don't handicap me, bitch. Make it for real."

Adam sighed at Darlo's stupidity. In water, you saved your strength. You didn't yell out taunts at the top of your lungs.

"Always staring at me!" Darlo yelled. "Fucking say something!"

"Save your strength," he said.

In response, Darlo sang in a bellow, as if he already stood atop Crow Head, pounding his chest in victory. "Wish I...was ocean size! They cannot move you, man—no one tries!"

The drummer drifted away from Crow Head, which loomed above them like a piton. The steel drums rained on them in a flange of sonic mist.

"Fucking love that song!" Darlo yelled. "Makes me feel so fucking alive!"

"Good for you," Adam grumbled.

The sound of Jet-Skidiots came across the water.

"Come on!" Darlo yelled, and started swimming again, his strokes becoming more like flailing. He didn't know the water any better than he knew the inside of a homeless shelter.

Adam changed to a crawl, his movements in time with the rhythm of the bay. Steel drum notes drifted above him like guiding gulls, and he experienced a moment of total bliss, rudely interrupted when he slapped Darlo in the face.

"Whoa, sorry," Adam said, turning away, waiting for a promise of retribution. None came, and he looked back.

The drummer looked at him. His eyes were wide open. His tongue pushed out his lower lip.

"Darlo?"

Darlo did a water dance. The panic Watusi. And then, silent and straight as an arrow, he dropped.

Now the steel drums turned to carrion vultures and dove in sharp. Adam took a second—a sinful, very un-Adam kind of second—to confirm that the song was indeed "Don't Worry, Be Happy." During this second he was the king; he ran the show, and complete freedom was his to slice into any shape he wanted, because Darlo was moving beneath the surface, drowning. Then Adam dove down to save the scourge of his existence.

Once Adam had rescued a child from the deep end of a pool in Bakersfield, and the child had thrashed in the same way that Darlo did as Adam grabbed his midsection and hoisted him.

Darlo tried to climb on top of him in a piggyback, as if Adam stood on concrete. The drummer whimpered and shivered in Adam's arms and then toppled off. Adam grabbed his midsection again, feeling a cramp in his back from having to support their collective weight. The water grew syrupy. In Darlo's eyes he saw nothing but black; the drummer was in shock and somewhere else. Adam needed to bring him back. He couldn't do this alone.

"Get it together, Darlo."

Darlo shook his head and made a wheezy grunt. Beachside, an impossible quarter-mile away, people laughed over their vacations. The clouds laughed over their ability to change shape. The sky laughed over its ability to reflect all colors save the most gorgeous blue. Laughter laughter laughter.

"Oh no," Darlo peeped, in about the most unharmonious, choked-up wail. "Oh no no no."

"You need to help me with this. You need to help me."

The drummer started to cry. "I don't want to die. I don't—"

And then he took in some water and started coughing.

Reality spread its billowing blanket and blocked out the sun. Darlo would kill them both if Adam didn't get his attention, so he grabbed Darlo's hair and pulled as hard as he could. The drummer cried out like a newborn, slipping off Adam's shoulders.

"My fucking hair—Jesus!"

"Do you want to live?"

"Fucking prick, I don't want to die!"

Then Darlo took in more water, coughed it up, thrashed about. Adam tried to get him on his back, navigating the tangle of arms, but then he started flailing too, because suddenly he was sure, absolutely sure, that the drummer had given up and was trying to drag them both down. The desire to live overtook the desire to help, and Adam threw Darlo off, completely certain that if there was one person not worth the trouble, it was Darlo, so fuck him, just *fuck him*, when he banged his arm into Crow Head. They had blundered their way right into the finish line, and they had tied.

Darlo's shoulder slammed into Crow Head, which was riddled

with guano. The steel drum god-echoes rose all around, wings turning white.

"I don't want to die," the drummer said. Blood ran down his tanned, sinewy shoulder. Adam smarted at how much Darlo looked like an illustration from a book of Greek myths. "What are we going to do?"

"Just shut up and hold on."

"But what are we going to do?"

Amazing things happened when you were out of your watery depth and totally fucked. Amazing things showed up from the deeps of one's personality.

"I can't swim, Adam. I mean, I really can't swim!"

"You swam here!"

"No, no, I didn't!"

Adam grabbed Darlo's nonbleeding shoulder, feeling the rock nick and cut at his legs. "Calm down."

"I don't want to die!"

Adam looked up at the craggy rock god. A mouth could be made out, full of jagged teeth. The sun hid behind the prehistoric silhouette.

Darlo was going on and on about how little he wanted to die, which was music to Adam's wet ears. If Adam hadn't been in mortal peril, he would have felt bad about thinking this way. What freedom there was in mortal peril!

He grabbed Darlo's flailing arm. "It's only fifty yards, Darlo."

"No way. And fuck you for getting me out here!"

"Getting *you* out here?"

White piles of bird shit lay there, ruining everything for him.

"I never got you out here," he said. "How can you blame this on me?"

And that was when the dirty French Jet-Skidiots showed up.

"French french fra-french, french ha ha ha!" They laughed. "French french!"

They wore green fluorescent bathing suits, and each had a shark's tooth on wire hanging from his neck.

"French french french ha ha ha!"

They circled around, making a wake. Their voices battled for airspace with the steel drums.

"You guys are in need of some assistahnce?" one of them said. "You 'mericans lost yer way?"

"Help us!" Darlo yelled, as if they were a plume of smoke on a dark and stormy horizon. "Help us!"

"Ahh!" one said. "French french bleeding!"

Riding back on a Jet-Ski, his arms around a Frenchie's skinny waist, Adam felt his relief soon turn to disgust. There was no evidence that anyone had saved anyone, and that galled him. He could never prove it. Darlo would probably say that *he* had saved Adam. Another good deed about to go punished.

Not to mention that the tide was coming in. He watched the crystal-clear water run over the sandbar in lengthening rivulets. His notebook slid in, tipping upward like the nose of a ship as it sinks to the bottom of the ocean.

Adam thought, I should have let him die.

But when they got back to shore, Darlo said nothing. He disappeared into town, and surfaced the next morning when he stumbled into the studio, smelling like he'd fucked half the island. Which he probably had. But he never said a thing.

Except one time, in the middle of the last American tour, when Darlo woke from a dream on I-5 near Grants Pass, woke up yelling so loudly that Bobby practically took the van into the guardrail.

"I don't want to die!"

They looked at the drummer as if he'd just appeared from another world, covered in cross-dimensional jelly, stinking of the astral plane. He rubbed his eyes, made an expression of awe, and reached over to hit Adam on the shoulder.

"Hey," he whispered. "Come here."

Adam put down his copy of *The Onion* and moved close. "What?"

"I remember," Darlo said, breath stinking of cigarettes. "I *remember.*"

Adam nodded, just barely.

"I was dreaming about it," Darlo said. "But you weren't there and I was fucked. The Crow Head laughed at me. I was a goner."

"But you're OK."

Darlo nodded. "You saved my ass."

"I did."

"Thanks, man," he said, and rolled over.

Now, in Vondelpark, Pizza Face was under Darlo and the drummer's fists were covered in blood and he held that knife up in the air. Red jumped into Adam's vision like in a two-color photograph, like a Barbara Kruger photo he had seen in a friend's dorm room.

The skinhead gurgled under Darlo. The other one writhed on the ground, pulling at his face, trying to tear off the pepper spray, trying to get up, falling down, getting up, like an old blind man without his cane. Joey ran over and sprayed him again.

"Die, motherfucker!"

Darlo held the Magic Wand above his head for a moment. He seemed to be stretching, as if to imitate a guillotine.

Defying all gimpy-legged reality, Joey kicked the knife out of Darlo's hand, yelling for him to run, pulling at him as he collapsed. The autumn breeze smelled like roasted chestnuts, and all the screaming was hail banging and bouncing upon a smooth roof.

Pizza Face rolled on the ground, and his friend bowed down, sort of crawled over, and wailed like a mother over the corpse of her son. Adam could not see the details, could not see Darlo's anger mapped out and laid bare in all its momentum and leverage. The skinheads looked as if they had absorbed the force of an explosion.

Adam ran forward, grabbing his bag, ducking in the line of fire. He jumped on his bicycle, and for a second wondered if he should turn around and ride his rickety Dutch three-speed into the melee. But shock and disgust smothered the notion. What did he owe them? When had they ever cut him a break? Just for that moment, he wanted them to die. He wanted Joey and Darlo to vanish from the earth and had no interest in helping out, being loyal, lowering their chances for an early burial. As his brothers loved to say, *Mea culpa, Caesar.* Under the hail of shrieking, he rode away.

21

OUTSIDE DR. GUTTFRIEND'S OFFICE, Bobby decided that maybe Amsterdam wasn't so bad after all. His hands would heal—someday—and until then he would be all right. Life wasn't a complete bust, really; here was this girl, this sweet girl with hennaed hair, classy-tarty outfit, dusty blue eyes, and a full smile. She smoked Players and giggled at his every joke and acted as least as affectionate as the other girls with whom he had shared meaningful physical relationships.

Maybe the four of them would all be friends in a few years. They could come visit him here. They could come visit and see him and Sarah living in some four-hundred-year-old building full of modern Dutch architecture. He'd be, uh, working in a café, a bar, sure, bartending is a thing you can do anywhere, and his hands would be eczema-free. They'd have a bunch of fun Dutch friends with names like Bergitt and Hans, Saskia and Maarten, and each day would be a Euro blessing, kind and nonconfrontational.

He would play his bass in times of doubt. He would play his bass, normally hidden in the closet, when he began to forget how awful it had been. His fingers on the frets would bring Blood Orphans back to him, and he would shudder, put away childish things, and skip, dance, and hop toward a European thirty.

His phone rang, breaking off the daydream. Shane.

"Captain Vision Quest!" he yelled.

"Just wanted to thank you for leaving me to die."

"Well, you and I both know that if you see the Buddha coming down the road, you're supposed to kill him. But really, I'm just beside myself with shame."

"I can tell. You are such a piece —"

"Hey, wait. Did you hear that?"

"What?"

"The sound of your bullshit hitting the karmic fan."

Sarah gave him a freshly lit cigarette, which promptly fell out of his hands. She looked at him with angelic sympathy and rubbed his face. The touch filled him with a dose of sunny wrath.

Shane groaned. "Fucking screwed me over is what you did. Just like you always do."

"What the fuck are you talking about?"

Shane mumbled.

"Don't mumble, bitch. How have I always let you down? Take your time. I'll be here, wiggling my fake front tooth." He paused. "I'm waiting, Darlo."

"Don't call me Darlo." Shane snickered. Bicycles flew by, bearing young beauties in scarves of fine merino. "You'd love to be Darlo. It's pathetic."

"In remedial English that's called a non sequitur."

"Always the smartass," Shane said. "Always so smart."

"Compared to what, your stupid, faux-theological Orange County ass?"

Click.

Bobby inhaled. He smelled a field of blooming flowers.

"Who was that?" Sarah asked.

"The singer. Shane. The Jesus Buddhist dreadlocked bullshit artist."

"I like Buddhism."

"Me too. But Shane wouldn't know Buddhism if it walked right up and split his duality in two."

She giggled, and some of her rosy perfume boarded his nose.

He pointed at one of his front teeth. "See this tooth? The fucker knocked it out."

"Why?"

"No reason," he said, because telling the pretty girl who just may be your salvation that you destroyed someone's childhood Bible was a bad strategy. "Maybe he got his dharma screwed up with his karma. Maybe because there were green M&Ms in the candy bowl. Maybe because he sold out his Christian faith to play in a sex-drugs-and-rock-and-roll band."

"You're cute when you're mad," she said.

"Good," he replied, "because I'm mad a lot."

She threw her shoulder into him, all playful.

"I want to take you somewhere," she said. "Do you like Van Gogh?"

Sarah was beginning to remind him of Phoebe, whom he'd dated at UCLA. She too dyed her hair with henna and had pixie features that clashed with big lips. Their relationship ended when she made it clear that she didn't want to be with a rock musician. She didn't want a guy who didn't care about health insurance, who smoked a pack a day, who still thought Bruce Lee was a giant among men.

But then, not long after the band signed to Warners, she showed up at Spaceland for a sold-out show. Darlo snuck her in. He claimed he didn't know she was Bobby's ex until after they'd slept together.

"Just proves that women cannot be trusted," the drummer said.

"I'll kill you!" Bobby said, and took a swing at him.

That was two exes of his that Darlo had fucked. Unbelievable.

"If you wanted me to apologize, you can forget it now!" Darlo said after they'd been separated. "She's the one you should punch."

Actually, he thought, maybe Sarah didn't look like Phoebe. Maybe he just needed a reason to do his thrice-daily self-torturing, in which Darlo vanquished him time and time again, in which the drummer stumbled his tall, dark, sex-addicted way into the pants of girls Bobby loved.

His hands throbbed, as if to say, We'd like our afternoon changing now.

Trying to reconcile this problem with Darlo, Bobby thought, was like being Bilbo Baggins in *The Hobbit*, in which Bilbo has to find a few measly arrows with which he has to pierce the hide of Smaug, the great dragon of Middle-earth. Smaug had one missing scale in his vast skin-armor, one stupid scale where Bilbo's missile could find fatal purchase. The task was too large for him, but elves were depending upon him to make it so. The elves of his fearful, tour-sapped mind were counting upon him to slay the beast.

Somewhere back there, hiding behind the trees in tunics and slipper boots, Shane and Adam were waiting for him to make it right.

Darlo didn't think about the band as a brotherhood. Shane didn't think about anything but himself. Adam had his painting and his precious sensibility, being the fruity friend of all creatures large and small. Joey was racing her way from bindle to bindle, talking to herself about world dominance.

So he was alone in his groupiedom. He was the guy who still saw glitter on their name underneath all that resin. He was the chump happily lashed to the mast of the ghost ship.

For the others the band was a means, but to him it was an end. From the first fantastic practice in Darlo's porn-set basement to tonight, when they would take the stage like prehistoric amphibians coming up from the slime, this clichéd, stuttering, rinky-dink epic was all he had ever wanted.

Damn it.

Now they were headed down Paulus Potterstraat. He let his phone ring and ring. Fuck Shane for even trying to get him out of this fantastic stroke of female luck.

They approached the Van Gogh Museum.

"He's *my* rock and roll, man," Sarah said. "He's my Mick Jagger."

"Van Gogh? Old one-ear, live-like-a-suicide Van Gogh?"

She hit his shoulder. "No joking!"

An ambulance drove by.

"Sorry," he said, cracking his knuckles, popping open a bandage so it hung on his thumb like a flag at half-mast. "I can't wait."

"He's a god to me," she said, waving a finger in his face. "Be nice!"

Once Blood Orphans had met their gods. Once they had met Aerosmith backstage at the LA Forum. Well, they were supposed to, but then Aerosmith's personal attaché showed up in their stead, showed up in some waiting area underneath the arena, near the locker rooms, and said that Steven and Joe and even Tom Hamilton had a personal emergency, and that they wouldn't be able to make it.

"They are *so* fucking excited to go on tour with you," the attaché said, and made a fist of rock-and-roll solidarity. "They wanted me to say that they love the record. They love how hungry you sound. So much hunger."

"But where are they?" Darlo said. "How come they couldn't make it?"

"Totally love the record," said the attaché, who wore a black suit, a black shirt, and a black tie. "Totally psyched for you guys to get on the bus."

"But where," Darlo said, "are they?"

"Awesome record," the attaché said, turning on his heel. "Awesome, and they can't wait to meet you."

Darlo had brought a T-shirt from the *Pump* tour—his first show—for signage. He chucked the old black rag at the skinny Aero-lackey, who disappeared down the tunnel.

"But *where* are they?" Darlo yelled, and his voice echoed off the steel walls.

A month later, after they had been dropped from the tour, Darlo took matters into his own hands.

"My dad used to be tight with Tyler," he said. "Before Tyler went AA."

They were driving to Tyler's mansion, Bobby, Joey, and Darlo. The address and phone number of said mansion were in David Cox's Rolodex.

"Tyler had the tastes," Darlo said. "He loved the cocaine and the anus." He shifted hard into fifth. "Male anus."

"The cocaine, maybe," Joey said. "But dude's not *gay*. Damn he was hot before all the Botox."

"There are things I can't tell you, babe," Darlo warned. "You wouldn't believe the stories Dad told me."

"Yeah, *stories*," Bobby said. "Fiction. You probably don't even have the right address."

Chez Tyler was one of those Topanga Canyon jobs where the gate stood a mile away from the house, overgrown with flora to keep the freaks out, to daunt their personal star maps.

They rang the buzzer. Darlo made claims to someone in Tyler's employ. "We're old friends," he said. "Darlo Cox. Son of David Cox."

A few minutes later a patrol car arrived, featuring a cop who resembled Wilford Brimley if he had actually gone and eaten his oats.

"Get out of here," the cop said.

"I'm a family friend," Darlo said. "Steve knows me."

Tyler must have had the cop on a sweet retainer. He went at Darlo like an old Green Beret, a real hand-to-hand-combat pro. Bobby thought he was going to remove his badge and break both the drummer's arms.

"I said get the fuck out of here, punk, before I twist you into a pretzel and shove you into the back of that car." He waved at the others like they were flies. "And take your faggot friends with you."

Now Bobby shrugged.

"There was talk of meeting with Rod Stewart as well," he told Sarah. "Stewart didn't care about the racism thing, or the fact that we sucked. Stewart's been making a career out of bad taste since he went disco."

"He's very gross," Sarah replied. "He's letchy. You shouldn't mind that it didn't work out."

"I do mind, though," he said. He had spent half of the eighth grade singing "Maggie May," and one cute girl's disdain wasn't going to shake that strange love. "This was my big chance to meet rock stars, and now it's done. Sounds ridiculous, right?"

She nodded. "Very ridiculous."

They waited in line at the museum. Bobby had never liked Van Gogh. Sure, *Starry Night* was good, but people who disfigured themselves, no matter how brilliant, were six shades of stupid. He opened his mouth to share his opinion with Sarah, then realized that he'd formulated that opinion at twelve, while singing "Whole Lotta Love," gorging on Doritos, and listening to Rush around the clock.

Soon he was going to need to change his Band-Aids.

"I come here at least once a month," she said. "It's a church for me."

"That's awesome," he said, because he had lost his train of thought. Across the street, Darlo and Joey ran down the sidewalk.

"Totally awe...some," he said. "What the fuck?"

It was them all right. Joey hobbled crazily, making some pretty amazing time, kind of pulling Darlo forward. And was that blood on their hands?

"What's wrong?" Sarah asked. "Bobby?"

Amazing how the simplest image can grow monumental, sum up everything. Amazing how you can just float in oily understanding.

His drummer and his manager, running down a leaf-blown, five-hundred-year-old street, their hands covered in blood. And he, bearing witness.

What were the chances?

"Bobby?" she said again.

A chill ran through him. A chill and a splash of melancholy, curdling on contact, like milk when it falls into a cup of tea with lemon.

You look familiar. Are you in a band?

He'd had a feeling like this the day they signed to Warners. No blood was involved—in retrospect it was a pound of flesh—but he'd had that sense of complete emotional summation. The drummer and the manager sprinted from an invisible terror, and he wanted to sprint with them; whatever lay ahead, he wanted to be part of it. Their terrors were his terrors. He felt left out of a big secret; the solution lay in falling in line. But the gravity of the female fantasia kept him still.

"Hey." She shook his jacket. "Are you OK?"

"Yeah, sorry." They locked eyes. "I don't...Forget it."

"You sure?"

If he was going to miss out on being where the real action was, then he sure as shit was going to throw caution. He kissed her, and she leaned in, whispering his name in her cute little accent. *Buuby. Buuby.*

So far, so good. But then under the museum's pleasant lights, Bobby went numb. Under normal circumstances, numb would have been nice, giving his hands a break, cutting out the itchiness, the discomfort, the damp grossitude of flesh taking its time to spume and rot. But this wasn't nice. He had just witnessed his drummer and his manager running down the street in dreamtime. Their hands were bloodied, which in said dreamtime was incontrovertible proof of a higher symbolism. Not that Bobby understood the image; but nonetheless he was possessed by it, and suddenly unsure of the, you know, dude, the *reality* of things. When does the myopic vacuum of living the touring life change one's perspective into unreliability? When do you cease to trust what you see?

"Isn't this lovely?" Sarah asked. They stood in front of a painting called *The Potato Eaters*. Bobby did not think it was lovely. At that moment, a new job as Pete Townshend's valet would not have been lovely.

"Yeah," he said, and couldn't feel his neck connecting head to torso. "Sure."

"What I love about it," she said, leaning against him, "is the way that the people seem to be decaying right in front of us. The toll of their unhappy lives is right there on their faces."

"Totally," he said.

"And the colors too," she continued, pointing. "The tones are so ... how do you say it in English? *Mournful.* It looks like a family planning a funeral."

He really had no idea what she was talking about. It was just some bunch of peasants looking bored. He could smell the mildew, though.

"Yeah," he said. "I have to go to the bathroom."

She hit him and smiled. "That's what all guys say when they're bored with a girl in a museum."

But he was already moving. He walked into the bathroom for show and then snuck outside. He had to have another look at the scene, had to understand why he felt as if part of him had disappeared. And so he stood, staring into the street, a series of questions coming at him. Where the fuck were those two running, covered in blood? How come he never got to play the dramatic moments? How come he got the shitty role? How come his only talent was to be the guy who was abrasive enough for the assholes, and smart enough for the artists?

Because I can't play the bass very well and I'm not talented. Because I was just the guy who was around that owned the right equipment. Because I'm the one who bought the dream wholesale and I didn't even deserve to dream it.

He knew these realities to be hard and true, but still, the desire to ditch was there. But then if he ditched there would be no new Euro life with the Euro cherry blossom. And so, while his mind was already bolting after them, his feet stayed put.

Those two, running right by him while love kept him stuck in place.

What were the fucking chances?

He couldn't stand being left out like this. As feeling returned to his hands, he dialed Joey's number.

22

SHANE HAD DISCOVERED *SIDDHARTHA* on the candle-wax-covered table of a girl he had fucked in Austin. Her name was Lana. She was an English major at the university and had nipples the size of small pancakes. Blood Orphans was on its third tour of America, the one that gave them bragging rights that they'd humiliated themselves in the entire lower forty-eight. Even North Dakota. Even Vermont. Even fucking Wyoming. Warner Bros. was using them to game out every bad tour-routing idea. They were free R&D for the label.

So, Austin. Princess Goth Big Nipples grabbed the book, sitting up in bed. Candles guttered all over her apartment. Black light was giving off faint rays. The smell of sex, sandalwood, and cloves. Amateur dread-mats of hair slathered in aloe vera gel fell over her face. The bed sagged.

"Oh, man, this's a beautiful book," she said, her big tits firm, apples on the tree of carnal knowledge. "Changed my life."

He swept back his hair, which had been dyed black a week before by some hairdresser he'd slept with in Kansas City. "What's it about?"

"The awakening of a spiritual being that changed the world." She did some stupid little hand-dance. "You should read it."

"But what's it about?"

"Are you religious?"

"Not like I used to be."

She made moony eyes. "What happened?"

"Just tell me what it's about."

She climbed on him, ending the conversation. Later she gave him the book, which he read in the break before the first trip to Europe, while killing time at his aunt's house in North Carolina. His aunt, a librarian and Southern Baptist, could not believe what had become of him.

"You have copped quite a bit of an attitude," she said. "Is that what being in the spotlight teaches you?"

"We're not in the spotlight," he said. "That's the problem. May I please take my dinner to the TV room?"

"No. You'll say grace and eat with us. Your mother would faint if she saw you like this, Shane."

The book blew his mind. Such a simple story, told with such quiet force! Siddhartha, a seeker like him. A kindred spirit trying to find his way through the morass of worldly desires. Touring had leached the seeker out of him, or so he had thought. But it was still alive. His desire for a higher truth had sprung from the cover of this blessed tome; he'd outgrown the angry father bit, the one God hanging over all of us. It made the beauty of Jesus seem like a good-cop sham, running interference for an ugly majordomo in the sky. But Buddhism, this was more to his liking. He was desperate for a fresh way to organize his life, something to counteract the filthy, rotting reality of Blood Orphans. He needed a new engine of hope, something to propel his singing back into a place of caring, eyes on the prize, out of the filth and lust.

Siddhartha. Buddha.

He told everyone about his magical discovery, his new path. All the time. From the stage. No one cared.

A few weeks later, Shane tacked "Tantric" onto the front of "Buddhist" after sleeping with a skinny American girl studying abroad in Edinburgh. She introduced him to this age-old sex strategy at her flat in Old Town. She chose him over Darlo, quite publicly.

"You're a pig," she told the drummer, and grabbed Shane's arm. "Let's go."

For that, Shane was ready to do anything she wanted, even if it meant holding off on coming for like a fucking hour.

"Hold still," she said, and slid slowly up and down his cock. "Breathe with me. It has to be synchronized. A hundred times, a hundred breaths."

Her muscle control made Michael Jordan look like a stroke victim.

"I don't think I can—"

"Hold it, Shane. Slow, slow. Your lingam and my yoni. Tighten, then loosen. Tighten. Then loosen."

Belle and Sebastian sussed from the stereo. Judy with her dream of horses.

"Breathe with me. Put your hand to my chest."

She started to go.

"Your ha. Nd. On my. Ch. Es. T."

When he came, he kicked back like an old shotgun, cried out like he'd witnessed the Revelation. "Hoh-whoa-whoa!"

There was fear, too. He wasn't sure if his heart was going to be able to take such an intense, all-body rush.

"Yo-haha-yo-God-whoa-God!"

On top of him, an almost perfect stranger grabbed hold, her body shaking in waves, and took out whatever chest hair he had. Years of tension rushed out of his crotch.

He cobbled together two autonomous philosophies into a theological Frankenstein, one that would never walk. Darlo indicated his approval.

"If it's sex, that's cool. I tried Tantra. Fuckin' A."

Shane wondered what had happened to that girl. Maybe somewhere in the back of his sour suitcase, a little sheet of paper held her number, blurred with sweat, Gatorade, and beer. So many numbers, castaways, in every pocket.

He called Adam and got Joey's hotel info. Adam sounded the way he always did, as if the misery through which the rest of them swam never touched him. Shane envied the way Adam could keep his head stuck in his art, as if the band were merely a cloudy day in an otherwise beautiful summer. He had that thing, what was it called, he learned it from a French girl he'd had in Lyon...

"Joie de vivre," he grumbled, and stomped down the street.

A shower, a shave, a few hours on a hotel bed watching a television in a white hotel robe, and then everything would coalesce back into recognizable shapes. His ears ached, and he felt something squish in his boots. Peanut butter? Dog shit? He couldn't bring himself to look. But he did pull out Danika's panties from his pocket, take one last delicious whiff, and chuck them in the trash.

When he saw the Krasnapolsky, looming in Dutch glitter, a fresh wave of Joey-hatred crested over him. "Freeloader," he said, walking through the palatial lobby, where people laughed and rejoiced, simple like new snow.

He planted his ass at an e-mail kiosk and drummed up Yahoo. The Proust Personality Test from Rachel—with a different, longer cover letter from the one the others had received because Rachel thought Shane was *so* cute—awaited him. The first fucking interview in months. Shane couldn't help but be excited.

"Thanks to Buddha," he said, and opened the file.

Boy, was Rachel a friendly-sounding girl. A girl this friendly, Shane thought, must be fat. Without pussy power, you had to rely on the lesser weapon of personality.

"...and I think," she wrote, "that people miss the joke, in the best sense of the word! People think of Blood Orphans as a parody, but my friends and I, we see the sincerity in what you do..."

The guy next to him curled his nose at Shane's stink, but Shane would not take the worldly bait. He was firmly back in Buddha-state and could resist the disgust.

"Seriously, *Rocket Heart* is mos def the mos underrated record of 2004 and 2003 and 200—you get the picture. I mean, I'm not gonna say that my friends and I weren't, ahem, challenged by the lyrics—I still don't really get 'Hella-Prosthetica,' sorry!—but soon the utter rock-and-roll awesomeness had me hooked, lined, and sinkered. So, on to Proust!"

His eyes were heavy suddenly, and his hands felt like lead. Why did this praise unsettle him? He inhaled deeply, which attuned his nose to the radical, utterly godless nature of his body odor, and addressed the questions at hand.

What, for you, is the idea of total happiness?

He remembered when Warners had put them up in the Four Seasons in Seattle to make their video. That was happiness, all right. Shane had never been in a hotel that didn't have a Bible in every room. Warners had been all too happy to put them in swank hotels back then. Now he stared at the lobby chandelier and imagined Joey hanging in the glittering filaments of light.

His attention was diverted by the sight of a band checking in. They hauled in suitcases and guitars, joshing around, wreathed in denim, scarves, and cowboy boots, framed by groupies. They had that alt-country-boogie thing going on, the love child of Johnny Cash and Rod Stewart, post-irony Black Crowes. They wore their dirt and filth in an elegant, offhand way. Posers, Shane thought. I bet they smell like rose musk. I bet they smell the same as every promise-ring-wearing, Awesome God–worshipping coed at Pepperdine. That's how authentic they are.

One of the groupies, wearing a cowboy hat and a buckskin jacket, slapped her own ass to demonstrate a point. "And then he went like *that!*" she said, and they all laughed.

These fuckers were at the beginning of the journey and he was some carcass on the side of the road, miles from the finish line. The knowledge circled him in a predatory way.

He went back to the e-mail and answered the question: "Total happiness, for me, would be a greater understanding of the spiritual forces that guide life. Such happiness would provide me with more love for my band and a compass to guide me, and hopefully us, in figuring out..."

Jealousy distracted him. Who was this band? He wanted to bust in, get some of that new shine.

He walked over and grabbed the guy who appeared to be the drummer by the shoulders. When trying to insinuate yourself into a band, always hit up the drummer first. With the glaring exception of Darlo, the drummer was always more than happy to have a stranger talk to him. Chances were he'd spent the last month being ignored.

"Hey, what's up, man?" Shane said. "What's going on?"

From under that floppy cowboy hat, the dude's eyes lit up. Bingo. "Oh, uh, hey!"

"Where're you playing tonight?"

"Oh, uh, the Paradiso."

A dagger in his heart. The Paradiso. That big beautiful hall.

"Oh, that's awesome!" Shane said. "That's the fucking place to play!"

"Yeah?" the drummer said, a little unsure. Drummers could be so cute. "Really?"

"Oh, yeah, totally."

The drummer's nose wrinkled. He smelled what Shane's body was cooking, but Shane didn't care.

"You guys going to party before the show?"

"Yeah."

"Excellent," Shane said. "What room are you in?"

"Uh…"

"Probably got the suite, huh? Probably gave you the best room in the house, overlooking Dam Square."

"Um, yeah."

"I know, man. We stayed there the first time. It was sweet, no pun intended."

Shane watched as none of the bandmates took notice of him. Someone talking to the drummer? Who cares.

"You stayed here?" the drummer asked. "Are you in a band?"

"Yeah, what room are you guys in?"

So many calculations running behind those naive drummer eyes. To invite the letch or not invite the letch, who maybe wasn't a letch after all, who maybe was in, like, a famous band, and wouldn't the rest of the band think it was cool that he befriended a famous guy? Wouldn't it be great, the drummer was thinking, if they paid attention to him for once?

"Sorry," Shane said. "I didn't get the room. What room?"

Wouldn't it be great if they actually acknowledged his fucking existence?

"What room, man?"

Wouldn't it?

"Three-two-two." He glanced at the key. "The Rodin Suite."

"Sweet, I'll bring all the boys!"

And then he scurried away, fast, because he knew from the plaintive grunt that the drummer knew he had made a mistake, was thinking, What am I doing, that guy smelled like old peanut butter and doggy doo. Jesus, they're gonna give me such shit for this. I just want them to like me.

"Hey!" he yelled to Shane's back. "What band are you in?"

I just want them to like me. The lament of drummers worldwide.

"Who was that?" someone asked, and Shane escaped into a stairwell.

23

WHAT SHOULD HE DO NOW? Stop a policeman, stop some strolling tourists, stop anyone and tell them what had happened, get help, be a good person, do the right thing?

No. Ride, Adam, ride.

Two years and change he had been in cahoots with Darlo Cox. For over two years he had been under the control of the caveman, but always he had found some dishonest elegance to paint on the drummer, even just the thinnest membrane of vibrant color to humanize him, put the *noble* back in *noble savage*. Now he knew what was real. He wished he had not seen that horror, that misery, wished he had not been the instigator for the truth laid bare. He cursed himself for entering into this den of idiot thieves, for willingly sharing the gold forged in the mint of complete denial. He cursed himself for ever having met Darlo Cox, Joey Fredericks, Bobby Campbell, and Shane Warner.

Two cars swerved around him as he went through a red light.

"Shit!" he yelled, his front wheel going every which way. He lost control and headed into a group of pedestrians, but then at the last moment they parted, revealing a side street, and sheer luck rolled him through, good fortune threading the needle. At the other side of the traffic was an alleyway, and he turned in to it before he half smashed into a perfectly restored fifteenth-century brick wall and skidded to a stop.

Dutchies crowded around on this pretty alley, built when men wore chain-mail slippers and women wore bone corsets. All the Dutch people who'd almost run him over all day, who'd kept their noses high as he moved through them, focused upon the boy with the Fu Manchu. For the first time their eyes acknowledged Adam's existence. A face smeared with blood will do that.

"Oh my Gott!" said a middle-aged businessman. "Gott!"

They hovered around him. He tasted iron in his mouth. He'd thought it was sweat.

"What happened?" they asked.

Feelings bubbled up. He started to shake.

"Tell us," they said, touching him. "Tell us what happened."

Adam imagined his bandmates burrowing into Amsterdam, hiding from the imminent, impending end. He thought of Shane on the phone, hair matted, head down like a junkie's; of Bobby, with chopped-up hands and constant doubt; of Darlo, unsatisfiable Darlo, burning from the inside out; of Joey, the fifth Beatle, trying to make it all right, find some restitution for all the mistakes she had made. And finally he saw himself, a murky reflection in the dank, ageless water of his mind's eye.

He turned around. He swore he heard the Sharpie Shakes jingle. He spun a few times. Sound from a window. Fun in the sun, you betcha.

"What happened?" the people said.

All this time he had held out for the idea that he had made it out of Blood Orphans unchanged, intact, that the rest of them were lost but he was only the wiser for it, that he had carried in his heart a paint of pure calm, one that could be moved over any nasty scene and would coat it with a redemptive sheen.

But he hadn't avoided it. Blood on his face was proof. His inability to speak his mind was proof. His excessive daily rituals of silence, silence as the only defense against the hourly rush of insult, was proof. His cowardice in the park, the way he had left those who had saved his life to fend for themselves, was full-on proof.

"Are you all right?" they repeated.

He pictured the four of them, in their modes of suffering.

"No," he said. "Do I fucking look all right?"

24

WHAT WAS IMPORTANT WAS to get them cleaned up, get the blood off, avoid explanation. Joey carried way too much cocaine in her bag to want anyone to stop and inquire. So when she and Darlo blasted through the door of Patrick O'Byrne's, a pub in the Irish style, she knew she just had to keep moving, not make eye contact, make it so the patrons could just mind their own faux-Celtic business. And so she and Darlo went through the doors in a fury and panic, and she didn't stop for directions.

She held on to Darlo so he wouldn't deviate from the course as they pitched into the men's room, barreled into a stall smelling of antiseptic and lemons, banging their heads as two businessmen scurried out of there, drying their hands off with much deliberate speed and giving a wide berth to the girl in the suit and her friend in the leather jacket with blood strafed across his cheeks.

Joey knew that Darlo had been cut away from something, had experienced some sort of psychic cleaving, was down in the ancestral darkness, navigating issues that went to the core of him, issues that language could not assuage, and she felt that she had started it by making fun of his love declarations. She had lit the wick on some serious familial dynamite.

In the stall, he gazed upon her, daft and spaced out. That gaze melted her. Above his head, on the toilet paper dispenser, someone had scrawled, *Amsterdam = overrated.*

Yes, that gaze and its mixed meanings. But the analysis would have to wait for the hotel room. First she had to bring the crying son of the porn king back from the deep space of airless grief.

"Darlo!" she yelled, and slapped him across the face.

Darlo came back, sniffling. His leather pants made crunchy noises. She took his face in her hands. She felt the squareness of his jaw. What a jaw.

"We clean up and get out of here, yeah?"

The prince nodded. Wavelets of black hair fell over his face. He sniffled and wiped his nose on his jacket. Snot streaked his face, and Joey wiped it off.

"Do you understand what I'm saying?"

He nodded. To make sure, Joey slapped him again, which turned her on.

"We cannot have any problems. We are in serious jeopardy. OK?" Was it rain on his face, or tears? Had it been raining? She slapped him once more; this was fun. "OK?"

He nodded and grabbed her arm. "Just quit hitting me."

They washed off over ornate fixtures as Joey contemplated her next steps. Now, on top of breaking his spirit completely with the label droppage, she was going to have to navigate his affection for her, the subject broached without ironic qualifiers and out in the open. Not pleasant; she'd never been in a situation, so long in coming to painful fruition, that she couldn't act upon. One kiss and her power over him, her Pure Spell of Physical Withholding, would be broken forever. She couldn't risk it.

Darlo looked over. They locked eyes. He nodded and held up his hands, water running down his sleeves.

"Blood's gone," he said.

A man came in and drew back when he saw the beat-up tourists. "Are you all right?"

"Yes, thanks," Joey said, and rejected the idea of yelling about skinheads attacking them and Amsterdam's unreal hypocrisies. Pulling Darlo along, she pushed past the man, threw open the pub doors, and continued on to the hotel.

Darlo started babbling about his dad. That was fine. Better for him to babble about his dad than his feelings for her. She cursed herself; here was her best friend and theoretical lover finally opening up, finally vulnerable. But with Darlo preoccupied with the tax-evading slimeball, she could gather her head, put away the trauma of the past hour, and go back to thinking about dinner, trying to make a mad dash into some hidden corner of her consciousness where shitty reality could not track her. Now dread overcame her. The altercation with the skinheads took on an inexplicable glow in comparison. She had never grown so nostalgic so fast. She had never seen just what a crock of shit nostalgia really was, when you could sugarcoat something horrible in less than an hour's time.

When she got back to her empty West Hollywood office, she'd send Arthur St. What-the-Fuck at *Spin* an e-mail and tell him about the big payback. They beat up some skinheads. They vanquished the racist element. How about running another review? Could you turn back time? Could you find some way?

The lights were up on the Leidesplein. They took the scenic route. Amsterdam would be a great place to come back to one day, she thought, when I am in love with someone who is not in my band, and maybe even someone who is not in the music business. Pretty lights. So pretty. What if *pretty* could be the word that ran her life, instead of *poser?*

But for now, back to seating arrangements. Who, when they got the bad news, would be least likely to physically attack her? Adam and Bobby; she ought to put them next to her. Let them get knifed. Let them get whiskey thrown in their faces. She would have Poncy-Pants and the Mummy as her front line to absorb the first wave of heat off Darlo and Shane's breath. She thought of the scene in that movie about the Who, in which Keith Moon talked about weathering the rotten vegetables that people threw at him during shows. The cymbals were key to avoiding a mess on his face.

"I just turn them up," Moon said, wearing a frilly white shirt and a black beard, "and at the end of the night I have a delicious salad. It's quite nice, really."

Adam and Bobby would be the cymbals, deflecting the rancid praise. She could hide behind them. She didn't owe them shit. Maybe she would end up with a salad.

"Completely," she said, agreeing to the logic of an unknown assertion that Darlo, in his babbletude, was making. "Absolutely."

"Just so fucking stupid is all!" Darlo crescendoed, and grabbed the manager. "So stupid of the old sick fuck, right?"

"Totally. Seriously."

"Are you listening?"

"To you?" She grabbed the leather sleeves and dust rose off them. "All ears, babe."

With night coming on, the air grew cold and damp, but that didn't deter the scarved-out Dutchies from their high-nosed happiness. They moved in a lilt, swinging kid-leather briefcases, riding old three-speeds like they were ready for the Tour de France.

Darlo shrugged at a phone booth. "Can I use that eight-pound phone again?"

She reached into her bag. "Here," she said. "Use a credit card. It's cheaper."

"Thanks, babe," he said, and ran off.

With Darlo out of earshot, Joey took out the phone and dialed Adam. She felt preemptive guilt, as in, We should have gone after him. We should have protected him. I'm a bad person and a bad manager. I'm a terrible fucking person. I'm a—

"Joey?" Adam said. "Are you all right?"

"I'm fine. Are you? Are you in shock? You sound too calm."

"I've said like four words."

She lit a smoke and realized that she was sober. "Four words?"

"What's wrong, Joey?"

"You're all right?"

"Yeah. Some people took me into a restaurant and got me washed up."

"Roger that, we sort of found a restaurant too, it was OK, are you OK?"

"*Yes.*"

Joey watched Darlo in the green KPN booth, pointing his finger at someone thousands of miles away, spinning around. "Was just so terrible, what happened."

"Yeah. I feel good, actually. I shouldn't, but I feel exhilarated."

I don't, she thought. They're going to kill me when I tell them that Warners said fuck off and die. They'll never forgive *or* forget.

John Hackney's handsome face reared up. "What could we do?" he said, in that dream-echo used for cheesy television murder mysteries, when the detective recalls a key moment. "There's nothing we could do. Noth-ing. Nu-huh-huh-thing-ing-ing."

That echo had some monumental acoustics. Ripples in the screen. It would be better to quit this phone conversation before she blurted out the truth.

"Just wanted to make sure you're all right," she said. "You're all exhilarated because you're in shock. Enjoy it, because after you come down, you might get more than a little freaked out."

"I know. I'm going to Morten's to take a nap."

"Roger that."

"Sounds like you need a nap too."

"I do," she said. "A dirt nap. Hey, had these people who helped you out heard of us?"

"No. But they're going to come to the show tonight."

"Paying customers," Joey said, as Darlo spun faster in the booth, gaining velocity, gaining torque. "How novel."

25

STANDING OUTSIDE THE IRISH BAR while Joey sniffed out their direction, Darlo realized what had happened. When he was on that skinhead, mashing his face into the earth, he'd come in his pants.

Yes, he had. Couldn't believe it. Pounding that guy, softening him up for the kill, and then a warm sensation in his crotch. Warm tears of rage on his face, warm sex tears down below.

But it felt as natural as wind off the back of his hand. It felt like something a person goes through now and then, perennial and unchanging. Getting on top of a person, beating him to the brink of death, and coming in your pants. What could be more natural?

A genetic code was a funky thing. That double helix had shady sides, a half that curved inward, away from light. You could see it in any diagram. That explained something.

The wetness on his face and in his crotch — now that was some kind of scary symmetry. And it had happened before. This one time after a show at Spaceland, he brought two girls home, got on top of one, and started strangling her. She had said that she liked getting strangled. It made her come harder. "Yeah, baby," she promised. "Makes me shudder like a fucking earthquake."

He strangled her, and she began to make hard guttering croaks. And then the warmth and wetness above and below. Both above and below, as the other girl threw herself on him because her friend was turning blue. She scratched at him, and the other girl coughed and screamed. He backed into a corner, lashing out at nothing, swinging at the air, grabbing at his own neck in shame.

After that, he went a whole week without sex. He lost five pounds. Every time he put food in his mouth, he retched.

He should have known this would happen again. But he wouldn't have imagined it would be on top of some dude, in a park, while saving your guitar player's ass. Violence on top of violence was a compound force that turned him on while gazing further into that shady side of the double helix, where the truth lay in fetid genetic ponds.

On top of that, he'd let himself go and told Joey what he thought of her, shared his feelings for once, unguarded, and she had called him faggy. She knew damn well how much it meant, and she had mocked him. Just beyond belief.

Darlo had, on the lit side of that wending series of nucleotides, a desire for the forward thrust, all engines go and don't look back. But now the engine unraveled; he felt the unspooling, a sensation through him of the mechanism going loose. Since the moment that first ATM card had failed, all the latent, beaten-down worries—the band, his dad, his mom, his entire *nature*—had stormed his steel-skinned castle of righteous good times. Now, when he looked back weeks, months, years, this unraveling became visible.

So much to try to figure out. How was this trouble with his dad going to shake out with Warners? They wouldn't love the fact that the drummer's father was a sex slaver tax evader—not a bad name for the next record—but he imagined all kinds of positive spin emerging out of the swirl. Blood Orphans were bad boys, so what difference did it make? That would only add to their mystique, would be a selling point for the next record. When the first Aerosmith record had come out, it wouldn't have mattered if

Steven Tyler's dad had been a porn-collar felon. Nothing stopped Tyler and nothing would stop Darlo.

No, dude, he thought. You're so off.

"This way," Joey said, and they bolted down the Leidesplein.

He and Joey walked at a fast clip toward the hotel. Streetlamps lit up the canals in a diffuse glow, but he longed for the winding sweat and heat of Sunset Boulevard, the cool salty breeze down on Venice Pier, the panoramic view from the Griffith Observatory. Just walking the LA streets, hour after hour, would help make things right.

So much to figure out, and no help from the manager. What was she hiding from him, behind her beautiful sloe eyes, besides her love? Worst-case scenario: Adam was leaving the band. Best-case scenario: Bobby was leaving the band. Now, at the end of the touring cycle, would be the ideal time to let him go. Who needed a Root-Note Ronnie with hands of mud to hold the music back? So why wouldn't Joey just tell him about it? Bobby leaving the band was *great* news.

Two skinheads, taller than the other ones, walked past them, and he floated in his shoes a little. They were probably friends with the kid he'd pulverized, with the kid upon whom he'd released more than just his rage. Self-disgust coated his thoughts.

Joey took his arm. "Are you cold?"

"No."

"Well, you're shaking like an old fucking engine."

He wanted to grab her, hold her, try a little tenderness. But no way would she reject him again. No way would she make him feel like a chump for emerging from the darkness of the double helix to throw light.

Another green phone booth beckoned, and he secured Joey's credit card, a nice break from the ridiculaphone. He dialed Jesse; the ship was not going to sink with all his coke, speed, and unlicensed guns aboard. He would *not* be greeted at Long Beach by an ATF agent holding a mug shot of his dad and a warrant for his arrest.

In a fiber-optic sleeze-itude, he shot over the North Pole, ripped through clouds above Ellesmere Island, pounded down pine forests outside Calgary, bounced off radio towers in Nevada, repelled static in Sacramento, and landed in Jesse's soft, small-time drug-dealing palm.

"Dude," the dealer said. "I'm in my Benz. Bad news and good news. Which do you—"

"What are you eating?"

"A burger from In-N-Out. Got the Double-Double and a chocolate shake. Breakfast of champions, bitch!"

"I'd kill for one of those. So what's the good news?"

"There's no cops at the house." He sucked down ice cream. "The windows in the back were open and I just hopped right in. Didn't the old man make bail?"

Dad was hiding, Darlo knew, down in the dungeon, and probably not alone.

"Bad news," Jesse said, "is that I didn't find a thing."

"Did you look where I told you to look?"

"No, I looked where you *didn't* tell me to look. What the fuck do you think?"

Darlo formed a vision of his room, saw the red walls, the G-Swing hanging in the corner, and the four-poster bed that Dad had assured him had belonged to Jayne Mansfield. He saw the scratches on the poles where hundreds of girls had run their nails, stretching their hands out, reaching, grabbing, coming.

"Darlo?"

"Hold on, I'm fucking thinking."

He saw the closet, hanging clothes, big-buckle belts of Harley-Davidson, Wall Drug, Queen, Aerosmith, the state of Texas, shirts of silk and satin. On the shelf above his clothes lay the velvet shotgun box, wherein lay the doobage, the powders, the apparatus, and the several illegal firearms.

"You got up there and really looked? It could have got pushed back. You're short—did you get a chair and look all the way in the back?"

"Nothing was there, bro."

"Are you sure?" Darlo asked. "Are you sure you're not lying to me?"

"Are you crazy? Why would I lie to you?"

"You're a fucking drug dealer, that's why."

"And you're a fucking drug *user*. So that makes us even."

He looked down at his hands. Joey was right. Shaking real hard.

"Don't fucking lie to me, Jesse. I'll fucking kill you."

Jesse laughed as if someone had slipped on a banana peel, light and surprised and joyous. "Dude," he said. "Come on, now. Jesus in fucking heaven, man."

Joey tapped on the booth, then tapped her watch. Darlo turned away.

"Maybe you put it somewhere else in the house," Jesse said. "What about the pool cabana? Isn't that where you keep it sometimes?"

Darlo cringed. Bad memories tracked him. On his last trip home, the pool cabana was where he had found his father fucking some coed from UCLA whom Darlo had brought home a few times. The man's face loomed up out of his mind's murk, popping around every corner, a paternal Whac-a-Mole. Was there a location he could think of in which his father did not hide?

"Too much chlorine in the pool." His dad had laughed as the girl, Shirelle, had shrugged, like Who cares. "Better go fix the balance and let Mr. Rooter finish cleaning the pipes."

"Darlo?" Jesse said. "Suggestions?"

"Try the pool," he said. "Have you seen anything about all this shit on the news?"

"Do you want me to say no?"

"What channels?"

"I just saw something on the Entertainment Network. What the hell's a racketeer?"

"Racketeer?"

"Oops."

Darlo banged the phone on the glass. What about all the other girls in the dungeon? What about every time he hadn't gone down there to stop the screams, and what about the year—no, *years*—he had been away?

Someone had to get down there. Someone without a badge.

Darlo told him. He spoke of the stairway, way down. He spoke of hidden rooms and dungeons and a girl there, and screams through the canyon.

"So I need you to go down there," he said. "The combination on the lock is 664. Neighbor of the beast—664."

"No way, dude." Jesse's voice had gone sharp. "Even if I did believe you, no way."

"You don't believe me?"

"A girl, hidden in a dungeon, part of a sex-slave ring, your dad?" He said this with the cadence of *a man, a plan, a canal, panama*. "No, I fucking don't."

"Why is that hard to fucking imagine?"

"Because if it's true, I don't want to know, dude. I don't want to get the fuck involved with your sick family."

Darlo knew Jesse was serious. He heard the jaunty tone leave his voice.

"How could you do this to me?" Darlo said. "I thought you had my back. After all we've been through."

"What have we been through, exactly, besides squillions of drugs?"

"I'll call you back," he said, because Jesse had him cornered. "Just sit tight. Can you at least do that?"

"Sure. I'll help you whatever way I can. But no way I'm going—"

"I heard you the first time."

26

SARAH FOUND BOBBY on the sidewalk outside the Van Gogh.

"Sorry," he said. "Let's go back inside."

"You've gone pale," she said, and stopped him. "What's happening? I can tell when something is wrong."

"I don't want to bore you," he said, and heard the sound of people chanting, marching down a nearby boulevard. "Seriously, Sarah, I'd put you to sleep with my patheticness."

"What would I be doing here if I was bored, huh?" She shook her head. "Now come on, tell me what's wrong."

He spoke of band woes, and laid it on pretty thick, trying to get her to shut him up with a kiss. That was the way they did it in movies; if he didn't know which way was up, then fuck if he was going to go gently through this confusion.

"I hate the band, but it's my life," he was saying. "I dream of slicing up Darlo and—"

"Darlo?" she said, as if he'd never said the word before. "That's a nice name."

"Nice name?" He nodded though the back of his head pulsed. "Yeah, I guess it is. But just wait until you meet him."

"What do you mean?"

He stood on a precipice of envy. The wind blew in his eyes. An icy cliff. Would he fall?

"Look at that," she said, getting him off the hook. "Right on."

From the direction of Vondelpark came a few hundred protesters, small in number but making a racket. Even from a distance, Bobby noticed how nicely their skin glowed. They looked as if they were on a school field trip.

"I should be marching today," Sarah said. "That sick war."

"My brother, Darren, was in Seattle during the WTO," Bobby said. "He went down there just to see what was happening and ended up right in the middle of it. The National Guard was out, and they carried, like, five-foot blocking poles."

"I've seen books about that," she said. "People running and screaming while clouds of tear gas hover in the air. The pictures are beautiful, which is crazy. But they are beautiful."

The kids marched by, lightly singing.

Bobby's phone rang. He let it vibrate in the dark of his pocket and watched the protesters skip on. She took his hands by the wrists and looked them over. Band-Aids fluttered, discolored. Raw flesh glistened in stygian pools of lymph.

"We need to get you some new bandages," she said. "My house is not far. Ugh, you poor thing — they are falling apart."

"What about Van Gogh?"

"He'll always be here, but your hands may fall off. Come now."

They walked half a mile. The neighborhood turned to single-family houses that looked like the pictures of where the Beatles grew up, which to Bobby, in their ponderous black-and-white exposures, were Dickensian and foreboding, as if the electricity were always out and the gardens always dead and the air-raid sirens always ten seconds away. Sarah stopped at one of these bleak houses, but up close the signs of children appeared: child-painted doors, washable rainbows on the panes. Toys littered the yard like flowers. A few empty garbage-can lids were strewn on the grass.

They went through the main hall. The smell of sausage cooking held dominion, mingled with that of tobacco. Cigarette smoke radiated from the kitchen.

"Marcus is home," she said, annoyed. "My stepfather."

Marcus had a bushy mustache and sat at the table reading the newspaper. His glasses covered half his face; they were the kind worn only by biology teachers and mass murderers. On top of that, he wore a lumberjack shirt that was pure Green River Killer.

"I hope you're nicer than the boy I met this morning," Marcus said when Sarah introduced them. "Your sister really outdid herself. She brought home a boy who looked like a junkie. Disgusting." He waved his hands around, dragged on his cigarette. "But what can I do — she is not my daughter. There is nothing I can do to make her more like you, sweet Sarah."

Sarah smiled in a way that indicated that she was both the good girl of the two and no fan of Marcus. Bobby kind of liked him. He liked guys who looked like one-hundred-percent highway-roaming psychopaths.

"We're just stopping by to get Bobby some bandages," Sarah said.

"Nothing like you," Marcus said, not to be interrupted in his groove. He lit a cigarette and cupped it in his hand. "Why can't she be?"

Sarah pulled two bottles of Heineken from the fridge. She cracked one for Marcus and one for her and Bobby to share, then proceeded to stroke the man's head as he talked to himself, becoming more heated as he recounted how fed up he was with Danika, her sister, and how this guy she'd brought home had matted blond hair and looked as if he'd been living out of a Dumpster. Stroking his head had the effect of turning down a burner.

"He looked like slime from the Dam," Marcus said, his face tightening into a twisted modulation of the permanently upset. "But I showed him."

"What's for dinner?" she asked. "Are you cooking?"

"I followed him outside and showed him."

"Is Mom going to be home for dinner?"

"Clapped him around the ears is what I did."

Sarah tapped on the beer bottle. "I think we should wait for her before we eat, don't you?"

"He was asking for it. Little punk."

She smiled at Bobby and rolled her eyes. "Yeah," she said. "We should wait for her."

Family life. He hadn't seen it in so long in any form. He hadn't been around fathers and daughters interacting. He had forgotten about fathers and daughters and taking out the garbage and ruminating at the dinner table and every other shade of the domestic spectrum. Never before had families seemed enviable. The heat of reassessment pulsed through his mind.

Bobby wondered how a dysfunctional Dutch family differed from a dysfunctional American family. What were the mores by which this dynamic occurred? Could a young American woman cook up the cocktail—two parts coddling, one part ignoring, a splash of disgust—that constituted Sarah's strategy with her stepfather?

"We'll be upstairs," Sarah said when Marcus took a breath. "OK?"

"Fine," he said, and winked at Bobby. "See you, boss."

Climbing the stairs, Bobby stared at the curve of Sarah's ass. "Nice guy," he said, imagining her crotch in his mouth.

Sarah stuck out her tongue so it lolled at the side and made the crazy sign with her hand. "Speaks English for you," she said. "Wants to impress you."

After Bobby had covered his hands in a new set of bandages, he sat on a chair in her room and marveled at this Dutch plot of IKEA modern, soft spongy couches and clear glass tables and a bed of the finest Swedish pine. He wondered if he could stay in here while everything shook out. It wasn't a cozy room, but he would be fine here. He would hide while Darlo and Shane fought, Joey fudged and frittered, and Adam ran out the clock.

On her blue dresser stood a bunch of pictures. One was of Sarah and some dude locked in a kiss of clear passion. He looked like Shane.

"Boyfriend?" he said, motioning to the picture.

"Ex-boyfriend," she said, and smiled, a little bit sad. The room went warm all of a sudden.

"I've got an hour before I have to go to dinner," he said. "It's going to be like a last supper."

Sarah lay on the bed. "Come over here."

He lay down next to her. Her covers portrayed some kind of ironic scene involving deer in the forest. Well, he hoped it was ironic. If it wasn't, they should just put him in handcuffs for being such a chicken hawk.

She leaned up on her elbow. A chain-linked onyx bracelet hung from her wrist. "When I saw you at that café," she said, "I thought you were so cute."

"Really?" He tried to hide his hands behind his body, but it just looked like he was arresting himself. "Seriously?"

"Mm-hmm. I thought, how am I going to get his attention? I didn't need to check my e-mail, just killing time before school, but I sat down and checked it anyway, and then you sat down opposite me but wouldn't make eye contact." She played with a stitch in the comforter, looked down, looked up. "Very hard to get. So I went outside to have a cigarette, but you didn't take the hint, kept looking up at me but didn't get up. I was just about to leave when you had that tantrum and Ullee kicked you out."

"He's a nice man," Bobby said. "That was shitty of me."

"He's a perv," she said. "He stares at my tits. Those computers are shit. And his dreads — nasty."

Bobby started picking at the stitching too, bringing his hand closer and closer to hers, moving among oak trees and Bambis, woodchucks and daisies.

"And then I came stumbling out," he said. "A mess."

Their fingers touched, took apart a seam.

"And there you were," she said. "And here we are."

She dimmed the lights. Stars covered her ceiling, glow-in-the-dark constellations. She rolled over him softly, throwing off her shirt, and as her shadow grew on the wall, he thought of Roy Batty, the replicant played by Rutger Hauer in *Blade Runner*, and the soliloquy he gives in the moments before his death.

Her tongue was hot and slick. His hands went all over her. She didn't care about their condition.

"Press lightly," she said. "Slow and light now, Bobby."

At the end of *Blade Runner*, Batty stands on the top of a building, having just saved the life of Deckard, the man hunting him down, played with a most potent dude-itude by Harrison Ford. Batty's quest to stay alive, to escape the internal robotic clock that marks him for imminent expiration, is over. Atop the rain-soaked roof of some rotting art deco building, the lights of dystopian progress sputter in their vision. Handfuls of vapor sheet down their faces. Batty rises over Deckard, who looks up in terror and wonder. He rises over him, as thunder and lightning spit sound and light. He rises over him, mountain-sized.

"I have seen things," Batty says, "you people would not believe."

He understands that he cannot fight against the predestined, understands certain inevitabilities, finally, completely.

"Attack ships on fire off the shoulder of Orion," he continues. "I've watched C-beams glitter in the dark near the Tannhauser Gate."

Sarah removed his shirt, ran her hands along Bobby's spotty-haired chest, got on top and pinned him down. The replicant's face loomed in his sight. But the replicant was him, come to rest once and for all.

"All those moments," Batty whispers, "will be lost in time. Like tears in rain."

In Bobby's eyes, the room dropped away in the tunnel vision of desire and flight. Sarah was a burning little star, dwarfing the Milky Way behind her, moving, unhurried, in the dimmed-down gloaming.

"Lost," Batty says, lowering his eyes. "Like tears. In rain."

But still, streaming over her henna-red head like a halo, Bobby saw the Big Dipper, and the spindly necklace of Cassiopeia, and, poised like a little diamond earring, the North Star.

"Like tears," he said, stretching to meet her. "In rain."

She reared up. Had she heard him at all?

"You smell like vanilla," she whispered. "What do I smell like?"

"Salt," he said. "Water. Fire, baby. Fire."

She laughed, and her teeth glinted, and further off, past her, lay oceans of stars, oceans that had lain upon so many ceilings, from all the vantage points, on skies painted in blue and white, oxblood and sea green. On beds in countless states and cities, foreign and domestic, these glow-in-the-dark constellations, these dioramas, couched him and the numerous burning feminine celestias that had hovered and crested and zoomed in his vision, creating points of bearing by which he navigated all the differences of escape. She and he, coasting and grooving, up into the night sky.

PART

III

1

SOMETIMES THE BUDDHA HAD a tough day. No problem. Shane was in rags, a fucking Untouchable, but some roles were worth the humiliation.

His ears were really ringing now. That Dutch bastard had popped him good. But it made the suffering more complete, richer, gave the experience more bragging rights.

He stood in Joey's hotel room, a real nice spread, still a little bit stunned that she'd actually left their names at the front desk.

"Yes, Mr. Warner," the petite suited punk-rock boy with the nose stud had said, and handed him a key. "Enjoy your stay."

Shane grabbed the boy's arm. "Is there a wet bar in the room?"

"Yes, sir," the clerk said, in the blandest nonconfrontational monotone. "Please let go of me."

And what a wet bar it was. Big-ass mother. Little gimp tramp.

Joey's tan Vuitton suitcase lay next to the bed. Shane wondered where the rest of her luggage was — that bitch would take a suitcase to buy a pack of cigarettes — and pondered the worth of rifling through the contents. Who knew what he'd find, besides unsent love letters to Darlo. Next to the suitcase lay a box of thirty CDs, right from the printing plant. A Post-it note stuck to the box said *For Revvy at Guild Records.*

Shane had no idea who Revvy or Guild Records was. He ripped open the box and grabbed a CD; their four faces in that Queen-wannabe pose, looking up from darkness.

"Wow," he said, stroking the cover, like an old crone looking upon an image of her princess self. "*Man.*"

He regarded the opulence of Joey's suite. If she cared at all about us, Shane thought, she would have gotten each of us a room. That would have been a nice thing, a generous thing, but the manager wasn't nice or generous. She was a sewer rat, chewing away with her spiked rodent teeth at the bottom of their mighty rock-and-roll vessel, doing nothing while Darlo steered it right into the shoals of show-biz breakdown.

In the sparkling clean shower, dirt and peanut butter fell off him in a sheet, making a putty on the five-star porcelain. He pleasure-groaned until water ran into his right ear and imitated a ballpoint pen going jab-jab-jab. His knees buckled and he cried out, but he loved the pain too. Ear stigmata to the max. He steadied himself. Rode it out.

"And I have suffered," he sang into the detachable brass showerhead, trying to croon like Sinatra, his only croon frame of reference. "Oh za-za-zoom I have suffered. Oh I hate Darlo, za-za-zoom, and I hate Bobby, ya-za-ba-za boom, thank you, New York, thank you so much. No, you're much too kind, no, please, I don't deserve it!"

Steam filled up the shower, reminding him of a certain moment in a shower in a hotel in Portland, where two Reed coeds had taken him on. He leaned against the wall, jerking off, and remembered the brunette's shattered heart tattoo across her shoulder, and how he had gotten down on his knees and played the part of the sexual penitent as they offered soft, complex communion. He leaned against the wall and grew stiff as a board in the desert.

Then a jet of water blasted his ear. The pain this time left no room for reminiscence, bisected his head in a nonnegotiable agony, a sharp, burning lance straight through to his brain. His legs gave out and he fell to the floor. The position he assumed was similar to that of prostration at New Fundamentalist Baptist Church, Anaheim, the church where he'd tithed away his fortune, the holy house at which he'd been a once-and-future-king but where, now, if he entered in his peanut butter aura, he'd be immediately and forcefully ejected. But the position was also an evolutionary still life, of one headed out of, or back into, the silty tide pools of some Mesopotamian floodplain.

The agony, he knew, was guided by the invisible, all-powerful hand of God, malignant and devious, never showing its face, piercing and playing, halving and quartering. Shane coughed up water and pounded the tile floor in theological frustration.

"Why is this happening?" he said. "Why are You doing this to me? Why are You doing this? I have tried so fucking hard! I have looked for You everywhere!"

He leaned against the wall. The showerhead, high above him like the nourisher of all things, rained down. Water dripped from his lips.

"But where are You? You are nowhere. Show Your face to me."

The pain delivered him no knowledge. Nothing from the wellspring but an empty echo of pitter-patter covering his tears. His ears settled back into a steady, numbing thump, and he looked up to the Teledyne altar. Water poured down like silver.

"Show Your face to me!"

He exited from the stall and donned a plush terrycloth robe that fell down to his ankles. But luxury, even this slight, went against his unshakeably shitty mood; within a minute he was out of the robe and back into his nasty clothes, which, sad smells and all, felt like part of his body, felt like armor. Certain things were indispensable in the seeker's quest, but terrycloth was not one of them.

He tuned the TV to VH1 Europe, broke the seal on the wet bar, and mixed a bourbon and water. Ordered a cheeseburger from room service, because veganism suddenly seemed like a dumb thing when you had free meat at the snap of your fingers. Felt a hot hum in his crotch and marveled at the everpresence of sin in his heart.

Watching twilit Amsterdam from the window, he was filled with serenity as he used to be in church, when he would turn to his left and see his whole family there, dressed and buffed: his sister, Jane, his brother, Tom, both of them still in high school and showing little interest in rock and roll, or any form of self-expression; his mother, Catherine, happily born, bred, and set to die in Orange County; and his dad, the old engineer, whose intellectual curiosity was as narrow as Paris Hilton's waistline. Shane stared down the pew and they looked at him, waiting for a cue.

"I should meditate," he said. "I should be thankful."

He assumed a poor man's lotus position on the bed, put his palms up in the air like he was checking for rain, and closed his eyes, focusing his anxieties into a ball and sending them down the trash hole of his consciousness. But ear pain, pulsing and spiked, plugged the hole like a clump of rotting food and sent the anxieties back up at him.

His cell phone rang. The disgusting world called the seeker back.

"Fuck it," he said, and opened his eyes.

A local number. What the fuck?

"Shane, it's Danika. From last night." She giggled. "Remember me?"

Remember me? They always said that.

"What do you want?"

She kept giggling. She was in on all kinds of jokes he'd been left out of. "You're funny, man."

He said nothing. She breathed into the phone. His crotch kept humming. His ears rang like a starting bell.

Remember when you were earnest and sincere, Shane? Remember when you thought that callous was something you had on the heel of your foot?

"Your fucking dad attacked me," he said. "He attacked me and banged up my ears. Did you know that?"

She laughed. "He's not my dad. He's my stepdad."

"That explains a lot."

"Sorry?"

Shane recalled the intimacy, however perverse, between stepfather and stepdaughter. Out the window, a crow took off from a tree. He poured a shot of Jack Daniel's and took a manly slug.

"He's a dick either way," he said. "He came at me with two fucking garbage —"

"Hey, so are you going to put me on the guest list tonight?"

He took another slug but missed. Bourbon ran down his shirt. He said nothing.

"But come on!" Her voice grew heavy. "Come on, baby."

He imagined all kinds of geometry, and physics, and most of all biology.

"OK," she said. "See you tonight?"

He grunted.

"OK, see you later!"

He threw the phone to the floor, reflected on temptation, rubbed his temples. When he returned to Los Angeles, he was going to figure this out. He would separate the seeker from the horndog, even try to make his parents understand that he was still their prodigal son, even though he looked like their worst nightmare and no way was he going to go back to singing about Christ. But for now he was going to find that band from the lobby. He wanted to be around them, and that felt pathetic but fuck it, he could show them how it was done. He was a veteran and they were obviously green. No band was that happy unless they were green, or Aerosmith.

His cheeseburger came. The Dutch bellhop waited for a tip, so he signed over twenty euros. Fuck Joey. It was probably their money anyway. Managers made their living skimming cream off the top.

Though Shane enjoyed his cheeseburger, a heaviness in his mouth warned him of great wrath to come; so much unfamiliar animal protein in one day was bound to cause a hydrochloric shitstorm. The meat tasted fantastic, but across the wilds of gastrointestinal time, he felt the faint charge of acidic explosion. He had eaten, in five hours, more animal flesh than he'd had in the preceding two years. Some serious blowback was coming down the pike.

He chased it down with another shot of Jack, putting a sting on his throat. Was there any meal more rock and roll than burgers and whiskey?

"No," he said, and some of the brown drool escaped from his mouth. The taste hit his brain like a sloppy wet kiss from a beautiful girl.

Rifling though Joey's suitcase in search of money, he found a copy of *Hustler*, a half-used carton of Players, and a dime bag. Wrapped up in a bunch of panties lay a wad of twenties, from which he took two bills. He wrapped the rest up tight, trying to make it look like he'd never been there. Then he decided that Joey could go fuck herself and dumped the entire suitcase on the floor. A pack of cigarettes covered up a beaver shot like two sins trying to go clean. Damning his loss of control, he tried to put everything back the way it had been, but he only succeeded in unraveling the twenties from the panties. He grabbed a CD to give to that band he had met in the lobby. His ears hummed as if he lay underneath a Marshall stack. On VH1 Europe, Motley Crüe talked about their triumphant comeback from the wasteland of drugs and alcohol.

"I was dead for five minutes flat," Nikki Sixx said. "Like, for real, man, absolutely dead. Flatline. Seriously!"

2

WALKING IN THE HEART of the red-light district with Darlo, Joey watched the girls in their windows. They exerted a certain allure, all that impure skin promising absolution from tension, all those bodies without context. Though she wasn't into pay-to-cum, she understood its power in the way she understood all the times people ordered Jägermeister; nasty shit could really blow your mind, but that didn't mean you'd escape the consequences.

Darlo, zombiefied, didn't seem to notice any of it. She couldn't be sure how much of his semi-catatonia had to do with her rejection of his advances, but she had to bring him back.

Only one option lay before her. The logic of what she was about to do would reveal itself to her one day, maybe when they finally lay together.

"We need to get you laid," she said. "Come on."

Darlo perked up. "You sure?"

"Of course I am," she said, nodding hard before she could change her mind. Her leg began to ache again. She dry-popped Tylenol. Darlo, suddenly and distressingly back from the grave, started looking for someone specific.

"She was, like, yea tall, and had a mass of black hair and full ruby lips. She was a real wet dream, and my credit card wouldn't fucking go through."

Joey couldn't believe how fast the prospect of pussy turned the drummer into a shaggy dog. Hackney's face loomed up at her, all her failure summarized in the sultry gaze of an English stranger.

Soccer hooligans were out in full force. "Glory, glory, Man United!" they sang, red in the face, happy as new millionaires.

"I think she was over here," Darlo said, pointing at a few windows, getting warmer. "She had the hottest curves, fuckin' A, man, yeah, over here, the hottest little piece. I hope her fucking heavy is out to dinner. What a prick!"

The drummer pointed at a girl in a candy-pink window. She looked just the way he described her and wore a color-coordinated negligee. She stared at Darlo in a hostile way, confirming their history. Her stare made Joey jealous. The drummer held out his palm.

"That's her," he said, tongue almost lolling. "Whatcha got?"

Joey removed a few hundred-euro notes from her pocket and handed them over.

"Here goes nothing," she said. "That ought to take care of it."

Darlo snatched the bills with a piratical giggle and skipped over to the prostitute's door. Ms. Pink glared at him through the glass, and he waved the cash like a white flag.

"Hey, remember me?"

Candy Pink shook her head.

"No, look, I have money now! Look, I have money right here!"

Dutchies on their way home from work took in the scene, expressionless; no doubt they saw an American Puritan prostrating himself at the legal pussy altar every day. Two dark-skinned guys in peacoats, smoking outside a fry joint, noted the situation with a Turkish call of encouragement. Joey watched the broken son of the porn king beg at the feet of this little pink-emblazoned Dutch lady. She battled back her jealousy and took a mental photograph.

Candy Pink opened the door. The peacoated fellows clapped. Joey envied Darlo and his simple wants; all the drummer needed was some tail and he was all right. He could point at something in the physical world and see a solution. Joey's satisfaction concerned slippery slopes of success, reputation, and power. You couldn't grasp any of that in the palm of your hand. You could only piece together events and try to find a pattern. And the pattern for her was blind alleys, missed opportunities, possibilities squandered, a brand name that couldn't buy respect, a bunch of bands that everyone ridiculed. And tonight she had to put the fucking franchise to rest. Tonight she had to preside at a dinner that would end as a total roasting, no matter who she put at either side of her.

The Sharpie Shakes jingle wafted up from a radio passing by. Its bone-crunching tones surrounded Joey in a vise grip. That fucking jingle. They'd be swimming in hard licensing cash. But she had talked them out of it.

> Fun in the sun...you betcha...good times ahead...it'll
> getcha!

The jingle faded down the street like Fischer-Price thunder. Darlo had disappeared into the brothel. They were supposed to be at the hotel for dinner in less than an hour. She lit a Players and pulled from her jacket pocket her nickel-plated Warner Bros. flask, swag of good times long gone. She'd promised herself she'd go to dinner sober, but that jingle, tracking her, haunting her, burning her, had tipped over what was left in the wet, cold barrel of her resolve. Resolve seeped out of her pores, ran down the street in rank rivulets.

She gulped her brandy. Applejack. She'd read somewhere that Ronnie Van Zant drank it constantly, strutted the stage aflame with it, wrote "Freebird" doused in it. So there had to be some magic in its bitter, chemical tones. She gulped again, blew smoke rings, and waited for his beautiful backcountry ghost to take her by the soul. When it did, she formulated one last, desperate gambit.

3

SHANE HEARD THE PARTY from way on down the hall. Good thing; he couldn't remember the room number that sucker of a drummer had told him in the lobby. The copy of *Rocket Heart* weighed down his jacket. He knocked on the door of the Rodin Suite.

A young woman dressed in impeccable turn-of-the-seventies cowgirl hippie chic answered the door. "Can I help you?"

Little groupie, out of my way. I am Shane James Warner of Blood Orphans. I am the recipient of dirty money and negative press. I have scoured the earth, always seeking truth and God. I can teach you a thing or two. I am a veteran of the scene. I am a valuable resource.

"What's that smell?" she said. "Oh, man!"

A chill went through him. He took a whiff. She was right. Why did he still smell like rotting peanut butter?

The members of the band looked up from their couches, their sterling mirrors, their fashion magazines. They looked up from their fantasyland and saw the Ghost of Christmas Past. Shane might as well have been wearing chains and moaning. Parts of him might as well have been falling off.

They pointed at him, exultant.

"Hey, Dave, get out here! It's Peanut Butter Bob!"

"PB and J!"

"Peanut fucking Butter Bob! Man, what's up!"

The drummer came out of the bathroom, zipping up. When he saw Shane he began to apologize. "I didn't really think he'd come up here, I swear, I just —"

But they waved him off.

"Forget about it, Dave, all the freaks want to get to know you. Well, shit, PB and J, Dave said you smelled like peanut butter and damn if he wasn't right, but have a fucking seat, take a motherfucking load off, we got too much good shit anyway, why be a hoarder? Why bogart all the goodness? Nay, we shall not! Nay, we shall smote our hoardage with equal and opposite kindness! A seat, smelly PB and J, take a seat!"

Shane sat down at the fortress of white leather couches arranged in a square around the big glass table, which was littered with drug paraphernalia, cans of Heineken, and several bindles of coke. What would the Buddha say? Is all of this yin or is it yang? Stick or serpent? Heaven or hell?

A girl emerged from the bathroom right behind the drummer, wiping her mouth.

"Dave's got a monster load in that little thing!" she said, and they laughed.

"Even the drummer gets laid in this band!" yelled the guy who was certainly not the bass player; he had a shine on him that said, I stand at the front of the stage every fucking night. My crotch stares down young girls. I am a made man. "Are we not charitable? Are we not kind? Does Virgin Records not so completely own our ass? Are we not utter happy whores? Does Warner/Chappell not so completely own Ron's songs?"

Ron came up from the cocaine like a wave cresting. Taller than the others, with broad shoulders and big muttonchops framing his full lips, he appeared to be the natural leader of the group.

"I am *so* owned, dudes." He put his mouth on the cleavage of a young lady who wore red suede pants and had a bit of a roving eye. Then he grabbed both her tits and cradled them while she protested too much, falling into giggles and play slaps.

"Oh, yes, oh my God, yes." He laughed. "I am so owned. These are the fruits of my bounty. I am a whore in Babylon."

"No, Ron," she said, thick eyebrows and all. "*I* am the whore of Babylon."

"Damn your eyes!" Ron said, apparently to himself.

Another guy, whose mottled skin belied his happy vibe, laughed so hard he fell to the floor, coughing.

Shane knew this scene, remembered the room at the Chateau Marmont they'd wrecked after their CD release show at the Wiltern, mayhem and bedlam and ahem, pass the cocaine. But even at the time Shane knew he'd been trying too hard, been too tense about it, as if someone were filming the destruction. Here in the Rodin Suite, the vibe was somehow mellow. There was no sense, even in the ribbing they gave Dave the drummer, that they meant any harm or gave two shits about how it all looked; he just sat there enjoying himself, having accepted his lot, like Ringo in *A Hard Day's Night*. Shane liked that movie. Ringo was the jester and he took some shit from the other three, but you could tell they loved him. Even Paul, that smarmy little bitch. Why did everyone say to Shane that if they were the Beatles, Shane would be Paul? How come Adam got to be George? Shane was the spiritual one, goddamnit. He was the seeker. Adam wasn't spiritual. It wasn't fucking fair.

"Do a line, Peanut Butter Nutter Fucker," Ron said, pushing the small mirror at him. "Give it a go, Holmes."

"Much obliged," Shane said, and bore down on it like a champ. "Hoover!"

The sting in his ears pulled against the sting in his nose, which pulled against the cheers from the room.

"Hoover-on-o-mous Bosch! He's an artist!"

The sting pulled him three ways until Wednesday, pulled

him taut and turned him into an electric amphetamine Bermuda Triangle.

"Hoover mover and shaker!"

A slap on his back. Congratulatory cheers.

"Peanut Butter equals Hoover! Hoover-a-lanimous! Born in Hoovlakhastan!"

He recognized that they had all kinds of sayings and codes. Blood Orphans had no codes, no secret handshakes, no winks, no shared anything. Except bitterness.

He hit another line before they could stop him.

"Lord have mercy! Good God, will someone testify for the Hoover Man!"

Down there, riding that white rail, he saw the record cover. Four faces alone, staring away from each other. Four faces, zero friendship. Created just for the joke of Mammon. Created for a deadly sin. Staring up to the ground, to the earth. Down in limbo. Four faces in a devil's bargain.

"Hoover, damn *it!*"

Four faces. No shared anything.

"Wow!"

He fell back on the couch, heart beating.

"You son of a gun!"

His stomach rumbled. That cheeseburger. Maybe he should go to the bathroom. But then the dudes were enacting a story from their recent airplane ride over here from America. They were called Tennessee, recently signed to Virgin and here on a press junket.

"Tennessee what?" Shane asked, wiping his nose.

"Just Tennessee," said Dave the drummer.

"After a state?"

"Of mind."

Postnasal drip kicked in. Stimulant stalactites.

"But you guys aren't from Tennessee, right?"

"Shut up, PB and J!" said Ron. "We're telling a story!"

Cocaine popped open his eyes. He just wanted to sit here forever, sit and be around their happiness, sit in rock-and-roll fellowship. For once.

Ron told a story of his entrance into the Mile High Club and acted it out, twisting his body wildly, propping up his legs, thrusting.

"I was like... *this*, and she was like... *that*, and we were like... God, man, can I do this!... We were like *that!*" Ron motioned to one of the ladies. "Baby, get under me to complete the image."

She assumed a position and he began to dry-hump her. No compromise of character was involved.

"So then we had to prop ourselves up... like... oh shit!"

Ron lost his balance, teetered in the air. Laughter propped him up for a second. Laughter freed him of gravity for a blessed moment before he went crashing, on his back, into the oak side table, breaking it in two.

"Fuck, Ron! Jesus!"

Splinters of faux-antique wood cracked; drinks ran onto the white carpet. They fell over in hysterics, bowed their heads in prayer to the rock-and-roll gods, for which destruction of hotel property was the surest sign of Providence.

Shane couldn't manage a smile.

"Oh my fuckin' God!" Ron laughed from the floor. "Oh man! Ouch!"

"Oh baby!" said the girl who'd been under him, after falling to the floor in mock worry. "Sweet lord!" she said, and stroked his scruffy face.

Shane felt old. He'd never felt old before. Ten minutes with Tennessee had aged him ten years.

"Excuse me," he said, and rushed to the bathroom.

He could have been taking a shit on the couch and they wouldn't have noticed. Fun was a big fucking wall of sound protecting them from the feedback screech of reality. Fun was a brand-spanking-new record deal from Virgin.

"Oh damn!"

"My head!"

"Oh baby, baby!"

"Shit, dude, that was a fucking *table!*"

Cocaine. What was he thinking? Cocaine was for Darlo and Joey and the otherwise vacant, a drug that catered not to the enlargement of the spirit, like ecstasy, for example, which put you in tune with loving one another, accepting the faults, finding the good. Cocaine was a crash course in coveting, a fast track to envy and hubris and fake possibility.

Also it gave him a rotten headache and made his eyes expand, like maybe they'd burst out of their sockets, and made his throat close up.

"Now look at you," he said to the bathroom mirror, shaking a little, throwing water on his face. "Now you just look at you look at you look at you!"

There was a knock on the door. Room service. The clanging of plates and pots ricocheted off his punctured eardrums, and he slid to the floor, covering them. His stomach rumbled like a fucking alien was in there.

His phone rang. Bobby. "What do *you* want?"

"Hold, please, for an atheist!" Bobby laughed. "Hold, please, for the Enlightenment!"

Bobby, I won't let you mock me.

"Hold, please, for the theory of evolution!" Bobby yelled. "Hold, please, for Newton and Copernicus!"

This is what you get, he thought, when you punch a man's

tooth from his face. This is what violence begets. A transmission, a sign, at the bottom of life's well.

"Nama rama ho-ho ding-dong!" Bobby laughed. "Nama navaho yodel-ay-hee-who!"

A knock at the bathroom door. He snapped the phone shut. Dave the drummer came shuffling in. "Sorry, dude," he said, and his groupie followed behind him for blowjob numero duh.

Shane stumbled back out to Gomorrah Central. Tennessee writ large sat there, gorging on platters of fried chicken and french fries. The smell of grease made Shane's stomach hiccup, but he kept it together, sat down, and opened a Coca-Cola.

Ron motioned to the food. "You OK, PB and J?"

Shane nodded.

"Damn, this is good chicken!" another one said. "Some fine, fine music!"

Chicken grease sprayed around as their teeth ripped and tore. It was a slaughterhouse in here.

Shane sipped his Coke and picked up an acoustic guitar, a Gibson Hummingbird Custom, list price four thousand American, a six-string signing bonus. Out of tune, it still sounded like the ghost of Segovia.

"Play something, baby," one of the girls said, pulling on a wing. "What band did you say you were in?"

Shane took out the CD and dropped it on the table. "Blood Orphans."

They stopped with their chewing and ripping and stared at him.

"*No*," said the girl who'd been Ron's Mile High prop, and licked her fingers. "Didn't you guys, like, break up?"

"No."

"I thought you broke up," Ron said. "I swear I read it in *Spin*."

"I read it in *Magnet*," the smooth guitar player said.

"I read it in *Rolling Stone*," said Dave the drummer, emerging from the bathroom and zipping up his pants. "I saw it on MTV."

"I'm the singer," Shane said. "I'm Shane Warner, and I can promise you we're still together."

"You're the preacher's kid!" said one of the girls, a blonde with glitter on her eyelids who hadn't yet said a thing, who'd just giggled her way through the last half-hour. "I read about you on Pitchfork. You're the Christian!"

"Uh…"

"Yeah, there's four of you, right? There's a preacher's kid, that's you, there's the guy whose parents are in porn…and who are the two other guys?"

"Adam and Bobby. I'm not a preacher's kid."

"Far out!" She raised her chicken leg, waved it like a judge with a gavel. "Right on!"

Ron started dancing around with the tops of the silver food trays, clanging them together lightly, but in Shane's estimation he'd become possessed by Danika's stepdad. His ears rose to the bait and started pulsing.

"You guys are *infamous!*" Ron said, dancing around, forming a conga line with four of the girls. "In-fa-mous pricks, hey!"

"It's just Darlo," Shane said. "Darlo's the prick."

"Oh yeah, now I remember!" said Dave's blowjob queen. "You threw pies at some Warners execs. I read about that in *Rolling Stone.*"

Shane wondered why every time he met people who knew about the band, they dredged up yet another bad memory.

"Pies," Ron said. "What was that all about?"

The idea was to have a record release party in the grand old tradition of the sixties and seventies, when such things were a cultural event. So they had arranged, a week after that horrible trip down Fifth Avenue in the back of a flatbed, to get dressed up like dudes out of a circus and have a medieval feast, like the Rolling Stones did for the release of *Beggars Banquet*.

They rented out Tavern on the Green. All the Warners execs came, because Blood Orphans was going to be the money truck and this was a way to grease the wheels, another fully recoupable sendoff the suits would make back before the band saw a penny of royalties. They hired some conceptual artist who had thrown theme parties for Aerosmith and Sting, turned the Tavern into a silk-and-satin Renaissance Fair, filled it with news media from seven countries. The gluttony angle was a lock on pages in entertainment sections all over the Western world. Even the Norwegians sent over one of their best tall thin blond men to watch from the back.

The band sat on a dais against the wall. On the dais lay a pig with an apple stuffed in its mouth, various game laid out in bounty, and cornucopias to the max, just like in Merry Olde England. They looked like sixteenth-century lords, ripped at turkey legs, and smiled for the camera.

"I'm gonna get drunk," Darlo had said into Shane's ear. "And then you and I are going to double-team a few of these college journalists."

Shane switched seats with Adam.

After much merrymaking, the pies came out. A hundred cream pies. A regular pyramid o' pies, because that's the way the Stones had done it.

"What are those for?" someone yelled out.

"For throwing," Bobby said, and bashed one into Darlo's ear.

"Do that again!" a photographer yelled.

"I have a better idea!" Darlo said, and chucked one at the crowd.

Joey, who wore a Comme des Garçons dress that made her look like a slut Cinderella, threw pies like Nolan-fucking-Ryan.

The crowd of international correspondents ducked, but it was no use. They strafed the place with whipped cream and sugar. Enough people became involved that the scene degenerated into crust-and-cream anarchy, covering the band in pie-errata, ruining their expensive medieval costume clothes. To top it off, Darlo pie-pounded the president of the Warner Music Group square in the face.

"And the guy's face bled, right?" Ron said, strumming on another guitar. "I read about that in *Blender*. I was working in the Tower on Sunset and I showed that to everyone. Oh shit, it was a fucking mess!"

"Darlo's always out of control," Shane said.

"Every time we bring up an idea like that," Dave the drummer said, "they mention you guys. You made it hard for the rest of us to have any fun. Thanks for making our lives so damn boring."

Dave wasn't using that pathetic drummer tone anymore. A blowjob an hour put some weight into a guy's voice.

"Oh, yeah, you have it so tough!" said his girlfriend du jour. "My pretty mouth is just a living hell."

"No, it's heaven," Dave said, getting down on his knees. "Heavenly!"

But look at me, Shane thought, moving in his clothes like moldy meat in between stale bread. *Look at what happened to me.*

The broken table was a bummer, so they moved to some white couches near the window. They smoked and fiddled with guitars.

Shane dozed off and dreamed that he was running from disasters. Sometimes the disasters could not be escaped. A man beat on him in the alleyway of a major American city. There were cataclysms. He sank into a hole during an earthquake. Hands reached up to him, covered in sewage.

He sat up straight. His jeans felt oily on his legs.

"I'm like Job," Shane blurted out. "That's the thing."

They passed a pipe around. Ron, who seemed to be the guitar player, played "Creep." Everyone sighed and joined in.

"I want a perfect body," they sang, "I want a perfect soul."

They were half-watching a large TV embedded in the wall. The skunky stink of weed floated on a stench of fried food.

Ron stopped playing and turned to him, hazy-eyed. He wagged his finger as if it moved through mayonnaise. "You sound like my dad, man. *Job?* What do you mean you're like Job? You're nothing like Job."

Shane shrugged. "Feel like I am. God has brought travails upon my head."

"Travails? Stoned Peanut Butter. Old stony Peanut Butter Bob."

"Stop calling me that."

"Well, stop smelling like a can of old Skippy."

"It was Danika's fault. Dan-ee-ka."

Shane had his hands in the air, imagining them covered in eczema. Ron grabbed at them.

"Stop with that, dude," he said. "It's freaking me out."

Shane put his hands down. When he did, Darlo's dad's face stared at him from the television.

It took him a few seconds to get it. An MTV news exclusive. A man in a three-piece suit led away in handcuffs. A shot of the Cox estate. Mug shots of two men with thick necks and slicked-back hair.

"Fucking no fucking way."

He grabbed the remote and turned the volume up.

"...in a scheme that involves a regular checklist of white-collar crime—money laundering, racketeering, and falsification of documents to the SEC. Cox, whose name is synonymous with a type of adult entertainment known as extreme porn, has been under surveillance by the district attorney's office for over six months."

Cut to a man in a suit at a lectern emblazoned with the DA's coat of arms. Skinny, bald, like Ed Harris.

"Mr. Cox has been arrested on charges stemming from an investigation of convicted West Coast drug lord Joel Savage, who in the past helped with the financing of some of Mr. Cox's ventures. One of them, a store called Grimly Fiendish, was, we believe, the key business through which Mr. Cox and his various confrères structured their fraudulence."

"Confrères," Ron said. "I like it."

"Mr. Cox," the narrator continued, "has a long history of dancing near the edge of the criminal underworld. In 1981 he was associated with the victims of a gangland-style killing in Laurel Canyon, known as the Wonderland murders."

"Shit," a groupie said, holding her smoke. "That's fucked up."

"That's my drummer's dad," Shane said. "That's Darlo's fucking father."

Shane turned up the volume. A picture of Cox swirled toward the screen. He was at a party, with a table full of strippers. Raised glasses hid parts of their faces.

"Mr. Cox's name has been under a cloud since the 1997 overdose of Alice Jarvis, an eighteen-year-old-woman, at his mansion in the Hollywood Hills. Ms. Jarvis, who spent two weeks in a coma, claimed that Cox had tried to kill her because she had overheard discussions between him and several men regarding their various schemes. Cox claimed that she was a hanger-on, a party girl who just happened to overdose in his house."

Grainy footage of Cox framed against surf and palm trees. Winds galed but didn't do a thing to his perma-glued, too-black pompadour. "She was," he said, "a very unfortunate girl. I wish her the best. But I maybe met her once, twice, before I found her lying on my bathroom floor."

"Slimy," one of the girls said. "El Creep-o."

Shane looked out the window. Darlo must know. Against all judgment, sympathy rose in him.

"Mr. Cox is also under investigation regarding allegations that he was part of a sex-slave ring. A woman named Daniella Spencer—"

Ron clicked off the TV. "Bad vibes," he said, licking his fingers for chicken grease. "Lame, huh? That sucks for your drummer."

"Fuck him," Shane said. "He's a sodomy-obsessed misogynist with a mean streak a mile wide."

"Sodomy?" one of the girls said. "What's his number?"

It really signaled the end, didn't it? The father, in his wretched but fiery unstoppable glory, was the coal that stoked the son's engine. With the old fuck busted, the drummer's flame would surely peter out, flicker, and die.

As went Darlo, so went Blood Orphans. It was a hated, non-negotiable law, an immutable covenant of their lives.

Despair grew in Shane. Despair made fireworks in his stomach, made the red meat and whiskey grind the hydrochloric gears.

"Dude, play us some Blood Orphans," Ron said, handing Shane that zillion-dollar guitar and patting him on the shoulder. "That'll make you feel better."

He felt a house of suffering upon his seeker's spirit. His vision quest? Bullshit. Your journey to oneness with God, Buddha, whatever? A joke. Your absolute belief that life has meaning, that struggles are part of His plan, that setbacks are signs of Providence not yet earned? A lie.

"Sing...us a song," Ron sang. "A song to keep...us warm..."

"Love that one," one of the girls said, shivering in her buckskin and taking another hit off a joint. "Heartbreaking."

The truth was, Shane barely knew any chords. He never played the guitar onstage; Darlo and Joey wouldn't allow it.

"No way are you going to be a dilettante guitar player," they'd said, for their voices often blended together, Darlo low, Joey high, making a harmony of nemesis. "You stand there and rock out with your cock out. None of that now-I'm-a-sensitive-guy-with-the-guitar shit."

He ran his hands up the neck. The strings were sharp.

"You just sing," Darlo-Joey said. "You leave the guitar playing to Adam. Fucking Bono shit. Does Steven Tyler strap on a guitar? I think not!"

Another way they'd kept him down.

"So play something, PB and J," Ron said.

Shane shook his head. "All our songs are disgusting."

"True," Dave said. "I have the record."

Shane did a double-take. "You have *Rocket Heart?*"

"Sure."

"You bought it?"

"Yeah."

"No one gave you a review copy? Really?"

"Yeah, really."

A minor miracle.

"Then you name a song," Shane said.

Everyone looked at Dave. He appeared to enjoy the attention, the lowly drummer. He tapped his finger on his chin for an extra second.

"'Hella-Prosthetica,'" he said.

One of the girls made a face of wondering. "Nice name," she said. "What the hell's that about?"

In answer, Shane began to strum. The room grew warm under his dulcet tones. Rhythm was a little hard to come by, no, it was a lot hard to come by, but he tried to channel the higher powers, the Gautama and the Jesus and the spirit of the seeker. These ethereal guidance counselors were the only things keeping him from utter spiritual truancy, from failing out of God School for good. Darlo's lyrics fought Shane, but Shane pushed the words to a transcendence of meaning, finding their inner glory:

> Once upon a time I knew a girl who liked to beg.
> That was tough: she had no legs.
> She was a trooper, I never made her ask twice.
> Sex with amputees is really quite nice.

Just like every other time they had played the song, the audience froze a little. Even the Tennessee rock-and-roll idiots were caught in the crossfire of irony and bad taste. This little tune redefined audience reticence.

> Are you familiar with a position called The Stump?
> It's just about the best way to pump, pump, pump.
> She told me it's so nice to be understood.
> Now get over here and give this cripple some wood.

For the refrain, Darlo and Shane did a little call-and-response. Darlo was the boy and Shane the girl. Neither understood how creepy this was, because it constituted their intimate moment. Even Steadman had wondered if the duet was a good idea. So now Shane took on two voices. It felt right.

> I'm a cute little girl.
>> Crab-walk that rump over here!
> I'm the girl without feet.
>> How 'bout a piece of my meat?
> You're so good to me.
>> Ah well, I aim to please.
> You're the best, big boy.
>> I wish you had some knees.

He raised his voice and hollered in a galloping double-time:

Hella-Prosthetica, I love you,
for all the strange and funny things that you do.
Your love's so good that it's a fucking crime.
Drag your way over to my house any time.

Shane took a look at their openmouthed expressions, curling into dull smiles, turning into a recognition of his ability to turn this lyrical shit into sugar. That's right, he thought, I can be a transformative agent for good. I'm hitting all the right notes. I'm totally rocking this room. Without Darlo or Bobby or Adam. I don't need them at all. Look at the wide eyes and the bouncing in the seats. They get me. They understand how I transcend the stupid lyrics, set them alight with a higher truth. He thought of Bible camp up in the Sierra Nevadas, when they would gather around the campfire and sing songs — "Michael Row Your Boat Ashore" and "Nearer, My God, to Thee" and "She Loves You" and "Cathy's Clown." Those were fantastic times; play on, play on, there's nothing here but the Good Lord and us.

He yelled out in merry song. He threw his dreads around. He channeled the rock-and-roll furies. No Bobby or Darlo or Adam.

Hella-Prosthetica, take me down.
When I'm with you, I'm just your lovin' clown.
I thank the gods for bringing you to me.
I'll carry you anyplace you need to be!

He paused and looked around the room with utter supreme mastery. Just like at Bible camp.

Hella-hella-hella!...Hella-hella-hella!...Prosthetica!
Prosthetica!

Utter supreme transcendence. He slammed down the last lines.

Hella-hella-hella!...Hella-hella-hella!...Prosthetica!
Prosthetica!

A steam tower of peanut butter power wafted up from his body. He rose with it to greet the triumphant silence. The hotel room sparkled, shimmering, humid. He held himself up for the adoration of this transcendent moment.

One by one, like a row of synchronized swimmers diving into a pool, they fell over laughing. Like warped dominoes, they banged against each other and buckled, the eight of them, until Shane was the only one still sitting, bent against the winds of derision.

Dave surfaced and propped himself up.

"Oh my God, that was so bad!" He coughed and turned red. "Oh my God, that was so bad, but you...oh man...oh, that was beautiful!"

Shane thought back to Bible campfires. Girls adored him—wholesome girls, not the ones Darlo had brought to him, rotting his virtue.

"Oh, but what can a poor boy do?" Ron sang, "'cept to sing for a rock-and-roll band?"

Wholesome girls.

"Stop him," one of the girls said, laughing. "Stop him before he kills again!"

Such a pathetic attempt he had made, trying so hard to impress these strangers in their newly minted bubble of limitless and fully recoupable expense account. So lame to have come all this way to curry some favor, to try and jump someone else's train right as his went completely off the rails. But he was no train-jumper, no acrobat, no stuntman. He was tied to the front of the Blood Orphans crazy train, the mascot, the very face of it, as if flew off the tracks and headed for reality's hard rock mountainside. He could do nothing but close his eyes and prepare for the impact.

4

ADAM EXAMINED THE TOURING VAN that sat outside Morten's, a shiny black Sprinter without a trailer. Band stickers covered the bumper, a little too obviously crooked, as if some A&R intern had put them on that way, going for maximum cred. Adam groaned; Morten had double-booked and now he'd be stuck navigating the choppy waters of rock musician autism.

He climbed the stairs, waiting to hear the hollow tones of dudes cracking open beers, claiming beds, strumming guitars, lighting up the bong.

"Hello?" he yelled up the creaky staircase. "Hello?"

In the kitchen, a male body stood in shadow. For a second he thought this shadow was Bobby, but then he saw that the guy had his hands in his pockets, something the bass player's condition would not allow. The guy wore a black suit, had gel in his wavy black hair, and was trying to navigate that nasty-ass coffeemaker.

"It doesn't work," Adam said, and introduced himself.

"John Bridges," said the man, in a reformed Cockney. "You in Blood Orphans?"

"Yeah. Have you heard of us?"

"Just a little." He poured some ground coffee. "I'm the manager for Deena Freeze."

"That's me," said a voice behind him. On a bed that had previously been defiled by Darlo, a young woman tuned a Martin acoustic. She looked as if she'd just walked out of a *Vogue* photo shoot of fairies dancing and flying in the verdant British countryside, black hair tied up in small braids at the front but hasty at the back. Makeup glittered around her eyes. She wore a long, tight patchwork skirt and a black peasant blouse. Around her slim neck a string of shiny golden stones.

"We were warned about you," she said, in a throaty king's English.

"By who?"

"Marta at Full Bore."

"We have the same publicist?"

"And the same label," she said, strumming. "My record's out in a month on Warners. I'm opening for you tonight."

Adam watched Bridges lean against the wall in a way that Joey never could, as if the wall had a crush on him and had been waiting the whole damn school year for him to make his move. Behind him, glued to the window, lay the dried, smashed carcass of a wasp.

"Excuse me," Adam said, because he suddenly wanted to make sure he didn't still have blood on his face. "Be right back."

In the bathroom, he washed up and looked in the mirror. His faraway eyes brought to mind those pictures from *Life* magazine's book of photographs that he had had as a kid, of war veterans. He stared at his beat-up face and thought of the picture of a GI from the Korean War, wrapped in blankets out in the rain, head shrouded in wet flannel, looking to the sky, hopeless.

When he'd crashed his bike into the brick wall, the crowd of Dutchies had paid him a surprising amount of attention, and a pair of swish designers had taken him into some café, expressed their sympathies for his condition, the cause of which the guitar player would not divulge. They bought him toast, jam, and espresso. "I'm a vegetarian," he said, turning down the ham.

Adam examined his blackening eye, and the crud on Morten's mirror, and the shower curtain with all those superheroes looking cocksure but flying toward the floor at ridiculous angles, useless vectors.

When he emerged, Deena and her slick, brassy manager were staring beatifically into space.

"Sorry," he said. "Not feeling so great."

"No worries," she said. "Is your face all right?"

"I'd rather not talk about it."

"Cor," she said, and batted her eyes. "You know, I wasn't expecting such a polite young man. Marta said you were some rough crack."

"I'm the exception," Adam said. "The rest of them have a real appetite for self-destruction."

"Tough tough boys," Bridges said, smoking. "That's what Marta said. A regular wrecking crew. Kept talking about some lad whose hands are terribly fucked up. Bandages covering them?"

"Bobby," Adam said. "He has terrible eczema. We call him the Mummy."

"Ugh!" Deena laughed. "A perfect segue for tea!"

Deena told him she'd been on Warners for close to a year. The label's strategy was to release an acoustic disc and send her off with Bridges for three months of low-overhead, getting-to-know-you touring, playing in small clubs and cashing in on her ragamuffin looks and angel eyes. Then she'd make a record with a band and they'd give her the full push.

"I was a model," she said, "but music is everything to me. Let me play you something?"

Adam nodded. Guileless as he was, he had been doing this long enough to recognize her harmless calculation.

When she started singing, Adam saw the angle, half Sarah McLachlan and half P. J. Harvey, sweet but edgy, a little bit will-o'-the-wisp, but mostly Ophelia starting to burn up, burn up beautifully.

"Kiss me down your lips," she sang in midtempo. "Fuel me with your fire. Harbor your tall ship. Moor me on desire."

Jagged chords. An angry firefly.

"Burn down the reef," she chorused. "I am with you still. Scorch the port, damn the launch, I am the oil spilled."

Bridges, her number-one fan, watched with adoration, continuing to lean sensuously against the wall in his black suit, smoke curling up from his meaty, long-fingered hands adorned with thick rings, Liberace meets the Krays. Deena bore down on the guitar, cradled the Martin as if it were her mortally wounded child.

Adam had seen plenty of girls like this in Los Angeles, at open mike nights and Tuesday evening chump slots, opening for other bands without a draw, but who was he to judge? She was the one with the fresh Warners contract, at the very start, setting sail, the Royal Deena Britannia. And so he clapped and smiled, glad to be a guest on this sparkling new vessel.

"Nice work, love," Bridges said.

"Cheers," she said, and handed the guitar to Adam. "Now you play something."

A good guitar had a certain amazing weight distribution; the Martin practically floated in his hands. He bowed his head and played a section from Bach's *Well-Tempered Clavier*. He wouldn't have played such an intricate, showy number, but he wanted to impress them, so he played with more than a little mastery. He played as if Segovia had reached across the spectral divide and taken hold of his rock-and-roll fingers. He could do that.

Steam blew through the radiators with the clang of pipes. Valves opened and closed, putting a rhythm to his playing.

This piece was one of his favorites. Growing up, Adam would play it over and over again on the cheap Ovation he'd bought at Bakersfield Pawn, while his brothers stood outside, revving engines. "Hey, Hendrix!" they'd yell. "Why don't you come down here and show us your latest tricks? Play your guitar behind your back and shit." They laughed from the lawn, revving the new V-8 they'd put in an old Corvair. They were illustrated men, bear-arm muscles rippling under the ink, sinews storming up through portraits of samurai warriors and iron crosses. "Show us your moves, pretty boy!"

He threw in jazzy notes and power-chord riffage on a theme. He juggled phrases in the air like swords on fire, catching them without a care. He turned Bach's melodies into an expression of endless life. When he finished, sweat ran down his face, stung his cuts. The two strangers clapped and exhaled.

"Brilliant," Deena said. "Fantastic!"

Bridges had upped himself off the wall. "Fuckin' A," the manager said. "Bloody amazing."

Adam looked out the window at Amsterdam descending into night. But his sight flickered for a moment, and he watched his brothers stare at him from atop their Corvair, framed in the fading California sun. Light ran down their faces in a tearlike translucence.

"Hey, man," Bridges said. "How come you never do that in Blood Orphans?"

Adam wiped down the guitar with the sheet. "Darlo would never allow it."

"He's the manager?" Bridges asked.

"The drummer. The dictator."

Bridges scrunched up his face. "That's a lot of shit, man," he replied without raising his voice. "Any band you're in that you can't do that, you shouldn't be in."

Deena took the guitar from Adam and held it as if Adam had brought her child back from the dead.

"I just can't believe," Bridges said, "that a brilliant guitar player like you is stuck playing that stock trash."

Adam agreed, even though he'd written said stock trash. "Sometimes I can't believe it either."

"Sometimes? No, man, you must be walking around in a grand state of bloody world-class denial. You can play like fucking Clapton and you're in Blood Orphans? From your band's bad rep, I would have thought the last thing I'd find would be a bloke who could play a fucking Bach fugue as if he wrote it yesterday during sound check." He looked at Deena. "We should take Adam to dinner."

"Cor," she said.

"I can't," Adam said. "I have to go to dinner with the band. Our manager's in town."

"Who's your manager?" Bridges said, lighting a Players.

"Joey Fredericks. DreamDare Management. Bottle blonde with a gimp leg. Heard of her?"

Bridges waved his cigarette and tightened his smiling face. "No," he said, his voice louder, on pitch. "But you tell her that John Bridges heard you play today. You tell her that John Bridges from Avatar Management, who has fifteen artists on five major labels and a most excellent licensing portfolio, who makes stars out of mere glistening grains of sand—you tell her that she should be ashamed of herself for not letting you do what you do because the drummer's got a small cock."

"Here he goes," Deena said, smiling.

Bridges blew smoke in the air and laughed. They lived in a world of calm and light.

"Yeah, you tell her that," Bridges said, shaking his head. "And tell her I'll see her tonight to shake her skirt. Jesus fucking Christ. Bloody joke-metal prison. Rattle your bars, Adam. Rattle your bars!"

5

WHEN JOEY OFFERED UP some pay-to-cum, Darlo almost declined. He almost grabbed her by that dirty platinum scruff, the short wire-hairs at the back of her slight neck, and made his move. He knew damn well that whatever was between them had grown, just as he had. But he didn't grab her. He didn't say no to her wad of euros. Because she understood him. She knew him inside out and had considered the obvious nature of his heart and crotch. Appreciation was as rare an emotion for Darlo as doubt, but through his body the two feelings crashed and coursed. Back in LA, he would make things right with her. They would even go on a real date, with flowers and candy; he'd go down on her before dinner, whatever she wanted. But for now she knew that he needed her surrogate.

After he got the lead out, he would get back to logistics and plans, call Jesse and get an update, call McFadden and give him some hard truth about his dad, and then he really ought to call the cops. Right? He wavered on the notion of being such a full-on Judas.

"I'm not him," he said. "Fuck him."

But now he would show that little black-haired Winona-frau. He would present her with the Cox magic, the mad Darlo science, ride her hard and leave her wet and begging for more. He had the euros and could get whatever he wanted. Northern Euro girls, with their tight glottal moans, like they were choking on the smallest little bit of pride. He'd make her his little black-haired autobahn and take her curves real tight.

Without warning or provocation, he thought of Shane standing on some nameless stage, stuck in a ridiculous pose of rock god, trying to be Robert Plant and Perry Farrell, skinny chest out and stupid short white dreads sprouting from his head like eyes on a potato.

Why did his mind have to fucking go and ruin the moment?

There she was. In the pink window. He marched over.

"See you later," he told Joey, who was standing in the street uncapping that flask of awful apple ripple she loved. "Thanks, babe."

The girl in the window recognized him immediately and began shaking her head. He flashed his money and yelled out his contrition for all to see. The remnants of the loogie that he'd spit earlier were still congealed on the glass. She waved her finger, like, Not a chance. He waved the bills in the air furiously.

"Look, please, come on, how can you say no to this. Look!"

She spent a few moments thinking it over, then spoke through the glass. "Hold on, please," she said, and disappeared through her black curtain.

Oh fuck, was he going to give it to her. The longer she held him back, the harder she was going to make it for herself. Shane's pasty chest continued to block pleasing images from his mind's eye. That fucking poser pussy. When he saw the singer later, he would lay down ultimata. Get rid of those ridiculous dreads or you're fired. Not another mention of Buddhist Tantric Zen chickenshit or you can find another band on a major fucking label.

He turned and looked back for Joey, but she was gone.

"Huh," he said as the girl opened the door. He bore his gaze into hers and put the cash in her hand. "I wasn't kidding. There it is. So I can do whatever I want with you now."

"American boy," she said, looking at the money, "you'll do what I tell you that you can do. Understand?"

Some spit almost fell from his mouth as he took in her milky breasts, soft, rolling hills in the northern dells of green-fielded, thatched-roof Holland.

"Because that's how it's done here," she said. "Or we don't play. You act nice. No second chances."

"You got it, baby," he said, closing the door. "Fucking sweet."

She walked behind the curtain. The room smelled of cedar. Darlo's stomach grumbled. A strobe light came on and he felt alone, back in the canyon, stepping on sharp sticks, crying out for that girl.

"All right," he said. "Don't keep me waiting, baby."

She came out with a can of Coke. She smiled and cracked it open. "I love this stuff," she said, took a gulp, set it down next to the bed. "Now take off your clothes, boy."

"It's Darlo."

"What kind of name is that?"

"A stud's name."

She laughed, but not with him, and said something in Dutch. Darlo's feet felt numb. "Take your clothes off, Darlo."

"You first. I'm paying."

She smiled and swept off her top, revealing small, rounded breasts and a thin silver chain hanging from her belly button. She sat on the bed, spread her legs, and rubbed herself.

"Your turn," she said, speaking in monotone. "Show me that big American muscle."

He took off his jacket and his T-shirt, showing the skinny, broad-shouldered, bare-chested figure that had always served him so well. A little bit of belly sat there, like a badly thought-out addition to a mansion. Then he dropped his pants. A minute before, his cock had raged against the inside of his leathers, harder than water from a copper mine. Now he was soft as a piece of Play-Doh.

"What the fuck?" he said, pink walls closing in. "Wait a second."

She rubbed at her pussy some more. Darlo tried to concentrate.

"What's wrong?" she asked. "Stressed out about something?"

"No, I just..." He stared at his cock like they'd never met. "Just wait a minute."

The strobe light powered over them. Some saxophone-ridden smoky jazz came out of the stereo.

She moved to the floor and crawled toward him, coming alive a little. "I can help, boy," she said, and stuck out her tongue. "I can bring you my soft, sweet little mouth." She stopped every few moments to bring her hand against her crotch, reaching in, bowing her head down. "So soft and wet. Wet," she whispered, and her voice blended into the music. When the strobe hit her face, sweat appeared on her alabaster cheeks.

"Wet, boy. Stroke your cock, baby."

He touched it and felt nothing. Her belly-button chain dangled.

"My mouth is soft and wet," she said. "Stroke."

She was almost below him, but Darlo wasn't getting any harder. He was still thinking about that girl hiding in the canyon woods, blood running down her legs, the bramble cutting her up as she crouched, hid from the Cox Leatherman. Hid from Darlo's cries of help.

She looked at me, Darlo thought, and saw him. She saw me through the brush and thought, It's a trick. They'll kill me.

"Baby, come on," Ms. Pink said. "I'm getting closer, baby. Stroke that cock, big boy."

The police would ransack the house, but they wouldn't know the combination on the door to the dungeon. His dad wouldn't tell them the combination and McFadden wouldn't make him, so they wouldn't find them in time. When they broke through, they would find bones and flesh. He would be the inheritor of all this death and suffering. Uncovering the Cox family plot, they would find rot and worms. He would be connected to this forever. How could he save them?

"Here is my mouth, baby," she said, and her breath was on his crotch. She looked up at him with complete commitment. "Give me that cock."

Staring down her throat was like staring down the stairs of his father's snuff cave. Into the dark. Flickers of tonsils. Mouths without bodies. Mouths ripped apart. He was connected to this. He had installed the door. He had screwed in the bolt.

"Give it to me," she said.

Deep in the dark of her mouth, girls tied up, hidden. Deep in the dark of her mouth, rotting bodies, sorrow and hurt. And him.

"Give it to me," she said, the strobe over her mouth as if she were a pole dancer at the Peppermint Castle. "All the way down, baby. All the way down there."

"No," he said, and moved away. "No, shit, no."

Somewhere down there. All of them. Bodies in pieces. Connected to him forever. He was soft. Her face was wet.

"What's wrong?" she said. "Are you all right?"

He fell to the floor. He crumpled up.

6

AN HOUR AFTER MEETING Deena Freeze, Adam sat in the office of Fritz Mallgroom, from whom Blood Orphans rented all their equipment. He'd come from Morten's with two guitars, a Les Paul and a Telecaster, that belonged to Fritz, in the hope that he could quickly drop them off and head to the bar of the Krasnapolsky. Adam thought it would be nice to have a drink on Joey's tab before dinner. Fuck Joey, right? Everybody else says fuck Joey, so to speak, so why can't I?

But nothing happened fast with stony Fritz, who was taking care of a band of skinny-tied emo fops named Praise Chorus. They were arguing with each other over the size of their amps, and Fritz refused to weigh in.

"Internal affairs," he said. "Utterly, man."

His office, at the end of the equipment catacombs, was overrun with instruments. Here, collecting dust and half covered with papers and exotic stringed instruments, were Hammond B-3s, Wurlitzers, a mellotron. On top of an Ashdown amp, two lutes balanced with a bag of apples. Fritz ate apples constantly so he wouldn't smoke. Through the doorway, Praise Chorus argued on and on while Fritz, in his leonine shag, Golden Delicious in hand, sat serenely on a Marshall cab.

"That Marshall Fritz is sitting on is too big, dude!"

"Well, it's the only thing that can counter your Vox!"

"We just can't fit it in the van unless James gets a smaller set of drums."

"Fuck that, dude. Why am I always the one who has to sacrifice?"

The first time Blood Orphans rented from Fritz, they spent all afternoon pulling this prima donna shit. Fritz's slow, contemplative ways had driven Darlo insane; every time the drummer raised his voice, Fritz shushed him. "Quiet," he said, as if a giant slept next door. "Must keep it quiet, man."

"But why can't I have that old Gretsch?" Darlo said, pointing at a burnished gold set on the shelf that looked good as new. "You have to give me a reason."

"Too much noise," Fritz said, and bit into the crunchiest apple ever. "So loud somewhere. Can you hear it?"

The others loved watching Fritz gibberish Darlo into submission.

Fritz was a Christian man, which endeared Shane to him. Upon his desk lay a rosary wrapped around an old silver clock. Next to that was a portrait of his two hot blond daughters dressed as Santa's elves on a ski slope, their feet bound up in Rossignols. Next to that was a signed portrait of Jimmy Page.

Adam went into the bathroom, hidden behind keyboard cases. He washed his face and looked in the mirror. A large scratch, as if from a dog, bisected his left cheek. His right eye had puffed and was almost black. Caked blood nested under a few fingernails.

He remembered the feel of hard ground and the huge weight on his arms when the Nazi pinned him. The boy had had nostrils that flared up like a bull's. Adam wondered what had happened earlier to his attackers during the day, but figured that humanizing the assaulters would only lead down his default road of feeling bad for those who had fucked him.

When he emerged from the bathroom, Praise Chorus were loading their stuff into the freight elevator and Fritz was sitting cross-legged on a Marshall cabinet in his vest—brocade and silk, Fritz's Amazing Technicolor Dreamcoat—eating another apple, silver cross hovering above his New Age Christian bling.

One of the kids came back and practically begged Fritz for the lime-green Danelectro hanging with the other very fine guitars, between a gold-top Les Paul and a brown Gretsch Country Gentleman.

"Next time," Fritz said. "Next time when you've brought everything else back. Can't just lend out any old thing, no?"

The kid looked about fifteen, but he had a fire in his eyes. "I'll have our manager wire collateral," the boy said. "Please."

Fritz crossed his legs tighter and chomped the apple. "You must earn trust from a man, you know. Trust is like a glue that creates calm between men. That is the only way."

The kid nodded, confused, and retreated into the elevator. The back of his leather jacket had a cross on it, with the words *Solidarity and Faith* in florid lettering rainbowed over the top.

Fritz uncurled from the amp. The guy could shrink and expand at will, like a real superhero. His kingly mane was suspended above his head like a crown.

"Ah, Adam," he said. "Finally the little kiddies are gone."

"I'm not much older than them," the guitar player said.

"Ah, but you are." He lit a clove cigarette, sickly sweet. The smell of a million Goth dreams floated up to the vaulted ceiling. "They are just on their first time out, I think. You have braved the wilds. You are a logger of miles in the van. Age is immaterial, man, not a measurement of anything." He plunked down in his leather chair and touched the picture of his daughters skiing as if lighting a devotional candle. "So, what of Blood Orphans? How is Shane?"

"Tired. We're all tired. Shane is into Buddhism now. I don't know. We don't really get along."

"Shane is a seeker."

"That's what he says."

"I am quoting him," Fritz said, and smiled. "He cornered me by the bass amplifiers and asked me about my journey. He is a seeker, though, that is true. I am not sure what he will find. He is a ragtag boy of many colors."

Adam had no idea what that meant, but it sounded nice. The man's voice was a lullaby.

"And what of Darlo, sad Darlo? When will he come back with half of what he borrowed?" He crunched his apple. "When do you think his reckoning will come?"

"Probably never. Nothing bad could happen to him."

"Don't believe it," Fritz said. "Not...a word. For so much bad has already happened. Listen. He is telling you."

Fritz motioned to a stack of CDs on his desk, and there, in between Pavement and Evanescence, lay *Rocket Heart*. Adam put it in the boom box.

"Darlo is not the boy-king that you perceive," he said. "He is the one confounded in pain. Wrapped up in a stasis of suffering."

Rocket Heart's lead-off track, "Beretta-Couda," began, with a stomping rhythm not unlike half of the AC/DC catalogue. It was the second song Darlo and Adam had written in the basement rec room of the Cox mansion, sitting on the pool table and drinking Buds. The thousand-dollar-a-day sound of Paradise exploded through the tinny old Sony speakers.

She's got a love-stunner gun-tail move like a shark.
I love her and I hate her but she keeps me in the dark.
I swim along her reef to try to find the hidden treasure,
But my bones break on her rocks. When will I get her
    secret pleasure?

Insert roaring guitar solo to punctuate said waterbound frustration. Insert Adam, finding his way through Darlo's inability to put his sexual frustration to words, trying to perform a solo that approximated the metaphor of woman-as-ocean, vast tidebound taunting.

"Darlo loves that song," Adam said over the din. "He says it's the closest he's ever come to putting his sex addiction down on paper."

Fritz crunched his apple and bobbed his head along, shaking blond hair loose, and unveiled a red bong from behind some keyboards. At the base, in some kind of tropical font, were the words *Happy Notions.*

"The funny thing is," Adam said, "he can't swim."

"That *is* funny," Fritz said. "The ironies of this turning world. God and all of his follies. All of the many ways, man, the countless ways He shows that we are silly and after a fashion of the times. Our laments. The messes that show His glory in contrast."

"Beretta-Couda" finished and "Double Mocha Lattay" began.

Fritz climbed up on a Marshall four-by-twelve and crossed his legs. "All of these songs, man," he said. "Darlo and his unconquerable women, Darlo and his elusive feminines, the anger, the torment." He chewed the apple. "Such sadness in the boy. Can you hear it?"

Adam imagined Darlo as a little kid, sitting in some palatial room while the whole house moaned orgasmically around him. But he couldn't imagine Darlo as a little kid. Instead he saw the adult Darlo, in giant OshKosh overalls, sucking his thumb, rocking back and forth.

"Now it is all over," Fritz said. "Blood Orphans goes kaput. What will happen when little Darlo has to open that door and march downstairs?"

Fritz turned off the boom box and tapped at the cross on his neck. Behind him, Amsterdam's lights twinkled. "What about Shane? He's a Buddhist now, you say?"

"Ever since some girl he had sex with gave him a copy of *Siddhartha*."

"The seeker," he said. "He told me he was a seeker. And good for you, I told him. But work on your attitude." His voice got a little rough. "Arrogance is the fastest way to slow down the quest."

Adam found Fritz's interest in Shane's well-being to be unjustified and aggravating. Truth be told, he had always thought that Shane was the band lightweight. Bobby couldn't really play, but Shane wasn't really very smart. If Darlo hadn't come along, he'd still be playing in The Dragon Slayed, trying to turn psalms into lyrics. And those lectures he gave from the stage were just disgusting. Often Adam would get some serious feedback going, in the hope of drowning the lectures out. Darlo cheered him on; it was the only time he felt like he and the drummer were communicating at all.

"Let's give the seeker a call," Fritz said. "I want to talk to him."

7

SHANE STUMBLED BACK toward Joey's room. Had he ever felt so low? Certainly when his father expressed displeasure at Blood Orphans, Shane had felt as if he had deeply betrayed his morality...No he hadn't. He hadn't cared what his father had thought, that pious engineer with his fireside family bullshit. Who needed a fireplace in Orange County? The man lived inside a Royal Doulton miniature world, where everything was tidy and bodies were really made of gingerbread and bathrooms didn't have toilets and crotches were smooth. A fucking fireplace in Orange County, where it never got cold enough to put on a cotton sweater.

The muscles in his calves quivered a little. Two maids walked by, providing faint dirty looks. He could not bear to be a beggar just now, and kept his head down until they walked away. His phone rang.

Fritz?

"I am calling to check on my Christian brother," said the renter of musical goods. "Adam says you are struggling with questions of theology."

"Yes," he said, dumbstruck by the timing, wondering if it was more than mere accident, if perhaps this was a prelude to a vision. Accidents had to be visions now. Accidents were all he had.

"Adam is sitting here," Fritz said, "telling me of the end of days."

"It's true. We're fucked."

"Have faith," Fritz said, and crunched an apple in Shane's ear.

"In every end is a beginning. Like when I stopped drinking, man. Like when I stopped whoring."

"I have been whoring," Shane said. "I have been cruel. What can I do, Fritz?"

"Be kind."

The face of Fritz appeared to him from the ceiling. Fritz with his mole on his chin, his gaggle of crow's-feet, his slowly browning teeth. Fritz peering down at him as he squatted against the wall, shielding his eyes a little from the man's spectral light. The overseer of the rock-and-roll junkyard, outfitter of almost-rans and pretend-to-bes. Adam hovered somewhere in that awesome haze, somewhere beneath, between, behind Fritz's magic countenance, and Shane had to give the guitar player credit for that.

"I tried everything," the singer said. "I tried all the routes and nothing worked. We're no good. Our songs suck. We suck. I suck."

"Hey, man, listen," Fritz said. "You have to keep your eyes on the road, you know. It is the journey, not the destination."

"No, Fritz, I have to tell you, actually it *is* the destination."

Fritz laughed up in the ceiling. His holy maw dissolved Shane's resistance. Celestial smoke billowed from his ears. "The engineer's son," he said. "The stubborn boy."

"I have no right to complain," Shane said. "But I've fallen from God's grace faster than Lucifer himself. You know what I mean? Hello?"

His sweaty fingers had slipped and hung up on Fritz. He looked at the ceiling; no holy vision up there. Frantically he punched in Fritz's number, but it wasn't Fritz on the other end.

"Shane?" Adam said. "Fritz will be right back. He went to talk to this other band that just showed up. Are you OK?"

Now would be a perfect time to be thankful, to turn a corner on Adam and his precious, touchy-feely bullshit. But that voice was so fucking soft.

Wandering in the forest, did the Buddha, in his most sacred moments, ever experience this disjunction? Was there a scene like that in the book? He really should have read the last thirty pages. But a seeker didn't need to depend on words. A seeker was able to distill the—

"Shane?" Adam said.

"I have another call," Shane said, and switched over to the blinking Dutch digits. "Danika, what do you want?"

"Blondie boy," she said. "I am walking in the street and thinking of you."

The smell of her voodoo butter rolled up his nose.

"Thought about you all day in school," she purred. "Thought about you so much I had to take a special little break with my pocket rocket."

"Look, I'm a little busy right now, Danika."

"So moody." She giggled. He got a hard-on, which flailed in his pants like a broken weather vane.

"See you tonight?" she asked. "Guest list?"

All the girls he had known, and what good had they done him? All the twisting and turning and sweating and spewing and Tantric waiting and fast against the wall heaving and moaning and swearing and occasionally bleeding and sometimes begging, all the time looking for God this and God that. And to what spiritual profit?

Collages of wretched pleasure contorted and spun around him. He crawled across the hall. He crawled without destination, lost in the wilderness.

8

JOEY WENT MARCHING down the street, dry-popped a few Tylenols, hoped that analgesics and shit-grade alcohol didn't totally knock her out. The falling snow, which a moment ago had been freezing rain, refined her general sense of renewal and mission. She took out the slip of paper Hackney had given her with the name of his hotel on it.

"Near here," she said. "Right on."

Managers did everything for their band. Sometimes you just had to whore yourself out. She had always wanted to fuck Hackney, but now she had utility and purpose to underwrite her lust. There had to be some way around Warners' dropping them, at least here in Europe. Euros liked cheesy stuff; they liked what American companies told them to like. All it would take was for Warners to show a little marketing muscle. All it would take was for her to ride Hackney hard enough for him to forget everything he had previously thought about them, so he'd line up with her plan and start parroting the new gospel.

"That's right," she said. "Here I come, Clive fucking Owen."

Applejack never tasted so good. She gulped it down. Her phone rang. "Adam?"

"Hey, Joey. I'm outside of Fritz's. He says you owe him a whole bunch of money."

"So now you're his errand boy?"

"Looks that way."

Joey didn't like this at all. Adam sounded happy and carefree, not like he'd just had the shit kicked out of him.

"Tell Fritz to go eat a bag of apples," she said. "Is that it?"

"Sure. Uh, actually," Adam continued, all jaunty-like, "I was wondering what time you wanted us at the hotel for dinner."

"Six. How's your face?"

"Puffed up but OK. Hey, I met the people who're staying at Morten's after us. A singer-songwriter named Deena Freeze and her manager. She just got signed to Warners and she's opening for us tonight."

Joey's stomach rolled a little. "Oh yeah?" she said, faking nonchalance. "Had they heard of us?"

Hesitation on the line said it all. In that millisecond of hesitation lay the difference between hitting the ball out of the park and striking out. "Yeah, they had."

"And what did they say?"

Another second of hesitation, a dagger in her heart.

"They said that they liked us. I played them a Bach fugue."

"On the guitar."

"No, on the stereo. Yes, on the guitar."

"Why?"

"I don't know. So they'd take us seriously."

The word *traitor* rushed up in her throat like a surging crowd at Riverfront Stadium, ready to trample all her remaining hope. Take *us* seriously. Oh, please. This is the thanks I get—I help stop two thugs from eating your velvet-covered ass and you go and audition for some Euro Tori Amos ripoff. Little sneaky fuck.

Blood Orphans without Adam. *Great.*

"Dinner," she said. "Don't be late for it."

Adam was saying something plaintive, but Joey hung up.

"You suck, Nickerson," she said. "How could you do that to me?"

Truth be told, when they all got back to LA, she planned on getting Adam into Natalia's Edge, one of her new bands, but she still wanted all her options open. Just her luck to have Adam find a little confidence. Though better late than early; if he had any sense of his power as a shredder, Blood Orphans would never have happened. He'd be in a band called Adam Orphans, full of songs centered around long, silly, pyro guitar solos. He'd be the twenty-first-century Robert Fripp, and Darlo would still be hanging out at Spaceland, trying to get in her pants. Shane would still be in New Testament Express, or whatever the fuck his Christian Nation band was called. And Bobby would be scratching his hands in his apartment, watching Guy Ritchie films and feeling sorry for himself.

Adam. The prime mover. Who knew?

She neared the Grand Amsterdam, which resembled an in-city manor for kings and queens wedged between two canals off Dam Square. Hackney had done quite well for himself. She'd make him understand how much Blood Orphans meant to her. She'd get him down with the concept.

She dialed his number.

"Joey," he said, sounding smooth and sleepy. "Hello, love."

"I'm walking into the lobby of your baronial mansion," she said. "We need to talk. We need some privacy. Know what I'm saying, babe?"

He just laughed.

"Cur," she said, and felt a little dizzy.

Joey had once had a boyfriend, a musician of no talent but fine Sid Vicious–type looks, who liked the old trick-and-hooker role-play. She'd don her grandmother's above-the-knee rabbit coat, gold stiletto heels, and not much else, plaster her face in rust-colored glitter and flesh-colored lipstick, and take a walk over to the Renaissance Hollywood. Those stilettos fucked her bum leg up pretty bad, but by the time she made it up the elevator, her hoop earrings swinging and nose ice-cold from the coke, she was soaked all the way through and ready to move on him like a butter churn.

Yes, acting like a ho on occasion really got her slick. So why, in the elevator of the Grand Amsterdam, was she dry as the Gobi? Coming here, she assured herself, was a good idea. She was saving her band, her career, her reputation, by whatever means necessary. She saw herself across the arc of the past few years, a highlight film of decree-making, fast talking, and other heroic business-related acts that required her to wave her arms around and prove significant points. She pepped herself to the task, looking at her distorted cute-as-a-button face in the elevator mirror, lost in the funhouse.

The elevator door opened. She marched on down the hallway of chrome and vanilla carpet, an odd color she had never seen in the States, and banged on the door of room 305.

"Candygram," she said, turning the knob. "Love bunny."

He sat at the foot of the bed, in slacks but shirtless, lit cigarette in mouth. He looked twice as good half naked as fully clothed—just the perfect spot of black chest hair, thick at the sternum and lightly spreading toward his nipples. Broad chest. Washboard abs.

"Damn," she said. "Aren't you a sight."

"As are you. What a surprise."

She put hands on hips in a bratty pose, pulling up the skirt a little so the hem lay halfway between knee and crotch.

"Wondered all day what you and me were all about," she said, though she had no idea what that meant. "Wondered how maybe we could"—she unzipped her skirt—"get along a little better. I just don't think that we..." She blinked, wondered what to say that could come across as witty. "...understand each other."

Hackney snickered and stood up.

"We understand each other just fine," he said, and went to her.

Across the room he came. Hackney took her in, a smile growing on his face, and Joey thought about how many times this scene had been presented to him: a young woman, in nicer clothes than she could afford, offering up her body. She wondered if anything she did to, for, or with this man would be different from what the other pieces of ass that had come to one of his hundreds of five-star hotel rooms had done. She wondered where that sense of righteous mission had gone. She wondered what the hell she was doing here, and why she felt as if, for the first time in her life, she was being unfaithful.

The manager put her hands up. "No," she said. "No."

Hackney stuck out his lower lip. "No what?"

"Fucking you…This, this stupid…"

Hackney smiled, put his hand on her shoulder, and kissed her. For a moment she saw it all, was on top of him, riding that rock-hard Midlands steed. She kept her tongue in his mouth long enough to get wet, but when she didn't, her suspicions were confirmed, and she pushed him off.

"Seriously," she said. "I'm sorry. Your mouth is a wonderland and I'm sure your body is too, but—"

"Joey," he said, nodding in sympathy. "Fine, love."

"And my leg is fucking killing me. Can I sit down?"

Hackney cleared a chair of some clothes and walked back to his bed. The dim lighting in here, Joey thought, really worked. All the elements—the color of the walls, the placing of the lamps, the type of bulbs—brought out the bronze in a person's skin, the smoothness, the health.

"Do you want some water?" he asked, and put on a white undershirt.

Joey still wanted to fuck him. She also most definitely did not want to fuck him. Phantoms of ambiguity made plays for her soul. She felt sick from not knowing what to do, here in this stranger's room, late in the afternoon.

She lit a cigarette and took out her flask of Applejack. "All day I've been mulling it over in my head. But I'm here because I just don't get it."

He sat back in his chair. Black hair fell forward, covered one of his eyes. He brushed it back. "Get what?"

"Why we're being dropped."

"Joey," he said, in a *you're drunk* kind of voice. "Come on, love."

She kicked off her shoes and massaged her feet, which had gone numb. Fashion over comfort was a raw deal. "You should come to dinner and tell them," she said, waving the flask near her lips. "Break their dreams down."

"Joey, please, stop with this."

She took another slug. Bitter apple syrup coated her throat. "What about that tour with the Killers? Like, two months ago you promised us that. Like, two months ago you promised one more shot. People don't even remember the racism bit anymore. People have half-lives for memories."

"We've been through this."

"Let me tell them it might happen."

"It won't."

"Why not?"

Hackney's expression hardened. "Shall I spell it out? Do you know that I can't even mention you guys to my boss? It's the fastest way to put him in a fit."

"How's that my fault?"

"Enough," he said, and began to put on a shirt. Suddenly Hackney was her dad, and she was on the losing end of trying to get him to change his mind about her curfew.

"Look," she said, and watched, through the squeaky-clean window, as snow came down in Disneyland drifts, as if she were back in Pasadena and riding the new kiddie ride called Amsterdam Snowglobe. "It's a terrible thing, telling your friends that you have failed them. It really is, John. And I have failed them, man. It was my idea. My concept. My vision. I got all of them on board for it, and you could say that the stakes weren't high, you could say that who cares, they're just dopy kids who aren't giving up a thing to do this, but now I have to say, Sorry, I have failed you, it was a bad concept, it was a ruse, it was a bill of goods, it was shit, utter shit. Please don't make me do this. Please don't, John."

Tears came down her face, mixing with her makeup, rolling together like lovers between the sheets. "Are you listening, babe? Because I'm begging you."

She sobbed. Her leg ached.

"One more chance," she said, and looked deep in his eyes. "Please?"

But his eyes weren't registering. Whatever she had done here on this fucking fool's errand, whatever slutty heroics she was peddling, had failed. She could tell that he was neither angry nor disgusted. He was just bored, and in that boredom, Hackney had severed the last line between Blood Orphans and the record biz. Untethered, the entire gambit floated off into history.

"I wish you well, Joey," he said, reasonable and calm, smoothing his tie. "I really do. But you have to go."

Riding the elevator, she stared into the distorting mirrors and tried not to give herself a hard time about her pathetic attempt at a power play. An American family, decked out for a big night on the town, got in on the third floor. The parents couldn't have been much older than her. Their two blond children were adorable. "How are you?" she asked the tykes, but the parents looked at her like she was covered in come.

Outside, she lit a cigarette and fought back some tears. Disneyland snow powdered her hay-hair. Her phone began to ring. Darlo on the line. The fucking reason for all this confusion. She had done it for him, and then not done it for him. Her leg ached.

She held her satellite phone out into the snow, her thousand-dollar-a-month flotation device in the sea of the hustle. Always another portal to the possible. Always another angle to be played. But it had always been a prop anyway, always a practice pad. Even the day they had signed their contract. There had always been real people to take care of the real business. Even that lawyer-freak McFadden looked like Richard Branson in comparison. She had been allowed the amusement of her own fantasy, but she was just part of the brand. She was just a serif in the signage.

And now he wanted to find out why she had ditched him. Post-prostitute, he wanted to know just where the fuck she was.

"Eat me," she said, and smashed the phone into the cobble-stone street. It made a mad pop. Pieces shot in every direction.

9

WHEN BOBBY WALKED INTO JOEY'S ROOM and found Shane passed out on the bed, he thought the singer was dead.

"How exciting!" he said, peering closer.

Splayed out on his back, Shane really did look dead, body twisted like it had been dropped from four stories up, tongue out of his mouth, head pushed upward.

Shane groaned and stretched, releasing a cloud of stink, but Bobby knelt close, studying his rival, who looked like he had aged a year in one day. Wrinkles snaked out from Shane's eyes, and his ears were swelled up, like they'd been cuffed. Look at this, Bobby thought, at the very end of the road, look at how far the little self-righteous Christian rocker has fallen. Look at how he wears all his countercultural accouterments like they're a fucking funeral suit. Look at those dreads, gnarly things, with those stupid beads in them like decorations on the most rotted of Christmas trees.

"What the fuck happened to you?" Bobby said, grabbing an open bottle of Jim Beam off the nightstand and pouring himself a glass.

"Everything," Shane said, and turned away.

The bathroom floor was piled high with Dutch towels and dirty American clothes. *Joey is a pussy* had been scrawled in lipstick on the side of the mirror. Bobby washed his hands, took out his Tiger Balm, and applied a new set of bandages. His hands felt pretty all right, actually, and he reckoned that that had to do with the mass reduction of tension in his body, courtesy of

Sarah—pointy-nosed, brown hair dusting her underarms, and shivering when she came—grinding in a magic rut on top of him.

Also, she had bitten his shoulder hard enough to leave marks.

"Shine on, you crazy diamond," he'd said, and kissed her hands.

Shane's jewelry lay on the sink—a cross, a tiny brass Buddha, and a silver steer head with ivory horns, given to him by a young girl in Austin.

Bobby lowered his fist onto the necklace, but it didn't budge. His hand split open in numerous places. "Damn," he said, examining the damage, quickly reapplying the balm and bandages Dr. Guttfriend had provided. Then he shoved the steer necklace into his pocket.

"Are you still here?" Shane yelled.

Bobby peeked his head out. Shane sat up. They greeted each other with the silence of inmates. The singer's dreads were puffed up on one side and flat on the other, as if he'd been ironed.

"You look like shit," Bobby said.

"Nice hands," Shane replied.

Bobby felt the stolen amulet through the denim. "What time is dinner?"

"Like an hour." Shane rubbed his face, then touched his ears.

Bobby opened the wet bar, removed a bottle of twist-off red wine, and took a few quick quaffs. Then he sat on the bed and grabbed the remote.

"Dinner's gonna be fun," he said. "Joey'll have all kinds of good news, I'm sure, present her laundry list of all the ways we've fucked up, show off her new Prada suede bag and Gucci shoes."

"I wish she'd stayed in LA," Shane said. "What the fuck good does her being here do?"

"Makes her feel better," Bobby said. "She can pretend she's still a manager. She can think she still has a purpose on this planet."

Propped up on pillows, they sat on the bed and watched VH1 Europe, the end of an hour-long celebration of Kylie Minogue. Then came a news story about Aerosmith's new record and the first night of their world tour, a three-month affair of football stadiums, with intimate club shows in New York, Los Angeles, and Chicago for members of their fan club. *Intimate* in Aerosmith-speak meant Carnegie Hall, the Henry Fonda, and The Metro. Steven Tyler and Joe Perry's flat faces stretched across the screen.

"We're excited to get back to our roots," Tyler said. All that plastic surgery had given him a goofball Muppet patina. "Playing clubs really reminds all of us why we started doing this in the first place. You get up close and personal with your number-one fans, and that's a gas, man. A gee-ass!"

Bass player and singer sat in their cell, watching the lovely old fleshbags provide the deep rock knowledge.

"We're going to have a great light show on this tour, man," Perry said, brushing his hair out of his eyes. "It's all computerized now. Amazing." He looked at Tyler. "Long way from the Brookline High gymnasium, huh?"

Tyler laughed and brushed hair off his face. Perry flicked something from his eye.

"Man, no kidding, Joe," he said. "No kidding."

They watched new gods come and go: 50 Cent, Black Eyed Peas, Coldplay. That last band was, to Bobby, an especially galling example of midtempo, medium-talented, watery-emotioned light beer.

"It's probably a good thing we got dropped from the Aerosmith tour," Shane said. "Can you imagine being that terrible in front of twenty thousand people?"

"Seppuku," Bobby said. "Suicide."

Shane flipped through channels as Bobby stole glances at the singer, marking the new wrinkles, beginning to see the dull glimmers of someone whose chance has passed him by, the kind of guy whose face shows that he doesn't understand that the fame game is long over and that he lost. Hanging out at Spaceland in the old days, they had watched show after show of loser desperadoes, secure that the hammer of the gods would forever drive their ships to new lands.

If Shane looked a little like that now, Bobby knew he did too.

"Oh man," Shane said. He turned the volume up and wiped dreads from his face like they were seaweed. "You're gonna shit, dude."

On E! Entertainment Television, Darlo's dad was being led out of his house in handcuffs. He wore clothes that marked him in deep porn time—fat polyester collar, gold chain, ambervision aviators—and appeared not the least bit upset, his chest out in defiance.

"No fucking way," Bobby said, and leaned forward.

"Today," the announcer said, "in Beverly Hills, shockwaves through the porn industry. David Cox, owner of Dirty Darling Pictures and a living legend in the world of adult film, was arrested and charged with seven counts of tax evasion and racketeering. But there's more. In a double doozy, Mr. Cox was also arraigned on contributing false testimony in the disappearance of a young woman in 2003."

A picture of a young girl, a head shot, appeared on the screen.

"Daniella Spencer, an adult-film actress who went missing over a year ago, resurfaced yesterday at an Encino police station, claiming that for the past eleven months she'd been a captive of Jeffrey Brown, the owner of Feels Real, makers of high-tech, lifelike plastic dolls."

Cut to a picture of Daniella Spencer, blond and surly, in what looked like a mug shot.

"Looking sickly and exhausted, Miss Spencer went on to

claim that Mr. Brown and several associates, including Mr. Cox, were part of a sex-slave ring, complete with hidden basements and dungeons."

Cut to a shot of Brown's French Normandie mansion. Cut to Brown, a schlump in a tracksuit, smiling at some tropical bar.

"Mr. Brown, who is in a Los Angeles hospital with an undisclosed ailment, could not be reached for comment, but his attorneys deny all charges."

Cut to a man in front of a podium marked LAPD, Vice Division, who looked more or less like Tom Selleck.

"Upon searching Mr. Cox's house, we did find evidence that backed up the assertions of Miss Spencer, very specific assertions that we cannot at this time comment upon."

Then, another picture of David Cox, in a tuxedo, onstage at the AVN Awards, the porn Oscars, hoisting high the bronze. Younger and feather-haired, he looked like any suburban dentist.

"Mr. Cox is, quite simply, a porn legend. The first to comprehend the effect that video, and then digital video, would have on the industry, he made Dirty Darling into the Coca-Cola of hardcore adult entertainment. His knack for understanding how to make money, and to continue to make money, has resulted over the years in some interesting crossover into the mainstream business world as well as the political arena."

Cut to an assembly line, a warehouse in Pasadena piled high with video boxes, DVD boxes, sex toys, lubes, all the spoils.

"Mr. Cox was for many years a consultant to the Cato Institute, and through lobbying efforts to ease regulations in the cable television business forged questionable relationships with a group of congressmen, split evenly across the political spectrum, who in 1999 became known as the Cox Eleven for their now-dissolved association with the porn maven."

Cut to a white-haired fellow in front of a bank of reporters on the floor of some sanctified marble hall on Capitol Hill, identified as Representative Peter McDonough, Democrat of California, ranking minority member of the House Ways and Means Committee.

"My relationship with Mr. Cox was perfectly appropriate. Like all citizens in this country, even those whose businesses, be they munitions or adult entertainment, some may find distasteful, he is perfectly entitled under the First Amendment to advocate his interests."

Cut to Cox with his arm around Bruce Willis. Then another one, on safari with Burt Reynolds. Then another one, arm wrestling with Hulk Hogan. Then another one, jamming with Motley Crüe.

"A colorful, tall, strapping man, Cox has long served as the modern-day Hugh Hefner, sans the grotto and the toupee. He is known for his love of firearms and his stable of Rhodesian Ridgebacks. His reputation precedes him. But for now, that reputation is shrinking under a hail of allegations, allegations that sent the stock of his parent company, the publicly traded DD Holdings, plummeting."

Cut to Cox in a masculine embrace with Vince Neil, and then a fade.

Bobby flexed his hands and thought, What a great day. First I get my Dutch angel, and now this. And just imagine what that will do, has already done, to Darlo, off somewhere in that twinkle of snowy Dutch city lights. Just imagine how that news will pull the spine right out of him, leave him on the floor, bleeding, confused, without a nucleus. All roads led to Dad, but Dad is closed for business. What would the drummer do without psychic Daddy energy? How would he even breathe under the weight of the news?

"Tax evasion," Bobby said, and got up. "Just like Capone." He searched through the wet bar.

"Grab me a bottle of vodka," Shane said.

Bobby found two minis of Stoli Lemon and chucked one at Shane. His hands tingled. "There you go, champ."

Shane snapped the top off and propped some more pillows. "You think this is serious?"

"Serious as a heart attack," Bobby replied. "Isn't it fucking great?"

"You bet your ass it is." Shane reached over and they clinked bottles.

Bobby sat in the Louis Quatorze chair. They swigged their vodka over the E! network din, which had moved on to Christina Aguilera's latest attempt at going high-class. They lay resplendent in glee at the Cox family's fortunes gone south, of the prince's misfortunes and the king's offenses, falling from divine right to regicide.

10

IN THE CANDY-PINK BROTHEL, Darlo zipped up his pants, all fired up, and it wasn't about pussy. He was going to save the lives of those girls, go down in porn history as the guy who busted up his own father's underground sex-slave trade. Forget about everything else, even his band—what difference did all of that make as long as he popped the sore on the busted ass that was his father's sorry, sadistic life? The cops would get involved. Leading them down the stairs into the dungeon would complete his journey from accomplice to hero. Maybe they'd even give him one of those LAPD Vice Windbreakers as a present for doing so much good so fast.

He put on his shoes. Ms. Pink sat on the bed in her pink negligee. Her lipstick was gone. Her hair was in place. Within leather trousers, his cock hung soft on the left side.

"You really fucking helped," he said. "Seriously. I think I figured out a lot. More than any other time hobbying."

She looked at him, anger clouding her perfect complexion. "Figured shit out, man? What the fuck are you talking about?"

"I'm talking about exposing a fucking sex-slave ring."

She rolled her eyes. "The ones like you are the weird ones, the ones who don't like sex."

"I love sex."

She wiped the corners of her mouth. "No," she said. "The ones like you just want to watch me undress and cry about it, or fucking moan, man, or talk to themselves." She lit up a cigarette. Smoke filled the room like dry ice before Aerosmith enters the building. "Creepy people who pay to be with a beautiful woman and then become crazy. Without the little bit of self-respect to follow through on the promise they make to their bodies. Can't fulfill the contract. Become little crazies instead, crying, whimpering. I hate that."

Signals starting jamming again in Darlo's emotional airspace. The idea of calling the police seemed full of false promises. He felt like he'd done an entire eightball on his own.

"If you had come in my mouth," she said, "I would not have minded. I would not have loved it, but you know, *whatever*. But crying in my mouth?"

"I didn't cry in your mouth."

She grimaced. "Yes you did, boy. You stared down into it real close and started to cry. I felt your tears on my tongue and gums before you fell back into that corner." She wiped at her wet face. "You think this is come? No. Tears." She took a drag and French-inhaled. Her Dutch accent pinned the English down, flattened it out in the molten smithy of dialect. "That's fucking real, man. That's a shared fucking experience. That's gonna stay with us forever, and you should have paid me a thousand fucking euros for that kind of intimacy."

Signals jamming. Tears?

"Now just get out," she said. "Go."

Darlo fought back the creeping numbness, the misery revving somewhere in his heart, popping into first, ready to roll below the horizon.

"I said, go, boy." She adjusted her top. "Now."

He adjusted his Harley belt buckle. Fighting back the numbness.

"Hey," he said. "You like rock and roll?"

She stared right through him.

"'Cause I'm in a rock band. We're playing at the Star Club tonight."

"That's fucking Disneyland, man."

"Just give me a name," he said, sweaty, jumpy. "Just pick a name and I'll put it down. You're really foxy, you know that?"

Still with the cigarette between her lips, she leaned back on the bed. The skin on her shoulders shone. Maybe he had cried on them too.

"What do you say?"

She waved a little. "Goodbye now."

"We're called Blood Orphans."

"So long."

"Blood Orphans," he said, like a sheriff who'd just busted up the ruffians. "See you there."

He would never say it like the rest of them did. He would never be ashamed, like Adam, or aloof, like Shane, or mocking, like Bobby. He would be proud of it until the bitter fucking end, which, if he had anything to do with it, wouldn't be anytime soon.

"Blood Orphans," he repeated.

She shrugged and spit his tears into a tissue.

11

JOEY STOOD IN THE LOBBY of the Krasnapolsky. A half-hour early for dinner, she had gone into the restaurant—a silly atrium full of pallid plants—and waited for the four stooges at their table, but nerves soon dictated that she pace around. And she had that post-bad-sex feeling, which she hadn't known you could have without actually *having* sex. Darlo came through the revolving doors and marched over to her. Joey felt jealous and disgusted.

"Do you have any change?" she asked.

"What happened to you?" he said, not so much indignant as let down. "You ditched me. Where'd you go?"

"Not telling you."

"Fine," he said. "Where's your phone?"

"All over some street somewhere. I smashed it up."

"What do you mean you smashed it up?"

"I decided it was ruining my life."

The drummer looked at her, cocked his head, shook it. Dust billowed out in the bright lobby lighting.

"You used to be a person I could depend on," he said. "You used to be the fucking foresight."

She lit a cigarette. "It's all a mess is all."

"What is?"

"The band, you idiot. You. Me. The whole fucking thing."

Joey saw herself back behind the bar at Spaceland, having to suffer the looks of those making their way through the crowd, who whispered into each other's ears, Dude, that girl is *the* walking joke of Los Angeles rock and roll. She took out her flask of apple ripple, swigged, and offered it to Darlo. Never one to say no, he followed suit.

"I really need that phone," he said, and wiped his mouth. "I need to call LA. I think my dad is hiding some girl in a basement."

"Come again?"

"My dad...babe, you just don't know."

"Try me."

Joey liked the word *dungeon*. It sounded pretty fresh. And a false wall? With, like, a button located behind a fake copy of *The Story of O?* You mean, like a fucking horror movie?

"No, babe, worse, because it's real."

Anything was possible, she knew, when it came to Darlo's dad. But that tone in his voice, that new righteous do-gooder shit, made her laugh.

"Ooo," she said. "Scary."

The drummer didn't have time for Joey's lack of faith and went stomping off. She watched him walk away, admiring his ass. Sure was cute how he was on a new mission. Sure was sweet that he'd discovered morality as it passed by on his emotional conveyor belt. A dungeon? Oh, sure. Shackle me the fuck up. Put my nipples in a twist. She took a breath, sickened by the saccharine, flip nature of her sense of humor, and hobbled over to a couch.

12

DARLO COULDN'T BELIEVE JOEY. What kind of person destroyed her phone just because her leg hurt all the time? Back in LA, on that date he would take her on, they'd get to the bottom of her aimless defeatism. But now he needed a phone. Spying Adam in the lobby, he felt a troika of unfamiliar emotions: loyalty, regret, and contrition.

He marched over, gripped Adam, and stared at the guitar player's blackening eye. Adam gripped him back.

"You're OK?" Darlo asked.

"OK," Adam said. "Good, actually. Thank you."

"No, thank *you*." Darlo felt shivery. The new emotions shook through his body, turning up bedrock. "I wanted to fucking kill them," he said. "I would have killed them with my knife. They would have died a most painful fucking death at the hands of the Magic Wand, and you better fucking believe it."

"I know." Adam smiled to keep El Loco under control. "I hear you."

Darlo gripped his shoulder harder. "OK. Good. Now I just need to find a phone. Joey broke hers. Bitch is crazy."

Adam pulled out a silver Samsung. "Use mine," he said. "It's a quad-band. It gets America."

Darlo felt water well in his eyes. "Bless you," he said, taking the phone. "Dude, I would have killed them."

He would get the LAPD on the horn and start talking. He would spill and spew information. But then he wasn't sure. Maybe calling the cops was a bad idea. There might be all kinds of drugs he couldn't remember all over the house. He didn't want everything to spiral out of control while he was an ocean away. If he ratted on his dad, he'd get immunity. But they'd still drop all his coke down the toilet and confiscate his guns.

Hmm. Call Jesse instead. It would be like seven in the morning in LA. Jesse owed him.

"About time you called," Jesse said.

"I'm a little busy over here," Darlo said, "trying to save my ass. So listen—"

"No, *you* listen. I've been up all the rest of the night waiting for you, and there's *nothing* good on the Comcast. Keeping me up like this, like I'm your fucking assistant. Fucking bullshit."

Darlo paced, bumping into people in furs and suits. "At least you're in fucking LA," he said. "At least you're not losing your mind here in who-gives-a-fuck-ville. Did you ever think that maybe I wish I was in LA? That maybe if I was, I wouldn't hassle you? Did you? Fucking did you?"

Adam was still waiting at the elevator. He looked over. Darlo saw his black eye and felt completely responsible for the first time in his life. His hand that held the phone was wet.

"So are you going to help me out?" Darlo said. "Are you going to—"

"—go looking for your dad's dungeon? No, I'm not."

Darlo felt pressure well up in his temples. His eyes lost focus. "I cried in a girl's mouth today," he said. "I went to a hooker and I was staring into her mouth and I don't remember it, but she said I cried into it."

"Jesus, dude."

"That's why I need your help, Jesse. I'm fucking freaking out. And now I'm crying again. Oh my God, what is going on?"

A catatonia was setting in. A numbness. Nerve blockers shot up over dendrites. Can't cry. Don't cry.

This numbness had happened to him before. When he had met his mother.

They had been writing all these letters and he had been starting to get all fucked up with a question: Who was she?

"Go, Darlo," his father said, sucking down a Bloody Mary and looking for talent at Cheetahs. "I'm sick of hearing about your curiosities about your mother. It's a real buzzkill, man. It makes me go soft like Silly Putty."

"You afraid of me finding out something?"

"Yeah, I'm fucking terrified," Cox said, picking some girl with a glance and a nod. "It'll be your own little trip down the rabbit hole. Take a copy of *Poppycock,* with my best wishes."

During the flight to Des Moines, drowsiness had overcome him and his body had gone numb. You ride things out, he thought, looking around the cabin. That's life, bitch. Get tough. Beat that terror upside its head. Look at all the weak people in their suits and dresses. Are you them? No. The world is run by the people who tough it out.

The airport in Des Moines was flat, moonish. Two college-aged boys picked him up in a Ford Escort. They were dressed like Latter-Day Saints on holiday—blue polo shirts, khakis, loafers. They had thick, wheat-colored hair, rolling amber waves of grain, purple fucking mountains majesty.

"I guess we're your stepbrothers," one of them said. "Jump on in."

He could barely breathe by the time they arrived at the farm. Horse stables. A woman who looked like him, and still beautiful. His eyes were open, but a vise was crushing his chest. His dad was in there, grinding him up.

"You are so lovely," she said in their living room, a well-worn, comfortable parlor festooned with portraits of her family in various active pursuits, and smelling of paperwhites. "Twenty years and here you are. Almost twenty years I have not seen my baby."

"Hi," he said, and wheezed.

His bravado had left him somewhere in the Pacific time zone. How could he be part of this, part of her? How could he have half his genes from this stranger who killed her own food and talked about the slaughter of the unborn at dinner? She was a monolith of mystery towering in front of him. He lay awake the whole night in a stiff bed — one she said had been used in a Civil War hospital — stared at the ceiling, and listened to the wind whip through nothing. What was the wind doing?

In the morning, he and the two wheat-headed brothers, John and Robert, went horseback riding. This was the first time Darlo could identify with them; his dad had taken him to stables up in Malibu belonging to friends who kept horses, and he loved to ride. They trotted around on the five acres, access roads surrounding fields of the amber waves.

"Such a beautiful day," John said.

"Heck, yes," Robert said. "What do you think of God's country, Darlo?"

I hate it, he thought. No way could the Sunset Strip and this fruited plain coexist on the same spinner.

"It's a gas," he said. "It's all right."

When they returned, their father, the head of the Des Moines branch of Allstate, greeted Darlo without any of that midwestern condescension that his father had warned him about.

"Well, if it isn't Darlo," he said. "So pleased to meet you!"

The two fathers were connected now whether he liked it or not, and that night in his Civil War bed Darlo dreamed of his dad planting his Venus flytrap mouth on the man's ear and sucking everything out, until he fell to the ground like a deflated balloon at a Thanksgiving parade. His dad had the eyes of a hornet and pincers for hands. He woke up covered in sweat.

What was it with the wind here?

"You cried in a girl's mouth?" Jesse said. "What are you talking about?"

"I don't *know*, dude," Darlo said. "I'm falling apart. So what do you say? Please go look down there. Please?"

He waited. He waded through static and gulls and satellites.

"Sorry, man," Jesse said. "I just can't get involved."

"You're *already* involved, shithead," he said. "You've been involved for years. And I'll fucking tip you off to the fucking LAPD if you say no. They'll be my new best friends after I bust this sex-slave ring. I'll fucking do it, Jesse."

"Will you?"

"Yeah, I will. This is a big deal. Lives are at stake, man, and you are not going to get in the way by playing it like a fucking Boy Scout!"

The silence between them ferried Darlo's righteousness. He smiled and waited for contrition.

"Fuck you, Darlo," Jesse said, and hung up.

Darlo waited for Jesse to call back. He wasn't serious. He wouldn't dare. But no call came.

All that pimping for the drug dealer and this is how he got thanked.

Some band that looked like the Black Crowes came strutting out of the elevator. They had their fake furs and revealed chests and greasy haircuts, not to mention an entire modeling agency on their arms. Anger roiled his guts. These dudes weren't sleeping in some stranger's cold apartment; they probably had the entire top floor of the Krasna-go-fuck-yourself. They laughed together in a way Blood Orphans never had.

Joey came rushing by, hobbling with gimpy grace. "Come on, babe," she said. "Dinner."

"In five," Darlo said, and dialed McFadden. He had to redial five times before the lawyer picked up the phone.

"Peek-a-boo," Darlo said. "Me again."

He heard traffic. He smelled LA all over the phone.

"Why are you calling again?" McFadden said. "I haven't done anything since we talked but sleep, and barely that. Your dad—"

Darlo stopped him with the theory.

"Jesus, Darlo."

"It's true. You think that girl's lying?"

"They're trying to scare him. It's bait to get him talking. To get *me* talking."

"No, Bob, all true. You think she made the whole fucking thing up?"

"I'll say that when they find who knows what in her system, it'll be very hard to establish probable cause for a warrant. Goddamnit, I'm his lawyer, Darlo. I'm not...I'm in traffic here...I can't even have this conversation."

"The fuck you can't. You've been having *these* conversations for years."

McFadden hung up on him. Darlo called back. "Don't hang up on me!"

"I went into a tunnel, Darlo."

"Oh."

Static over the Irish Sea. Snow in the Rockies.

"So what do you think? I'm not crazy, Bob."

McFadden yelled at another driver. The high pitch of a horn passed. "I give you huge marks for creativity, Darlo," he said. "But forget it."

"The fuck I will. Put two and two together. How long have you known my dad? Are you about to tell me that the old fuck is above some kind of reproach?"

"Ah, what a beautiful day it is, here, Darlo," McFadden said. "Let's talk about the weather instead."

"And you know what he's into," Darlo continued. "You know that he likes to hurt girls, how he likes to tie them up and gang-bang them. He pays them for group fucking, but then he gets scary."

McFadden made a sort of negating moan. Darlo felt himself struggle over that familial horizon, pour light onto the surface of his soul, trying to resist his damned ancestral latitude just one extra moment yet feeling the turning of the earth, the turning of the sky.

"I haven't even had my orange juice yet," McFadden said. "You're losing me, Darlo."

"I'll say it again. There was this girl—"

"I'll say it again, I can't have this conversation."

"—and she was in the dungeon that I told you about—"

"Darlo."

"—and Dad had those fucking mobsters over, and I helped him install the damn thing so I *know* it's there—No, don't hang up on me again, dude!"

He dialed McFadden again. A message.

"What tunnel are you in now, dude? Well, when you get out of it, why don't you call the police, because there's a girl, at least one girl, probably more, and she's in trouble, she's being held against her will. Damn it, Bob, if only for the thirty grand you got handed for waving your hand over our contract, fucking get on it. Do something! Save those girls! Help me!"

All the fine-suited people, Dutchies and tourists alike, tried to ignore him, but curiosity forced them to stare. And so he turned to the silent crowd and told them to call the media in Los Angeles, call every police officer they knew, tell them that the son of the porn king David Cox says there's a dungeon below their house at 21 Camellia Drive, a hidden dungeon where girls are imprisoned, just call everyone you know there and tell them that his father is a psychopath. Tell them he's the sickest fuck in a city of sick fucks. Tell them to excavate that basement!

Salt in his mouth. Wet eyes. Was he yelling? Was he?

"Oh my fucking God!" one of the members of that Black Crowes band said as their groupies covered their mouths, amazed.

The ancestral line snapped and set him free from the horizon. He heard the shatter of wire, felt the tether fray to nothing, dissolve, burn off. He floated up over the world. His latitude changed. His meridian altered. More sky. More sun. Up from the canyon. Not running anymore. Not running.

13

TWENTY MINUTES LATER, Bobby sat at their table in the Krasnapolsky restaurant, thinking how close he was to pulling off this day of extreme good fortune. All he had to do was get through the show and make sure Sarah didn't meet Darlo, or if she did, to keep it short. Across the table, the drummer sipped a beer, peeled the bottle, looking as if he'd crawled up out of his own grave. This was El Darlo? This was the conqueror of pussy, the Ayatollah of Rock and Rolla?

Dad gets busted. Kryptonite. See ya.

They sat in the restaurant, the four of them, waiting for Joey to come back from the bathroom. Bobby had been the first there; then Shane came down stinking of Joey's perfume, which was just fine because the guy stank of beer wrestling with body odor wrestling with a nasty hint of old peanut butter; then Adam, with that default expression of dull politeness; and then Joey and Darlo. The manager made Adam and Bobby change seats.

"I have this all planned out," she said, a mad scientist wiping her little button nose. "You can't sit there. Sit here. Bobby, you have to." She wiped her eyes. "Adam, get over here, please. I have this all planned out."

"Planned out?" Shane said. "What's wrong with you? And who's Revvy at Guild Records?"

"He has a label based in Rotterdam," she said. "He's supposed to come to the show tonight. So play well."

"Why?" Bobby asked. "So we can be the next big thing in a country no one cares about? I'd rather sweep the floors in hell."

Joey ignored him. She touched her fork and knife and looked solemnly at Adam. "Are you OK?"

He nodded.

"OK about what?" Shane asked. "What happened to your face?"

Joey jumped up, smoothed out her suit, adjusted her earrings.

"Be right back. OK. Order some drinks. Be right back."

Adam's expression wasn't one Bobby had seen before. Despite the cuts on his face and his black eye, the old velvet emperor had some kind of serene glow, the kind Shane had spent his whole life searching for, the state of oneness the singer constantly spoke about, lecturing everyone in reverential terms. The guitar player had scored a red-hot dose of fat Buddha science, and floated in waves of peace.

Bobby wanted to taunt Shane with this, but found himself unable, in deference to Adam's vibe.

"I was attacked by skinheads," Adam said, the way you say, *Not a creature was stirring, not even a mouse.* "I thought they were going to kill me. Joey and Darlo kicked their fucking asses."

"Did you just curse?" Bobby said. "Holy shit, the fairy godmother just cursed."

"Those fucking pricks," Darlo growled, surfacing. "I would have eaten their fucking faces."

Bobby and Shane exchanged comic buddy glances. Another first.

"I don't forget when people help me," Darlo said. "I am loyal. I am really fucking loyal. I am not my dad. Fucking really loyal and sometimes that sucks, but sometimes I can actually help someone. And that's what I wanted to do, Adam. Help you, dude."

Adam nodded, and whispered affirmatives. Darlo looked at Adam with something like affection. Another first. Everyone was trying on new emotions, preparing themselves for a post–Blood Orphans world.

"Ouch," Shane said, and touched his ears. A big, flaky piece of something dropped from his scalp.

"What the hell is that?" Bobby stared at the reddish chunk. "Is that blood?"

"Peanut butter."

"Why is it red?"

Shane looked up, touching his ears as if he didn't think they were there. "I got beat up, sort of, by this crazy dad."

"Dude." Bobby reached out and touched Shane's shoulder. "*Dude.*"

"I am loyal," Darlo said once more. "I *am.*"

When Joey returned, wiping coke from her nose, the era of good feeling went dead. Her failure vibe brought it all back home. Bobby felt his fake tooth, remembered the punch, the blood, the utter humiliation the singer had hoisted upon him in that Super 8, day after day, the Mummy this and Darlo's Right-Hand-Man that, the embarrassment every show when Shane went into his pathetic religious screeds, strutting around like some preacher at the school of Jesus Is Way Cool. And so he retreated from the borders of Kindlakhastan and back into his embattled fiefdom, into his damp castle, where eczema lined the walls like matted moss.

"This is like a last fucking supper, huh?"

Shane's smile disappeared, and he looked confused.

"If one of us is Jesus," the singer said.

"I bet you'd like that," Bobby replied. "If you were Jesus."

"Uh…" Shane shrugged. "Sure?"

"*Yeah,*" the bass player said, not really sure what he was talking about. The retreat to the castle was going badly; his feet were stuck in the boggy moat of change. He had managed to confuse even himself. His hands pulsed as confirmation of this flailing strategy, this failure ever to assume power in the band enacted in miniature. All this change between them, happening so fast, portending the end of them as a functioning traveling unit of misery. Without misery, they weren't a band. Which he wanted. Which he didn't want. Which he dreaded. He dipped his hand into a glass of water, leaving behind a film of muck and moisturizer, and flicked water at Darlo.

"How's your dad?" Bobby asked. "Heard he got bizusted."

Darlo looked up. The drummer's eyes were teary. The drummer had feelings.

"Dude," Darlo said with uncustomary low volume. "Give it a rest."

"What do you mean?"

"I mean you're doing that thing where you just talk and make no sense. Where your fucking mood changes on a dime."

"I don't do that."

Shane laughed.

"Just kill it," Darlo said, and even though his voice was still and soft, each word felt like a hand rubbing Bobby's face deeper into shit shame. "Spare us the extended tour into your pathetic, fucked-up mind."

The emotional space into which Bobby fell was soft, silty, moist. He looked at Adam, who still had that new map of Happyville drawn on his face, quickening the trajectory of Bobby's fall. While they were busy falling apart, Adam had acquired some clear, well-lit pathway to another world. The guitar player had a look on his face that was pure future tense.

All the other group dinners with Joey had been triumphs. Deal this and licensing that and tour with just take a guess you will be so fucking psyched. It hurt all of them to be here, to sing fucking "Taps."

"Dude," Darlo asked Shane, "what do you want to play tonight?"

"Are you asking me what I want to play?" Shane said, amazed. "Are you really *asking* me? Because I will tell you."

"Don't labor it," Bobby said. "Just tell him."

Darlo turned and looked at him like a dragon rudely awakened from sleep, looking for bones with which to pick his teeth. Smaug was here, and Bobby had forgotten his bow and arrow.

"I wasn't asking you," the drummer said. "No one gives a fuck what you think."

Shane nodded, like, *Damn.* Adam sipped water. Bobby's throat went tight.

"No one," Darlo said, "has *ever* cared what you think. Not from the first note we played. Not when we were trying to figure out what to call the record. Not when we were constructing song lists. Not when we were having a good time way the fuck back when, when we all pretended to give a good hard shit about what the fuck you thought." Darlo closed his eyes and fluttered them open as if he were trying to stay awake. "Do you know what Sheridan said about you? He said you wouldn't know a good bass melody if Paul McCartney fucked you in the ass with it. Mr. Producer-Man said you were a fucking passenger."

The P-word.

"We laughed about it all the time. I mean, Sheridan and I hated each other, that stoner moron, but we could always bond over what a passenger you were. He asked when I was going to fire you."

Pathetic. Poseur. Perfunctory.

"'When are you going to get a real bass player?' he said. 'Bobby just can't go the distance.'"

Bobby fell down and down. The drummer's voice snatched up every bit of his happiness in its dragon maw and crushed it.

"Kind of fucked up to say it at all," Darlo said. "Kind of point-less. But you oughta know, Bobby, that no one cared whether or not you made the cut. You just got lucky is all. You just got lucky."

14

WHATEVER BAD NEWS JOEY HAD for them, Adam was feeling pretty fucking great right now. The worse the news, the better, really. A sense of freedom had lit in Adam as the tour drew to a close, like a little pilot light looking for some gas to turn it into a full flame. That flame had been stoked by Deena Freeze and her slick manager, awed by his chops and stunned by his talent. That flame had been the look the two had given each other, a look of surprise, and joy. So the worse the news out of Joey, who sat there chewing her nails, a condemned woman about to receive her punishment, the better.

When he returned to LA, he would do a series of paintings called *The Bidding War,* in which these lowly apostles were visited by various spirits of the rock-and-roll ether, demons both petty and grand, like old wraiths of biblical temptation: the hoary Witch of Warner Bros., the black-winged Saruman of Sire, the dank Balrog of Bertelsmann, come as emissaries from worlds of wonder with contracts and codicils. These tempters all had the Vision and swore they also had the Execution. In the painting, they would sit in the reverse formation of how they now sat, with Darlo and Shane near the A&R action and Bobby and Adam at the fringes. Of course, this time the action was no action at all. It was just their manager, Joey Jane Fredericks, having just come back from a twenty-minute trip to the bathroom, here to untie the knot for good.

"Warners dropped Blood Orphans today," she said. "They sent John Hackney. Remember him?" She swigged her Grolsch and bent over the table as if they were wily thieves in a medieval tavern, plotting a highway heist over steins of hearty grog. "I want you to know I'm going to fight it. With all my heart and soul, I'm going to fight to keep Blood Orphans on the Warner roster. We will prevail." She banged the table. "We will *prevail*."

She sat back, arms crossed, expecting someone to join the insurrection. But no one did. Adam thought of Instructor Samuels in his second-year atelier, talking about how every painting must construct a narrative. Joey was trying to create a portrait of defiance, but no one was going along.

"You guys aren't just going to roll over, are you?" She held up her hands. "Is that all that this band means to you?"

Four faces, exhausted, stared her down.

"Amazing," she said. "I was thinking that you guys would care about staying with a label with global reach and distribution. I was thinking that maybe you'd want the giant steel arm of the Time Warner empire at your back. I thought that maybe—"

"Shut up, Joey," Bobby said. "I can't take the speech right now."

She looked at them, furious. "That's it?" she said. "No fight left? That's *it*?"

"What do you want us to say?" Shane said. "Fuck Warners? What choice do we have?"

Tears ran down her face. "The choice to fight."

They just laughed at that one.

She threw down her napkin, got up, and hobbled out of there. Adam saw how Joey had changed; she who had once loomed huge now resembled a hollow piece of show-biz balsa wood. In the end, he thought, she was the one who had lost the most in the whole mess. At least they had lived the dream. They'd carry that with them forever. All Joey had were the receipts, sums due and owing.

"Assholes!" she yelled, her voice echoing through the atrium.

15

JOEY STORMED OFF in a furious hobble. They watched the gimp clip-clop away, yelling obscenities and bumping into tables.

Dropped? Darlo thought. Sure, Joey, whatever. He had bigger problems right now.

But then he got stuck on that word. Dropped?

Oh, that's what it was. A ploy. They were just trying to cut her out. When he got back to the States and charged up his cell phone, there'd be a message from Steadman, long-lost Steadman, waiting for him with the score. They were cleaning house and wanted to bring in a new manager. It was a Joey purge. Their lawyers had it all planned out. McFadden was withholding until his return. Joey's lost her touch, he'd say. We have to let her go. But we still believe in Blood Orphans.

Belief. The longer the word floated up there in his head, flapping like a tattered flag, the realer it became.

Darlo turned to Bobby and grinned. He actually felt shitty about unloading on him. Dude was just too easy to pick on. Dude was a stationary target.

"Dropped?" Darlo said. "No."

Bobby turned to him, red in the face, still smarting. "Fuck you, Darlo," he said, and stormed off too.

Shane and Adam looked at him with their stock expressions, unimpressed and amused, but Darlo had been stuck with them long enough to detect their disgust for picking on the weak. This disgust really hurt. He felt…what was it called? Vulnerable? He turned to Adam.

"Quad-band," he said. "One more time."

Adam handed the phone over. "Bobby," he said. "Too bad."

"He'll be back," Darlo said, with a false confidence essential to maintaining his sanity. "I'd like to see him go start a new band."

"We're all going to have to start a new band," Shane said, and wolfed his scotch in one big non-Buddhist gulp. "We're toast. Man, my ears are killing me."

Dropped? Darlo turned the word over in his mind. He opened his mouth but could not say it, felt a dryness at the back of his throat, and returned to the memory of hovering over that prostitute's throat in her little cum-'n-go. He had felt tears running down his face and thought that he might be bleeding. She had been trying to suppress a laugh, but when the tears started falling into her mouth, she started to show panic. And the more panic she showed, the more he cried. He had found himself in a loop there, a vicious cycle; the worse her discomfort, the more despairing he became, but he couldn't stop because he was finally in a moment he had been searching for, looking down into her mouth for all those lost girls. Here he was, staring down the dark cave of memory, falling into loss.

"Darlo," Shane said. "Be careful."

His hand strangled the water glass. "Dropped? What the fuck?"

"You're going to fucking destroy your hand, dude."

The drummer imagined himself as handless. He imagined life as a handless porn maker, inheritor of his dad's fortune after the fucker died awaiting trial for the deaths of numerous women, their bones found in the basement of his house. Their bones found directly below Darlo's bedroom. Their bones found directly below his guns and his knives. Sitting on a throne of flesh.

He had installed the lock. A secret door behind a fake-fronted bookcase. Six sixty-four. Neighbor of the beast. They had laughed over that one.

Run a pole straight down from his bedroom floor and it would nestle in tibula and fibula. Run a pole from the den, where he'd fucked countless teenage girls, and find bones. Run dancer's poles down through any point in the house. Find bones everywhere.

Bones everywhere. Darlo handless, trying to sift through them.

Find a graveyard under the house. Find Darlo the Handless, inheritor of ghosts, sifting through, on his flesh throne. Find him. This is his fate. Bone sifter.

He got up and raced out to the street. Standing outside the hotel, snow in his face, he dialed McFadden.

"Jesus, Darlo," McFadden said. "This has to stop."

"Hope I didn't catch you in the middle of a really important squash game, Bob," he said. "It's just that you need to hear me out."

He explained the theory again.

"Darlo, I'm really starting to worry about you. Are you losing it?"

"You fucking bet I am. How could I have ignored all those screams? Did I hear them from the kitchen while I was making dinner?"

"Darlo..."

"Like, what was I thinking the next morning, after that girl escaped and I went down to breakfast? Where the fuck was I when Dad took his Viagra and muttered, Well, shit, she was a cooze anyway. Where was I? All the times Dad was making his slap-and-burn movies, the ones that aren't sold at the fucking Hustler store, the ones where he paid a lot of girls to get burned with cigarettes while they were taking on two guys. And where was I, besides upstairs jerking off or watching some fucking Bruce Willis movie? Where did I go, man? Those screams were like engines revving in a ditch."

He bent forward, tears falling onto the flat Dutch earth. "How did this all happen, Bob?"

"Darlo," McFadden said. "Just calm down."

"Like revving engines," he said, sobbing. "Bob, I'm part of it. Bob, my therapist, he said I was part of it and I laughed, but he was right." He made his own turbine sound. He made his own grinding hum, sputtering and sliding down an incline, falling, white smoke floating away. "You have to help me, and help those girls in those dungeons. Help me."

Spitting up dirt off the tires, fusing rubber with earth.

"Look, OK," McFadden said. "Darlo, you need to calm down."

"He wants to take them apart," he said. "He wants them dismembered. He's my dad, Bob. He's my dad."

McFadden's breath on the line was a puffy, useless cloud. Seagulls flying through it.

"Darlo," he said. "What I can do is..." but Darlo went numb again. Numbness overtook him, down in his own dungeon. Numbness fermenting, growing, distending, and now bursting forth with a hideous strength. So he tried to separate from it, tried to float away, tried to snap the line again and move high into the sky, but his body held him to the horizon. No new meridian. Same old latitude. The dungeon chains held him. Handless and sifting through those bones. Chained up.

An ocher swell of ancestral filth rolled him over. McFadden couldn't help. Jesse couldn't help. No one could help. Who knew what his father hid? Who knew and who cared? No one could help him avoid the wave of garbage and shit that was his life, that kept his sunlight low in the sky, that pinned his sunlight down.

16

IF SHANE HAD KNOWN Blood Orphans was being dropped at the start of the day, he would have been surprised, upset, defiant. But on the other side of this *dies horribilis,* after getting his ears clubbed by Danika's stepfather, after the Starbucks baristas treated him like a worm, and after the humiliation at the hands of Tennessee and the vision of Fritz in the Dutch hallway, defiance had no bearing. That quadrant of bad experiences provided the tipping point for his distress, sent the treacle of failure cascading down over every pore of his frail, paper-thin confidence.

He left the restaurant without eating—they all did—and walked to the Star Club. Amsterdam was lit up in festive lights. Dutch Christmas season was in full force, and their take on the holiday was considerably more Brothers Grimm than New Testament. In front of a department store, handfuls of Dutchies were dressed as elves, but in blackface. These ebony goblins were called Black Peter—he had learned about them in church—and they gave out candy to children. One of them scurried up to the singer, yelled something happily in Dutch, and handed him a big swirl lollipop.

"Racist," Shane said, and threw the lolly back in Black Peter's face.

In the months before *Rocket Heart*'s release, Shane had lived in a spare room at Joey's house in Silver Lake. The band had a residency at Spaceland, playing every Monday night, and he'd enjoyed walking from his temporary lodgings on Crestmont Avenue to the club. Life ran smooth as silk; girls were swallowing his sperm, the band was pretending to be a united front, and Silver Lake was just one of the lovely wildernesses upon which the seeker would travel, a place blessed with eternal, lovely light.

He pretended on these walks that he was a character in a Bible story, enacting some outtake from the rough draft, not good enough to make the final cut but still worthy of consideration in the best-selling book of all time.

Passing by the black-faced elves and on to the Star Club, he grafted that memory onto this evening's walk. All it took was a little faith. He imbued the scene with that biblical outtake vibe.

The Star Club, which lay in a tricked-out basement on the Amstel, was set up with the bar on the right, pool tables on a raised platform to the left, and the stage through swinging doors. It didn't look anything like a place the Beatles would have played, with red velvet, marble tables, and brass handles. The Beatles would have had to pay five kroner just to peer inside. Bobby stood against the wall with a cute girl who looked like a kinky Raggedy Ann. She wore a tight skirt that appeared to be the skimpy remains of an Amish quilt, socks striped in yellow and purple, and well-kept crimson hair.

His tenuous generosity of spirit flagged when he saw Bobby, but Shane rallied. Bobby's eternally grating personality wasn't going to let him break ranks with his good mood. They'd actually had a nice time at the hotel room, hadn't they? The singer appealed to the beat-up better angels of his nature.

"Nice to meet you, Sarah," Shane said. "How did you and Bobby meet?"

"I think I picked him up today in a café."

"Sounds good to me," Bobby said, braying.

"Bobby is a great bass player," Shane said. "He's solid as a rock, even with his hands the way they are. He's really someone you can depend on in the musical trenches. Have I ever told you that, man?"

Bobby look confused, rubbed his ass against the wall, breathed a little heavily. Shane realized he should have killed him with kindness from the beginning. Still, against all desire to the contrary, witnessing Bobby's new love affair sent Shane's good mood straight out his ass. The bass player had found his Narnia, had blundered into that magic wardrobe. But Shane had no such escape hatch. He had never found love in his time in Blood Orphans. He'd found Tantra and deep throat, threesomes and twins and bondage, but not love. He'd plowed almost as many female fields as Darlo, but not one of them had yielded a single flower of inner peace. Bobby mocked the honest travails of the vision quest, yet here he was, all up in this girl, their connection simple and effortless. It's all I've ever wanted, Shane thought. What the fuck do I have to do?

Sarah's eyes widened. "Danika?"

Shane turned around. Danika stood there, her dreads back-lit like a teen Medusa. "Sarah?"

They said a few things in Dutch and broke into laughter.

"This is my little sister!" Sarah said. "Little troublemaker!"

"You're *sisters?*" Shane said.

"What a coincidence, no?" Sarah said.

"And how!" Danika said. She clutched Shane's arm as if he'd escaped and she would never let that happen again. He'd dealt with crazy girls before, whose ability to fuck was inversely proportionate to their ability to function, but the way she put the grip on portended a whole new level of nutty-bitch bullshit.

"I saw them last night, right here." Danika giggled. "I stood over there and stared at Shane all night. I knew he would be mine. And then, the poor thing..." She pouted and shook her head, releasing right under Shane's nose that particular batch of pheromones that, to his dismay, had lost all their magic; now she just smelled like old roses. "Marcus found him in my bed and chased him out."

"We heard," Bobby said. "Marcus is a real live wire."

Shane looked at Bobby. "You *met* him?"

"He's not our father," Danika said. "So he's powerless. Mother won't let him lay a hand. All he can do is whine."

"And perforate eardrums," Shane said. "He can do that. He's real sharp with the tops of garbage cans."

He thought that would be enough to break the happy spirit of the conversation. But they didn't even notice.

"He seems like he's been through a lot," Bobby said.

"A lot of drugs," Danika said.

"But he loves our mother," Sarah said. "He's good to her. He treats her like gold. Our regular dad is a hothead too, but no nice side."

"They're both idiots," Danika said happily, squeezing his arm hard enough to cut off the flow of blood. "We'll see you later. Shane and I have to go have sex in the alleyway."

"No," he said. "I can't. I, uh—"

"Have to go talk to the Buddha?" Bobby said.

"The Buddha?" Danika said, and closed Shane's mouth. "I am your little Shiva right here, baby. You don't need no Buddha, let the motherfucker burn!"

Danika led him around back, past the knowing glances of dudes without dates. Never before had he found the certainty of sex in an alleyway to be unappealing. He tried to beg off. "I'm not up for it," he said.

"Sure you're not!" she said, and shoved him between two Dumpsters. "Give it to me!"

The alley stank of rotting meat and old beer. There was just no way. But she pushed against him, grinding in her best cat-in-heat, so he couldn't move. She reached and fondled.

"Hands off," he said. "It's not an orange."

She really put the grip on him, as if his complaint were a dare to continue.

"Fucking cut it out," he said. "Let go, Danika."

"Sure, baby," she said, her breath smelling a little bit of licorice. "I'm a freak."

"I think there's a language barrier problem here. I think we're having—"

She squeezed tighter. His hand grabbed the offending arm. "What the fuck is wrong with you?"

"You like it," she said. "That's what your lyrics are about."

"What?"

"Rough sex."

"This isn't rough sex. It's torture. And I don't write the fucking lyrics."

She pulled at him like he was a cow.

"That's enough!" he said, and shoved her off.

She lunged, grabbing at both sides of his head in another attempt at a hot embrace, so that her hands cuffed his ears, sending a shock of pain through him. Like stepfather, like stepdaughter. Shane was squeezed through some aperture, pulled though and squashed. He fell in pieces, in symmetry, crumbling like the demolition of an old building. No smoke rose from the sides, though. No professionals rushed in to assess success. No one shook in awe. No one whooped at the majesty.

17

JOEY STOOD IN THE STAR CLUB, drinking Jim Beam and fuming. All that planning and worry, she thought, and they don't care. She had plotted out a seating arrangement, fretted all day, and worried that she might get physically assaulted. But they had barely noticed. All she got was attitude. What was wrong with these people? They were so undeserving of her anxiety. After all the work she'd done, this was how much they loved her?

A head full of snow didn't make her feel any better.

You care too much, Joey, she thought. At the end of the day, you care too fucking much to ever be a very good manager. And now you're stuck drinking cheap whiskey in a glass that smells like detergent.

She really wished she hadn't destroyed that phone. Without it she could barely breathe.

All the work she had done, and they were ready to roll over. They were just *so* unimpressed with her call to arms. No guts at all, this band.

She sipped her drink. Shane came rushing by, clutching his ears. Behind him ran a young girl in black dreads, calling his name. The little baby Jesus stopped and turned around.

"Leave me alone! Crazy bitch! Crazy fucking family!"

"Shane!"

"Leave me alone!"

The singer and his Dutch black-dreaded girlfriend shot apart, moved as if a wave had cast them to separate shores. The girl lifted her hands to the sky and ran from the club. Shane grabbed at his ears and howled and ran through the swinging doors, out of sight. The bartenders, loading up the well, shared a laugh.

"Christ, Shane," she said, and chewed on some ice.

Then Adam walked in. Without his Fu Manchu.

"You didn't," she said. "But you fucking did."

He smiled, and she couldn't believe her eyes. Without the fuzzy caterpillar 'tache, Adam was really cute.

"I needed a fucking change," he said, eyes glowing. "I should have done it a long time ago."

"But where?"

"Your hotel room."

"Damn." She took a drag, squinting. "Did you put it in a bag? Like a fucking memento?"

He nodded. "You're creepy, Joey."

She crouched down, looked at him like an anthropologist poring over a specimen of some ur-creature. "Dude, I think you're taller, too. That thing on your face was dragging you down." She shook her head. "Keeping you hunched and hidden. You look *good*."

He hugged her; it was like in movies when people overcome addiction and embrace the person who got them straight. She kept her arms in the air like she was sticking 'em up. She was just that stunned.

"Don't tell the others," he said. "It's a surprise."

He walked off into the club's shadows. Joey sucked down her drink and ordered another. Fucking betrayer, she thought. You're totally leaving me, us, the band. You finally figured out what was what. Good for you and fuck you and damn, Adam, you are a foxy piece of poncy ass, aren't you?

Right on the heels of this scene, a young woman of staggering Black Irish beauty strode in with a guitar. Her ebony hair shimmered in the semidarkness, as if attracting all the visible light in the room. Behind her came a stylish-looking roadie who resembled Sting in *Quadrophenia*—she couldn't remember his character's name—with short white hair, a glossy two-hundred-dollar red Windbreaker, and cheekbones that cut glass.

Roadies, Joey thought. One more thing we never had.

Behind him came the manager, completing this triumvirate of gorgeous Anglos. He wore a black suit, a white shirt, and a shiny blue tie. A handkerchief stuck out from his breast pocket. Creases ran in fear from this guy.

That's a rock-and-roll manager, Joey thought, wobbling on her heels. That's a pro.

To her chagrin and excitement, the pro came over and ordered a drink. "Campari and soda," he said, in a rough, all-business brogue. The bartender, who'd been insouciant to Joey, moved as if this guy were his boss.

Joey's palms went sweaty. She wondered, Maybe I should fuck him. Maybe, through the osmosis of sweat and flesh, he'll impart some managerial science. He'll make me come and then he'll call his good friend John Hackney and they can double-team me, thereby saving my career. Cowabunga.

She and the Hackneyette exchanged glances. He extended a hand. "You must be Joey Fredericks."

"What makes you say that?"

"I heard you were short, blond, and beautiful."

"Guilty as charged," she said, and took his hand. "Who are you?"

"I'm John Bridges. I manage Deena Freeze." He motioned to the stage. "We're opening for you tonight."

"Welcome to the funeral. Thanks for wearing black."

Bridges laughed politely, because that was default behavior.

"We were dropped today," she said, pushing it. "Warners dropped us. I just told the guys at dinner. So I'm feeling a little low."

"Sorry to hear that," Bridges said. "Terrible."

Bridges took a little sip of his Campari—very classy, Joey thought, very sexy—took out his Palm, and started scheduling things. Here a tap and there a tap. Joey bristled; she had dropped her Palm off the Venice Pier last week when she'd been trying to use it with greasy post–hot dog hands. Damn thing had sunk to the bottom of the bay.

"They told us they would always be there," Joey said, "and then they acted as if we didn't exist. Oh, sure, people say that we screwed ourselves, that I should have kept a muzzle on Darlo. But how do you keep a muzzle on the mouthpiece?"

Diarrhea of the mouth flowed in a stream from her lips. Bridges was caught, if only for a minute. She'd better whine fast.

"You don't muzzle the mouthpiece," she continued. "That's what you don't do. You can't change what you are. You're dealt the cards and that's what you play. We played them wrong." She took a sip. "Why don't you tell me what cards you were dealt, John?"

Bridges put away his Palm, and with just as much calm as confidence—an unnerving, royal confidence—he told Joey exactly what cards he and Miss Deena Freeze had been dealt: not as good as the one that Blood Orphans had been given, but Deena was the Lady of the Lake, and no doubt she and Slick Rick here would know exactly what to do. She wouldn't, say, take the cards, shit on them, and wipe them in the dealer's face.

"That is *so* great," Joey said, feeling like the incredible shrinking woman. "If you'll excuse me, I have to go blow my brains out."

Bridges smiled, sipped his Campari all sexy-like, took his Palm back out. "Aim for the temple, Joey," he said. "The skull's softer there."

"Any other advice?"

He pulled out a business card from his wallet. "I'll be in LA in a few weeks. Maybe I can help you sort out all this business with the label."

She stared at the card. White lettering against a gold backing. So tacky it worked. "What kind of power do you have that I don't know about?"

"I have the good faith of the label," he said. "It goes a long way."

"We have a long way to go." She fixed a gaze on him. "All right. Sure. I mean, there's nothing to be done, we're fucked harder that a Hollywood hooker at dawn, but maybe you're a magic man."

"I was thinking more about you," he said. "Not so much Blood Orphans. They're beyond help, but you might need a job, eh?"

At that moment Joey saw it in his eyes. The player. She had no idea what he was talking about, but a tight rush up her spine told her nothing good could come of it. She was being taken; she was sure of it. She was a minor pawn in some bigger scene. For once she stood on the other side of total calculation, and felt its burning breeze on her face.

"I have to go, London Bridges," she said, and handed the card back. "Have to go see which member of my band needs my help. Someone must. While we still exist. While I still get to play the part."

He shrugged, like, Shoot yourself in the foot if that's what you want, and smiled in a way that revealed that he might only have been trying to help out. Joey wondered when her bullshit detector had gone south on her, but then figured she'd only fooled herself into thinking she'd ever had one.

18

ALL THE PEP TALKS Bobby had given himself about Darlo were useless. Day after day, month after month, for almost three years, every time he had locked horns with the drummer, his horns had snapped right off.

Passenger. He'd sat through the whole thing, and when it was over, all he'd been able to manage to do was storm off, tight in the throat, wanting to burst, to sob. I'm a runt of a man, he thought, the smallest of the litter.

Now he stood in the Star Club, chain-smoking, drinking free Stella. Interesting that his hands didn't itch.

Sarah showed up. She wore some kind of handbags-and-glad-rags outfit, though the angles were still pretty tight. She gave him a big kiss.

"How's my rock-and-roll star?" she said, and embraced him. "How are your poor little hands?"

"We were dropped," he said. "Warners dropped us."

She frowned, and for a moment he assumed the worst. Star-fucker, he thought. Now that I'm out of business, she won't want me. She was slumming.

"You must be very sad," she said, and gave a reassuring kiss. "Sorry."

"No, no," he said, emboldened. "I'm psyched. Now I can do whatever I want. I was a fucking prisoner and now I'm free. This is great fucking news."

Practice nonambiguity, he thought. It's awful news but pretend it's the best thing ever. Standing there with a bullshit smile on his face, Bobby thought of himself as the Terminator. He was going to have his skin stripped off, his metal guts laid bare, and get crushed in the trash compactor of failure before his desire to be famous would die.

Thinking of himself this way, as a towering monster from the bleakest future, lifted his spirits.

And then it turned out that her sister was fucking Shane, and psycho Marcus had cuffed Shane's ears. That he and Shane had dipped their wicks into a very tight gene pool made him queasy, but he had gotten the good end of the deal. Clearly Danika was a thespian to the marrow, annoying and grandiose. The thespians always went for Shane. The bad girls went for Darlo. Adam got the wallflowers out on a dare. Bobby got...Darlo's leftovers?

No more. Never again.

He bought Sarah a drink as Shane rushed back into the club, screaming and clutching his ears. "Fuck!" he cried, and ran into the green room.

They waited for Danika to come barging in after him. She did not.

"She drove him nuts," Sarah said, and adjusted her skirt. "She suffocates her lovers. Happens all the time."

A few minutes later, Joey hobbled over, favoring her right leg hard, as if her left one were a prosthesis with a fracture right up the middle. She shook Sarah's hand and then proceeded to complain about her phone.

"I smashed it up," she said. "It was crazy, Sarah, but I just felt like, I'm such a failure, why don't I just kill it, sever the line, cut the cord. Just have it be me and Joey Fredericks, alone in the world. But now that I don't have that umbilical cord, I really have to say I think I'm dying. Without that phone, I'm starving. I can't find my other bands to see how they're doing. That's, like, part of my identity." She lit a cigarette. "I'm totally without the tether. It's, like, ground control to Major Tom!"

"I have a cell phone," Bobby said. With Sarah's heat up against him, magnanimity was easy. "If you want to use it."

Joey stared at it, and another blond lock fell forward from her wilted Mohawk. "What's the point?" The manager shook her head. "Forget it."

From far off in the distance, they heard Shane scream. Everyone turned for a second, then went back to what they were doing.

Joey held up her hands. "Leave him for me," she said. "I'll take care of this."

Bobby and Sarah stood there rubbing up on each other as Joey hobbled off, banged through the swinging doors, and yelled to Shane that help was on the way and stop your bitching and whining. Sarah expressed amazement at the state of Blood Orphans.

"You guys are wrecked, man." She sipped her rum and Coke. "I thought you were kidding, but no. Just a mess."

"Told you."

She lit them cigarettes. "Have you ever seen the Géricault painting *Raft of the Medusa?*" She passed a smoke over. "Heard of him?"

"No. Why?"

"It reminds me of you all."

"How's that?"

She bounced on her heels and moved her hands in the air, as if to unfold the scene. "On rough seas in the nowhere of the Atlantic," she said, "a group of survivors from a shipwreck float on a rotting raft. They are gripping each other. Some of them are dead. Some of the dead have been eaten by the survivors. They look up at the black sky like saints, cannibal saints, God's forgotten favorites. And at the farthest corner of the horizon there is the blip of something—a ship, maybe? They have made themselves into a human pile to get higher, and at the top of it, one man holds aloft a white handkerchief, waving to the dot they hope will be their salvation." She rocked on her heels, and her eyes lit up.

"We know it's folly," she said. "We know that this is their last cry to heaven, to fate, which has damned them, to the smallest bit of their hope, drifting away, almost invisible." She lowered her voice. "But is it really? Sometimes I wonder about the colors in the painting. Sometimes I imagine that the colors are so beautiful because God is there, the colors are proof that soon he will swoop in and enact a miracle. Sometimes I think they will somehow manage to survive."

19

JOEY FOUND SHANE in the green room, on the couch, head in hands, weeping. "Are you OK, dude?"

"Great!" he said into his hands. "Bitch clapped me right on the ear!"

He stumbled up, but then collapsed onto a bronze sink so big it looked like a trough. "Why?" he asked, slamming his arm into the wall. "Why why why?"

Joey had never expected any of them to weep in front of her. Even Adam. A surge of usefulness overcame her.

"Shane," she said. "I'm so sorry."

Whatever anger existed in Shane's cries quickly yielded to heartache. Whatever defiance lay there, housed in the low registers of misery, changed to fast, rhythmic pulses of surrender. Listening to it, Joey thought of watching snow change to rain. Something disappeared.

She grabbed her singer. The peanut butter smell would not stop her from giving aid. Nor the faintest hint of dog shit. She held him with much force and love.

I must remember something happy, she thought. I must think of a good time that we have had, present a ring of good memories around him, so that these vibes will soak down through me and into him. What else can I do?

A memory came to her—their photo shoot for the aborted *Rolling Stone* cover, the band dressed in silver suits with blue piping, white shirts, and blue ties on the beach in Venice. The magazine had commissioned someone to create a large papier-mâché heart, which wasn't exactly red—more like see-through rose—and resembled an alien pod. They were to surround it, lean on it, climb aboard it, jam it into the sand like a surfboard. The picture would capture all its various prismatic features, shafts of light raining down from the sky as if to say, These fuckers are channeling it all. These four have found the ultimate delivery system of rock accuracy and beatitude. They are the inheritors of a master plan.

The final pictures had never been shown to Joey, because in between, the racism charge had been leveled and no radio station, from Clear Channel to Infinity Broadcasting to XML Satellite, could be paid enough to run the record. But that day, no one could have imagined any of that. On that day, eighty degrees and not a cloud in the sky, they ran on the beach while onlookers gathered round, kicking sand in each other's face, drinking beers and laughing and thinking, We will always get along because we are all members of the Elect of the Firmament of Electric Guitar, in the constellation of common time. Makeup artists painted glyphs in the corners of their eyes, floating above the subtlest of passion-red lip gloss. Adam taught Bobby how to play "Stairway to Heaven"—tried to, at least—and Darlo told stories of life on the Big Porn Candy Mountain, before giving Joey a big hug and saying, I will love you forever, babe, you've made this all fucking happen. Hey, everyone, she's made this all fucking happen. She's the one responsible! Which one of you hot bitches is going to give the manager a kiss? Shane laughed, sitting in the director's chair, messing with the megaphone; lithe and thin-lipped, he was really starting to look like the bass player from Jane's Addiction, skinny and sleek. He raised his megaphone to Joey and smiled.

"OK, Blood Orphans!" the director-singer said, his voice a smooth caress. "Are you ready for your closeup?"

Nothing bad would ever come of them. They had time for everything to happen. They had so much time to get it right. They had the entire length of life in front of them to enjoy this massive blessing. What could possibly go wrong?

20

SHANE WOULDN'T HAVE CHOSEN Joey's shoulder to cry on, but wrapped up in the manager's little hug — her body radiating a balm of lilac and lavender, her perky B-cups pressing into him — calm began to return and he went limp.

While he cried, with Joey holding him up like a wet sack of wheat, he thought about his family. He wondered whether, upon his return, they would greet him with open arms or with judgment. He wondered if they would ask him to go to church. He thought about all his old friends, and his dog, Ranger Rick, and everything else that he had dismissed in this devil's bargain as foul, stupid, and provincial.

Dropped from Warner Bros. He knew it was inevitable, but now that it was here, the reality overwhelmed him. No Buddha was going to comfort him now. He felt like donkey shit on the bottom of Jesus' sandal.

He slid out of Joey's clutch and fell to the thousand-euro leather couch.

Joey lit up two cigarettes and passed one over. "Enjoy."

He took the smoke and watched her French-inhale, legs crossed, regal somehow in her crushed zillion-dollar suit.

"I'm such an idiot," he said, puffing. "I'm such a joke."

"Join the club," she said. "We are all so fucking equally responsible, and, I should add, not fucking responsible for this fucking disaster. Blame is just cold comfort. Too complicated for it. Too many cooks with all their poisons, jumping over each other to throw their poison into the pot."

"If you say so."

"I do." Joey stood up, smoothed herself out, adjusted her stilettos, stretched her limpy leg. "Have you seen the opening act?"

"No. Who are they?"

"The next big thing," she said. "Some hot girl with an expensive stylist."

Shane rose, rubbed his eyes, touched his ears.

"Sounds good," he said. "Let's go watch her blow us off the stage."

21

BOBBY LIT A CIGARETTE. His bandages were coming loose; soon the unholy itch would begin. He and Sarah watched the opening act, who looked like the love child of Johnny Depp and Kate Bush.

"I like her," Sarah said. "What do you think?"

"I don't like airy-fairy music."

She rolled her eyes. "Little tough man with his bandaged hands."

The room had around forty people in it now, which was about thirty more than last night. The reason was onstage in all her glamtastic glory. Once she exited, the crowd would too.

"Did you call any of your friends?" he asked Sarah. "As you can see, we could use the crowd."

"I did," she said. "They said they would try."

"I've heard that before."

Deena Freeze finished another song and stepped to the mike. "I want to welcome a very special guest," she said over the applause, tuning her guitar, "and a new friend up to the stage. All the way from the end of the bloody line, please welcome Adam Nickerson!"

Adam emerged out of the shadows and took the stage. His body language was extremely un-Adam—straight-backed, long-strided, big-smiling—and he was tall. That's right. Adam was about six foot one. Bobby had completely forgotten. Why did he look so much taller?

"His Fu Manchu is gone," he said. "Holy shit."

Fucker was up there looking twice his size, all because he'd shaved. He really looked, like, ten times better. He didn't even look like a pussy. And then Bobby really thought he was dreaming, because Adam, who normally turned to ash within two feet of a live microphone, went right up to that vintage SM57 and spoke without one iota of nerves.

"Thanks, Deena," he said. "Thanks a whole lot."

Who was this guy? Where had his wimpy guitar player gone?

Adam's not-mustachioed face scanned the crowd and found Joey and Shane, who were equally stunned by Adam's new look, and then Bobby, who shrank back a little, as if he were a mole, blind and brainless, and Adam were the sun, come to snuff him out. "This song goes out to my band," he said. "It's an old spiritual."

Bobby hadn't watched Adam from the audience since the earliest days of Blood Orphans, which only increased his sense of awe. The guy really could shred; the effortlessness covered up the utter mastery of his slide technique. You could close your eyes and think that Leadbelly was up there. Leadbelly by way of Bakersfield, in that tough, swaggering sound.

A sense of abandonment came over the bass player. Adam had already left them. Adam was an orphan in this family too. The difference was, this family wouldn't work without him. And they could keep the mustache.

How could he not root for the guy?

"Yes!" Joey yelled as Adam nailed a crazy Stevie-Ray-Vaughn-meets-Jimmy-Page kind of solo, the kind every teenage kid alone in his room with a cheap Japanese Strat and a Fender Twin aspired to approximate for half a second. But Adam didn't even need to glance at the fretboard.

"Awesome!" Shane yelled out. Bobby watched the singer double- and triple-take, his expression one of total delight. "Way to go!"

"Yeah, Adam!" Joey said, standing next to Shane. She held up her drink. "All right all right all right!"

The singer and the manager banged glasses together, and Bobby saw that time would do what it pleased with them. Their bullshit was going to melt in the convection of their shared traumas. Something dazzling might come of it. A strange hope for his band of brothers filled him.

I've seen things you people wouldn't believe, he thought, and flexed his hands. *All lost, like tears in rain.*

Then he saw Darlo coming toward them. His body tightened up, goodness flooded out, and he asked himself, Are you going to roll over again? Are you ever going to stand up and be heard? Are you ever going to show Darlo your stones? Are you ever are you ever are you ever?

22

PLAYING THE DRUMS would be nice. Playing the drums would be an island, a shore to wash up on. His band, his stupid band, coming to an end, but there would be other bands. Maybe they wouldn't have a name as good as Blood Orphans, but at least he could get Adam involved. He had to be nicer to Adam. He would try to be nicer to everyone.

Here was a chance to be nice. Entering the club, here was Bobby, the pitiful passenger—that had been a low blow, but it was true—here was Bobby standing at the side of the stage with his disgusting hands and some hot girl he'd managed to fool into liking him. Be nicer to everyone. Forever break the tether on that ancestral latitude. Find that new latitude through kindness.

Why did Bobby always treat him like an enemy? Apparently Bobby didn't recall how he'd saved his ass in that jail in Omaha, how the bass player had whimpered that his whole life was ruined, that he was going to embarrass his whole family of Sherman Oaks lawyers, doctors, and dentists, that he was going to have something called a permanent record. He had whimpered so that the other drunks and punks in the holding tank had started to imitate him, which only made him whimper more. Then he had started scratching at his hands like they were covered in hornets.

"What's with your girlfriend?" said some guy with a platinum crew-cut like Eminem's, complete with the little hoop earring. "You want to get baby some wet wipes?"

What a shitty night that had been. They were there because some guy had jumped Darlo backstage. A personal gripe.

"My sister lost her legs in an accident!" he'd yelled. "'Hella-Prosthetica' this, you prick."

Darlo gave the guy one hard shot to the face and sent him off. Bobby threw in a kick just to be cool.

"It's a song, bitch," the bass player said. "Go back to Moron School!"

Too bad the guy's brother was an Omaha cop.

"Better hurry up," Eminem said, back in the pen. "Baby might shit his pants."

Darlo was up and off the long bench. He had the guy's shirt balled up in his fist. "Scum-fucker!" he said, and banged Eminem's head against the wall.

And what thanks did he get? Not much. When Eminem's friends jumped up and beat his ass, Bobby yelled to the warden for help while Darlo covered his head.

And what thanks did he get? That look, as he approached under pale light, the bass player clutching at this girl like she was a fucking tow rope.

"What's up?" Darlo said. Bobby said nothing, tight-lipped, and the girl smiled a little. "I said, what's up, Bobby?"

"Fuck you, Darlo."

"Bobby," he said. "Just cool it."

"Don't tell me to fucking cool it." Bobby's lips quivered. "Calling me a passenger."

"Can we just call a truce?" the drummer said, laughing to try to show what a nice guy he was. "Come on, dude, what do you say?"

"Keep moving, you ass-wipe."

"Baby," the girl said, moving a little in his Mummy grip. "Take it easy."

"That's right," Darlo said. "Listen to your girlfriend." He stuck out a hand. "I'm Darlo Cox."

Bobby knocked him down and started kicking. Darlo melted into the blows; a beating was just what he wanted, really, and what he deserved. After all, he was complicit in the pain and death of, like, a hundred girls. He had tuned out all their screams. He had pretended they were crickets fighting over leaves and dirt. He had sat at the pool, stoned and staring at trees in the wind, while his dad did his dirty work. He deserved a beating bigger than an army of Bobbys could give.

Some great chain held him still, the dauphin of the devil hung out and swatted. It felt right. Tethered. Low in the sky. No sunlight.

"Monster!" Bobby yelled, and nailed him in the head.

23

WHEN BOBBY PUNCHED DARLO, his bandages shot off, revealing his hands in all of their lymph-and-pus majesty. Skin rose up through wet infection and glistened like a damned newborn.

He absolutely meant to kill him. He absolutely meant to silence the monster forever. Guttural screams were the best he could do. Bandages snapped free like restraints on Frankenstein.

Darlo didn't put up a fight. He just curled up on the floor, covered his head with his hands, defended his soft parts. Bobby heard Darlo crying but didn't believe it for a second.

Shane and Joey pulled him off. Adam had jumped offstage but stopped before joining in, standing there as if he were unsure whether he was now participant or spectator.

The unkillable, on the floor, curled up in a ball. The Blob.

As manager and singer dragged him back into the green room, with Sarah following, Bobby thought about the Omaha jail cell where he and Darlo had shared incarceration, hearing the Sharpie Shakes jingle come out from the night warden's radio before Darlo got beat up for no clear reason. Such real times, in that hot Nebraska clink. He missed the drummer already.

They threw him to the couch, tsk-tsking him.

"I just wanna fucking *kill* him," Bobby said.

"Well, *don't*," Shane said. "Fucking get over it. Right, Sarah?"

"Yes, yes," Sarah said, stroking Bobby's hair. "It's crazy, babe."

Bobby harumphed and flexed his mitts.

"Your hands," Joey said. "I can't remember the last time I saw them without Band-Aids."

"Pretty disgusting, huh?"

Applause went up for Deena Freeze and the former guitar player of Blood Orphans. They sat there like pallbearers on a smoke break.

"He's pretty amazing," Shane said, touching his ears as if they were precariously glued to his head. "I've never seen him onstage. He's a wizard."

"And he's gone," Bobby said. "Long time gone. Can you believe he shaved the fucker off?"

"Weirds me out," Joey said. "End of a fucking era."

Shane plopped down on the black leather couch and took a Stella from the ice chest. Then he took a few hundred-dollar towels and gingerly propped them behind his head. Joey cracked open a bottle of Jack Daniel's with a ribbon around the spout, on which was scrawled, "Welcome Blood Orphans."

"I've been expecting you to snap like that for months," Shane said. "But I thought when you did I'd be the one you came after."

"He called me a passenger," Bobby said. "He used the fucking P-word, dude."

An awkward silence ensued. Shane picked at the label of his beer. Joey nodded slowly and popped another Tylenol.

"Maybe I am a fucking passenger," Bobby said. "Fine. I can handle that. I mean, I can try to handle it. But it was a cheap shot."

Having rejoined Deena Freeze onstage, Adam broke into another taunting shredder of a solo. They looked at each other with the collective awareness of the abandoned.

"Let's get you some Band-Aids," Joey said, rummaging through the cabinet, grabbing a first-aid kit. She started in with the nurse act. Shane cracked a beer and handed it to Bobby, grimacing at the Mummy unplugged.

Adam showed up, looking triumphant. His black eye was

perfect and huge, like he'd paid a pro to pop him, some weird masochism kink. They applauded.

"Nice job, man," Shane said. "You kicked a lot of ass up there."

"Hear, hear," Joey said. "Looks like you got yourself a job."

"I don't know," Adam said, but smiled like, Yeah, absolutely.

"You deserve it," Bobby said, looking up from bandage application. "After all the abuse we put you through."

"She's hot, too," Shane said. "She doesn't need a backup singer, does she?"

Adam hedged for a second, then wiped his mouth, looking for a mustache that wasn't there.

"No," he said. "She doesn't."

24

DARLO HALF-CRAWLED UP THE Star Club stairs and stumbled into the snowy Dutch night. His nose bled. Blood had a nice tang. Iron was a rush. He fell onto a bench and pulled Adam's quad-band from his pocket.

He was coming out of the ring of a fight that had lasted years. In the last round, the champion had fallen. In the last round, the challenger had fucking *arrived*. It always came down to the size of the fight in the man.

Could he snap the tether? Could he float above the earth, once and for all?

There was one last way to jump free. Here was a last shot he could take to understand, one last way to cut the Daddy cord, one last way he could rise, rise, rise over the horizon, shine all day, never be pulled down into ancestral night.

How strange it was that some numbers came together in the mind. Like a chronic condition just waiting for the right moment.

In a white-walled, natural wood-grain midwestern kitchen, a middle-aged woman with long black hair answered the phone.

"Mom?" he said. "Mom?"

25

AS THEY SET UP, Adam watched the crowd thin out to...no-body. Nobody watched them set up. Nobody hollered out their name. Twenty-some people hovered on the fringes, here to see a friend, here to cut a deal, here to do anything but see Blood Orphans.

Shaving that mustache off his face had left him feeling heady and giggly. He'd gone up to Joey's room after she'd tried to shock them with the label droppage news—watching her stammer at their collective lack of giving a shit had been rough—and stared at himself in the mirror. He realized that the mustache had been a way out of being seen, a way for people to very quickly come to the same opinion his brothers had come to every time they looked in his direction; that he was some stupid geek loser. It was his way of staying subjugated, staying down. But Deena Freeze had been blown away. And so had her swank manager. And so had he, sitting on Morten's bed and blasting through Bach like an after-thought, wondering, Yeah, why *are* you in this band, really? Why do you insist on playing the fool? So he put soap and water to the Fu Manchu and said, See you later, crutch.

Still, he reached for it every five minutes and came up blank, stroking air.

Bobby's cute girlfriend sat on a stool, bopping up and down with a drink. Maybe, Adam thought, he would do a painting of the two of them and present it to the bass player for his next birth-day. Of all of them, he liked Bobby the most, and that made no sense at all.

The bass player came waltzing over. His new Band-Aids had hermetically sealed off all skin.

"This is the end," he sang. "Beautiful friend."

"This is the end," Adam sang back. "My only friend."

They noodled together, laughing.

"That's the Doors, right?" Shane asked, adjusting the mic stand. "We can do the Doors if you want. Let's just not do any of our fucking songs. I *never* want to sing them again."

"Amen to that, bitch," Bobby said. "You in on that, Adam?"

"Sure." He looked at Shane. "Think tonight you could skip the religion?"

"Sure," Shane said, "if you'll turn down your amp. For once."

Bobby did a few bass runs, then walked over and threw a good-time shoulder into Shane. Smiles crossed their mouths like low, fast-moving clouds.

Joey speed-hobbled to the stage. She still had her heels on.

"Can I do an introduction tonight?" she said. "Just for old times' sake."

"Find Darlo," Shane said. "Find Darlo and you can sing lead for the whole fucking set."

Adam watched Bobby noodle on the bass, testing out parts way past his ability. That was the thing about passengers; they just wanted their ideas to be heard. Adam was ridiculed, but he sure as shit wasn't ignored. Half the licensing royalties were no better proof.

"You want to bend that last E," he said. "And then slide your index finger up the fret a little slower. It's wobbly right now."

"Check," Bobby said, nodding, a student. "Cool."

But still, Adam understood the pathology of the passenger. No one in his family had thought him useful. No one had thought him a contributing member of the Nickerson Motorcycle Club. He was the familial whatever, never needed and never noticed.

Watching Bobby tangled up in blue, Adam recognized that it was the duty of one passenger to be sympathetic to another.

Bobby gazed up from the hard translucence of perceived identity, through the years of psyching himself out, once soft and pliable, but now solidified in a prism of nonnegotiable second-classdom. Maybe being back in Los Angeles would soften up the resin and set Bobby free, but for now, Adam knew, camaraderie could only operate as a little hammer tap on the hardened orange casing, the echoes of which would fracture the distance. He threw vibes at the bass player. He threw vibes like daggers, trying to pierce through to something real. Arise, bass player, from your persona prison. Arise, and leave your hands behind. Arise.

26

DARLO CLUTCHED THE PHONE to his ear and listened to his mother recount his birth, how he had been tangled up in his umbilical cord. The doctors had panicked, but according to Ann Atchison, from whom Darlo inherited his shaggy black hair, tall frame, and natural sense of rhythm, he had fought and screamed his way out of it.

"You kicked hard," his mother said over the static. "You weren't going to let anything stop you from being born. It hurt like heck, but you were a fighter. You were determined as all get-out to live. Your father was there. Don't think he wasn't. And he was terrified. He was scared to death for my life and yours. He was doing his best."

She tried to explain the roots of David Cox's limitations, what made him a man so determined to hurt and exploit, but it was all pop psychology to Darlo, his dad's distant father and deathly quiet mother, an upbringing of total order and no dissent in postwar Canoga Park. No questions were being answered. Only excuses to explain away the ancestral latitude.

When he told her about the arrest, her voice lost composure. "Do you remember the Wonderland murders?" she asked.

He wiped his cheeks, and bit his lip so he wouldn't start crying again. "Dad likes to talk about them," he said. "He talks about them like they're an anniversary for something."

"Yes, Darlo. An anniversary. Do you know that we used to have some of the people who died at Wonderland over for dinner all the time, back in the house on Mount Olympus? They were friends of John Holmes, so your father welcomed them in, even though they were mad with poison in their bodies, wide-eyed. John was a lost soul, looking for a reason to be. He was a drifter, and a liar, and he didn't have a real friend in the whole wide world."

ther had most probably had sex
is would have been a point of
't make sense of the separation

pened," she continued, "your
e of John's friends. They were
ver to the Wonderland house.
et me blow your mind. I was
wasn't feeling well. Your dad
uch, but he was crazy about
f his child could stop him a
loodline and how you would
to validate the good side of

$= \left| \frac{1}{2} \right|$

him, that through y   ve his ghosts behind. And so I played sick, because Lanius and his friends terrified me, and I knew that sooner than later something awful was going to happen to them. It was a card I played. I had no idea what was going to happen that night, but I knew that at the very least your father would come home with a lot of drugs in him and a bad attitude."

"You saved his life."

"I don't want that responsibility. I didn't tell people about it."

"He has a wall devoted to pictures of the murders. He said that they were friends of his. Why didn't I ever think there was more to it?"

"The idea of you," she said, "wiped clean some curse. The idea of you, floating in the air, an angel to him already, an angel."

She drifted from the phone. He waited.

"Angel," she said, and he heard his mother weeping, free of Christian Iowa static. "My angel."

A world of explanations about his dad, and his role in their sad life together in that Normandie mansion materialized around him, began to take shape, mysterious, permeable, thawing.

"I'm lost, Mom."

She wept, or maybe it was static coming back. "Pick yourself up now. Get up from where you're standing. Breathe, Darlo. It's OK now. I love you."

Those four Wonderland victims, those girls in the basement, the desperate pull at his heart when he had sex — these were connected, part of some through-line, and Darlo felt a growing cohesion to some system that ran him, some resolution in this sequence of suffering, some minor order. A shift occurred inside his emotional bedrock, loosening up what lay strangled beneath the hard sediment. This system was a part of him and was his responsibility to fix, untangle, make right. He wiped his eyes and breathed. He breathed easy, as if some weight had been released.

"I'll call you when I'm home, Mom," he said. "I'm sorry."

"Darlo," she said, "you have your whole life ahead of you."

He hung up, holding Adam's phone in his palm like a broken bird as tears ran down his face. On tour a few months before, he had sat in a Minneapolis multiplex on a day off and watched a movie about the Wonderland murders, with Val Kilmer as John Holmes. He'd laughed at the utter farce-itude of the film, full of bumbling meth monsters and stock organized criminals, with Holmes portrayed as Wile E. Coyote on speed, goofy, loose-tongued, full of big dreams. But now he saw unvarnished scenes of despair, gore, and gloom, a world of misery, a world with no way out. That was his father's world, the anatomy of porn melancholy, without light or hope, long days in a white shag-carpeted house, trying to stave off the hollow choices and their brittle, empty consequences.

Joey came stumbling out, looking deranged. Darlo expected her to rustle him up, pull at him, get him to hurry the fuck up, fucking loser, fucking fool. But she just looked at him, eyes wide. Then she marched over, grabbed his face, and kissed him.

Darlo grabbed her by that little waist, hoisted her up. She wrapped her legs around him. His whole body rushed to her. She put a vise grip on him.

"Your leg," he said. "Be careful."

"Fuck careful," she said, and shoved her tongue down his throat.

Her breath had days of liquor and chocolate on it. He breathed it in.

"I fucking love you," he said. "You crazy bitch."

"Shut up," she said, and bit his lower lip, her breath shaking. "Shut the fuck up and fucking hold me."

Darlo had felt this passion with Jenni Feingold, and he had felt it, in a way he did not understand, with his dad. That there was precedent for this swooping, encompassing feeling, that he wasn't just trying the emotion on, made it something he could trust.

"OK, my leg hurts now," she said.

He put her down. They stared at each other. She barely came up to Darlo's chest. He grabbed her faux hawk and tugged. She grabbed his black mane and tugged harder. Some animal ritual was satisfied.

"My dad should have died at Wonderland," he said. "He was supposed to be there that night."

"Who told you that?"

"My mother."

She nodded, squinting.

"Ignominy," Joey said. "Pure ignominy. Pure impetuosity. You OK?"

"Yeah. I fucking love you."

She pulled him down and licked his lips. "I fucking love you too. You fucking mess."

"Cokehead gimp bitch," he said, and smelled her breath.

Darlo looked around at the Dutch Christmastime throng, glittering with purpose and life. The whole day was a dream. Everything was a dream. What was it with the snow here?

Joey pulled away and started doing a slithering little Axl Rose–esque dance on a pole of cold Dutch air.

"I'm practicing to introduce Blood Orphans," she said. "You heard of them?"

"They opened for Aerosmith, right?"

Joey swayed, drunk on some kind of crazy wisdom. "That's right. And now they're finishing their triumphant two-year world tour with an intimate club date at the very not-at-all-posh Stoor Cloob. Their entire fan base of cripples, fat white boys in *Babylon 5* T-shirts, and nose-picking sex offenders will be there. Plus exactly zero A&R and no representatives from the Sharpie Shakes company, from whom the band mistakenly did not take several hundred thousand dollars."

"Would it really have been that much?"

"Try not to hold it against me," she said, and went back to her stripper aerobics.

The Dutch nighttime bustle was in full swing. A whole new army of cyclists, trams, and blond kids dressed as elves, faces covered in bootblack.

"Why couldn't we have ended the tour in a city just a tad less stuck-up?" Darlo said. "Why did we have to end the tour in Yawnlakhastan?"

"Why go out on a good note?" the manager said. "Why operate in denial?"

He lowered his eyes at Joey. "You used to make sense. Back in the day."

"Oh yeah?" Joey said, spinning on that invisible pole. "What was it like?"

Darlo didn't know. Joey put her hand out, and he took it.

"You think about that, lover-boy," she said. "I'm curious about what the hell that could mean. But in the meantime, let's rock."

27

BOBBY STOOD ONSTAGE, still noodling on his bass. He looked at his bandmates. He looked at the middling crowd. He looked at a girl who'd better be turned on by needy confused fuckers. He looked back at his singer.

"I'm really sorry, Shane, for being such a shit to you."

Shane smiled and nodded like a priest on television. "It's no problem, Bobby. So am I, dude." He tapped the microphone. "You have no idea."

"We fucked it all up."

"Sure we did." Something fell off Shane's hair. "What did we know, though? What did we know at all?"

"Come on, you fuckers!" the Dutch bartender yelled. "Kiss and make up, fuckers! Play dirty rock!"

Adam emerged from behind his amp, walked his velvet-panted, Fu-Manchu-less way over. The guitar player's new swagger hit Bobby in the heart.

"It's like part of you is missing," he said. "You did yourself a world of good by shaving that thing off."

"Thanks," Adam said, and stared soulfully at Bobby's hands.

Joey and Darlo walked in, arm in arm. Bobby wondered what that was all about, and thought of the ice caps melting. Darlo got behind the drums and winked at him.

"We're gonna play a bunch of covers tonight," Shane said.

"Fine," the drummer replied.

"Doors and Stones?" Bobby said.

"Whatever," he said.

"'Dead Flowers'?" Adam said. "'Miss You'?"

"Fuckin' A." He craned his neck. "Holy shit, you shaved off your—"

"Play the dirty rock musak!" the two bartenders chanted. "Dirty rock muzak. Dirty rock muzak!" They held up copies of *Rocket Heart.* Joey and her tricks. Bobby's heart warmed to the incompetent manager, who now, under the chant of the Dutchies, strode the stage like Don-fucking-King at Madison Square Garden, as if the whole damn world were waiting for her voice to ring out in sterling introduction.

She grabbed the microphone, swatting away disappointment and fatigue, swatting all the pain away.

"Good evening, blond people of Amsterdam. Hello! My name is Joey Fredericks, and I am the manager of the band standing here, who are about to entertain you with their tales of sexual and psychic woe and plunder, who have traveled the world in a wee little tour van to evangelize hidden truths of men and women put to jolly martial song. Can I get some fucking lights on us, please?"

Lights shifted upon Joey's five-foot frame. She had a frothy drink in one hand, and that limp was full on.

"Thank you, sir," Joey said, feeding back. "Now you may be wondering, fine international people, what makes you so very lucky. You may be wondering, How did I end up in a nice but unimpressive tableau of rock-and-roll mythmaking? You may be wondering, Was it something special that brought me here tonight? And the answer is yes! The answer is yes! You have been brought here by the universe to witness the end of a long, exciting journey. To witness the start of another chapter. To witness the denouement of a dream."

"Tell it!" the bartenders yelled. "Tell it!"

"How long ago we started on this journey, lads." She surveyed the four of them, holding her glass. "How long ago in the palm groves of darkest lost angels, in the shallow spires of the kingdom of the Pacific. How long ago did we meet: an art student, a Christian folk-seeker, a careerist with a skin condition, and the son of a pornographer. How long ago was it that we plotted the course of empire, delved into the delineations of delight, deemed the fiefdoms, carved up the land of our future leisure!"

It had been forever since Bobby had heard one of these speeches, back when Blood Orphans was just another name for Party Down. He'd forgotten that Joey had the circus-barker-meets-poetry-slammer in her. Yet after all this time, her spiel still rang in heroic tones, and her voice was the sound of an Elysian wind come to bless them.

"And off they went, off we went, into the complexities of contract, emerging as handmaidens to Aerosmith, interns in the office of international pop-stardom, squires at the round table of rock and roll. But the waters of whimsy turned against us. What was once smooth sailing became a racist riptide, pulling us down and down, descending into the maelstrom of uncoolitude. We were branded bigots, stupidos, morons. Our crown of jewels was replaced with a crown of thorns, and yes, we were punished for all the sins of the lifestyle, we were the railway children, the left-behind, the dashed-away."

Darlo started up a jazzy midtempo beat, and the rest of them followed into a solid little vamp. Shane picked up a tambourine and shook in time, wincing from his busted ears but keeping the shake going. They locked in behind their manager as she sang their elegy, stirred up the attendants of this wake, made it glorious and shimmery. Like that, they were Joey's backing band.

"But on we trudged, still faithful to the times when posters filled our rooms, when every night as we lay in pubescent anticipation, Jagger stared at us, Lennon stared at us, Rotten and Page and Osbourne stared at us from glossy shitty-stocked four-color photographs crookedly taped to our walls, the poses of kings! Of kings, my friends, of kings!"

For once, Bobby could get his stinging fingers to make all the changes. If he could only stay locked in this groove forever, he wouldn't need anything. If he could just stay on this root-note plane, he would be happy and content. He had purpose here. He had peace and love. On Joey went, swinging her glass from hand to hand, then clutching at the mike like the Boston Strangler.

"On we trudged, across time zones in a shitty van, across countries where no one cared, across the stunted dead tundra of an unfairly ruined reputation. To make it right. To make it worthwhile. To say to the world, We may be down, but we are sure as hot shit not out. And so here we are, washed upon the pointy-roofed medieval shores of Ye Olde Amsterdam, here to perform our last rites. And so I present to you, unimaginable, unfathomable, unpossessable, I present to you the very definition of a type of genius not yet recognized. I give you the stomp and hue and cry of the power-poppermost of the hard-hitting rockermost. Here at last, bloody, unbowed, and unsilenced, I give you tomorrow's future bastards. I bid you sleep tight, my babies! Sleep tight, my darlings! I give you Blood Orphans!"

A spark came up from the microphone. Joey reeled back, sending her drink in a wild arc to the middle of the room, sailing through the lights, descending into the maelstrom. The manager stumbled for a moment, looked at Bobby as if something amazing had been revealed to her eyes, and dropped to the floor.

28

WHEN JOEY LIFTED INTO THE AIR, Shane thought of that
time at Christian camp when that young preacher had become
engulfed with the spirit. They had taken a bus to the Redwoods,
and Pastor Duncan had brought a friend from the sister South — he
couldn't have been more than twenty-five — to do a guest sermon
as they ate grapes and held hands. Preacher-boy was a cocky dude
from Louisiana, and his sermon had taken a hard turn toward
Pentecostal weirditude; he began speaking in tongues, something they all considered a form of undue attention toward oneself
in the eyes of the Lord. Hitting a crescendo, Preacher-boy had
thrown himself back, and for just a moment under those ancient
massive trees, for just a moment in that calm clearing, he had left
this world. They all reeled, the entire contingent of the Christian
youth, Shane and Donna, his girlfriend — who, in the tent the
night before, would not swallow his sperm — and all their friends,
cheery and wearing their new Eddie Bauer gear and Teva san-
dals. Their eyes went wide as the strange southern dude flew back
and popped his head against some thousand-year-old stump. And
yes, of course, could one avoid, when thrown back and flailing,
chucking one's arms perpendicular to one's body? The southern
preacher hadn't been able to help himself, hobbled with the crutch
of calculation. Maybe, Shane thought later, after Preacher-boy
was driven away in a Yosemite EMT van to get his concussion
treated, he was not what he had seemed. And now, as Joey lifted
up her forsaken arms, flying on the wings of electric angels before
falling to the stage, Shane knew that the young preacher on that

Redwoods retreat had been consummately full of shit. For unlike him, Joey definitely bore the brunt of their sins.

They rushed forward. Darlo, climbing over his drums, shoved them out of the way. "Move!" he said. "Oh, God!"

Joey's mouth was open, her tongue hung out the side, and her blond hair poofed straight up. Darlo grabbed her and shook her. Joey grunted and swung her arms, slapping Darlo across the face.

"Joey?" Darlo said, getting really close. "Baby, are you all right?"

She nodded. The two locked eyes and kissed.

"No way," Bobby said. Shane and Adam grunted, like, About time.

Darlo carried her back to the green room with the rest of them in tow, and Shane thought about that Pentecostal soldier again, how he had recovered awfully fast from his spiritual shock. Faster than you could say massive scam, he had started in on how God had just touched him, yes, my friends, he had just received a shock from the greatest power source of all, and it was a mighty charge, a mighty wattage indeed. And then he had clutched at his head and dropped. But Joey, Shane knew, was the real thing.

Darlo lowered her to the couch.

"Maybe too much booze," she said. "In my head and on the mike. Wet hands maybe. So fucking embarrassing."

"Are you kidding?" Bobby said. "That was like the most badass bit of rock-and-roll theater I've ever seen. And you're following in a great tradition. Bill Wyman and Keith Richards were both electrocuted onstage."

"Sweet," she croaked. "Keith's hot."

"Babe, I saw you fall," Darlo said. "I heard that pop and I saw you fall. Jesus, are you sure you're all right? Adam, are you sure she's all right?"

"I'm fine," Joey said, and threw an Altoid into her mouth.

"I just have a headache and I'm still a little sick, but I'm fine." She propped herself up. "You guys need to go play your set." She winked. "Even though after me it'll be one hell of an anticlimax."

Going back up there was the last thing Shane wanted to do, but when he opened his mouth to make the case to ditch, he had a change of heart. His ears ached, his hair was disgusting, and his faith was a stretched-out carcass of belief, but this was his life. This was where the quest had led him, to the masturbatory, soulless dream of some millionaire, but he had to honor that. Maybe this band was the purgatory for the next life and he was about to pass through, but maybe Blood Orphans could be salvaged, made new, made real for once.

Either way, everything had led to this moment. He rose out of some surface that had formerly held him down in concrete clutches.

"I know a party," he said. "Let's play the set and get the fuck out of here."

29

THEY APPROACHED THE RODIN SUITE like a bunch of refugees. Shane stood at the front and banged on the door. Joey and Darlo flanked him like dime-store devils, broken ornaments you'd hang on Satan's Christmas tree. Adam stood behind them, smoothing his phantom Fu Manchu, his eye ringed in black, dark but diffuse, like an espresso stain on a cheap napkin. At the back, Bobby had his arm around Sarah. He hoped for cacophony and good times, felt sentimental about this final moment of togetherness, which was not so different from the first time they had stood together in public, outside Spaceland with their amps, waiting for entry into a sacred celebration of the rock-and-roll high life. That for a time they'd been the ones on the other side of the golden equation seemed impossible.

The door opened, and the sound nearly blew them back. A guy stood there, double-fisting Stella. Shrouded in buckskin fringe and leather pants, his beard spotty and blond, he could have been in charge of rigging the lights at Woodstock.

"Ron," Shane said. "You stoned fucker."

"Peanut Butter Bob!" he yelled. "And the rest of the Bloody mother-fricking Orphans. Entrez, mes amis, entrez!"

Like all good rock-and-roll parties, the Rodin Suite was a living exhibit of the vapid and exultant. On the stereo, Bon Scott rang out his clarion call of beer- and tail-chasing, rang the bell that Idiot School was in session. The Young brothers riffed around his gravel-bound voice. AC/DC were the Australian Ramones. They were holy.

"If you want blood," people sang, "you got it!"

"Did you have parties like this?" Sarah asked. "This is crazy shit."

"Back in the day," he said.

"You're sad."

"I am."

She took his hand and kissed it gently.

"Will you come visit me?" he asked. "Will you come to Los Angeles?"

"Certainly," she said. "As long as we go to the Getty."

Ron stood atop a couch and yelled for attention. Bobby couldn't believe this guy; his Gram Parsons *Electric Horseman* look, straight off the case at Nudies, was so incredibly lame. Then Bobby remembered that he was in a band that, for most of their existence, had worn enough eye shadow to sell out the MAC counter.

"Yo, bitches!" Ron shouted. "I have an announcement to make!"

The whole room applauded.

"You fuckers don't even know what I'm going to say, man!" He laughed, and his buckskin fringe went back and forth, and then he swigged from a bottle of Jack Daniel's. He had the whole routine down, and Bobby saw a pretty prominent hard-on through his two-hundred-dollar jeans, which hugged his jewels just like Keith's on the cover of *Sticky Fingers*.

"We're in the presence of major rock infamy right now, people!" he yelled. "We're in the presence of a group of dudes that got the most royal and criminal screwing by a major label!" He scanned the crowd and found Shane, who stood with the younger sister of Daisy Duke. Everyone here had grown up in Hazzard County.

"Peanut Butter Bob!" he yelled. "All right!"

Shane raised his beer, put his arm around the little Daisyette.

"Get to the point!" Joey yelled.

"And to the point I will get, yes!" Ron said. "The point is, that they were never given a fair shake, and were royally screwed, these brilliant ironists of rock-and-roll stereotype, and"—he belched—"were terrorized by the fucking whims of fame! But they are here tonight to party with us, these hard-rocking phantoms, impart some hard-learned wisdom and easy love, and that is an honor indeed. Cue up that stereo and play me some Blood Orphans!"

The room erupted in cheers, and the first chords of "Hella-Prosthetica" rang out. Ironists my ass: it was a damn good thing no one could hear the lyrics. That the song existed at all seemed ridiculous to Bobby now, but at the time they had been storming some imagined barricade of taboo, with this paean to horny amputees as the battering ram.

Apparently the guys in Tennessee knew all the lyrics.

Darlo walked over with two cans of Heineken. "Some songs land people in jail," he said, and handed one to Bobby. "Ain't that a bitch?"

"'Tis," Bobby said, knowing that the bringing of beer was an apology of sorts. Darlo's face was still puffed up from tears, and Bobby let his anger go. Maybe, just for a night, he ought to cut the drummer some slack.

People sang the song out. It was cute. They sipped their beers.

"Shit is fucked up," Darlo said. "Shit is so fucked up right now, Bobby. I ain't got no label and I ain't got no dad."

"Sorry about the news."

"Whatever." He shrugged. "Or not whatever. Doesn't make a difference. Fucker's been a real dirtbag, and if I can help send him to the clink, that's fine. Oh shit, hold on." He took out Adam's phone and stared at it. "Thought it was ringing," he said. "I'm waiting to hear back from that asshole Jesse."

"He's an asshole, all right," Bobby said. "Fucker sold me an eightball of powdered sugar."

Darlo winced. "I told him to do that."

"You're a real piece of work, Darlo."

"I'm gonna try to be better. Don't look at me like that—I mean it."

Bobby nodded, rolling his eyes, and watched Sarah talk to Adam and Shane over at the keg. They were telling her some story that involved a large object falling on their heads, laughing as they ducked for cover. Maybe it was the bird of happiness taking a big dump. Either way, he warmed to the image—his brothers, protecting her.

"That wasn't such a bad show tonight," Darlo said. "Though I think we lost them when we tried 'L.A. Woman.'"

"For sure," Bobby said. "Shane isn't exactly Mr. Mojo Risin'. Though Adam nailed all those snaky guitar parts."

"Doesn't he always," Darlo said. "Fucking slayer, that guy. Even without the Fu Manchu."

Bobby grunted. Darlo picked at the tab on his Heineken.

"So," the drummer said. "What the fuck are you gonna do when we get home? 'Cause I want to figure this whole thing out, bro. I want us to not fuckin' hate each other." He lowered his eyes. "We should hang out."

Bobby made to scoff, and then he thought, This is a peace offering. Who knows what might come of it? A certain sense of satisfaction dawned in him. Had Bobby not watched the drummer fall apart? Had he not, by all appearances, gotten the girl? His customary hatred and envy were absent; instead, he felt a vague, diffuse affection for Darlo, and the knowledge that he had no idea what was coming next.

"Fine," he said. "Just don't make fun of my hands. And I want a hundred bucks for that faux-caine."

Darlo nodded in contrition. They listened to the song, bobbed their heads up and down. Bobby felt like he was on a blind date.

"I still think you and me got mixed wrong," Darlo said. "Fucking Sheridan. Mixed us too far down, that fucking jam-band idiot. You and me. No fuckin' thunder. What's rock and roll without a whole lotta thunder?"

"Jazz," Bobby said. "Ugly, despicable jazz."

"Word," Darlo said, and they clanked cans.

The song rose toward the crescendo. All four members of Tennessee were gathered up, arms on each other, singing about having sex with girls who were missing their legs. Bobby watched Adam and Joey bob their heads and laugh like they'd never heard the song before, like they couldn't believe anyone could have such bad taste. Then one of the guys in Tennessee grabbed Shane and screamed for him to take it, right as the final chorus kicked in. The dreadlocked Christian Buddha seeker-fool pogoed up and down. He guzzled some beer, hugged his new boyz, then poured the rest of the can on them as they shook in rapture. He counted off the lead-in, held his arms high like a spirit risen gloriously from limbo, and threw his body into it. From the very top of his lungs, he sang the song back to heaven.

ACKNOWLEDGMENTS

Thanks to Eileen Pollack and Laura Kasischke for helping make this book shine.

Thanks to Peter Ho Davies, Ray McDaniel, Patsy Yaeger, Michael Byers, and Nicholas Delbanco for advice on matters critical, creative, and theoretical, and the University of Michigan, Helen Zell, and the Rackham School of Graduate Studies for essential and generous support.

Thanks to Ayesha Pande, dedicated agent of tireless energy and natural grace.

Thanks to Reagan Arthur, Michael Pietsch, and all at Little, Brown, for taking a chance on me and being so excited about it.

Thanks to Scott Michael for providing suggestions from the real world, as well as reminders on laws of physics and probability.

Thanks to the fellows with whom I have shared vans, stages, hotel rooms, and sunsets: Bo Gilliland, John Roderick, Jeramy Koepping, Cody Burns, Eric Corson, Chris Caniglia, and Sean Nelson. Well played, sirs, well played.

Final, profuse, and endless thanks to Anna Barker, for your love.

MICHAEL SHILLING is a lecturer at the University of Michigan, where he received his MFA in Creative Writing. His stories have appeared in *The Sun, Fugue,* and *Other Voices.* A recovering rock musician, he played the drums in The Long Winters, as well as in numerous other bands in Seattle. He is currently working on a novel set in Victorian England.

Reading Group Guide

Rock
Bottom

A NOVEL

Michael Shilling

A conversation with
Michael Shilling

You spent several years as a touring rock musician. What elements of your experience informed the writing of Rock Bottom?

There are two kinds of rock bands. The first is the young and skinny people in their twenties, drug Aardvarks with no nutritional needs except beer, cigarettes, and two hours of sleep who, day after day, wolf a bag of Doritos for dinner, blast through an hour-long set, and then abuse themselves all night with the help of total strangers. The other variety is usually older and always weaker of constitution. They need the occasional home-cooked meal and as much sleep as the next accountant or dentist, and like to argue for hours about what Gore would have done as president. That was the band I was in. You want to read that novel?

There are five different points of view in Rock Bottom. *Why did you choose this structure, and how did you go about finding the balance between these different vantages?*

After politicians, rock bands are the ultimate unreliable narrators. Though the comedy in *Rock Bottom* is what gets the reader's attention, at its heart I wanted the story to be about people coming to tough terms with the choices they had made, and how those choices affected others around them. By having such a varied set of viewpoints, I could accomplish this thematic objective and provide a sense of solidity to the narrative, so that any epiphany or understanding that a character arrived at could be emotionally cross-checked by another. To mangle the words of Joan Didion, people in vans have to construct stories in order to live, and those stories are often ridiculously self-serving. Nobody in Blood Orphans passes even the lowest bar of objectivity, so this way the reader is the final judge, which is not something I strive for, but in this case is what served the story.

Is this "emotional cross-checking" part of the motivation to have the manager play such an important role and *be a woman?*

Very much so, but it cuts both ways. Joey's carrying around her black-magic bag of delusions too, and having the four members of the band around to grab that bag and throw it into the nearest Dutch canal sends her on her own compelling journey of reckoning. Of course, having a woman's touch—even that of the coked-up, gimp-legged, bitter-as-horseradish variety—was essential to facilitate emotions from the dudes that they would never have experienced if left to their own, all-male devices.

Speaking of which, why did you choose to set the book in Amsterdam?

Originally, I thought that Amsterdam was a good setting because it mirrored the dynamics of rock band life—known for its sinful, libertine ways, but in its heart very buttoned up and, in terms of manners and social graces, surprisingly conservative. But by the time I realized what a dumb simplification that was, I was already knee-deep in the draft, so it never changed. In the end, I think I set it there because Amsterdam is very pretty, and if I'm going to spend two years in the same creative place, I'd prefer it to be pretty.

What were the challenges you faced by setting the novel over the course of a single day?

When you have less than twenty-four hours, a story line can easily become contrived and full of expedient moments. I didn't want the changes the characters went through to come cheap; so, certainly, creating an organic plot was difficult. Also, with such a tight time frame, the structure of the story seemed to either completely work or fall flat on its narrative ass. When you're telling a story that has weeks, or even days, of present action, you can move stuff around. With only one day, if you change the time that one character gets to one place, everything else has to shift. So revising was a bit scary. But when I was in Amsterdam I walked the routes of all the characters to make sure I wasn't creating any physical or temporal impossibilities, so that matter was pretty nailed down. That said, it took a while to get the sequence of events to work in a believable manner, but when I did I had one very tight story.

A while? How long did Rock Bottom *take to write?*

About ten months to draft and a year to revise. And revise. And revise. I'd written two, uh, "practice novels" already—just saying it makes my hands ache—so I had a pretty good understanding of what it feels like when you're on the right track and, even more important, what it feels like when you're on the wrong one. There is no greater gift to a writer than the sixth sense that what you're working on is genuinely bad. Of course, if I hadn't written that other stuff, I would have never been able to write something pretty decent. Or at least that's what I tell myself to stop from crying.

Any writing advice you'd care to share?

I read an interview with Peter Carey, whose work is a genuine treasure of narrative artistry and flat-out prose chops, in which he basically said that writing is a last-person-standing enterprise. If you do it long enough with some amount of regularity, you will probably produce something good that gets published. I think that's true, because if you stay at it for five, ten, fifteen years, you probably don't suck at it. And also, improvement is exponential in this line of work, which, because it's such a lonely endeavor, is a truth that is quite satisfying. The drafting I'm doing on the new novel is still pretty rough, but not anything like the crud I used to turn out. I don't have to drag the dream into existence as much anymore.

Care to share what you're working on?

I'm writing a novel set at the crossroads of Regency and Victorian England—the late 1820s—involving some of the characters and incidents from *Jane Eyre* and set at Thornfield Hall, but existing in a completely different narrative context with a whole new cast of strivers, connivers, grotesques, and romantics. I am trying to combine the dark fairy-tale fabulism of Angela Carter with the plot-driven, hard-boiled push-and-shove of James Ellroy, all the while keeping in mind British class dynamics to create, as Ellroy called it, a reckless verisimilitude. The beauty of a story like this is connecting the desires and motivations of all the characters—from the lowest scullery maid to Rochester himself—while keeping the plot organic and fluid. It's a large undertaking, but I like a challenge. If I go down in flames, at least it'll be in a blaze of glory.

Questions and topics for discussion

1. Of the five main characters in *Rock Bottom*, which one did you find the most compelling, and why? Which character did you find the most humorous?

2. Amsterdam plays an important role in the novel. Discuss the ways in which the city influences the actions of each band member.

3. *Rock Bottom* is a no-bruises-spared portrayal of the rock-and-roll world. In your opinion, which band member gains the most from the difficult experience the band endures?

4. What do you think of the "friendship" between the band members? Which characters did you feel were really friends at the beginning of *Rock Bottom*? Did that change in the course of the novel?

5. What is the importance of Joey in the story of Blood Orphans? What does she ultimately learn from her experience as manager of the band?

6. Discuss the idea of forgiveness in *Rock Bottom*. How important is forgiveness to the members of Blood Orphans?

7. Darlo starts off as a truly vile character, yet as the novel progresses he is forced to confront much of his past behavior. Does he eventually find a conscience?

8. The love story between Joey and Darlo is, to say the least, a fairly unconventional romance. In what ways does their relationship impact the lives of the other band members?

Suggestions for further reading

Some of Michael Shilling's favorite books:

The Bloody Chamber by Angela Carter
The White Album by Joan Didion
American Tabloid by James Ellroy
A Public Burning by Robert Coover
The Palm at the End of the Mind by Wallace Stevens
Bear and His Daughter by Robert Stone
Frank Zappa's Negative Dialectics of Poodle Play
   by Ben Watson
Amy and Isabelle by Elizabeth Strout
Salem's Lot by Stephen King
Among the Thugs by Bill Buford
Money by Martin Amis
The Production of Space by Henri Lefebvre
Self-Help by Lorrie Moore
Observatory Mansions by Edward Carey
The Violent Bear It Away by Flannery O'Connor
The True Adventures of the Rolling Stones by Stanley Booth
The Remains of the Day by Kazuo Ishiguro
Libra by Don Delillo
To Bedlam and Part Way Back by Anne Sexton
Mystery Train by Greil Marcus

Ariel by Sylvia Plath

The Medium Is the Massage by Marshall McLuhan

Mrs. Dalloway by Virginia Woolf

The Corrections by Jonathan Franzen

Teach Us to Outgrow Our Madness by Kenzaburo Oe

Chasing the Sea by Tom Bissell

Lord Weary's Castle by Robert Lowell

Titus Groan by Mervyn Peake

The Wind-Up Bird Chronicle by Haruki Murakami

Midnight's Children by Salman Rushdie

Rubicon Beach by Steve Erickson

Budding Prospects by T. C. Boyle

Wuthering Heights by Emily Brontë

The Executioner's Song by Norman Mailer